Praise for *Kanata*

"With the bravura of E.L. Doctorow and the elemental force of Cormac McCarthy, *Kanata* captures the heartbeat of a continent, in a language as visceral and raw as the landscape and lives it chronicles. This is history made flesh, unerring in its portrait of how we make history and are made by it."
— Nino Ricci, author of *The Origin of Species*

"Don Gillmor may well have written 'The Great Canadian Novel' here. In casting the country as the main character, in tracking Canada through the story and bloodlines of explorer David Thompson, he has shown Canadians their country as never before seen or imagined. Brilliantly written, *Kanata* is a breathtaking achievement—and one that should bury, forever, the ridiculous notion that Canadian history is dull. It is not; under Don Gillmor's hand, it is a page-turner."
— Roy MacGregor, author of *Canadians: A Portrait of a Country and Its People*

"Unforgettable [and] stunning … Gillmor has such a firm grip on his factual material and the story he's created to link those facts together. *Kanata* should be required reading for immigrants to Canada, but the beauty of the book is that it will also appeal to anyone looking for a good yarn rich with detail."
— *Edmonton Journal*

"Gillmor's descriptive writing sings of colour. He creates vivid portraits of a young land endeavouring to reach maturity, its inhabitants challenged by natural disasters, wars and natural disputes, but constantly struggling not to be defeated … it sure brings Canadian history to life."

—*Guelph Mercury*

"Don Gillmor dares to write nothing less than the history of the nation in novel form, with a legendary explorer up front … Gillmor['s] style—direct, wry and dramatically astute—might most reasonably be described as Pierre Berton by way of Don DeLillo and HBO."

—*Toronto Star*

"An ambitious Canadian novel … Fine and demanding reading."

—Randy Boyagoda, *National Post*

"[A] snappily written, fast-paced piece of historical fiction."

—*The Globe and Mail*

"You certainly can't fault Don Gillmor for lack of ambition … [*Kanata* is a] maple-flavoured match for that Great American Novel, John Dos Passos's *U.S.A.* (And to give Gillmor extra points for audacity, he aims to do in one book what took Dos Passos a trilogy) … A compelling work … *Kanata* will make you feel a little less lost when you think of your place in Canada."

—*Winnipeg Free Press*

PENGUIN CANADA

KANATA

DON GILLMOR is the author of *Canada: A People's History* and *The Desire of Every Living Thing*. The winner of nine National Magazine Awards, he is a frequent contributor to *The Walrus*, *Toronto Life*, and *The Globe and Mail*. He lives in Toronto.

KANATA

~ A Novel ~

Don Gillmor

PENGUIN
CANADA

PENGUIN CANADA

Published by the Penguin Group

Penguin Group (Canada), 90 Eglinton Avenue East, Suite 700, Toronto, Ontario, Canada M4P 2Y3
(a division of Pearson Canada Inc.)

Penguin Group (USA) Inc., 375 Hudson Street, New York, New York 10014, U.S.A.
Penguin Books Ltd, 80 Strand, London WC2R 0RL, England
Penguin Ireland, 25 St Stephen's Green, Dublin 2, Ireland (a division of Penguin Books Ltd)
Penguin Group (Australia), 250 Camberwell Road, Camberwell, Victoria 3124, Australia
(a division of Pearson Australia Group Pty Ltd)
Penguin Books India Pvt Ltd, 11 Community Centre, Panchsheel Park, New Delhi – 110 017, India
Penguin Group (NZ), 67 Apollo Drive, Rosedale, North Shore 0745, Auckland, New Zealand
(a division of Pearson New Zealand Ltd)
Penguin Books (South Africa) (Pty) Ltd, 24 Sturdee Avenue, Rosebank,
Johannesburg 2196, South Africa

Penguin Books Ltd, Registered Offices: 80 Strand, London WC2R 0RL, England

First published in Viking Canada hardcover by Penguin Group (Canada),
a division of Pearson Canada Inc., 2009
Published in this edition, 2010

1 2 3 4 5 6 7 8 9 10 (WEB)

Copyright © Don Gillmor, 2009

This book contains certain accounts of conversations and events involving historical figures.
Where necessary, facts and conversations involving such persons may have been altered.
Kanata is not intended to provide a historically accurate memorial but is a work of fiction
involving historical events and people.

Manufactured in Canada.

LIBRARY AND ARCHIVES CANADA CATALOGUING IN PUBLICATION

Gillmor, Don
Kanata : a novel / Don Gillmor.

ISBN 978-0-14-305442-9

1. Canada—History—Fiction. I. Title.

PS8563.I59K35 2010   C813'.54   C2010-905723-6

Visit the Penguin Group (Canada) website at **www.penguin.ca**

Special and corporate bulk purchase rates available; please see
www.penguin.ca/corporatesales or call 1-800-810-3104, ext. 2477 or 2474

FOR GRAZYNA

KANATA: Iroquoian for village or settlement, thought to be the origin of the word *Canada*.

"Longing on a large scale is what makes history."

Don DeLillo, *Underworld*

"Maps are slippery customers."

J.B. Harley, "Deconstructing the Map"

MICHAEL MOUNTAIN HORSE

1967

ALBERTA, 1967

The light leaked through red cirrus clouds over the eastern hills as two hawks floated in elliptic descent. To the south a large bowl rose to a narrow ridge defined by the millennial curves of a stream. The Blood had stampeded buffalo off the cliffs into the creek below, their thundering weight suddenly pointless. The Rocky Mountains were visible to the west, and the expansive sky evoked a sense of possibility, the hand of God on the tiller here in the tranquil lee of the oil industry. The wind rushed at the kitchen window where Michael Mountain Horse sat, percussive gusts punching the glass.

When they were children he and his brother Stanford used to wake early to fish the Jumping Pound Creek. It was a good trout stream but during spring runoff some years catfish ran as thick as logjams, their fat, prehistoric bodies filling the creek where it narrowed. One day in May,

Michael and Stanford piled rocks to narrow the creek even further then stood and swatted the fish out of the water like bears. They were slimy and firm and each swat had to be timed perfectly or the fish would slide by. Filled with adolescent purpose, they found a rhythm, the simple destructive fact of being able to do it a justification. After an hour dozens of catfish lay on the stones beside the water, a handful still tossing morbidly. The largest was two feet long, its heavy, monstrous face staring up. Neither of them cared to eat the spongy flesh; it was simply malevolent sport.

The creek was fed from glaciers in the Rockies and their feet were quickly numbed. When they got out of the water, the air stung the wet raw skin. They lay on a large rock that slanted toward the sun warming themselves, and finally slept. When Michael woke, Stanford was sitting up, surveying the fish littered on the stones below, magpies hopping delicately, taking the eyes, the most accessible (and shiniest) part. He remembered Stanford's face, its look of disappointment.

He and Stanford shared a bedroom and Michael recalled the door opening one night and their father standing there in a cloud of gin and they instinctively closed their eyes pretending to be asleep. Michael opened his eyes to slits and watched their father hovering over them, breathing heavily through his nose like a horse on a cold day, looking down, his face a puzzled wound, as if he wasn't sure what he had created and was examining them for clues.

It was Stanford who found their father, a nine-year-old boy led by his dog finding his bloody, peaceful form in the damp grass. He looked like something that had fallen from the heavens, which was true more or less. The dog licked his ruined face and Stanford just stood there for fifteen minutes, an odd farewell.

Michael's Thursday morning class stared at him, each pudding face empty of conviction. Baxter was curling her white blond hair with a pencil. Hector Grayson sat stonily, and August Purvue had his usual air of distraction. Billy Whitecloud's seat was empty, an absence that filled the room. How did he fly out of that car? Michael considered the stories that had surfaced: unreliable threads, rumours, bold uninformed certitude: "I told you. Guy's crazy. Didn't I say it."

The sun came in the eastern windows and flooded the room with a warmth that could put a third of the class to sleep in half an hour. Some of them lived on ranches and had been up since five doing chores. Michael taught grade twelve history at John G. Diefenbaker High School. He enjoyed the students, their complacency an amiable challenge. He told them stories. These children who had been lulled by stories, whose first worlds were made of dragons and princes and who had moved through cowboys, detectives, and plucky heroines, and finally heartache.

The class was drawing a map, a historical mural to mark Canada's centennial. Today they were painting the surrounding foothills and mountains. What is a mountain? A question too obvious for any of them to consider. Waves of stone that extended from the Pacific Ocean wrinkled into existence by the methodical war between crustal plates. At the bottom were the Proterozoic layers containing fossilized algae, then up through the Cambrian with its trilobites, past the Devonian and into the Mesozoic and Cenozoic. They held oil and natural gas created from lost worlds, and vast coal deposits formed by Cretaceous forests.

The Rockies weren't formed, like some mountains, by volcanic activity. They were the result of the meticulous creep of sedimentary shelves sliding inland, the horizontal compression pushing them into soft folds and continuing to push until the folds finally erupted with slow delicacy into jagged peaks. It was a middle-aged range with no history of violence. Its childhood, in short, was normal.

The foothills were the final folds, the geologic energy spent, a last marshalling of Mesozoic strength after the calm of Morley Flats to the west, the arching of the rock less severe, the folds intact as soft hills.

Once formed, however, the Rocky Mountains showed a flair for violence. They took the lives of hundreds of Chinese railway workers. People drowned when the spring runoff suddenly flooded the Bow River, the Elbow, or the Red Deer. They died of hunger or exposure, were gored by elk or mauled by bears, buried by avalanches. They skied into crevasses, were lost on glaciers, drove off embankments, and suffered heart attacks diving into the clear pools of melted snow.

It was Europeans who brought the idea that the mountains were an inconvenience, an obstacle to trade, the barrier between Europe and the mythic wealth of the Orient. The drawing of a mountain, Michael told the blank, blotchy faces in his class, is more than a child's simple geometry, that triangle with a cap of snow indicated by a bisecting squiggly line. It has a history.

Mrs. Grayson had talked to the principal about Michael's class. Her son Hector was a corn-fed giant moving awkwardly into adulthood, a rancher's son, and like all mothers, she was trying to protect her child. From what? Michael wondered. From change, perhaps. Change in these parts had been measured in small doses for more than a century. But now it was gushing out, and perhaps she saw his history class as part of that. The culture was in upheaval and she was worried that what had been built might fall. But she was safe. These children were immune to the slogans and fashions from the Summer of Love, from the privileged revolution playing out in the cities. They were certainly immune to his history class. Hector will go away to university, Michael thought, drink beer, perhaps try marijuana, and stare with doleful love at the first girl who undresses in his presence. He and his new girl will go everywhere together, to the library, to classes, walking and talking and drinking coffee and staring at the miracle of themselves. Hector's body, which moved as if it was operated by two different owners, will be invested with a new authority and confidence. And what will he do with this confidence? Search for a prettier girl to sleep with. He'll finish two years of university and then drift back to the ranch to become his parents and his grandparents: hard-working, independent, unimaginative, resourceful, capable of delivering a calf at 2 A.M. on a January night, changing the timing chain on his Ford half-ton, digging wells, repairing pumps, butchering a steer. This was his history, Michael thought, he just hasn't lived it yet.

The pale yellow cinderblock hallway of the school was filled with essays that sang the praises of prime ministers, medical researchers, and suffragettes, all taped to the walls in orderly rows. A red and white banner stretched across the hallway. One hundred years old, an infant among countries. Michael's mother was ninety-seven.

The map project had begun last term, and the idea had metastasized into two hundred and fifty square feet of ragged narrative. Twenty-five feet long and ten feet high, it laid out the country in all of its idiosyncrasies—earnest drawings of founders, explorers, politicians, rebels, local landmarks, distorted aerial views, a few gracefully rendered portraits, crude battle scenes, and a ghastly rendering of Christ bleeding on the cross. It contained all the baroque whimsy of a fifteenth-century map. Initially, Michael had offered some direction, but it had grown into a monumental piece of folk art and he was comfortable with its cheerful chaos. It was his last year of teaching. He was sixty-nine, past retirement age, teaching because of a severe shortage of teachers and because it sustained him. There had been questions about his methods, but they were largely perfunctory. What choice did they have?

Did it matter who taught them history? Most of the students spent their days trying to kill the past. They lived in an age that prized the present and the future. In two weeks there would be a faster car, a new Rolling Stones album, personal jet packs. The present had all the joys of revolution without the blood.

At some point every teacher was talking to himself. You got to a point where the age gap was simply too large, or you became bored with your own stories. Or you lost the student you felt you were talking to, the life you thought you might be affecting. Michael wondered if that student was Billy Whitecloud. Now that Billy was no longer in his class, with his patient, inscrutable face and epic detachment, perhaps Michael was remaking him as someone who had promise. Some of the kids would move to Calgary and disappear into the oil business. Others would simply take over the ranch or marry a rancher. Billy's future was less clear. That ancient lament—when, in real life, will I ever need art/math/history?—had genuine currency here.

In the sixteenth century, Michael told the class, London was like most of you: The British didn't have much interest in exploration; they were content to stare at one another and silently find flaws or love or both. They listened to music, drank beer, pissed in the street. Anyway, why explore? Londoners assumed they were the centre of the world, content with public floggings and the glory of themselves. Meanwhile, the Spanish sailed across the ocean to spread Christianity and disease, returning with gold.

But at some point you have to embrace the world. How else to define yourself?

So the British take the leap. In 1576, Martin Frobisher leaves to find a passage to China. He's handsome, ambitious, essentially a pirate. One of his backers hires a balladeer to write songs about his bravery before he even leaves. Frobisher has maps that are partly rumours and fantasy, drawn by people who have never left London, who rely on traders and travellers and fabulists for their information. On the maps are drawings of sea monsters, fish, game, grape vines, and spice trees. This is the map we all begin with, filled with faith and doubt and error and fear, and with that imperfect document, we sail away.

Frobisher sails to Baffin Island where there are Inuit in their kayaks bouncing on the waves, and when he gets close and sees those weathered, narrow-eyed faces, he is filled with joy. These must be Chinese people; he is close, though China is colder than he imagined. He sends five of his men to accompany the leather boats to shore. They land out of sight and then two of Frobisher's men appear on the shore and stand there, not moving. They turn away and disappear. Hours go by. Frobisher sends a search party to look for the men, but there is no sign of them or of the magical Chinese. The two men are never seen again.

On his way back to England, they encounter an Inuit in his kayak on the calm sea near Baffin Island. Frobisher dangles a bell over him and when the man reaches for it, they haul him and his boat on board as if they were fishing. The first thing the Inuit does in captivity is bite his tongue in half. Now he can't tell them anything in any language. Frobisher takes him to Queen Elizabeth, the perennial virgin, who had put up a thousand pounds for the voyage. He wants to show her what her money has bought: an authentic Oriental, living proof. The Inuit goes to Hampton Court and on its exquisitely manicured grounds he demonstrates his skill with a bow by shooting the Queen's swans. He dies a week later of heartbreak.

Frobisher goes back a second time and returns with ore and a family of three Inuit. The ore isn't gold, as it turns out, and the Inuit all die within a month.

He goes back a third time. To raise money, one of his backers sells tickets to see the dead Orientals. There are maps in London that have China on them now, located northeast of Newfoundland. This time Frobisher brings back 1,200 tons of ore. Gold, he says, and he parades some of the dark rock through the streets. It turns out to be iron pyrites: fool's gold. Frobisher returns to his old job of pirating, and London returns to hangings and floggings for entertainment. The maps are once more filled with monsters.

At the hospital the nurse stood in front of him, her grey face weary with the daily routine of cigarette breaks and human decay. "Third floor," she said.

"What do the doctors think?" Michael asked.

"Impossible to tell with these things. He could wake up in ten minutes or ten years."

Michael walked up the stairs. There were two other beds in the room and all three occupants were unconscious, their IVs dripping methodically. Michael sat on the metal chair and stared at Billy Whitecloud. His face was slightly swollen at the jaw, and a small patch of hair was missing on the side of his head where the stitches were. One arm was in a cast. He looked like a seven-year-old boy, untroubled in sleep. You could still see the child in them, even as they were almost grown, suddenly and regrettably gawky teenagers, resentful and insane, Michael thought, but a small gesture, the way their mouth sat in repose, the light catching their hair, and the perfect seven-year-old emerged. Billy was over six feet tall, stretched out on the bed, his feet pushing against the metal footboard.

His potential as a student was impossible to divine. He wasn't indifferent to history—the most common response in Michael's class—but was somehow unavailable to it, as if he hadn't decided what it was. There were glimpses of ability. There were glimpses of something in most students.

Ancient maps, he told his class, were seductions, the compiled lies of merchants, the half-truths of fishermen, tales from sailors swimming in ale, a fevered dream drawn on parchment. Most of the mapmakers sat in London or Lisbon or Genoa and in their foreshortened lives they didn't get any farther than the harbour. The empty spaces on those maps were filled with fear. What waited out there? Perhaps the Antipodeans, a race of devils who lived in flames near the equator. Or sea monsters, or men who had only one foot and hopped after their prey, their shark teeth gnashing. A race of giant women who shat gold, or winged monkeys.

The maps we have now, he told them, the ones you pick up at the gas station, are purely functional, for people travelling through those spaces. But early maps were made by people who had never gone there, for people who would never go. They were filled with larceny and rumour. Mapmakers stole from one another and distorted the truth to suit their interest.

Their mural had few supporters. The principal thought it was a fool's errand and had said as much. Each of the five panels was five by ten feet, and they worked on them in sequence, spreading them on the floor, the shoeless students congregating around the canvases like an overgrown kindergarten. He thought the act of doing, of translating talk into art, might help. The teenage brain, an endless subject in the teacher's lounge, was impervious to logic or reason, but a grateful host for whim and experience and, on occasion, narrative.

It was Purvue, a rancher's son, dark haired, twitchy and raw boned, usually attentive only to the unchanging view through the window, who put up his callused adult hand.

"If we wanted to draw a war on the map, Mr. Mountain Horse?"

"How would you paint a war, Purvue?"

"Blood. Dead guys."

For the exams, they had to memorize dates, and the dates usually corresponded to wars or treaties: Jay, Ghent, Boer, Civil, Holy.

"What war did you have in mind?"

"The Plains of Abraham. It was short. I think maybe an hour."

"Battles are short and wars are long."

"You were in a war."

"Yes."

"Did you paint it?"

"No, but others did." Picasso's *Guernica*, with its angled drama and calculated chaos. Paintings were once the only visual images of war. Da Vinci's idealized males with their perfect musculature, wielding swords, holding severed heads, dying nobly of their wounds in languid poses attended by angels. The audience craved nobility, the state demanded it. Artists were complicit for centuries. Frederick Varley's World War I paintings showed the same anguished faces as da Vinci's work, the gods or women or cherubs replaced by waste, decay, and futility in brown acres of mud. Of course, Varley was there. The Plains of Abraham produced several paintings, but one elbowed all others out of contention and became the visual reference for the next two hundred years. Inaccurate, perhaps, but catchy, like a pop song, it was called *The Death of General Wolfe.*

The first thing you have to understand about James Wolfe, Michael told the class, is that he was a tortured man. There isn't much disagreement about that.

In 1759, England and France are at war in Europe and the British are losing. The drearily named Seven Years' War.

Prime Minister William Pitt decides to send a large force to North America. Perhaps they'll have better luck there.

The man who will lead this force is Brigadier General James Wolfe, thirty-one years old, a frail and humourless man. He suffers from seasickness, a bladder infection, and rheumatism. He's a fatalist who believes he'll die young, a gift for a soldier. During a party at the prime minister's residence, Wolfe retrieves his sword and begins slashing at imaginary enemies. He isn't drunk. The dinner guests stare in reserved horror. "To think that I have committed the fate of my country and of my ministry into such hands," Pitt says after the demonstration. Wolfe is betrayed by his predatory name. He has a weak chin and the spindly build of a London clerk. There is nothing lupine about Jimmy Wolfe.

In the spring, Wolfe sails to Quebec with one-quarter of the British navy, 186 ships, a floating city. On board are fifteen thousand soldiers, as well as cooks, surgeons, butchers, sailors, children, prostitutes, pipers, cobblers, teachers, tailors, clerks, cattle, sheep, hens, dogs, rats, syphilis, and lice. They sail up the St. Lawrence River, a parade that is thirty miles long. The Canadiens who farm the banks of the St. Lawrence see the enemy arrive like a stately dream, one that goes on for days. Look at the power of Europe! There are more people on these ships than in the city they're invading. Canadien farm boys and old men lie down in the grass under the pleasant June sun and level their muskets at the ships, spend a leisurely day trying to kill something.

Wolfe arrives at Quebec, but it's a fortress, heavily walled and sitting on top of a steep hill. He can't figure out a way to attack it, and in September he's still sitting in his ship. Almost three months have gone by. He bombards the city

with mortar fire, but the French won't come out. Wolfe has
a fever and he's indecisive, forming plans then changing
them. He has just received news that his father has died,
which further depresses him. He reads obsessively from
Thomas Gray's *Elegy Written in a Country Churchyard*, "The
paths of glory lead but to the grave." His men draw pictures
of him, chinless caricatures, and pass them around like school
kids. They openly doubt his leadership. He writes to his
mother, telling her he'll quit the military when he returns to
England, that life is a misery.

If he doesn't do something soon the river will ice up and
trap them and they will slowly starve before spring. If he
returns now, taking this mighty fleet back to England
without having engaged the enemy, he'll be ridiculed, a
symbol of national impotence. His fiancée will deny him, his
colleagues will avoid him, his family will bear his failure with
quiet condemnation. But to charge the hill would be suicide.

Luckily, he is suicidal. This is his strongest quality as a
leader. At least that's what the men who had been with him
at Louisbourg thought. Louisbourg was the French fortress
that guarded the entrance to the St. Lawrence River, and a
detested symbol for the British. In 1758, they sent twelve
thousand men to destroy it, a battle that started with
European politesse: The British sent a gift of two pineap-
ples to the French governor's wife, and in return the
governor sent over several bottles of champagne. Then they
bombarded each other with cannon shot.

Wolfe was at Louisbourg and he decided to land a force on
the rocky shores of Île Royale, where Louisbourg was
perched. The piece of the coast where he chose to land was
so rough and rocky that it was undefended. Who could
possibly land there? But Wolfe did. He lost men as the boats

smashed on the rocks, but they landed. By then the walls of Louisbourg were so riddled with cannon shot they could just walk in. Wolfe made his mark, and that's what got him the job of invading Quebec.

Who is he facing in Quebec a year later? Wolfe's French counterpart is the Marquis de Montcalm, a forty-seven-year-old career officer who began his training at the age of nine and who comes from a distinguished French military family. He is short, impatient, vain, and as tortured as Wolfe. He misses his wife and France and is heavily in debt. He had tried, repeatedly and unsuccessfully, to be posted elsewhere, somewhere warm, and has just received word that one of his daughters has died, but he doesn't know which one, an agony that has all of them dead in his frail heart.

And Montcalm has another fear: that he'll lose his European soul. The French are allied with the Indians, whose style of warfare is to spread terror, to burn villages, kidnap women and children, and submit the male captives to inventive torture. These aren't the European rules of engagement. The Indian soul, Montcalm thinks, is as black as pitch, and some of the French soldiers have slid into this morass, have abandoned themselves, their country, and their God, and have become savage in this savage land. The French weren't spreading civilization, they were becoming barbaric, that seductive state.

Michael observed the class, his barbarians, a few faces following the story, eager for blood. So he continued. These two lost men face one another to decide the fate of a continent, Michael said. Wolfe with his impressive fleet and well-trained soldiers, Montcalm with his fortress. They sit, day after day, with their respective demons, wishing they were elsewhere, convinced they will lose the upcoming battle.

Wolfe keeps making plans to assault Quebec, but rejects them all. His officers lose faith. This feverish scarecrow will get them killed. Or humiliated. Or both.

Finally, on September 12, Wolfe announces his historic decision: to climb the steep face of Anse au Foulon at night, to move hundreds of men and guns up a sheer rock face in the dark a few hundred yards from the city.

It is suicidal. It's perfect.

At eleven that night the soldiers begin the climb, sliding in the mud in their leather-soled shoes, their hands torn from grasping the gnarled brush that grows on the hill, their rifles and shot weighing them down. They curse softly and pray the French sentries don't hear them, that the Iroquois—those lords of the forest—don't descend upon them with their godless tortures. It takes six hours to make the climb.

By five in the morning, five hundred British troops are standing on the Plains of Abraham in a light rain. Montcalm had been expecting an assault from the east, at Beauport, the more logical spot, and his troops have been awake for thirty-six hours, waiting for a night attack there. When Montcalm gets word that Wolfe is outside the gates, he marches the men back to Quebec. It takes an hour marching at double time. He has three thousand reinforcements coming from a position upriver, three hours away. If he simply waits, he'll have the British trapped in a crossfire.

But he doesn't wait. He takes his exhausted, underfed army out to the plain to engage the British. Why? Perhaps he needs the reassurance of those two lines facing one another, the nostalgic geometry of European death. Or maybe he's just as fatalistic as Wolfe.

The battle begins at eight with a volley of British shot. An hour later, the two armies move closer to one another.

At ten the battle begins in earnest. Both sides fire. Bodies slump, musket balls smashing bone. Wolfe is shot in the wrist by a sniper and his wound is bandaged with a handkerchief. At 10:15, Wolfe gives the order to fire once more. The French give way under the volley, and the Highlanders attack with their broadswords, hacking at the retreating French. A piper plays. Indian snipers shoot at the British from the woods. The stately format of European battle mixed with the guerrilla tactics of the New World.

Wolfe's injury gives him an appetite for the heroic death he craves. There is just enough pain for this moment to be glorious, a taste of mortality that whets his need for oblivion. He is hit again, this time in the groin. The pain is excruciating, and erases his thoughts of noble death. Suddenly he wants to live. As death circles, he craves life. He has no wife, no children, little experience of the world. He left a fiancée in London. If he had doubts about his love for her (and he did), he loves her now with a force that empties all impure thoughts of glory. Then he's hit again, this time in the chest, and is knocked backward and dies without another thought.

Montcalm is shot below the ribs and collapses. He's taken to the hospital, and as they scurry through the rubble of Quebec, he breathes out his love for his wife and his daughters. He is consumed by sadness at having lost that feminine world. It sits in him like a dark cloud as he dies. His reinforcements arrive at eleven but it's too late. The battle is over. Quebec has fallen.

The Canadiens attempt to bury their dead, but there are no more coffins in Quebec. Poor Montcalm is put into a box and lowered into a bomb crater in the chapel of the Ursuline nuns. The sisters cover him with earth and pray for his soul and hold one another and weep for an hour.

Wolfe is taken back to London for a hero's burial. But how to get him there? His small corpse will rot. They open a barrel of rum, drain half of it, and stuff the general inside like a rag doll. A waste of good rum, some of the men complain. He sails back to England and is uncorked at a funeral parlour near Westminster Abbey, his skin the colour of tobacco. His coffin is paraded slowly through the streets of London, the conquering hero.

The continent has been won. All that's left is to paint it.

The artists weren't there of course. They didn't see the Highlanders cleaving a man's arm at the shoulder with their broadswords, or Indians wrestling with a man's scalp as he screamed. They didn't see the mutilation, the doubt. They certainly didn't see the winter of starvation that followed, or the invalids begging for bread. They saw bravery and purpose and a nobility that could be hung in the galleries and palaces back home. Where did they see all this? In their artist's imagination. And what fed that imagination? Other paintings of war.

Montcalm is the losing general. So he gets the lesser artist and the inferior painting. *The Death of Montcalm* shows him dying beside a palm tree, flanked by what look like South American natives. In the background, if you squint, you can see Wolfe dying less nobly.

There are several mundane versions of Wolfe's death, of the battle, but none of them catch on.

What do we want from a death? That it mean something.

But then comes *The Death of General Wolfe*, painted by Benjamin West, an American. He has Wolfe propped by three aides. His face is uplifted, slightly anguished, beatific; he looks like a schoolgirl who has just fainted. An Indian warrior is in the foreground, staring at Wolfe in a classical pose of contemplation. The Indians, of course, fought for the other side. What is he doing in the painting? He is the noble savage, a popular European idea of aboriginal peoples uncorrupted by civilization. An idea held by Europeans who never left Europe.

West's painting is a hit. It is unveiled at the Royal Academy, and William Pitt, who had thought that Wolfe was mad, commissions a copy of it. King George III, who would soon go mad himself, also asks for a copy. West becomes rich from this one painting. His career is made. What was it about the painting that made it so popular? It certainly didn't tell the story of the battle, or even the story of Wolfe's death. What did it do?

It reaffirmed that there is nobility in war and purpose in life.

West's painting was finished in 1770, eleven years after Wolfe's death. It is a big year for history. In Boston, British soldiers open fire on a crowd of demonstrators, killing five of them. They are tried for murder and acquitted, and so begin the rumblings of the American Revolution. What else? James Cook circumnavigates the globe. The world is getting smaller. The British have won the top half of North America. The Americans will soon claim the lower half. The Spanish are retreating, the French dwindling. Ownership is being established, but the continent has yet to be discovered. Millions of square miles are still unseen, unmapped. They don't exist in the European mind.

And 1770 was the year that my great-great-grandfather was born, Michael tells the class. David Thompson, the greatest land geographer who ever lived, and in the tradition of greatness, a man who died in poverty and obscurity. He was a genius, both intuitive and scientific, largely self-taught, the Mozart of the plains. Driven by some inner force that is difficult to define, he mapped western Canada. It was a solitary passion. And the reward? Nothing really. Or almost nothing. What was his contribution? He helped create your world, the one you are now living in, with its Levi's, Ford pickups, longing, hormones, fear, and the exquisite boredom of this particular moment.

THE MAP

1777–1807

Today the hospital room had an emptiness, as if Billy himself wasn't there. His expression, Michael thought, was unchanged from the last visit. Did this mean that there was no activity in his brain, that no emotions were being experienced, that sadness, anger, and, as unlikely as it seemed, happiness had all been replaced by a void? Maybe these emotions were being felt but simply not communicated to his facial muscles. The signal was sent out and met with silence and Billy's mouth retained its enigmatic Mona Lisa cast.

He pulled the metal chair closer to the bed and examined Billy's face, checking to see if there was some flicker, someone to talk to. What if Billy could hear him and understood? What if his life was made up of long blank days and these visits were his only stimulation? At seventeen there wasn't enough experience and memory to fill the days. He couldn't look back on his life and replay scenes and decisions, mull through relationships. Seventeen is about longing, about becoming eighteen.

All stories begin in happenstance. What if Michael's mother

hadn't gone to Dexter, looking for work, what if she had looked elsewhere? Or what if his father had married one of the impressionable local girls? You can do this kind of math forever, calculating the variables, the coincidences that bring each of us to daylight (or darkness). What if Billy hadn't gotten into August Purvue's car?

The same is true of countries. They're born out of circumstance, necessity, greed, and negotiation, and then framed in terms of destiny and God's special love for their people.

And then what? Then you prayed and fought for them. Fifty years ago, a raven had followed Michael through the mud of France, hopping alongside him like a pet dog. An omen? A guardian? Or simply opportunistic nature sensing a fresh corpse? His mother had told him that the yellow grass to the west of their home was made of starlight knitted into a terrestrial carpet. The cows ate the grass, they ate the cows, and that light sat in all of us. And when our souls took their place in the skies, that's why they shone.

His mother would be a hundred soon. He had heard that the Queen phoned you on your hundredth birthday. What would the two of them talk about? Of course you had to have a phone, and his mother didn't. Perhaps the Queen would send a letter. My Dearest Catherine, congratulations on this ...

They came from opposite directions. The Indians from the west, the whites from the east. The Indians crossed the land bridge from Asia, across the Bering Isthmus thousands of years ago, and moved south along the coast, then went inland, crossed to the other side of the continent and continued in a long, gentle loop that brought them up the east coast and deposited them in the thick forests of New England and Ontario. They moved for the usual reasons: to find a better climate, to escape enemies, and to find food, and the Plains Indians crossed most of the country before settling in the lee of the Rocky Mountains.

The whites came from the east looking for furs. Some had ambitions—Alexander Mackenzie, the heroically efficient Scot, the less efficient Samuel Hearne, Simon Fraser, and others—but it was only with my great-great-grandfather, David Thompson, that the West was willed into existence. This is the conceit of every descendant, isn't it, that his ancestor is singular and remarkable; even if he was a sheep thief, he was the most notorious sheep thief. We sift through the ashes in search of celebrity. Thompson gave the West a shape and then watched it fill with European meaning. He helped create the boundary between the United States and Canada, and he mapped the northwestern states and most of the West and walked and paddled to the Pacific Ocean. He mapped more than two million square miles. In search of what? At first it was adventure. Then money, I suppose, in the form of furs. And knowledge certainly. Finally, though, I think it was enlightenment. In those travels my great-great-grandfather sought the spiritual, and not just in the sense of God (although he certainly believed in Him). It pushed him on, this particular search, past the point when fatigue or despair or fear had stopped those who went before him (or those who travelled with him). And in the end, perhaps that's what he found out there under that incessant sky: enlightenment.

If you look carefully at Thompson's map you can see his scientific mind, but there are traces of the Romantic too. And he was a Romantic, in his way. Who can understand the world? Who can divine the human heart? So we draw new maps.

1

LONDON, 1777

In the damp, windowless room David Thompson ate a thin soup that had limped along for a week, bolstered daily by one of his mother's desperate inventions (roots scrounged from the park, offal from the market). Her Welsh voice sang him to sleep each night, the clotted musical syllables lulling him. David was seven and had little memory of his father, who had died five years earlier. He dreamed of food, roasted turkey and potatoes, of heat. With his gift for numbers, a gift that had emerged even before his formal schooling began, he calculated when the soup would be gone, based on volume and the number of people it had to feed (one adult, two children). The answer appeared not as a figure but as an image, a fixed point in time with his family sitting at the desolate table.

It was autumn when his mother took him by the hand and they walked to the Grey Coat School of London near Westminster Abbey, a school that took the orphaned and indigent. They walked for more than an hour, their breath visible in the air, his mother talking the whole way, giving him a list of rules to live by: take the Christian path, avoid cold baths, be polite, practise thrift. Observe people closely and respond to them in kind. Don't eat foreign meats, wear a scarf, shun prostitutes and alcohol, read what you can. Never forsake your God, especially when it appears that He has forsaken you.

She left him in the care of an appropriately grey woman with a mournful face. Before leaving she buried her face against her son's shoulder, holding him for several minutes, squeezing the last of him before turning to go, walking quickly away on the dark cobblestones, hollowed in a way that hunger alone hadn't accomplished.

The young David tried to ignore the cruelties of the headmistress and the other children, and adapted happily to the food, which was coarse but regular. He slept on a pillow of such rough material that it chafed his face. But he loved the books that were now available to him. Once this world was opened, he stayed in it whenever he could, reading *Robinson Crusoe* and *Gulliver's Travels.* Another world, a world uninhabited by the other children, was opened with numbers. As he walked in Grey Coat's field he counted the paces it took to cover its periphery and calculated the number of steps it would take to walk to Wales. He assessed the school population, counting the number of teachers and figuring out how many strokes of the cane were delivered per teacher per student per week (eleven).

Thompson observed the other boys. Busby wept each

night; Wright was quarrelsome; Donner clever; Oliphant melancholy and unreliable; McWhey an untrustworthy ferret eager to report the misdeeds of others, a natural cleric. Thompson spent most of his holidays in Westminster Abbey, reading the inscriptions—"The shortness of the span of life forbids us to cherish remote hope; already night overtakes thee"—or wandering the cloisters, or sitting in his favourite place, the Henry VII chapel. On a day that drizzled rain, he watched a grave being dug, the shovelfuls of earth containing bone from the many dead that lay beneath the abbey, their bodies mingled with one another and the earth. The gravedigger had stringy hair and rotting teeth. He paused at his shovel and stared up at Thompson.

"Shall I dig one for you?" he said, and laughed.

In school they recited the names of the kings in order and studied their noble acts but none of their idiosyncrasies: the drunkenness, sexual peculiarities, physical deformities, mental shortcomings, inclinations toward incest or madness, their lack of both divinity and commonness. The great men were mourned by a nation that had only ever seen likenesses of them, portraits commissioned to flatter, the small corpses eclipsed by monument.

In April 1784, the Hudson's Bay Company sent a representative to Grey Coat looking for employees to work in the New World. Thompson was fourteen, a candidate. The Bay man was large and dark haired, with a deep voice, and as he surveyed the children in the field the teachers gave him brief profiles of boys they thought might be useful, inflating their abilities and neglecting their inadequacies. The Bay man watched them run stupidly in a herd, and pointed to Thompson.

"He has a facility with numbers and a gift for solitude," the teacher said.

Thompson was summoned and the Bay man looked at him, at his small shoulders and his face with its lack of cunning. Thompson stared up at the man, who smelled of sour clothes.

"Do you love adventure, boy?" he asked, baring his small grey teeth.

"Yes sir."

"Do you believe there are monsters at the edge of the world?"

"No sir."

"Well, there are."

Behind the Bay man, shapes began to move quietly on the horizon, striped circles that rose up from the dark spires of London. Thompson saw Busby pointing, his normally slack mouth even slacker. He followed Busby's finger to a sky filled with round balloons, bulbous on top, tapering down, each one carrying a basket. From the baskets, people waved and shouted. The hot-air balloons bobbed along the skyline, drifting east. They were madly incongruous with anything Thompson knew, the opposite of the sober facts and numbers that the teachers hammered into him. People flying through the air—the most wondrous thing he had ever seen! People could look down and see the world as God did. Thompson counted the balloons (twenty-nine), noted their colours, and observed their speed. Would they float to China? Could they continue around the world? How could you steer a round vessel that was moved by only wind? Perhaps you simply let nature guide you to whatever land it chose.

The Bay man watched the striped parade hovering over the city. "Foolishness," he said.

He spoke to seven boys, and in the end chose two. The other boy ran away when he realized the immensity of the task.

They sailed in May. Thompson imagined that the ship would sail to a magical portal on the horizon, and that on the other side would be a Gulliver world. Captain Cook's map of the world had just been published. Mankind knew the boundaries now, and had only to fill in the spaces. Cook himself had died five years earlier, and Oliphant had described the event with his usual authority: "Blackbeard drew his sword and cut off Cook's head, and Cook's mouth kept talking for an hour, a stream of pure filth."

The truth wasn't much less fanciful. Cook was killed on the Sandwich Islands by natives who had watched the large white-sailed ships congregate off their shore and regarded with suspicion the pale men who came to the beach in small boats. They didn't smell like gods. The natives were wary of friendship and indifferent to trade. They slaughtered Cook and his men and broiled them over a fire on the perfect white sand, and then ate their fears.

As the Hudson's Bay ship moved slowly away from England, Thompson wrote in his journal: *In the month of May, 1784 at the Port of London, I embarked in the ship Prince Rupert belonging to the Hudson's Bay Company, as apprentice and clerk to the said company, bound for Churchill Factory. I bid a long and sad farewell to my noble, my sacred country, an exile forever.*

2

CHURCHILL FACTORY, 1784

When Thompson arrived it was cold. They had navigated around icebergs in Hudson Bay, white and dignified, the opposite of the filthy ship after its weeks at sea. Thompson's small room at Churchill Factory was unfurnished except for a hard bed and crude table. The next morning he joined the grouse hunt, trapping two dozen of them under a net and then falling on the panicked birds and taking their necks in his teeth and snapping them without drawing blood.

"If the nets are stained with blood," the factor had said, a man with a dark smile named Guttins, "foxes eat them. And how will they get repaired? You'll be sitting in a circle like spinsters, sewing with cold fingers in the dark, my pretty idiots."

They caught sixty birds a day for a week. Thompson lay on his stomach, staring at his companions in their Crusoe poses, feathers in their mouths, their knees bloody.

"You're a long way from London, Mr. Thompson," Guttins said.

On Sunday morning, Samuel Hearne read a sermon of his own creation for the men. Hearne was six feet tall, a handsome, muscular man who had walked from Fort Churchill to the mouth of the Coppermine River at the Arctic Ocean guided by Copper natives, a journey of more than twelve hundred miles. He had hoped to find gold, but saw only pyrites and the grim slaughter of a band of Inuit. His presence was heroic, but his reputation was diminished by two events: the first was not finding gold, despite his hardships and effort; the second was letting the French capture Fort Churchill two years earlier without a shot being fired. He had allowed the French commander to advance on the fort with his small army, ignoring the pleas of his men to cut them down with grapeshot from their heavy guns, to shred these papists and send them to hell. Inexplicably, Hearne opened the gates and surrendered the fort, which the French burned, although the stones withstood the fire and were reclaimed, the fort rebuilt under the British flag. Even the French commander held Hearne in contempt. He was tainted now, a caricature of a hero, still golden looking but already fallen. Worse, he was a Voltairean, his only bible the writings of a French freethinker. He argued against the religious hierarchy of created beings, from ant to monkey to man to angel. He saw equality and a hell of one's own devising.

In Hearne's room, the only comfortable space at Churchill Factory, he read Voltaire's words in place of a Sunday sermon, his soothing voice penetrating the smell of labour-weary bodies. Thompson shifted uncomfortably in his seat, staring at his fellow men: the misshapen, reeking sailors, the failed husbands, the indebted and adventurous who had left England for the unknown. He had come upon Tetley and MacAvoy in the supply room, Tetley's back to him, MacAvoy kneeling in front. Tetley had looked over his shoulder with a defiant terrible face. Go away, boy.

"The Bible is a book much prized by sheep and invalids," Hearne said. He stood by his desk, holding a copy of Voltaire's *Philosophical Dictionary*. "This is my bible. I know no other."

Hearne took a few theatrical paces, preening. In London, they were summoning charges to sack him for cowardice.

"Voltaire himself only ever offered a single prayer," Hearne said. "'O Lord, make my enemies ridiculous.' And God granted his wish."

God granted the French commander the same wish, Thompson thought. How could such a man, this noble specimen who had explored the North with such purpose and surely with God's hand guiding him, how could he stand there, salving his own sins with the words of a Frenchman?

After an hour of Hearne's quiet blasphemies, they left the room. A young native woman was waiting, wrapped in skins, her brown eyes inscrutable. Lingerers would hear Hearne's satisfied grunting.

By October the marshes and swamps were frozen; by mid-November the river solid. December brought a cold that shivered everything. In the night, Thompson heard a rock split with the sound of a gunshot. He spent the morning collecting fuel for the fire. The stunted trees were no taller than Thompson and there was only enough fuel for a fire in the morning and another at night. In the afternoon he searched for game, which was scarcer than wood. The labour of moving through deep snow both warmed and tired him, and by late afternoon he collapsed in his room, still wearing his heavy coat. Ice had formed on the log walls, and he had given up chipping it away.

MacKay came to his door. An Orkneyman with a squat face, as if he had carried a great weight on his head all his life. He was slightly taller than Thompson, who guessed him to be a few years older, though it was difficult to say as the country aged a man.

"You've got the darkies," MacKay said. "Can't stay awake."

"I've no will to move."

"Your first taste of it. It gets worse. Birds falling out of the trees, stone dead. Frozen. You won't know if you're awake or dead."

"There must be other forts, other trading posts. I want to see the country."

"No one will ever see this country," MacKay said. "It goes on like Job's trials. Take fifteen lifetimes."

"What is out there?"

"There's buffalo herds with a million beasts. Power of God in them when they're moving. There's Indians can cut your heart out so fast they'll take a bite out of it before you're dead. I've seen the sky darken with birds, ten million in a flock, knocking the sun out of the sky."

"It can't all be this cold."

"There's no relief."

"Surely as you move south …"

"The mosquitoes get bigger."

"You're a clerk?" Thompson asked.

"When there's clerking," MacKay said. "A vile waste. But there are worse fates."

"How long have you been here?"

"Far too long."

"You miss home."

"The only thing worse."

Thompson guessed that MacKay was fleeing some grief in Orkney. He wanted to ask more, grateful for the company, but his eyes closed heavily and he slept.

In the morning he woke in his clothes and got up, wrapped the heavy buffalo coat around him, and walked along the coastline. On the shore he saw a polar bear, its white mass partly submerged in the guts of a white whale. Its head rose up, the red muzzle sniffing the air, and it growled like a mastiff, the massive forepaws resting on the whale, defending its kill.

The winter froze spit and piss; it froze Thompson's breath. The malevolent cold froze thoughts, and finally, time. Nothing moved in the darkness and each day cruelly mimicked the last. Sound was magnified; everything else shrank within itself. There were moments when he questioned his own existence. Had he been swallowed by the landscape?

He was sitting at the small table with the checkerboard on it when the devil sat down opposite him. He hadn't seen him appear: He was just suddenly sitting there, his features and colour those of a Spaniard. He had two short black horns on his forehead that pointed forward, and both his head and body to the waist (he saw no more) were covered with glossy black curling hair. His countenance was surprisingly mild. They played several games, the devil losing every one, yet each time keeping his temper. His movements were languorous, a lazy power, an evil strength coiled within. He uttered not a word. Then he got up or simply disappeared. At any rate, he was gone. Was it a dream? Thompson wondered. His eyes were open. There was a smell in the room, not sulphur, something else, like a singed animal.

Having defeated the devil in this black cold, Thompson began a dialogue with God, a conversation that reached a vividness in late February when He laid out the order of all things and Thompson's task: *You will map the land and its beasts and the fruits in the field and the men on the grasses, you will bear witness to My work.* Witness to God's work and man's struggle.

At the age of fifteen, Thompson had a mission.

Winter passed in solemn darkness, the light fading in mid-afternoon before it could bring any warmth, the land without horizon.

Spring arrived with its release, the relief of water, of warmth and movement. The ground turned to bog that took a man's leg up to the thigh. Rude boards were placed on the ground to walk on, but they sank into the wet earth.

In May, the Indians came with their beaver skins to trade. Thompson watched them arrive in canoes that were low in the water, laden with pelts.

"You want to know why you freeze all winter?" MacKay said. "Here it is."

"Do you suppose they are one of the lost tribes?" Thompson asked.

"Lost tribes?"

"The ten lost tribes of Israel. Descended from Joseph, perhaps."

"We're the lost tribe, Davy. They're in their homeland, happy as larks."

"It's possible," Thompson said.

"They're not lost now, but they will be. The factor will see to that."

Guttins offered the Indian chief a suit of clothes: a scarlet tunic, a pair of wool trousers, a linen shirt, and a hat with a feather. The chief put on this London attire and danced among his people. Indians and traders sat and smoked tobacco and began the long ceremony that marked the trading season. Guttins made sure the tin cups were filled with brandy, which he had watered down to make more palatable. The talks went on for nine hours, fuelled by drink. At dusk, the two camps broke apart for the evening.

Thompson observed two Indians in the meadow to the west, coupling drunkenly. A man stood and screamed at the sky and lurched sideways, stumbling downward, his head meeting rock. After two days of trading, the natives sat outside the fort, chastened and morose, their heads angry with a new pain, a sled piled with iron and copper implements sitting in the light rain. The chief's new clothes were covered in mud, the scarlet tunic torn at the arm, blood drying on the linen shirt, the hat gone. He led the children of Israel down to the river and they loaded their canoes and paddled westward with their prizes.

Summer was mosquitoes, the fall short, and the following winter a dismal repeat of the first. He had learned how to clerk, and had learned something of the Cree language. In spring Thompson was called into Hearne's room. The debauched hero stood in his leather pants and blue shirt, his golden hair matted. "Have you the stomach for discovery?" he asked.

Thompson stared at him. The Hudson's Bay Company, a fat fading monopoly, sat next to the frozen sea waiting for the Indians to arrive with their furs while its rival, the North West Company, took the trade inland, sending its men across the plains laden with copper and tobacco and kettles and brandy, seeking out the natives rather than waiting for the natives to seek them. The Hudson's Bay Company had a few inland trading posts, and Thompson worried that its trading operation was losing ground to the North West Company. In his view, it hadn't fully engaged its mandate to explore the North West and had become a palsied extension of an empire that was stretched thinly across the globe. Hearne, the great explorer, personified this lost purpose.

"I am a strong walker, sir, and a decent paddler, and I have some knowledge of navigation," Thompson said. He had left Grey Coat with a Hadley's quadrant and the two volumes of Robertson's *Elements of Navigation*. "I can speak a little of the native tongue and I've read a good deal."

"Fine, fine." Hearne examined Thompson's schoolboy face. "You will see things out there you've never read about."

"I hope so, sir."

"You won't always hope so."

Until then, what had he seen? A few bears. Too much cold. He was still a clerk, like thousands of boys his age in London, but instead of staring at a bleak, dark interior, he stared at a bleak, almost universal night. He made lists of everything the Hudson's Bay Company had and didn't have in alphabetical order: flannel, flints, gin, hatchets. He could have added: patience, purpose, time.

In October he left with MacKay and Welland, an Englishman whose fleshy face was collapsing, his large features moving downward with their own weight. It was before dawn and Welland sang a song about a woman in Glasgow with an unusual talent. "Oh Mary had a hunger for everyone that bunged her …" There were a dozen verses, each more ludicrous than the last: men disappeared inside her, as did canoes, and by the twelfth verse Westminster Abbey filled with parishioners, their voices lifted in choir. "You'll be next, Davy boy," Welland yelled. "Walking in upright, sin and salvation all of a piece."

Their intent was to establish contact with the Peigans who camped east of the mountains and who were allied by language and custom with the Blood and the Blackfoot. Thompson's facility for languages had already come to the House Master's attention in his dealings with the Cree around the fort, and he was being sent to learn the Blackfoot language. He examined his supplies: leather pants, blue cloth jacket, buffalo robe, rifle, forty rounds of ammunition, two long knives, six flints, two awls, needles, two pounds of tobacco, and one horse to carry it.

"You came from London?" MacKay asked Thompson.

"Yes. Wales before that."

"But London. Why would you leave London for this?"

"An opportunity to better myself. In London my life would be simply clerking."

"It's clerking here."

"What is in Orkney?"

"Wind. Too few sins shared among too many."

"But your family."

"I'm grateful for the distance."

Thompson wondered about his own family. How his mother was faring. She was without the burden of her children. She would be fine.

"You've never been with a woman, have you, Davy?"

Thompson was silent.

"You could die a virgin," MacKay said. "They used to sacrifice them, you know. I suppose they still do. You'll want to be careful."

Ahead the plain yawned uneventfully. An hour later a brown mass approached, massive, a herd of what Thompson took to be large deer. He fired into it and watched for five minutes before claiming his prize. MacKay helped him skin and quarter it, and they roasted a haunch over the fire and cut pieces with their long knives to eat.

The sky was a convex dome and the stars were unusually clear and close.

"You'd think you'd be able to see God on a night like this," Welland said.

"God is in England," MacKay said. "This is God's punishment."

Thompson sat silently. If he was in England, he would be sleeping with seven boys in a small room, boys who squirmed with one another in the night. Furtive clutchings that ended happily or sadly or under the cane. Days were spent listening to the impatient teachers, the Sisters of

Christ with their good intent and vicious energy. He was happy to be on the plains.

"It is my intention to map this country," Thompson said.

"If you draw lines around nothing," MacKay said, "it's still nothing."

"Perhaps drawing lines around it will make it something."

"The North West isn't a place, Thompson. It's a distance to be crossed to get to a place."

"You could draw me a map of Margaret Toomey's arse," Welland said, laughing. "A distance I'd like to cross and a place I'd like to go."

"This land has but one point," MacKay said. "The lowly beaver. Ugly as sin and just as plentiful."

"I have been commissioned by God," Thompson said, immediately regretting the words.

"By God?" MacKay said. "Thompson, this is the land God gave to Cain."

If he had a gift, and this was a land where gifts were prized, though not one where those with gifts were sent—among the industrious and moral there were Bay men with gifts for drink or rage or stupidity or bad luck—but if he had a gift, it was this: for observation. He watched. He watched the words that fell out of the mouths of men, the way lips moved to form the diphthongs of the Orkneymen, the rounded syllables of London, and he observed the forest in winter, the properties of snow as the temperature changed, the ingenious construction of the mosquito (exquisitely created for torment), the varying qualities of rock and ice, and the patterns of the stars, which appeared static but were symphonic in their movement. He watched the natives, studied their gait and their beliefs, and listened to their words, a grid of related sounds that met the world in a hierarchy of meaning.

In the morning, they walked the faded yellow prairie grass that stretched flat as a table, uninterrupted. The sun was high and Thompson welcomed the shade from a small stand of stunted poplar. He trudged across a coulee and found buffalo bones so white they shone. A few miles farther on were the bones of a man, his skull caved in and his hand some distance from the rest of him, as if it had inched away. A rabbit darted from a bush near Thompson and he took a shot at it but the rabbit was too fast.

"You'll need a better eye," MacKay said.

"Or larger game."

There was desert with stretches of sand and scattered carpets of low cheatgrass spiking up and pillowy cacti growing in small green patches. MacKay killed a rattlesnake with his long knife, skinned it, and laid the slick hide on a rock to dry in the sun. He tied it around his neck for a day, then abandoned it to the prairie. To the south there was a creek, and they followed its grassy banks until it gave out into alkali salts huddled in dusty hollows, the surrounding area brown and grey and spotted with prickly pear and sage. The sun stayed high in the sky, throwing off a pleasant late-autumn heat. Thompson saw a thunderstorm approach from seventy miles away, gathering itself, the spidery lightning visible in eccentric bursts. A coolness hit his face in advance of the storm that brought the angled sting of rain. The sound was overwhelming, a muffled roar that killed their voices. They were drenched within seconds. They sat down on the prairie, huddling like mushrooms as the lightning forked down.

"God's wrath," MacKay yelled, though he was only a foot away. "I expect it's Welland he's after. Either Welland or yourself. Stay close. God loves an Orkneyman. That's why he gave us such beauty."

When the sky finally cleared Thompson ate some salt meat and lay on the wet grass and stared upward. The light disappeared in quiet increments. He looked at the stars, the patterns that had been examined for thousands of years.

"Do you find comfort in them?" MacKay said.

"I suppose that I do." Thompson hadn't thought of them that way, but MacKay was right. They were companions of a sort.

"Take what comfort you can from these barrens," MacKay said.

The morning was damp, the sky still dark in the west. After a hurried breakfast, they marched. The men were weary. *If we keep walking*, Thompson thought, *if we persevere.*

The mountains came into sight like shining white clouds on the horizon.

3

THE NORTH WEST, 1787

A small party of Peigans rode out to meet them, the dust rising in billows that blew east, visible a mile away.

"Do you think they're friendly?" Thompson said.

"I don't think anyone's friendly," MacKay said. "But I think we can profit from them."

"They'll trade with us?" Thompson asked.

"They may cut out our hearts and trade those amongst themselves."

The Peigans escorted them to their camp, more than a hundred tents near the bank of the Bow River. The women said nothing and showed no expression. The children ran toward them and grasped at their clothes and hands and a few laughed. Thompson was led to a tent and ushered in.

Inside it smelled of smoke and the light was brown, filtered through the deer hide. A man of maybe ninety years sat motionless inside. Thompson examined his face, which was the colour of tea.

"I am David Thompson," he said in rudimentary Cree. "I am a representative of the Hudson's Bay Company." The man remained motionless. After two minutes Thompson wondered if he was dead.

"I am Saukamappee," the man finally said. "I am Cree but it is some time since I have heard their language. I find myself a stranger now in the land of my fathers."

Thompson sat down across from him, and Saukamappee sat there silently staring. Thompson wasn't sure if that was the end of their conversation or if he was gathering himself for more words.

After ten minutes of silence, Saukamappee quietly said, "When I returned from the battle with the Snake Indians I found my wife had given herself to another man and they had gone north to pass the winter. I was filled with grief and anger and walked to the white pine that stands alone on the plain and was thought to have great power. I slept beside it to see if it would grant me wisdom. If I had not gone to fight the Snake my wife would have stayed. But she never would have been mine. I only knew this by going away. So what had I lost? Someone I never had. I renounced my people and came to live with the Peigan who welcomed me. The chief gave me his eldest daughter for a wife. She is old now but she was beautiful and she was faithful, and yet I quarrelled with her and now I see that half my life was given to small battles of no meaning."

Saukamappee's voice had a small range, like church music, and he spoke staring straight ahead as if reciting a lesson. The fire flickered and changed the light within the tent. The air cooled and Thompson moved under the buffalo robes.

Saukamappee closed his eyes and Thompson wondered if this was the end of the story.

A few minutes later he opened his eyes. "Do you have a wife?" he asked Thompson.

"No."

"You should find one. Perhaps tomorrow."

When Thompson woke up, he was alone in the tent. Outside, the morning was bright and crisp, the yellow grass still damp. Shivering slightly in his clothes, he observed a young man applying paint to his face, using one of the small mirrors they had brought to trade. He worked patiently with the colours, absorbed in his own creation, a combination of ferocity and decoration.

Thompson spent the day walking the camp, which extended out toward the foothills. He was regarded with curiosity but no one approached him. MacKay had laid out trade goods on a blanket and was negotiating by pointing and holding up fingers. In the evening, they ate trout that had been taken from the river and roasted over the fire. A woman gave Thompson a bowl with berries and grease. As it grew dark, the Indians took their bowls to the river to wash them. Thompson washed his and then went into the tent.

Saukamappee was sitting in his usual spot, his eyes closed, but he opened them when Thompson came in. Thompson sat down, the audience that Saukamappee had been waiting for.

He described his first encounter with whites, with their silent gift that crept westward. He had led a party of warriors into an enemy Blackfoot camp one night. Five hundred men crept up to the tents and then slit them open to massacre the inhabitants.

"But our war whoop instantly stopped," he told Thompson. "Our eyes were filled with terror: there was no one to fight but the dead and the dying."

It was smallpox that had ravaged the Blackfoot, making its debut among the Plains natives. The warriors walked among the decomposing corpses and soundless, swollen children. They chose certain possessions and took them, the spoils of war.

"The second day after, this dreadful disease broke out in our camp and spread from one tent to another, as if the bad spirit carried it. We had no belief that one man could give it to another, any more than a wounded man could give his wound to another. We believed that the Good Spirit had forsaken us and allowed the Bad Spirit to become our master. Our hearts were low and dejected, and we shall never be again the same people."

The morning was unusually mild, the strong warm chinook coming down and eating the light covering of snow. Thompson walked the foothills with MacKay and surveyed the land. To the west, hogback ridges leaned out where the rock began in earnest. Clouds topped the southern range like a confection.

He had seen MacKay leaving a woman's tent before dawn. "You'll want to be careful, MacKay," he said.

"I am."

"We're trading with them."

"Some more than others."

"We can't put that trade in jeopardy."

MacKay stared to the south, squinting into the distance. "Look at this. I don't like it, Davy. It looks bad."

Thompson saw the group approach, perhaps two hundred and fifty men, some of them mounted, others walking. Saukamappee had told him that a war party had gone off two months earlier to avenge the death of four Peigan hunters who were murdered by Snake Indians. An advance horseman who rode back to get them to prepare a feast for their arrival had told Saukamappee the story. The party had ridden south in search of the Snake but didn't find them. But they came upon a silver caravan being led by black-faced men—Spaniards, Thompson surmised—moving up from Spanish Louisiana. They slaughtered the Spaniards and took their horses and mules, emptying the heavy, useless silver onto the desert.

"Who are they?" MacKay asked.

"A war party returning. The husbands."

"I walk in peace. I'm bloody Jesus."

"They aren't. Be careful."

"I will now."

Riding ahead of the horsemen was a tall man, six foot six, lean, his skin stretched over sinew. A crowd ran to greet him.

"Who's that?" MacKay asked.

"Kootenae Appee," Thompson said. "The war chief. He has five wives, twenty-two sons, and four daughters. MacKay, your odds aren't good."

"Jesus sake, man."

Appee's family gathered around him, and he stood in their midst like a maypole. The blood lust of the war party hadn't been sated; Thompson could see it buzzing around them like the nervous fluttering of a sparrow's wings.

Kootenae Appee saw Thompson and MacKay on the rise and got on his horse and approached them. Thompson shrank slightly as he neared, clutching his notebook tightly to his chest. MacKay retreated behind Thompson, who gathered himself and took a step forward, holding out his right hand.

"I am a member of the Hudson's Bay Company," Thompson said, his right hand wavering in the slight wind.

Appee didn't take the offered hand. "The hand that wields the knife," he observed. He leaned down, looming into Thompson's vision like something out of Gulliver, his face full of war. There were sharp markings on his face. He looked like a man constructed only for war, with no excess for any other purpose.

Appee examined Thompson, a white child clutching something to his chest, exposed on the prairie like a shining root from an uplifted tree.

"Perhaps you will bring us guns," he said.

"We will."

"And perhaps you will use your guns against us."

"No."

"A child on the plains trading guns," Appee said, and laughed. He turned and rode back to the camp. MacKay let out the breath he had been holding for more than a minute.

4

MANCHESTER HOUSE, SASKATCHEWAN RIVER, 1788

How many men saw death approach with its careless scythe? Thompson was eighteen, dying a fool's death. Who would mourn him? He lay on his back, drifting out of consciousness, a distant grey horizon overtaking him, small lights extinguished or blended with the snow that still held traces of the afternoon light. The thermometer at Manchester House had read eighteen below when he left, but it was colder now. His broken leg swelled horribly even in this cold. *This will be my death*, he thought, *some painful minutes, some numbness, then a comforting sleep from which I won't wake.*

He was resigned to this death when he felt himself being pulled. The rough hand of God.

"Davy, boy, you're fucked as a goose."

The voice of MacKay. Thompson looked at him and saw only darkness, his eyelids frozen shut. MacKay pulled him up the bank, struggling on the steep pitch that Thompson had fallen down while hauling a sled with deer meat on it. The pain was excruciating and he screamed. MacKay piled him on the sled with the deer meat and pulled him back to Manchester House.

MacKay laid him on the table and cut off his pant leg with a knife, tearing at the frozen material, which was stiff as wood.

"You're done for now, boy," he said. "Don't be looking at it."

Thompson forced himself to look. The femur of his right leg was jutting out, trying to break through the skin. MacKay made a crude splint and tied it to Thompson's leg with strips of a sheet and he lost consciousness. In the night he woke repeatedly, fevered, his leg feeling by turns numb (Was it gone?) or throbbing brightly. By morning, the poor limb was a sickly blue. He had a fever that lasted three days, and afterward he lay spent, able to eat only some thin broth. Days went by without any improvement.

"We may have to take it," MacKay said.

"No."

"It might be you or the leg."

What could he do without a leg? Work at Churchill Factory, counting supplies? He was clever at sums. Numbers would be his only companion. "You can't take the leg."

"Suit yourself. That leg'll dance on your grave, boy."

"Promise me you won't take the leg, MacKay, no matter what my condition. If I am fevered or unconscious. I need your word."

"You're asking me to kill you."

"I'm asking you to let God make the judgment. This is no country for a one-legged man."

"It's no country for a two-legged man."

Thompson clutched his Bible and drifted toward sleep. "Trust in God," he told MacKay.

"I'd sooner trust the devil."

After a month, Thompson was still unable to walk, or even to stand. He lay in his bed each night, his head filled with jagged dreams: he saw himself drowning, headed to the bottom alongside animals with benign smiles. During the day, the men brought him tea and he could sense their pity turning to scorn. He spent his time recording the weather in great detail in his notebook: wind speed and direction, temperature, the nature of the skies. In early July he tried to walk, but the next day his ankle was hideously swollen and he had to lie down. This country was no place for an invalid, with its plagues of mosquitoes and its heat and cold and fatal quarrels.

In the spring, MacKay took him to Cumberland House, another trading post, moving him downriver in the canoe, lying like a piece of meat. This was what he had become, a pile of tainted meat, unwanted, unusable, something to be left on the plain for the birds. He lay on his back, under the blue sky, staring at wispy clouds.

"You can't abandon me, MacKay," he said.

"I won't."

"If I take a fever."

"You won't."

"If I do. If it takes me."

"I'll sell your coat and feed you to the birds."

"You'll bury me."

"I will. Though it won't make a difference then."

"It does now."

"Then you'll be buried, Davy."

"Do you think about what your people are doing back in Orkney, MacKay?"

"Eating oats and staring into their graves. Cursing the wind."

"I have a brother," Thompson said. "I wonder sometimes who he is, what he has become." The riverbank went by in a pleasant tableau of grass and rock. The pale sky receded to white. Two hawks floated on the thermal winds. "Without a leg, I'll be no use in this land."

"There's men without a brain who are managing."

"If I can't walk."

"There's worse."

It was the last week in August before he could manage a few steps on a pair of crutches. Philip Turnor arrived at Cumberland House shortly afterward. He was the Hudson's Bay Company's surveyor and astronomer. Unable to do any work, Thompson became his pupil.

He hobbled to the common room where Turnor waited for him with a daunting pile of books. His teacher had an avuncular face and the manner of a missionary. Thompson sat down and waited for his lesson.

"Practical astronomy, Mr. Thompson," Turnor said, "requires knowledge of the skies. The position and movement of the planets are the basis for calculations. Latitude is calculated by measuring the altitude of the sun, or at night using a sextant to place a star, then referring to tables and formulas. Longitude is a more difficult matter. It is calculated by comparing local time to the exact time at prime meridian, which means keeping an accurate clock set to Greenwich Mean Time."

At sea, navigators used a chronometer, but that instrument was too delicate for land exploration, for rough travel by foot, on horse, or by canoe.

"So you must continually adjust the unreliable timepieces to Greenwich Mean Time," Turnor said. "The skies are a vast celestial clock. You can time the emergence and disappearance of one of Jupiter's moons, examining it through a telescope. Or you can use the Earth's moon, measuring its position against two fixed stars."

Thompson struggled diligently with this information, mastering the three hours of complex trigonometry that came with measurement. Astronomy required skill, determination, patience, a mathematical nature, and the ability to stare at the skies for hours in every kind of weather. And of course every calculation was threatened by human error and had to be done several times.

He studied the stars each night, marked positions, and made the meticulous calculations. He rarely slept and worked by candlelight. During the day, he examined the sun. He noticed that his right eye was swollen, perhaps from staring upward, or from the candlelight. MacKay looked at it and pronounced, "The beginnings of leprosy I'm sure. I don't want to think what part it wants next."

Within a week, Thompson could see little out of that eye. The world was clear through his left eye, but through the right everything was blurred and bordered by a dark frame. When he looked out onto the prairie, it undulated slightly, as if two versions of the landscape had been inexpertly put together to form a single image. After ten days the vision in his right eye was gone altogether. When he closed his left eye, all he could see were vague shapes the colour of darkness against a background of greater darkness.

And his right leg had yet to mend properly. In the night a wound had mysteriously opened above the fracture. Perhaps a piece of bone had broken off, still causing havoc. It was as though parts of him were trying to escape. He could walk only short distances, and that with difficulty. Perhaps he would never walk properly again. What kind of explorer would he make? A half-blind cripple limping through the New World, the north obscured as he walked west, the south obscured as he walked east. He looked at his calculations, pages of them, the neat numbers moving across the lines with logic and purpose. After a month of patient tutelage and experimentation, he had established his position: latitude 53°56′44″ N, longitude 102°13′ west of Greenwich, and the variation by the transits of the sun and a well-regulated watch is 11°30′ east.

His leg healed through the summer, though he had a pronounced limp that he was resigned to. He was given a brass compass, a thermometer, a case of instruments, four volumes of Dr. Johnson's *Rambler*, and a copy of Milton's *Paradise Lost*. He could speak French, two native languages, and had a little of two others. At eighteen, he had grown to his full, unimpressive height. He could establish his own location in the world, could place himself precisely under God's eye.

In December the air itself began to freeze, the kaleidoscopic crystals twinkling in the brittle sun. At the crude wooden table in the common room, Thompson sat in his heavy coat eating an indifferent meal of boiled venison. After dinner he went outside to view the stars through his quadrant, consulting his watch, making notes, a habit. He needed little sleep, or at least didn't notice its absence.

MacKay came out. "Do you see Him up there?" he asked. "Do you see God?"

"Sometimes," Thompson said.

"He talks to you, does He?"

"He talks to everyone."

"Perhaps I was out," MacKay said.

"I will tell you something, MacKay. I see no future with the Hudson's Bay Company. They've neglected their duty to explore. I'm preparing to leave. I've no more patience for these men."

"They'll begrudge you."

"I suppose they will. No matter. I'm going to take a position with the North West Company."

"A Nor'Wester. You'll be singing vile songs in French and fornicating without shame."

"You would fit, MacKay. You should think of it as well." MacKay had been a fine companion. He would be the only thing he missed. Was he turning his back on the British Empire? Perhaps it had turned its back on him. "They'll allow me to explore."

"Explore what."

"The country."

"I'll save you the bother, Davy. It's more of the same from here to China. More cold, more Indians, more mosquitoes. You can tell the Nor'Westers that."

The North West Company was based in Montreal, and was fuelled by energetic French who paddled thousands of miles to visit the Indians, undermining the Hudson's Bay Company's monopoly. They gave Thompson a sextant in a cork-lined box with quicksilver and parallel glasses, an achromatic telescope, drawing instruments, and two thermometers, and ordered him to go south and make contact with the Mandans, and to find the headwaters of the Mississippi River.

Thompson had persuaded MacKay to join the Nor'Westers, and MacKay stood before him, staring at this short, half-blind, half-lame explorer.

"I hear the Mandans eat the tongues of their enemy," MacKay said. "I hear everyone is their enemy. Watch yourself, Davy."

"I will."

"You'll only find more of the same. I could draw you the map now. Save you the grief."

"Grief is what makes a map, MacKay."

"You're still working for God, then? He traffics in grief."

"God and country."

"This isn't a country, Davy, and it will take a lot more than you to make it one."

Thompson left the next morning and camped beside a pine that was in the middle of the plain. There were faded red markings at the base of the tree, and beside it were the bleached bones of a horse. He fell asleep quickly and dreamed of a snake eating a larger snake in an English garden. Mice scurried among rotting vegetables. He awoke from the dream like a worm emerging from the earth. You cut a worm in half and you get two worms—two lives, twice the adventure, twice the misery. Or did all the misery stay with one half? The sun lingered below the horizon and a coyote paced fifty yards away.

He walked for five weeks into the hostile wind that came down from the mountains, and arrived in late December. The Mandan village had orderly lines and snow-covered fields where corn had been harvested. Only a few men were in the village, and Thompson sat with an elder who, through the pantomime that accompanied the story, told him that all the men were off at war.

A man with long dark hair tied up with bird skulls sat in the hut staring at Thompson while the old man talked. He came over, a walk that was European. He spoke French.

"You have come to study the savages," he said, and introduced himself as Michel Antoine.

"They grow corn?" Thompson asked.

"And beans, some pumpkins."

"How long have you been here?" Thompson asked. The man was dressed as a Mandan. His dark hair helped disguise him, and his face, with its slight, spotty beard, could pass as native. But he didn't move as they did.

"Fifteen years."

"What brought you here?"

"Love," he said.

"And that is what keeps you here?"

The man shook his head and laughed. "No," he said. "Habit."

The war party returned after dark, perhaps fifty men. Antoine conferred with them and told Thompson they had been fighting the Cheyenne to the south. They had entered an enemy village and killed everyone except three women, whom they took as prisoners and who now walked in their midst. Some of the Mandans carried leather bags. In the largest lodge they emptied their sacks and the heads of their enemies rolled out, the faces drained of blood, the mouths open and terrible.

One of the women prisoners held an eight-month-old baby. After hurried preparation, there was a war dance, and the three women stood inside a hostile circle of chanting men. Women and children banged pots. Thompson counted twenty-three heads lying at their feet. He watched as the woman with the infant picked up the head of her dead husband by the hair and kissed his drained lips and pressed the head to her baby's mouth. Two Mandan men quickly took the head away. One of them scalped it. The woman held up her child to heaven and sang a short song. She kissed her child and placed it on the ground and took a sharp knife from her deerskin garment and plunged it into her own heart and fell among the heads. One of the Mandan women picked up the baby and held it and sang softly into its ear.

In the morning, the slain woman was buried as a warrior. Thompson stared at her face. Where does such defiance come from? he wondered. Where did you find such faith, such love?

5

ÎLE-À-LA CROSSE,
NORTH WEST, 1799

In 1799 there was already the breathlessness of a new
century. Napoleon had seized power in France, the Corsican
peasant who embraced democracy, aristocracy, and the
military with equal fervour, who needed to swallow the
world and immersed himself in Josephine, whispering that
she was his homeland, he lived only in her, her smell of
drying leaves and damp mornings, leaving her wetness on
his chin at breakfast. It hadn't been that long—six years—
since Louis XVI had had his head removed by the heavy
blade of the guillotine, held up wigless and slack-faced to a
cheering crowd. Those pints of blood spraying over the
rough wooden shackles and cleaned up ten hours later by a

toothless woman using dirty water and a coarse broom. So ended a century of divine right.

In England, George III had lost part of an empire in America and was losing his mind. The monarch was now an amiable rustic, walking the countryside, admiring its orchards, his long hair unkempt, asking farmers' wives to share their recipes for apple dumplings, smiling like a simpleton.

The world was shifting, ancient hatreds and new appetites redrawing the borders. North America hadn't been concisely divided; it awaited a fresh war, treaties, and cartography.

Thompson thought that he would bring the North West into existence with hard lines. The land didn't come before the map, he thought: the map creates the land. A map was knowledge. At some point, there would be claims upon that land, as there were upon all lands. Thompson believed that the North would be the only part of the continent not taken from the Indians by fraud or by force, saved by its barrenness.

Thompson saw the future arrive like a starving wolf and he saw the poverty that would follow the destruction of the beaver, its death coming from over-trapping and an equally cruel predator—fashion, the beaver hats suddenly become barbarous anomalies in the closets of Europe. Elders already warned of a looming desert, of crows descending on a dying nation like a black wind.

Thompson needed a woman. This was God's purpose. What other point to this journey? He was God's witness, but who would be his?

Charlotte Small arrived like a revelation, as vivid as the devil at the checkerboard, tasting of earth and ashes. She was thirteen and Thompson was twenty-nine. Her father, Patrick, was a Scot, a Hudson's Bay man who had abandoned his country wife and family and retreated to England. Charlotte was tiny and well formed, with the dark eyes and luxuriant blue-black hair of her Cree mother. Thompson was observant, nondescript, his hair cut indifferently by a Cree named, through awkward translation, Kozdaw. He had the same dark eyes as Charlotte, although one of them was useless. He lacked the skills to woo her and simply asked her to be his wife.

The night before they were married—without benefit of clergy, *à la façon du pays*—on Île-à-la Crosse, Thompson took a wooden chair outside and set up his telescope and scanned the night sky, happy for the gentle breeze and the solitude. He focused the glass at the moon—the Mare Nubium, Nectaris, Imbrium, and Serenitatis—and stayed up most of the night, as he often did, putting off sleep like a chore.

The wedding was simple, a brief exchange of vows to be faithful. That night Thompson explored the soft expanse of Charlotte's perfect skin. She looked up at him as he fumbled for an opening, her eyes filled with fear. Holding this child in his arms after he was spent, Thompson wept along with her.

He took a bath the next day, pouring boiling water into the tin tub. Her smell was on his body, a scent both new and familiar. In the warm water, he surveyed the pale landscape of his body before scrubbing it with brisk strokes of the hard brush. His form was compact and wiry, a practical machine. His moments last night with Charlotte furthered God's plan. He lingered over the last scent of her before obliterating it with soap.

There had been one other before Charlotte, a hasty coupling more than a year earlier, his disappointing and long-delayed initiation. The following morning, the woman, a Cree, stared silently as Thompson left the trading post and walked west, carrying her stare inside him.

At Rocky Mountain House, Thompson spent each evening with Charlotte, teaching her to read English. He read from the Bible—"For the LORD thy God bringeth thee into a good land, a land of brooks of water, of fountains and depths that spring out of valleys and hills"—and taught her to write, guiding her child's hand. They spent hours spelling words.

"Tree."

"T-R-E," Charlotte said.

"E."

"Hills."

"H-I-L-S."

"H-I-L-L-S."

"David, my head is bad. I can't think of more words."

"Your head isn't bad. It will come. It takes time. We have time."

"I'll never understand them."

"You'll be teaching our children," he said. "Sky."

"S-K-I."

Each night, Thompson mapped her, her scent and movements, the small rises, the contours and stained hollows.

By spring, Charlotte was swollen. In the rough hut, she began to breathe irregularly. The child came in a rush of fluid, the hard breathing of Charlotte suspended briefly, as if gathering for a scream. Thompson cut the cord with a knife heated over a flame and looked at the girl who had gushed out, black haired and down covered, alien and inevitable. She slept in her mother's arms, and they all lay amid the wet bloody sheets. They named her Fanny.

With Charlotte, Thompson was no longer an exile. The fourteen-year-old mother of his child. His child and their child.

6

THE ROCKY MOUNTAINS, 1807

With nine voyageurs, among them MacKay, and two Iroquois named Charles and Ignace, Thompson took his family to cross the Rocky Mountains. There were three children now—Fanny, Samuel, and Emma. Thompson believed he could follow the Columbia River to its mouth at the Pacific Ocean and find a navigable route through the mountains, the culmination of three centuries of European dreams. The Americans were looking for the same thing. So, a race.

They paddled up the North Saskatchewan River, past Kootenay Plains and over Howse Pass, and arrived at Lake Windermere in mid-July. They built two cabins near the shore and spent the winter there, trading with the Kootenay Indians.

Thompson had heard that the Cree woman he had left had borne a child, a boy, that his name was Tristan, and that she was variable in her attentions. He appealed to a friend to try to take the child from its mother and to send him to the trading post at Fort Augustus, where Thompson would claim him. Thompson thought about him nightly, a salted wound. A boy conceived in sin and left to fate.

Meat was scarce, but Ignace found a dead horse in the forest. There were hundreds of wild horses in the mountains, their owners dead from smallpox. They banded together, ghostly herds that had lost any taste for servitude. The horse gave off a foul smell and they boiled the meat for an hour, but it made them all sick anyway.

A week later Thompson shot a whitetail deer. Ignace immediately cut off its head with his long knife, and the deer suddenly stood up, headless and awful, blood spouting from its neck. It remained standing for almost a minute, a visceral reprimand, then fell over.

"It's the devil," said Ignace, who was an occasional and confused Christian.

"It's only muscle and instinct," Thompson said, observing the body. "The devil is elsewhere."

"If you eat that meat, the devil will find his way inside you," Ignace said.

Thompson cut off a piece of its haunch, roasted it, and then ate it. The men regarded him with horror and suspicion. Ignace built up the coals and threw the carcass onto them.

"You can't burn the devil," Thompson said.

In the spring, Thompson left Charlotte and his family at Boggy Hall and tried to cross the mountains. A small band of Indians approached from the south. When they got closer, Thompson saw that it was Kootenae Appee, the Peigan war chief. He was still magnificent, a foot taller than Thompson, lean, his face dabbed in colour, a small mirror hanging from a leather strap around his neck so that his enemies could see themselves before they died.

"Koo Koo Sint," he said to Thompson, using his Indian name, and unfolding the smile that conveyed both friendship and menace. "The mountains are not yours."

"They aren't anyone's now," Thompson replied.

Kootenae Appee's world was shrinking. Like Napoleon, he was fighting wars on every front, stretched thin, his empire no longer easily defined and impossible to defend. His enemies had guns. The Kootenay, the Flathead, the Snake. Appee was fighting the North Westers and to the south, the Americans. He had sent a small party out to meet the explorers Lewis and Clark. In the raid, one Peigan was shot in the stomach by Lewis and another stabbed in the heart.

"How is Saukamappee?" Thompson asked.

"Dead," Kootenae Appee said. He had a rifle in a sheath. His men were armed. Thompson had armed the Snake Indians, enemy to the Peigan. He was arming everyone, partly the result of simple trade, but also to keep the plains in balance, to prevent unchristian slaughter. But he knew the plains were becoming unbalanced in new ways, that traders were pushing farther west, and the Indians were no longer as accommodating.

No one had accumulated as much knowledge of the terrain or the Indians as Thompson had. And this had given him a curious power, one he was increasingly aware of. The territory was held in a delicate balance and he worried that it wouldn't hold. When Fort Augustus had been attacked, Thompson had arrived there to find a man standing naked and bootless, a larval spectre squinting into the afternoon sun. A group of Blood Indians led by the brother of Old White Swan cleaned out everything: clothing, tobacco, guns, and shot. Thompson heard that the brother of Old White Swan used his new arsenal to make war upon the Crow Mountain Indians. He killed several men with his gun, but when it jammed he was set upon by a Crow with breath like lamp oil who cut off his ears and dug out his heart.

"The mountains are a dangerous place," Kootenae Appee said pleasantly. "Not like the grasses where you can see your enemy approach."

Thompson turned his men around. They would have to find another route in.

They went north and tried again. With him were MacKay, Ignace, Charles, Coté, Valade, Pareil, Grégoire, Bouland, DuNord, and a few others. Thompson had hired a Cree guide whom he didn't trust. Appropriately named the Rook, he had brought his wife, a silent, suffering woman whose face had the deepening lines of a rotting vegetable. On a night when the sky was partially clear, Thompson sat with his journal, making entries and marking their position through his instruments. The Rook came over, drunk on brandy, and sat heavily on the scrub, cross-legged, sweetly curious, his upper body listing in the mountain breeze.

"They talk to you, the stars?"

"They talk to me."

"What do they say about me?"

"That you will sleep badly and wake with two heads."

The Rook laughed and fell over and stared at the stars briefly and then fell asleep and snored heavily.

In the morning, the Rook sat blurry and quiet by the fire. He took his wife's arm and drew a sharp flint along the vein in her forearm, leaving a widening red line. His wife made no attempt to pull her arm away and didn't change her expression. The Rook drained some of her blood into a bowl and drank it in three long gulps.

Thompson looked at him with disgust.

"It's for my head," the Rook said.

Thompson got up and slapped him on the side of his head, and he fell over.

"That is for your head too," he said.

Thompson cut a piece of linen to bind her arm. They packed up the camp and walked west through a deadfall forest, the grey stalks angled in the half-light. The weather was turning colder, and the snow was deeper and more difficult to walk through. They moved along the Athabasca River, along the shoals and on ice that was crusted with snow though occasionally opened up to smooth, shiny sections thick enough that they looked black. The banks held stunted pine and willow. The dogs struggled in their traces and Thompson lightened their load, taking out food and making a crude wooden hoard to store it for when they returned. Eight sleds moved into a west wind that came over the peaks in violent gusts, and they came to the end of any grass for the horses. There were tufts that ringed a frozen pond, but the fields were bitten down by bison and half covered in snow. Thompson followed a line up to high land, through patches of dwarf pine. They needed snowshoes to move through the deep snow. It became clear to Thompson that the Rook was unfamiliar with the country, and in the morning he sent him and his wife away.

They needed firewood, and Thompson and MacKay spent the morning gathering it. In the afternoon they ventured farther, taking advantage of decent weather, to make caches of wood that could be retrieved later. Thompson narrowed his one good eye against the sun and avoided the horizon. He kept his head down. MacKay trudged, staring into the snow that reflected the sun with renewed intensity. When the sky began to darken in late afternoon he rubbed his eyes.

"It feels like there's hot sand in them," MacKay said. Ten minutes later, he was howling in pain.

Within an hour it was dark and MacKay was snowblind. He sobbed and stumbled, and tried to run, to escape his affliction. Thompson ran after him and tackled him in the snow. He looked at the Orkneyman's face, his lips drained of colour and eyes red as fire, the devil's face. MacKay began to scream and Thompson slapped him, the frozen glove leaving a mark on his face. A cruel thing to strike a blind man, Thompson thought, but necessary. MacKay lurched awkwardly to his feet and punched the air instinctively and wheeled into the needles of a blue spruce and collapsed. He struggled to his feet and stood there like a chastened schoolboy awaiting punishment.

"We are going to die out here, Davy," MacKay said. "Die a meaningless death in this meaningless land."

If there was no meaning, Thompson thought, there was utility. Their bodies would be food for something, the bear, the wolf, the coyote tearing their flesh away in bloody strips, the magpies and worms finishing their work. As for the land, it relied on Thompson to divine its meaning, to give it meaning with his map. Without that, the void.

"We won't die if we keep walking," Thompson said.

"Oh, we'll die, Davy. We'll die."

Thompson tied a length of rope around his waist and then to MacKay's belt beneath his heavy coat. "Walk behind me," he said. "Keep a regular pace."

It was getting late. Thompson could see Jupiter shining beside the moon. By tomorrow it would be on the other side.

"One eye between two men," MacKay said. "The one-eyed king."

"It's all we need, MacKay."

"Spoken like a man with one eye."

"We'll find the camp. We'll build a fire. We'll eat and remember this moment."

"Moses," MacKay muttered. "Leading me out of the wilderness."

They walked in the deep snow, breaking through the thin crust with each step, making slow progress. When they fell it was awkward getting up in their heavy, frozen coats. MacKay's imaginative curses were interspersed with pleas for mercy.

The aurora borealis lit up the night sky, the absurd colours moving vertically in smooth syncopation as Thompson watched. The sky an unread book. He scanned it as he led his profane duckling through the snow.

"*Jesus.* My. Fucking. Celtic. *Eyes,*" MacKay yelled.

"The blindness can be healed," Thompson said.

"Blindness can be healed. Thank you bloody Jesus."

For an hour, MacKay was quiet, rendered mute by the cold.

"We're dying," he finally whispered.

Thompson had a natural resistance to the elements, his mind elsewhere, observing the landscape, making calculations, or working out the elements of a new language. But he could feel its threat.

"What was my last sight of this world?" MacKay asked. "Was it the wet thighs of a brown Cree, staring into heaven with a belly full of ale? My last vision was grey sky and grey snow. A vision of nothing."

"The last thing you see is the last thing you want to see," Thompson said. "Picture your mother."

"A whore."

"Then picture a whore."

They marched, silent and fatigued. Thompson saw a deer ahead, its dignified, cautious movement. He untied the rope, whispered to MacKay to stay quiet, and walked downwind, cradling his rifle. He tracked the deer slowly, stopping when it stopped, gaining sixty yards. He feared that MacKay would bellow some new obscenity, scaring the animal. After ten nervous minutes Thompson stood next to a tree, within range, sighting along the barrel at the deer, which was facing him. He waited for the profile to present itself, then squeezed the trigger, and the deer fell softly into the snow, a shot that owed more to luck or God than skill. He went back to MacKay, who was dangerously asleep in the deep snow, resigned to a peaceful death. With some difficulty Thompson roused him and they trudged to the deer. He used his knife to slit it from throat to tail along the belly, and then took MacKay's hands and pushed them into the warm entrails before thrusting in his own. They massaged the slippery familiar shapes and breathed the warm visceral scent that came out of the steaming carcass. MacKay's face was turned upward to the sky, eyes closed in what looked like rapture.

It was past midnight when they returned, marching wearily, the blood frozen on their coats, MacKay's sightless face covered in ice crystals. Thompson made a fire and they sat silently around the heat. MacKay's face turned sickly shades of blue and red and then white, and Thompson noted a small dead patch on his cheek that would cause some grief. He wondered about his own face, then slept for fourteen hours.

Early Christmas morning DuNord beat one of his dogs to death with the copper handle of his knife, delivering heavy blows as he grunted curses. The moon was still reflected by the snow, a sepulchral dawn. He killed the dog out of anger and frustration and stupidity, but it was meat and they roasted it over a fire.

In the afternoon they walked through an alpine meadow into a blizzard driven by a hard northwest wind, the dogs plunging through the snow with every step, their eyes dulled by fatigue. The valley opened to a wide chasm between two high peaks, and Thompson's men were desolate at the sight. In five months it would be innocent with yellow dryas and sedge grass, but now it was a bleak gateway. As they walked through the snow, the men became so discouraged that they sat down, each in a separate melancholy.

Thompson plodded along the line, half ordering, half pleading. "Valade. Move yourself, man. Do you want to die here?"

"Better here than the next valley."

"Grégoire, where is your spirit?"

"In France. Fucking Lise Goulet in the bathtub of the whorehouse. And my spirit is much happier than I am."

DuNord was sitting in the snow, immune to orders and pleas. Thompson cuffed him on the head but he was indifferent to the blow. This enraged Thompson, who hit him repeatedly and finally broke his walking stick over DuNord's heavily padded body. "You useless bastard," he screamed. "You meat-eating burden. You're not fit for this land, you useless bloody bastard."

The attack exhausted Thompson entirely, and he collapsed in the snow beside the bloodied, silent DuNord. What did they care about discovery? Thompson thought. The land was the land. This valley as good as the next. Their hunger was for meat and women and stories. He sat with DuNord for half an hour. Then they made a dispirited camp.

In the night, four men deserted, among them DuNord, and Thompson was glad to be free of him. It was down to MacKay, Ignace, Charles, Coté, Valade, Pareil, Grégoire, and Bouland. The next day the men walked like plough horses, rarely looking up.

"Davy, DuNord's a swine, but he's heading in the right direction."

"Away from us."

"Even if we find a path, what godly use is it to anyone? No one is going to trade through here."

"There's a river," Thompson said.

"A bloody river. And this is the way to it, Davy? It's cursed, all of it."

"You can join DuNord if you want."

"DuNord's a fool. But even a fool is right sometimes."

In the afternoon, lenticular clouds swirled in wisps, a cursive warning that a warm wind would blow down. When it came, it was almost too strong to walk into. It made the snow heavier and walking even more difficult. A limestone wall a thousand yards high had threads of snow like veins. Black slate glistened in the afternoon sun as the water leaked out from the snow and dribbled down slabs that looked as if they had been cut with a knife.

In the morning the world was ice. They moved carefully past quartzite that ran in parallel lines angled downward as if dropped unevenly from heaven. They found tracks and followed them to a stand of trees, and killed the moose that was sheltered there. Pareil made a small fire and they roasted pieces and ate. Thompson opened the skull to examine the moose's small brain.

It was the last meat they saw for two weeks. They walked sullenly and came upon the frozen carcass of a moose that had been eaten by wolves. It lay in the snow like a prehistoric ruin. A few miles on they stopped and built a small wooden hut and spent a week in it, hunting, drying their clothes, and arguing about the futility of their journey.

Valade's face was dark, smeared with grease. "We won't live if we go further," he said.

"If we move south, we have a chance at better weather," Thompson said.

"We have a chance to die," MacKay said.

"There is the issue of empire."

"All empires are shit and they all come to shit."

The men refused to go farther. They built a larger structure and prepared to starve. After six weeks their faces had hollowed. They were filthy and gaunt, and ate a poor dinner of roots and the scrapings from a scavenged deer. Thompson wondered at the fortunes of his family. He ached for Charlotte, who now read well enough to teach the children. Civilization would follow them, and they would need skills.

Ignace stared at the fire and began talking. "A woman comes on the ships," he said. "She lives in a village where she is well fed and unhappy and lives in fear of the Iroquois and of the winters. She thinks both are trying to kill her. One night there is a raid; the Iroquois have come. Her husband, who she had no interest in and who she wished dead a hundred times as she sat freezing in their wooden house, is tortured in front of her. Finally his heart is cut out and cooked. She is taken to the Iroquois village and becomes the wife of the torturer. They have three children and the woman learns the ways of the Iroquois and comes to understand the forest as a man does. After ten years, she looks at her husband as he sleeps and plunges a long knife into his heart. She takes her children and escapes into the forest. Her husband is found the next morning, pinned to the ground by the knife.

"The woman gets to a white village. She is no longer young and her beauty is spent. She and her children are taken in by a man who uses them to work on his small farm. She works long hours and is treated poorly. Her children grow up and when the last one leaves, the woman bakes a pie for her master, and as he is eating she comes behind him and slashes his throat with a knife. She goes back into the forest. The men in the village follow her, bent on revenge, but she knows the ways of the forest too well. They can't find her trail. She has vanished.

"She survives by eating berries and plants, and as winter comes, she takes up with a bear. She lies with the bear in its cave and is warmed by it as it sleeps through the cold months. In April, the bear wakes up and sees the woman and can't remember that they were ever together. It kills her and eats her and her bones lie in the cave. Her hair, which became silver then white with age, continues to grow after she is dead. It grows out of the cave and through the forest, past the villages of the white men and the camps of the Iroquois. The white ribbon becomes a river that leads to the cave."

"Why aren't your stories ever true?" MacKay asked.

"They are true," Ignace said. "They just haven't happened yet."

April brought a scent of spring. Mornings were ashen and the clouds low. Thompson sent the men out to look for birchbark to build canoes, but there weren't any trees large enough. He had to abandon the idea and instead cut down cedar trees, and they began the unfamiliar job of building cedar boats. At first, they dug too deep with the auger and split the delicate wood. Some of it was too green and needed to be dried by the fire. They cut boards and laid them in overlapping vertical lengths and sealed the joints, but the first boat broke in half when they tried to move it. They spent sixteen days at this.

They pulled the boats along frozen sections of the Columbia River, paddling where it was open. The river moved north and then doubled back, going south, and they paddled into a reluctant spring.

On a morning when the river was running clear and the air was fine, they came to a village along the banks. The San Poil Indians were painted red and black. Thompson stopped and smoked with them. Bright red salmon littered the rocks, and Thompson traded tobacco for two fish and a basket filled with roots.

The Columbia River hosted a string of villages that depended on salmon. They drifted by the Wenatchees, Sahaptin, Solkulks, and the Sawpatins, where the chief wore a medal with the head of Thomas Jefferson engraved on it, a bad sign.

The river was wide and muddy with runoff. Past the mouth of the Snake River there was a village of twenty huts and no sign of life. Thompson put the boats ashore to survey the huts, which were crude and sat on dark volcanic soil as fine as dust. Two old men emerged from the pine forest, crawling naked over the rock. Behind them were three women on their knees, their hands lifted in supplication. Ignace spoke briefly to them. They had seen a white man (Meriwether Lewis, Thompson later discovered) shoot a sandhill crane out of the sky. They didn't know if Lewis was human. They didn't know what Thompson was.

Ignace told Thompson they had to leave, and when they were on the water, he refused to answer any of Thompson's questions.

The cedar boats moved downriver in an ethereal parade, the late-morning sun framing fifty men along the crest of a two-hundred-foot ridge, staring down at them, arrows poised in their bows. Thompson and his men moved slowly, glancing up at the painted faces as they passed.

"What do they want?" MacKay asked.

"I don't know," Thompson said. "I don't think they know, either."

"If they let those arrows go, we're done. There's no refuge."

"Don't look at them. Paddle steadily. They won't fire without cause."

"And what would bloody cause be, do you imagine? We reach for a drink? We paddle too slow? Too fast? We talk like the devil?"

They camped downstream, and Coté ate a red mushroom and became feverish. He began roaring, and waded into the river, screaming he was a fish, that he would fish for himself. *Pêche pêcheur ma pêche.* They dragged him out of the water and laid him near the fire. The fever faded and he slept for twenty hours.

Thompson wanted to see the ocean, to gaze toward China sitting invisible on the horizon.

The next morning, he saw a harbour seal sitting on a rock.

The Americans had gotten to the Pacific first. The *Tonquin* had left New York in September, provisioned by John Jacob Astor and crewed by adventurers, some of them former Nor'Westers, and they had sailed around the Horn and up the west coast. They arrived in spring and built Fort Astoria. Thompson came ashore and introduced himself, and he and the Americans stood at the edge of the Pacific, assessing one another as civilized men and enemies.

Thompson recognized one of the Indians at Fort Astoria. It was One-Standing-Lodge-Pole Woman, who had been Pareil's wife briefly. She was witchy and loose, and Thompson had ordered her out of the camp in the Flat Bow country after he found her naked, entertaining Bouland and Coté. He feared she would set his men against one another, less a moral decision than a strategic one. Thompson had heard that she'd since declared she was a man, and a prophet no less. She took a wife and left for the Oregon Country. And now here she was, dressed as a man in blue pants with a red sash, shells in her nose and a tattoo under one eye. She gave Thompson a look of recognition and disdain. The Americans told him that her name was Qanqon and that they wanted her out of camp—she was spooking the Indians and jeopardizing their trade. MacKay suggested sewing her into a bag and drowning her like a pup.

Qanqon walked over to Thompson. "A disease will move into your heart," she told him. "And live there forever."

LOST

1840–1857

What is a child? A simple question, you'd think. But there were nine-year-olds working sixteen-hour days in English factories. Such was childhood. Thompson was fifteen when he sailed off to the New World to work. He never knew his father—not that there was any model for fatherhood then. Children were sent away: to school, to work, to die. Thompson had thirteen children with Charlotte, and then there was Tristan. Fourteen children. He travelled with them, showed them the natural world, taught them how to write. He wanted to invent fatherhood, like everything else.

When Thompson was living among the Peigans, a young man announced he intended to eat his sister. He repeated this thought for several days. His parents became worried and sent his sister away and the young man said he would still need human flesh to eat. He said this calmly, as if deciding on fish for dinner. The council met and decided that a Weetego—an evil spirit—had entered the boy, and he was sentenced to death. The father was to be his executioner, not out of a sense of cruelty but to avoid any possibility of

*retaliation. The next day the father told his son of this decision
and the boy received the news without emotion. "I am willing to
die, Father," he said. He sat in a circle of men, and the father stood
behind him and wrapped a cord around his son's neck and stran-
gled him, his tears falling onto his son's head until he stopped
moving.*

*How to protect your children? From the natural world, from
strangers, from each other? From themselves.*

*Michael looked at Billy. Was he a child? A teenager, that
twentieth-century invention. The concept of childhood revolved
around innocence, a state that didn't last long in previous centuries.
Perhaps not in this one either. That idea of an innocence uncorrupted by civilization was what Rousseau had embraced. Who
knew how innocent Billy was? Not much was known about the
evening he got hurt. He was out with others, drinking. A small-
town Saturday night. His father was an oil worker, a big, sullen
man who was home rarely and when he was, he made people
nervous, including Billy, Michael guessed.*

*He had seen Billy's mother visiting, a small woman with blue-
black hair who hovered over her son. She might have been chanting
something. She didn't drive and lived twenty miles away and it
would be hard for her to visit. She had other children and her
husband was gone most of the time. She would come when she
could, unsure of whether she was visiting or mourning him.*

*Thompson had some money when he came to Montreal. This
was when you made your money in the country then retired to the
city. Now, of course, it's the opposite. Montreal was a city of
brilliant divisions: English/French; Protestant/Catholic; the
Scottish elite living in mansions on the hill while the Irish suffered
on the choleric floodplain below. It was a romantic place, though,
even then, and it drew restless villagers and young people who
want that sense of possibility that cities sell.*

Thompson flourished in the wilderness, where he made his own path. But he didn't have much luck in the city. Those paths had already been laid out. The city didn't offer possibility for Thompson; the wilderness did, with its epic space. The city was a narrowing of possibility. Cities were glorious if you were wealthy, hell if you were poor. Thompson had money when he arrived in Montreal and then lost it all. Like people, cities lurch toward oblivion even as they grow, the stones crumbling, systems failing. It's sometimes hard to tell progress from decline.

1

MONTREAL, 1840

Thompson rose early and uncertainly, his bad leg brittle in the cold. It had been bothering him more than usual lately. He dressed quickly, not waking Charlotte, who was asleep under the heavy covers. Her hair was still black at fifty-four. He couldn't remember the last time they had made love. Two years ago, perhaps. He left their small apartment, carefully negotiating the iron stairs. It was April, though there was still a foot of snow on the ground.

He had retired to Montreal in 1812, the year of the war. A war where both sides claimed victory, a modern idea. Thompson had seen the clash with the Americans coming, the lack of clarity about the border, the chafing of interests at the Pacific, the growing ambition in the American

Congress. It wasn't the numerical difference between the two countries that had worried him (Canada had only half a million people, some of them Americans, while the United States had seven million). No, the problem was that Canada had yet to become a country. It was still an idea, forming slowly. Who would fight for it? What would they be fighting for? The unarticulated nation that sits sublime and separate in each head.

That year he drew his map. In the rented home in Terrebonne (a blissful time, wondrous and almost incomprehensible now), he had approached his masterwork, drawing the imagined nation as the Americans marched over the border with their guns, their imperial hopes meeting with disaster at Crysler's Farm. Each section of rag linen paper was two feet by eighteen inches. He had stretched each one taut and fitted it into the frame and then scaled the outline. He made ink from oak apple galls boiled with iron sulphate and gum arabic and it went onto the paper in a rich oily stream and dried to a softer shade.

The flow of rivers was indicated with a feathered pattern and mountain elevations were noted. More than two million square miles of country laid out in a form that could be understood, settled, sold. He worked at night, by candlelight, for seven months. The twenty-five separate sheets glued together with mucilage, assembling the country even as it was being invaded. Was he mapping something that didn't exist?

In August 1814, as he was finishing the map, an army of four thousand British soldiers marched on Washington, setting fire to all that would burn, and like Moscow when Napoleon tried to take the city, it lit the night. The Library of Congress was burned to the ground, those pages of recent history floating softly like black snowflakes on the summer breeze. The White House was burned too, but President James Madison's wife, Dolley, had the presence of mind to save the original Declaration of Independence and a life-sized portrait of George Washington, aware, even as the Capitol burned, its written deeds obliterated, that nations are built on symbols, not history. The map had brought him satisfaction—the culmination of a life's work. But it hadn't brought profit.

There weren't many people about on the streets. A few horses moved along McGill Street, pulling coal and wood in the dark. He found it comforting to walk in the snow; it made the city more humane. There is equality in adversity, he thought. He walked briskly, his bad leg moving with a slight swing to it. His good eye was failing, and in the dawn light, images occasionally became muffled and indistinct, as if he was walking in a dream. A seventy-year-old man moving carefully in the dark.

The row houses of Griffintown were beginning to erupt. Behind each peeling door was a large family, sometimes two, desolate Irish who had fled famine. They had stayed in the immigrant sheds on Grosse Isle on the St. Lawrence River, herded like cattle into quarantine, and they died by the hundreds of cholera or typhus, pressed against each other in those rooms, staring into one another's doomed faces. The children of the dead were delivered to the city like dark gifts, raised by nuns or relatives or worse.

Thompson walked up the hill, past the mansions built by tobacco and fur and beer fortunes. He knew some of these men, had met them in the North West. The city had grown up around them like Nineveh, suddenly formidable, stupid with money.

The April snow was heavy and he pulled his leg through it with some effort. He saw a child bundled in dark clothes sitting on the back of a coal wagon, a girl whose face was dusted black. She might have been six, out with her father to make the morning deliveries. He thought about his daughter Emma, dead at seven, as innocent a being as ever walked this earth, and he was surprised to find himself crying. Her death remained incomprehensible to him, the severest test of his faith. For a week he held her, giving her calomel and castor oil, trying to kill the fever. Her small body was limp and then felt weightless, and finally, cold. She returned to him in a handful of images that had become like etchings, worn from so much use.

His son John had died a month before Emma, and perhaps he'd never been properly mourned. He hadn't spoken to his son Samuel in six years. Thompson had felt the boy's resentment building and hoped his son was merely going through a passage, would emerge a man, an equal, that their relationship would resume. Samuel would be silent for days, and then yell accusations at his father.

And of course Tristan was gone. The child he carried in his heart, never glimpsed, still perfect, the offspring of his only experience outside Charlotte. He would be forty-two now. Perhaps he had his own family, children, grandchildren even. Sometimes Thompson found himself staring into the faces of men Tristan's age on the streets of Montreal. His son could be anywhere, could be anyone. Occasionally he'd see a man with a dark face and an intense look, and Thompson wondered if this was indeed his son. Once, he stared so intently the man walked up and inquired if he was well. Thompson stared into the man's eyes, looked at his dark hair; there may be native blood, he thought. He wanted to ask him, but how to phrase it? Are you my son? Thompson couldn't manage a word, and the man simply walked away. Tristan was a ghost.

His money was gone too, invested in his children's unsuccessful schemes, and in his own ill-fated plan to supply the British army with firewood. He had left the employ of the North West Company with a share of the profits, not rich by any means, but comfortable. All of it was gone now. Arrowsmith, the British publisher, which had reprinted his map without his knowledge, had finally compensated him: 150 pounds for a life's work, and that too was gone. He had lobbied the British government for a modest pension, but his request was denied. He received the letter last week. *After diligent investigation, it is our view …* He hadn't shown it to Charlotte. He also hadn't told her about Washington Irving, the American writer who had offered to buy his journals and turn them into a novel. The idea that his work would be reduced to entertainment filled him with despair and he turned Irving down, even though he and Charlotte were living in penury.

Thompson had spent his life gathering: information, knowledge, miles, a family, and now each year brought fresh loss. He had lost four children, his money, and he was losing sight in his remaining eye. He might lose the use of his leg. On winter mornings, it felt as if it were a wooden crutch, inanimate, useful but limited, not really part of him. He had lost most of his friends, though perhaps *friends* was too grand a word for people you had spent a few months with more than two decades before.

He thought of Welland, drowned, a big man who thrashed in the Saskatchewan River like a harpooned whale must thrash. He was gone before they could reach him. He thought of MacKay often. They had travelled together through thousands of miles. He missed his cheer, his Orkney doubt, his companionship. He had married finally and settled at Fort Augustus, and then took a fever and slipped away, gone.

The sun was low in a morning sky smudged with winter clouds. People in dark clothes moved gingerly through the snow. Thompson was dressed in his best clothes, which were musty and mended and long out of fashion and could no longer mask his poverty. His appointment wasn't until nine, but he had left at six to avoid lying to Charlotte, and he walked the streets of Montreal for three hours.

The sheer boredom of clerking is what had driven him toward exploration. He mulled this irony as he finally trudged to the Hudson's Bay offices and was directed to the ill-lit office of a young man named Pritchett whose job it was to hire clerks. Companies needed an endless army of clerks. They got bored or left for more lucrative employment, or they drank or stole goods or met with misadventure. It was a full-time job replacing them.

"You are seventy years of age, sir?" Pritchett said, surveying Thompson's face and worn clothes, assessing his lifespan, his intelligence, his desperation. "It's not an age when most men seek employment."

"Most men are dead at seventy," Thompson said.

"Yes. Do you have any experience clerking, sir?"

"I worked as a clerk for the Hudson's Bay Company. It was some time ago."

"When, precisely."

"Seventeen hundred eighty-four."

"I see. Much has changed, sir."

Yes, thought Thompson. *The Hudson's Bay Company has been roused from its torpor by competition from the North West*

Company. A world has been discovered and mapped. And I am one of those who discovered it. I am the one who mapped it. In any event, what could have changed? Was there a new method of counting? Were there new numbers, new pens, new black notebooks to keep records in? Pritchett's office was filled with dark folders. His desk was dark oak and there was a faint smell of something like embalming fluid.

"I invented the North West," Thompson said, surprising himself.

"Indeed." Pritchett made a note in his black book. "I'm afraid, Mr. Thompson, that your services won't be required by the Hudson's Bay Company."

Thompson left the man's office. He wouldn't tell Charlotte of this new humiliation, though perhaps the job itself would have been more humiliating. He had once shared everything with her, but as his life veered into decline, he doled out his failure in small doses. He was protecting her, he thought. Perhaps he was protecting himself. She was sixteen years younger, a fact that had never been more glaring. She had borne their poverty without complaint. She would love him regardless of their circumstances, regardless of his occupation, or his infirmities, which were worsening. But these failures were adding up, and would soon present a terrible sum. He didn't want her to be faced with doubt. What was love? What could it be reduced to? Habit, certainly. The city was filled with marriages that were simply legal partnerships. Some of these men had had other wives in the country, and they had separated those two parts of themselves with some success. In the North West, there had been passion and lust, the warm scent of savagery. What man hasn't smelled it somewhere and embraced it as kin? But they moved back to the city, back to perfumed corsets, separate bedrooms, and a polite touch.

The light never quite arrived. One of those days that is held in abatement, a lengthy prelude to something that doesn't come. He recalled showing the constellations to Samuel when he was a boy, locating the pole star for him and showing him how to calculate their position. But the heavens were of no interest to Samuel; he saw only its emptiness, not its potential. There was no story up there for him. Surveying wasn't romantic work, but it was honest and it was outside, though neither of these advantages appealed to his son. Standing in an autumn rain, wet and shaking with cold, his face pale, his eyes hard and resentful, Samuel had yelled, "This is your world, not mine." The cry of most sons. Thompson supposed he was right. Samuel saw his father trudging other people's land, marking off the parameters of their wealth, a servant.

Thompson wondered if his son was still alive. There was a period when Samuel appeared in fevered dreams, dead on the prairie, stretched under the western sun, birds tugging at the wounds on his thin body. Thompson would wake up and convince himself that Samuel was simply a young man looking for a place in the world, like thousands of other young men, like Thompson himself, and that one day he would walk through the door, returned from the Orient with pockets filled with diamonds.

He remembered John sitting in the canoe at the age of four, seated on the blankets, watching the wilderness quietly go by, looking for dragons, clutching his father's leg instinctively. Save me from this savage world. But Thompson hadn't managed to do that. What father had? He hadn't saved John or Samuel or Tristan or Emma. Children go out into the world equipped with curiosity and naïveté and rage, and then seek a place where these things are welcome.

And now Henry was gone.

Henry was thirty-one, and the melancholy that Thompson had glimpsed in him when he was a child had fully flowered. It was a black mood that held no violence, unlike his brother.

Henry was a mapmaker. He had followed his father into a dying art. Ungifted, melancholy, and without work. When Thompson went to his rooms after hearing that he was missing, he was confronted by Henry's wife, Barbara, who was pregnant with their first child. She stood weeping, and she had a look that was both grateful and accusatory, suggesting that Thompson's blood was weak, and that she feared the same fate for their unborn child.

Thompson began looking for him in St. Charles, stopping in at shops and alehouses, asking after him. He walked for six hours in a meticulous grid, his leg stiffening. The winter light was fading, the deepening of afternoon. He had walked and paddled more than fifty thousand miles in the wilderness, and now he was once again an explorer. He turned down an alley streaked with urine. Three men squatted against the brick, sharing a cloudy bottle.

"Do you know Henry Thompson?" he asked them.

The men stared up at him, their eyes rheumy and empty. The question hung there and Thompson moved along the alley. A woman was splayed against the brick, her pale, bruised legs exposed. She gave Thompson an awful smile. There was a wooden door near the end of the alley, held on with rope hinges. Thompson opened it and went inside. A dozen men sat drinking out of pewter cups in the dim light. He asked them if they had seen his son. One of the men looked up.

"Henry Thompson?" he asked. "I know a Henry. Young man."

"He's lost."

"Lost," the man echoed dully.

"I intend to find him."

The man shrugged. Thompson continued looking until after nine, then walked home.

For four days, he walked the streets of Montreal, searched makeshift taverns that were hidden away, blighted spaces. In a few of them, Henry was known, but no one had seen him.

On the fourth day, Thompson found Henry in a dismal room in Lachine, sitting on the floor, his head resting at an angle against the stained wallpaper. His eyes were hollow and dark and filled with such despair that Thompson pulled his son's head to his chest and sat down and cradled him for an hour. He held him as he had held him through his sickness at the age of two, when the fever wouldn't break and Thompson had held him because he thought it was the last of him.

2

NEW YORK, 1850

New York was the colour of an old blanket. Thompson walked streets that were crowded with children selling chestnuts, heavy old women hawking stained material, and men selling roasted meat, tin plates, knives, hats, and hairless dogs. He couldn't fault this ragged army. He was there to sell as well, to find a buyer for his maps. He had written to Sir Robert Peel, the British prime minister, beseeching him to take the maps; they would be invaluable when negotiating a border with the Americans. Proof of what was there. How could you divide it up if you didn't know what it was?

London had refused him, perhaps America would embrace him. It embraced everyone, whether they wanted embracing or not. They had just embraced Texas, despite Mexico's protest. The new president, James Polk, favoured westward expansion. He coveted the Oregon Territory, and Thompson had drawn the most detailed map of the area. Perhaps Polk himself would buy the map, he thought, to see where he was expanding. On the northern border there was negotiation; on the southern, blood.

He remembered the dinner seven years ago with George Simpson, governor of the Hudson's Bay Company, a Highlander who had closed dozens of unprofitable trading posts and fired half the employees. A man of appetites and efficiency who abandoned his country wives and children when he moved to Montreal. Thompson wanted to sell him his maps of the Oregon Territory, and Simpson said he was interested and invited him to dinner. Simpson's house in Lachine was dark and opulent, and Thompson walked to it through ten miles of rain, clutching his rolled maps that were covered in oiled canvas. The dinner had been sumptuous and Simpson told him stories of his travels, throwing his head back to laugh at every absurdity. A Highlander in all things, he saw no point in paying Thompson for his maps. Those rivers and lakes and boundaries would surface elsewhere. Every occupied territory eventually yielded maps; pirated and inaccurate and marred by self-interest, perhaps, but delivered without charge. A miserable walk back to Montreal.

Thompson passed a dense huddle of buildings on Tenth Street and found Coleman in a shop that was five steps down from the sidewalk. He was bent over a desk, a thin, fluttery man who looked up and saw Thompson with his maps under his arm. Neither was buoyed by the other's appearance. Thompson introduced himself and tapped the large canvas roll.

"The maps I wrote of," he said.

"Yes, yes." It was clear Coleman didn't recall.

"The North West, the Oregon Territory."

"You're a mapmaker then."

"Yes."

"Do you map cities?"

"No."

"Cities are what people want now. New York grows so fast. Four hundred thousand people, half of them criminals."

"Your president, as you know, is keen on westward expansion …"

Coleman looked at him with a blank face. "There are several books on the North West. Have you read …"

Coleman went to the back of the shop and his hands circled the air in front of a shelf until he pulled a book out.

"Here it is. The man was captured by savages. Lived like one for years then escaped. Died in Philadelphia. The sort of thing you might like. The price is reasonable."

"My maps."

Coleman smiled slightly, a dark, unfortunate smile. "There isn't much call for maps at present. It's all adventure, it seems."

Coleman's face had a finality to it. Thompson had come to New York for nothing. Coleman gave him the name of another publisher, Wainscott and Son, who published maps. Thompson walked the fifteen blocks to Wainscott, who wasn't interested either.

"If you want to leave them, I'll take a look. I can't promise anything."

Thompson left with his maps, still unwrapped, and began to walk along Eighth Street, past a boy who was begging.

"Have you something, sir?" he pleaded, his hand, streaked with soot, thrust upward. Thompson had nothing for himself even, and kept walking. The boy yelled a string of curses after him.

He heard several languages around him, a coarse, rich cacophony, and observed faces, dark-eyed people who moved as if they were late for an appointment. The streets were filled with commerce, moving goods, selling them. Groups of young men lingered at corners, waiting for the cover of night. Laundry waved from staircases and railings, white underclothes and dark coats and dresses, giving the buildings an unfinished look. There was a row of buildings burned to the ground, charred timbers lying like giant sticks and a group of children played among them. Thompson had never seen such a concentration of people in such a small area. They competed for the same resources: work, food, money, water. It was a city filled with dire opportunity. The natural laws were stretched thinly and tribes huddled each night, bound by blood or religion or language or nation, waiting for morning. Lines were redrawn as the city slept.

How would he map this city? It was a grid, each block containing a separate constellation. He walked to Mrs. Ogilvie's boarding house, past her disapproving stare, through the smells of cooked cabbage and boiled meat to his small room. He spread his map of the Oregon Territory across the bed and ran his finger along the borders he had drawn. The Americans invaded as he was creating the map, and now he was trying to sell them maps of the country they weren't able to take. If they had taken the country, he thought, his maps might be worth a great deal.

The soft October evening light left long shadows, and the maples were the colour of fire. Thompson sat on the wooden chair and observed Montreal through the window of their rooms. Coleman was an ass. Arrowsmith were crooks. Mackenzie over-rewarded, the Americans untrustworthy, the British blockheads. The Peigans had guns, the Irish were dying.

"What?" Charlotte was nudging him gently. He hadn't realized he was talking out loud. The light was almost gone. They couldn't afford to light the lamp at night and the room became slowly black.

In the morning he went over the list of all he had sold: his surveyor's chains (twenty-six pounds), his theodolite, his good coat (five pounds, ten pence), a bed, the leggings of a Mandan dress, his navigator's instruments, books. Only his maps, it seemed, wouldn't sell. By October there was no money nor the promise of any. He and Charlotte moved in with his daughter Elizabeth and her husband, William Scott, an engineer, an efficient man who bore the presence of his in-laws with an air of pragmatism. Thompson had come to a decision. He would write his own book, not an entertainment, as Irving had intended, but an adventure nevertheless. He had hundreds of pages of journals. People read adventure, as Coleman had said.

The writing went slowly and his hand shook by late morning and by November the room was often too cold to work. His son-in-law rationed the lamp oil and he couldn't write at night. At any rate, he was too exhausted and his eye wasn't strong enough to work by lamplight.

On February 14, Thompson woke in the chill of their room, the residue of a dream—Saukamappee standing on Tenth Street in New York, eating roasted chestnuts and laughing—still in his head. He stared into blackness. There were a few seconds of suspended disbelief, followed by a flash of betrayal—Don't abandon your God especially when it seems He has abandoned you—then the simple fact of that darkness. Thompson was blind.

"Charlotte."

"Hmm."

"I'm blind. I can't see."

She sat up and looked at her husband, who was staring blankly at the far wall. She looked into his eye, looked at that solemn face, with its child's trust and fear. The blackness wasn't absolute. There were shades, blue-black, grey-black, a few pricks of light that appeared like stars and were quickly extinguished.

At nine that morning Charlotte led Thompson to Dr. Howard's office on Queen Street. In the small waiting room there was a child with a shirt wrapped around his head as a bandage. After an hour, Thompson and Charlotte went into Howard's office. He was a small, thin man with a large moustache. He sat in front of Thompson and lit a candle and passed it across his line of sight, moving closer and then withdrawing.

"What do you see, Mr. Thompson?"

"A glow, faint."

"Can you see shapes?"

"No."

"When did you lose your sight?"

"I lost the sight in my right eye when I was eighteen. Sixty years ago. The other eye, I awoke blind this morning."

Howard drew closer and stared into his eyes. Thompson could feel his presence, the human warmth, the proximate breath.

"Did you ever see a doctor regarding your right eye?"

"No. The sight was lost from working by candlelight and staring at the stars."

"You don't lose your eyesight from staring at the heavens, Mr. Thompson. You have cataracts. There is a chance your sight can be returned."

Howard rustled around the brown bottles that were against one wall.

"I'm going to fumigate your eyes with hydrocyanic acid," he said. He brushed Thompson's eyelids with veratria, and applied the acid. Then he set up a small machine that generated arcs of spidery light and moved it around the orbit of Thompson's eye. Thompson could see distant lightning. Charlotte watched this necromancy in silent horror.

"For the next two weeks, Mr. Thompson, every morning upon waking I would like you to drink a wine glass filled with a mixture of gentian, a small quantity of sulphate of magnesia, and sulphuric acid."

The mixture was predictably awful, a witch's brew that burned and sent bile upward. Thompson was glad he couldn't see it.

Three months later, he saw shapes moving on Craig Street as Charlotte led him on their daily walk. "Is that a carriage?" he asked her.

"Ahead of us. Yes."

"There are people passing."

"Yes. You can see."

"Not clearly. But there are shapes, dark shapes. I see movement."

"Your eyes are returning."

"Perhaps."

The shapes were indistinct, dark presences against a dark background.

After a month, he returned to his book, his sight returned, the unknowable hand of God surely. The mission begun at the age of fifteen was still unfinished. The writing was slow. He and Charlotte left Elizabeth's home, shunted to his son Joshua's house, where they felt equally unwelcome. Cholera arrived, killing a thousand Montrealers. Thompson was afflicted yet survived, a small miracle. His book languished. He was without a publisher, and finally without energy or hope. He abandoned the book, but continued to write in his journal. His last entry was February 1851, "Steady snow with ENE wind and drift. Bad weather."

He spoke less, and read the Bible. "The voice of one crying in the wilderness. Prepare ye the way of the Lord, make his paths straight." He supposed he had done that. What was cartography but making the path straight for the next traveller? There would be a trickle then a flood; the lines he had drawn would contain millions. He had done what God had asked of him and had received no reward on this earth.

It was still dark the morning Charlotte awoke and looked at her husband and knew that he had been claimed. She held him for three hours while the house slept, talking softly into his dead ear, telling him that she loved him when she was a child and loved him still. Her hand rested lightly on his chest. He was eighty-seven.

Elizabeth and Joshua buried him in the cemetery on Mount Royal. Five of his children were there, watching the simple wood lowered into the ground with a mixture of loss and relief.

Charlotte sat by his grave, ignoring the children's pleas to come home. They finally left her to her grief. When it was dark, she lay on the grave, felt the fresh earth on her back, and watched Jupiter's slow circuit before falling asleep.

THE DEAL

1864–1905

So it didn't end well.

Billy was alone in the room, but Michael still spoke in a low, almost conspiratorial voice. Thompson's maps were used into the twentieth century, though he was unacknowledged as the mapmaker. But they were his. You could tell because he made certain errors and they were repeated in the pirated editions; in a way, these mistakes were his signature. His journal—which ran to hundreds of pages—was eventually published in 1916, after it was discovered by a geologist named Joseph Burr Tyrrell. It was Tyrrell who pronounced Thompson "the greatest land geographer who ever lived." Fewer than five hundred copies of the book were sold; it was hardly news anymore and the country was at war and wasn't interested in the past.

How do I know Thompson was my great-great-grandfather? Especially given that I was descended from Tristan, the illegitimate son. Despite its pitfalls, the oral tradition has some benefits. My mother, Catherine, knew the story, the names, and I pieced it together from what I had read of Thompson. A tenuous claim? Of course. But people lay claim to brilliant ancestors (and exaggerate their brilliance) all the time; it's an epidemic. It gives us hope and something to pale beside.

But all history has pitfalls, including the one I'm telling you. Consider the sources. Diaries are self-serving, journalism is a narrow trade, witnesses are unreliable. Everything tainted by politics.

At any rate, with Thompson, the West was mapped: Now people knew what was there. The next question, of course, was: Who will govern it? At that moment, it was still owned by the Hudson's Bay Company, which had not yet become a department store, and which had five million square miles of land sitting on its books as a kind of perverse inventory. Rupert's Land (named for Prince Rupert, the King's cousin) was filled with Indians, an inconvenience that could become a burden or, worse, like in the U.S., a series of bloody wars. If you claimed the land, they would be a responsibility, an onerous one. But if you didn't claim it, the Americans surely would. And if they claimed the West, they might claim everything.

All empires are eventually undone. They collapse through war, attrition, debt, ambition, and finally, a lack of meaning. The Indians came to the idea too late, much too late, looking for an empire as Napoleon sought his own. It wasn't a great time for empires, as it turned out.

As Napoleon prepares for the slaughter at Borodino, the American president James Madison declares war on Britain and makes plans to invade Canada. The acquisition of Canada, Thomas Jefferson says, will be a mere matter of marching. Jefferson has read Alexander Mackenzie's Voyages to the Frozen and Pacific Oceans *(which contained uncredited versions of David Thompson's maps). So has Napoleon, both of them idly wondering if this new territory is worth conquering.*

But the Americans have to conquer their own territory first.

Tecumseh, the Shawnee chief, is travelling the U.S., trying to unite the Indians into one vast confederacy, a political and military force, a million warriors that could challenge Napoleon himself. Tecumseh is tall and well formed and a natural orator. He scours the country, going to the Wyandots, Delaware, Kickapoo, Seneca, Cherokee, Cheyenne, to the Mandans. He gathers the leaders of a dozen nations, chiefs who are streaked in vermillion, caked in blue clay, tattooed with battle scenes, enemies themselves but standing uncertainly together to hear Tecumseh's message: The white man will not be satisfied until he has all the land between the rising and the setting sun.

Tecumseh has a brother, a half-brother, Tenskwatawa, who spent the first part of his life in alcoholic despair. Picture him once more sprawled in a glade, his head bitten by alcohol made from potatoes, coloured with tea, and drunk from a molasses jar. He is instinctively searching for the swaying images that herald his greatness, that soothe his terrors, strengthen the hand that holds the bow, returns the eye that has been gouged out with an arrow, and, finally and most comfortingly, reassembles the bones of his mother, adding flesh, eyes, and the soft hand that pushes the damp hair away from his forehead as the fever rages. But that isn't the dream that arrives. Instead there's a new dream: black smoke drifts skyward, a thousand fires joined, and a white army rides across the plain where nothing lives, the water brown and dead, the sun the colour of mud, a yellow gas lifting off the rock. The army approaches, a million, more, so white they shine even under the dull sun, naked save for rifles, skeletal, the smell of burning metal in their noses, blood in their brains, united in a single scream.

When Tenskwatawa wakes up it's morning. He tells his brother of his vision, and then he tells everyone, a story that grows until there is a second vision that attaches itself to the first: a green perfect land where Indians sit at a table that stretches to sunrise in a feast with no end. He calls himself "The Prophet," and the name sticks. He shuns alcohol, and starts talking about a world where guns and whites are banished, where the Indians live as they have for millennia.

The Prophet wears a silver whistle in his hair, an amulet below his nose, has the moustache of a Frenchman, and his one useless eye is half-closed in a permanent droop that gives him a look of constant boredom. He follows in Tecumseh's wake, preaching a return to the Great Spirit, and he accuses doubters of witchcraft. In a Delaware village an eighty-year-old woman mocks his mystic words and the red silk scarf he uses to tie back his hair. He accuses her of being a witch and orders her roasted over a low fire. To his surprise, the village carries out his order. For a day she screams, naked and blackened, and each scream confirms his power. The Americans, he tells his followers, grew from the scum of the Great Water when it was troubled by the Evil Spirit. It was that spirit that found its way into the old woman: It's to blame for her death.

Michael looked at Billy. This was his history. A part of it anyway. If he didn't wake up, this was what he was, this accumulation of events.

*W*illiam H. Harrison *has a vision too: the West as empire. He controls millions of acres of land and sees the power of Tecumseh and the Prophet growing, threatening his dream. He rides out to the Delawares and denounces the Prophet as false. Have you seen his divinity? he asks the chief and his council. Ask him to alter the* course of the moon, to make the rivers stop, to make the dead rise, the sun stand still.

The Prophet hears of this challenge and announces that he will in fact make the sun stand still. The crowd in Greenville that day is large, waiting for the miracle. The Prophet stands and points upward, then raises his other arm and closes his eye. Ten minutes pass. Fifteen. The crowd is silent, their collective anticipation straining.

What happens? The sun disappears.

The Prophet feels the sudden shade and keeps his eye shut and calls out to the Great Spirit in a new language, alien syllables that come out in a high voice. The sun returns and the crowd lets out its breath. So it's true. He has the power. Who can dispute this? The Great Spirit has sent him. Perhaps the Great Spirit has arrived. Tenskwatawa looks over his crowd as the moon wanders from its brief eclipse of the sun and the noise recedes across the plain.

Harrison is looking for a place to strike in his campaign to make the West safe for settlement. And what better place than Prophets-town? It's here that the politician and his mystic brother live, the centre of this new religion. Harrison is a noble-looking man, a view he asserts before the mirror most mornings. He has a Napoleonic haircut, a high-collared uniform with gold braids, and with three thousand men, he rides in and razes Prophetstown, killing whatever is in their path. But neither Tecumseh nor the Prophet is among the bodies that are strewn like bloody toys over the prairie.

You could say that this was the first battle in the War of 1812, that unimaginatively named war where the Indians were used as a tactic, a bluff. The Canadian commander tells the American *commander: You and I are civilized men schooled in the rules of war, but these savages under my command, well, I can't control them once the fighting starts. God have mercy on you. It worked at Fort Detroit, where Tecumseh teamed up with the British commander Isaac Brock and the Americans surrendered to avoid a massacre.*

But now Tecumseh is on his way to Fort Malden on the Detroit River to join with British general Henry Procter, a fastidious man and reluctant leader. Tecumseh has a thousand warriors drawn from a dozen nations, feathered, painted in yellow and black and red, decorated with shells and silver and ornamental scars drawn with their own knives. They wait at Fort Malden for Harrison and his three thousand Americans. But Procter decides to retreat in the face of this threat.

"You are a fat animal that carries its tail upon its back as it is fleeing," Tecumseh tells him.

"It is tactical," Procter says, his red coat shining in the autumn sun.

"Leave us your arms and ammunition that you may run faster. We will stay."

"Bloody savages," Procter says, speaking dreamily as if to a third party, some neutral agent who can empathize with him. He tells Tecumseh, "You don't understand war, only killing."

"You don't understand that war is only killing."

Procter retreats to the Thames River and fails to assess the terrain, to gain advantage over Harrison, who is two days behind. His thoughts are scattered. He resents this war. To be in Europe, where the great battles are fought, where the glory lies.

His army is no happier than he is. They think Procter a plump fool, unable to define the war. It seems like someone else's fight, and they turn and run after the first volley is fired.

Tecumseh stands, but half of his men have also deserted, gone back to their respective nations, the autumn hunting season, and the comforting fiction that their world will endure.

Swarmed by Americans in the woods by the Thames, Tecumseh is shot through the chest. His body lies in a pleasant clearing near an oak grove, his skin carved off by souvenir hunters who sell the strips as razor strops. Flies congregate on the red mass. More than sixty men claim to have killed Tecumseh, a figure that grows over the years as neither his body nor his death is authenticated. Some are merely tavern drunks, vividly describing the great chief begging for his life; others use his death for political gain. Harrison rides Tecumseh all the way to the White House and becomes president.

After the victory, Harrison is filled with renewed purpose and his army marches on toward Upper Canada. But winter has come early, as it did for Napoleon. Supplies are scarce. The men trudge through drifts for two days, hungry, before turning back, defeated by the land and the snow.

Tecumseh is a martyr now and Tenskwatawa tries to use his brother to rally the Indians. I will cook their hearts, he tells the diminishing crowds. They used my brother's skin to sharpen their knives and we will feast on their hearts. Their blood will darken the rivers.

But this is the thing about leaders. Tecumseh filled the Indians with a sense of possibility; his half-brother, a one-eyed dandy with a flair for cruelty and the temper of an adolescent, doesn't have the same power. (Tenskwatawa screamed constantly as a baby, and was originally named—so many names ago—Lalawethika, the Noisemaker.) He fills them with doubt. The dream of an Indian Nation dies with Tecumseh, the prospect of empire gone.

*M*ichael stared at Billy's face, which was neither slack nor set in any specific expression but occupied some middle territory, a mask *that defended what lay behind it. His pale green cotton hospital gown was almost transparent in its thinness, the result of hundreds of industrial washings. How much information was getting through, and what, if anything, would be retained?*

This was, Michael assumed, the only news he was getting. Perhaps it was all being retained, as it didn't have to compete with books, TV, a mother's nagging, or annoying song lyrics that stuck to the brain like gum. These lectures were his only narrative.

Countries are like marriages, Michael told him. They are born in negotiation and remain an ongoing negotiation. They are unresolved, irresolvable. The next few decades were uneventful (like so many marriages). Then we had the Upper and Lower Canada Rebellions. Eventually the Americans descended into civil war, slaughtering one another with much more appetite and purpose than they showed in 1812. We returned to fighting ourselves, the most obvious enemy.

1

JOHN A. MACDONALD, OTTAWA, 1864

James McIlvoy woke in the grey light of his cramped room silently cursing his masters, the familiar salute of most mornings. The litany began, as it usually did, with the fact that Macdonald was a bulb-nosed drunk. Then D'Arcy McGee, as Irish as death, a reformed Fenian (though the most eloquent man in Canada, McIlvoy grudgingly conceded), all five foot three of him, face like a monkey and a poet into the bargain. In Quebec there was George-Étienne Cartier, French and Catholic, flaws enough for any man, having an affair of the heart with the pants-wearing, cheroot-smoking, aptly named Luce Cuvillier, a poorly held secret, though Ottawa was a city that had yet to develop

many secrets and suffered from the lack of mystery. And
George Brown (whom he always saved for last), the obsti-
nate, self-righteous saint of the newspaper business.

McIlvoy found his clothes and put them on, shivering.
This country was no place for civilized men. This country
was in fact no country. He could see why his masters (as he
had come to call them) wanted to create one. It was increasingly clear that Britain was tiring of these colonies. You
could sense it in their manner, read it in their editorials, hear
it in the speeches of Westminster. Their North American
holdings were both difficult and expensive to administer, and
almost impossible to defend, and it wasn't clear that the
people were even prepared to defend themselves. The
country's riches were subtle. To be rid of us, McIlvoy
thought, to be rid of the cost of us at least, would be a relief.

There were other reasons for the colonies to band
together. To the south, the United States, with its itch for
empire—that impulse that sat in the nation's soul, inalien-
able and God-granted—had come north before and would
come again. The British North American colonies needed to
unite to protect themselves from their friends.

McIlvoy had documents to prepare for Macdonald, eight
hours' work, probably more. It was one thing for them to
dream up a country, but you needed field soldiers to actually
carry it out. McIlvoy was one of those soldiers, fetching
documents, preparing reports, finding intelligence on a
variety of subjects, poring over constitutional law.

He ate a hasty breakfast of tea and toast, put on his thin
winter coat and walked through the small drifts of snow, his
boots wet before he reached the library, the wind moving
through his clothes. The library was poorly lit, and cold
enough that he kept his coat on.

It took until nightfall to find and digest all that Macdonald wanted, most of it obscure points of law. He had worked straight through, with only a short break to eat a meat pie, a lunch he immediately regretted. (McGee had told him they were made with dogs and he didn't know if the man was serious or not. It was difficult to tell with McGee. At any rate it was inside him now, dog or not. Or horse. Or worse.) McIlvoy bundled the documents together with string and put them inside his leather satchel and went out into the inhospitable evening. Macdonald would want these straight away. It would be almost eight by the time he got to Macdonald's home, and it would be an act of God if the man were sober.

McIlvoy remembered going to the house when Macdonald's wife, Isabella, was alive. She had an undiagnosed feminine malady that she combated with opium mixed with wine, and spent days in a state of nervous narcotic bliss. She would smile glassily at him and the two would wait for John A. to return, making strained conversation. "How was the law today?" she would ask him. "Is good still good and bad still bad?"

"I suppose."

"That's a Christian comfort," she said with her weak smile. All of her facial expressions had a peculiar weakness, as if she embarked on them—smile, frown, curiosity—but failed to arrive there, giving up before they took shape. It left the impression of a fearful blankness within her.

They would sit, Isabella sipping her medicine, McIlvoy counting the slow minutes until Macdonald's arrival. She and Macdonald had had a child that died at the age of thirteen months, and that grief sat between them always, McIlvoy supposed. They bore it in their way, each to his own medicine, though Macdonald would abandon drink for weeks on end without comment. Cartier had had a child who died at the same age, a curious coincidence. McIlvoy wondered if this somehow bound the two politicians, who on the surface cared little for one another.

McIlvoy trudged through the wet snow and finally reached Macdonald's modest home, which seemed out of keeping with his stature. "Do you know how indebted I am, McIlvoy?" he had once asked when nearing the end of a dreadful binge, a phase that always featured a large number of rhetorical questions. His response had been, "Neither do I, thank God."

Yet his energy was heroic. McIlvoy had seen him work through the night with few ill effects, and then deliver a rousing two-hour speech without notes. There was a genius to Macdonald, messy and turbulent, occasionally contrary, but a genius nonetheless. Perhaps that was the nature of genius; it was necessarily coupled with mess and tragedy. His mind was admirable. McIlvoy hoped this would be enough.

He pulled the heavy knocker back and let it fall on the oak door. After a minute the door opened and Macdonald stood there, tall, almost gaunt, his untamed hair listing to one side, his large nose a web of veins, resembling a (not too) minia-ture street map.

"McIlvoy. Good good. I'd almost abandoned hope. Come in."

It was August when they left for Charlottetown on board the *Queen Victoria*, a serviceable steamer. McIlvoy had person-ally supervised the loading of $13,000 worth of champagne, though he was against this luxury for several reasons. One was mere superstition: Preparing to celebrate an event that had not taken place and may not take place was bad luck. To convince the colonies, which were prosperous, or felt they were prosperous (which amounted to the same thing), to join in a federation, one that delivered benefits but also required sacrifice, would be no easy task. The second worry, of course, was that Macdonald and McGee would go through much of the supply before the ship reached Charlottetown. And there was the ominous coincidence of thirteen. Had that cursed number not been unlucky enough for Macdonald and Cartier? Perhaps they felt that between them they had exhausted its ill luck.

This infernal quadrangle. Brown, publisher of the *Globe* newspaper, hated Macdonald because he was a Conservative and a drunk. He hated Cartier because he was French and Catholic (and he disapproved of Cartier's arrangement with Luce Cuvillier, which he took as a valid impeachment of the Catholic faith). And he hated McGee because he was Irish, Catholic, and a drunk. Macdonald in turn hated Brown, whom he accused of being a self-righteous liberal, was wary of Cartier, and saw in McGee both an ally and a rival. Cartier, who had taken other transport from Quebec, a mercy, thought he was surrounded by English conspirators. Which was largely true. McGee dreamed of a land occupied by people like himself, poets and talkers, a private nationalism.

Macdonald surveyed his supporting cast, as he considered them, as they sat on the deck playing backgammon, idly chatting about whom they anticipated as allies and who would oppose union.

When they arrived at Charlottetown, the harbour was empty. The stillness was unsettling. They walked through deserted streets. Brown and McGee went to the hotel, but McIlvoy and Macdonald continued through the empty town, seeking the cause for this desertion.

"This isn't auspicious for our federation, McIlvoy," Macdonald said, the sound of their heels echoing off the walls of the buildings. At the edge of town they saw a large field. There was a massive tent set up and a banner that read, SLAYMAKER AND NICHOLS OLYMPIC CIRCUS. Outside the tent a giant in a striped suit paced stiffly, his acromegalic head topped by a tiny hat. A horse pranced, led by a woman in a shining dress. An elephant was guided carefully by a man in a purple suit. The elephant had a huge top hat that was attached with a rope tied under its chin, giving it a look of human melancholia. In a cage on wheels was a lion, old and scrofulous, lazily waving at flies with its tail.

They approached the tent and looked inside. What appeared to be most of the townspeople were there, enthralled. They were all staring up, and McIlvoy followed their gaze. A man was walking on a tightrope at the highest reaches of the tent. He held a long pole that jutted out on each side at right angles to the rope, and on his back he carried another man, who held something that McIlvoy couldn't make out. This strange apparition moved tentatively, balanced by the pole that bobbed up and down. There was a moment when the acrobat almost lost his footing, and the crowd gasped as one. McIlvoy wondered if it had been calculated. The tent was humid and close and smelled of animal dung and sawdust. McIlvoy estimated the distance from the rope to the ground to be thirty-five feet.

A mustachioed man in a red jacket stood in the centre of a black ring describing the peril that these two suspended men were in. "The Great Blondin faces a two-hundred-foot fall onto the hard, fatal ground," he said. "If the man he is carrying so much as sneezes, if his leg becomes itchy and he reaches to scratch it, it will be enough, good people of Charlottetown, to cause instant death." The pair on the rope got to the midway point and stopped, wavering slightly. The man on Blondin's back gave something to Blondin, who now had the long pole balanced on the rope itself. The man on top produced a small pan, and a small pot of cooking oil that he set aflame. He handed both of these to Blondin, then theatrically searched his pockets and produced three eggs, which he broke into the pan before throwing the shells over his shoulder. "What is this?" the ringleader boomed. "Faced with the most dangerous stroll on God's earth, they have decided *it is tea time. They are*, and I find this impossible to believe, *cooking an omelette!* Suspended halfway to heaven, *they are taking their supper!* You will *never* see anything as amazing as this!" McIlvoy watched as they did, indeed, make an omelette, and then ate it. He looked at Macdonald, who was staring at this curious feat without expression, one performer coldly assessing another.

The following afternoon, Macdonald stood at the pulpit and addressed six hundred of Charlottetown's quality in St. Jude's Church. An appropriate venue, McIlvoy thought; Macdonald was a preacher. At least on the issue of confederation. The audience was dressed in its finery, and McIlvoy detected a strain of defiance in the set of their faces and rigid postures. Sitting defiantly on hard wooden pews, they were unconvinced, perhaps inconvincible.

"You are content," Macdonald said to the assembled. "I see that contentment in your faces, in your homes and in

your streets. You have reason to be content. You are
prosperous. An enviable state." McIlvoy noted that when
Macdonald spoke publicly he seemed to undergo physical
change, becoming almost handsome. His face, which could
look like a gathering storm, or the wreckage of that storm,
or a startled bird, took on an august cast. His features had
the authority of his words. "It is a wonderful thing to be
prosperous. To be content." McIlvoy knew his rhythms,
knew how he would use that prosperity as a cudgel,
prodding them with such skill that they wouldn't know they
were being herded to the slaughterhouse. He spoke for an
hour and in the course of that hour, McIlvoy watched the
audience relax in their seats, leaning forward slightly, their
faces hanging in anticipation, almost swaying to his message,
which was: You have built something marvellous but it can
easily be lost. Confederation wasn't a way of improving their
lot but of keeping what they had built. He made it clear that
he needed them, needed their solid citizenry, their moral
decency, their guidance and purpose. What Macdonald
actually thought of these people was anyone's guess; he
hadn't visited any of the homes he had praised. He was a
curious combination of elitist and populist. Perhaps you
needed to be to become a successful politician. But by the
end of the sermon, they were swaying to the sound of salvation: The union would save them from the Americans, the
British, the French, the Indians, the devil, and themselves.

In the evening there was a grand ball and McIlvoy was
seated between a local butcher, a large man, prosperous it
appeared, and his equally large wife, safely out of conversational distance of anyone appealing. Across from him was a

man who owned a funeral parlour, a growing business in the New World. The food at least was excellent—pheasant and venison and jellied tongue, roasted potatoes and parsnips—and the wine was plentiful. McIlvoy's masters were all at separate tables, among different crowds, a strategic measure for them to talk to as many people as possible, and relief from the simmering animus that lingered after their days on the boat. They had had enough of one another. Across the room he could see McGee sitting between what appeared to be a mother and her grown daughter. McGee, the Irish raconteur, would be telling them a story in his fluid style, some story that had a hint of intrigue and innuendo, but not enough to offend them. Just the right degree of sauciness to make them feel sophisticated, as if McGee had recognized in them a kinship. McGee's large head seemed to float as it bobbed with his story. As dinner wore on, as conversation with the butcher came to its dismal, tapering conclusion ("Most people don't understand the beauty of the pig"), McIlvoy could see McGee's head getting heavier, bobbing more slowly now, as if his small body had suddenly realized what a weight that large head was. It was evident from this distance of some twenty yards that he was quite drunk. Partway through dinner McGee stood up to excuse himself, and his feet searched the marble floor like a blind man at a precipice. He moved with mechanical steps out of the ballroom, listing to one side, fighting to remain upright. A swirling darkness, McIlvoy guessed, was descending upon him, and he was fighting unconsciousness. McIlvoy prayed he would get to his room unharmed, and relatively unseen. His dinner partners would pass along this bit of news, gleefully to be sure, but he seemed to be escaping without too much notice.

Though he didn't escape Brown's critical eye. The man looked up from his dinner and watched McGee's progress as a chemist observes a failed experiment.

The dinner conversation was painful, though less painful than the dancing that followed. McIlvoy had no choice but to ask the butcher's wife, and he steered her around the floor like a river barge. Then the funeral director's wife, who was thin and dour and danced to the rapid fiddles as if every movement was a separate sin. Surprisingly graceful, Macdonald waltzed gaily with an attractive woman of perhaps twenty-five years, his long legs moving them both in an effortless glide.

This gaiety went on for several hours. McIlvoy was tired, grievously so, but felt duty bound to remain to the end, aware that there might be some mess to contend with.

It was well past midnight and the room was more than half empty. Macdonald stood at his table, laughing uproariously, very drunk. Earlier McIlvoy had seen him grab the coattails of Charlottetown's mayor and pull them hard, a schoolboy prank, then laugh at this wit. He now saw Macdonald pick up a piece of cake and throw it at a local judge, who laughed along with him. This begat cake throwing from several others and ended with Macdonald sitting on the marble floor, having slipped on cake he had thrown himself, his wineglass shattered beside him, screaming at the judge—"You pusillanimous piss-pot! You cake-eating harlot! Shitbird!"—and laughing so hard he began to choke, his stork legs kicking, his face the colour of a cranberry. The floor around him was littered with bottles and food and pieces of clothing that had been torn off in sport.

McIlvoy went to Macdonald and helped him to his feet, patting his back and suggesting that it was time to say goodnight. Macdonald went with him, wobbling toward his room. Cartier, the French fornicator as Brown called him, had left much earlier, and was in his room, his head no doubt resting on the naked breasts of Luce Cuvillier. McGee was unconscious in his clothes after charming then surely offending his dinner companions. And now Macdonald was being led away like a wartime casualty. McIlvoy saw Brown staring after them with an expression of Protestant disgust. From these flawed vessels, McIlvoy thought, a country will be born.

Oh, benighted land.

In the morning, he brought Macdonald tea and toast. He drank the tea and ignored the toast. "Only the innocent eat breakfast," Macdonald said, pouring more tea. "I gather the evening was quite a success."

After Charlottetown they went to Quebec and repeated the performance, which went on for days. Dinners, balls, drunkenness, apologies, beseechings, threats, logic, noble words, foul deeds. Macdonald, the only constitutional lawyer among them—another source of irritation for Brown—tinkered with the founding blueprint daily and in all manner of temperament, a country mapped in whiskied elation and dark suffering, in the optimism of morning and the dread of night. The nation would contain all of this, as all nations do.

Macdonald was drunk every night, and occasionally in the day, and McIlvoy wondered when he would simply collapse. His diplomatic skills, normally astute and effective, were fraying. When the lieutenant-governor of Nova Scotia approached him for concessions, Macdonald stared at the man through bleary eyes and replied, "Sir, if I had the gunpowder, I would blow you up." With the Civil War raging in the U.S., Macdonald wanted to be sure to craft a strong central government; concessions were a path to hell.

That night, McIlvoy went to Macdonald's room and found him standing in front of a mirror, a rug draped across his shoulders, steeped in alcohol, reciting Shakespeare. "What is a man, if his chief good and market of his time be but to sleep and feed? A beast, no more. Sure he that made us with such large discourse, looking before and after, gave us not that capability and godlike reason to fust in us unus'd."

The following night Macdonald was again in his rooms, suffering from his excesses, going through a point of law with McIlvoy when Brown burst in, his mountainous rectitude filling the room. The Old Testament given human form. It was confirmation of McIlvoy's lowly status that Brown didn't notice him, or chose to ignore him, or perhaps he had become one of those servants who were in fact invisible, and therefore somehow incapable of bearing witness himself. "You are a disgrace, Macdonald," he boomed. "And through your appalling behaviour, the behaviour of a schoolboy I should say, you are putting into jeopardy our very cause. For God's sake, man, can't you desist for a week at least."

Macdonald watched him with his half smile. "Perhaps it is you, sir, who jeopardizes our cause, with your self-righteousness," he said. "These colonies are entering a union, not the kingdom of heaven."

"Whatever they are entering, they don't want to be shepherded to the door by the town drunk."

"As the people occasionally remind you, Mr. Brown, they would rather have a drunken John A. Macdonald than a sober George Brown." Brown, along with Antoine-Aimé Dorion—a devil's bargain—had formed the government when Macdonald and Cartier resigned. The Brown government lasted four days, and Macdonald referred to it for months as "His Excellency's most ephemeral administration," something that still had the capacity to irritate the irritable Brown.

"Perhaps they haven't had the opportunity to see you throwing cake," Brown said. "Or sleeping amid the refuse of your debauchery, or other samples of your Highland wit."

"They still await samples of *your* wit, Mr. Brown," Macdonald said. "I'll wager they'll have to wait a good deal longer."

Brown stood there, volcanic in his rage. "You want to build a country that is founded on strength, Macdonald, yet you lack the strength to govern your own base impulses. That may be your downfall, sir, but it shouldn't be the nation's." With that, Brown turned and left. Macdonald resumed his conversation with McIlvoy as if nothing had interfered with it, then took a healthy sip of his brandy. Rather than act as a soporific, as it did with most men, it seemed to give him life.

"It is Brown's wife, Anne, I suppose, who bears the brunt of responsibility for this," Macdonald said. "Rescued him, you know. He spent months bedridden, overcome with nervous ailment, believing, for good reason, that his life had been for naught. A black despair, I'm told. Then he met Anne Nelson in Scotland, and the poor misdirected thing convinced him otherwise. Saved by a woman. A common occurrence, though tragic nonetheless."

As he so often did to McIlvoy, Macdonald spoke while staring slightly above and to the side of his head. "Of course the loss of a woman has the opposite effect. Isabella was my cousin, you know. She was five years older and her ailment was a third party that rarely left the room. Bliss eluded us." He stared upward. "Do you have children, McIlvoy?"

He didn't. He didn't have a wife, nor time for a wife. McIlvoy's life was contained in that one query, someone he had spent eight years with asking him if he had children, as if they had only just met. McIlvoy's invisibility was sometimes so profound that he believed in it himself, believed he could walk undetected among the people. Perhaps he could walk through walls. Who knew the lengths of this extraordinary power? He didn't answer, but of course that was answer enough for Macdonald.

"We are hostage to them," Macdonald said. "Brown has spent a lifetime trying to draw my blood, yet those cuts, hundreds of them, some of them well placed, have nothing like the effect of a single look from an infant. In that one look, you can see your shortcomings, your responsibilities, your wants, all reflected back, contained in our own blood. A mute child possessing greater power than the largest newspaper, with all its damnable lies, its vitriol and insistent daggers." McIlvoy knew that Macdonald kept a box of wooden toys that had been his son John's, dead at thirteen months. He had once come upon him holding them, drunk beyond reason or vanity, stuporous, weeping, a terrible thing to see.

2

LONDON, 1867

London was rendered in shades of black: dark skies, soot-stained buildings, the clothing of the people on Oxford Street, the very air charcoal-coloured in the rain. Macdonald stayed at the Westminster Palace Hotel near Westminster Abbey. The British government viewed him as they would a thirty-two-year-old son who is finally leaving home: with thinly veiled relief. Macdonald and Cartier worked on the British North America bill, and McIlvoy was sent off on errands, fetching this bit of legal history, that bit of constitutional lore. The weather was foul, but the city was an excitement. McIlvoy noticed that Macdonald was drinking less, constrained perhaps by the nearness of his mission. He knew that he had encountered Agnes Bernard, a woman he had tried to woo after Isabella's death. They had met by chance on Bond Street, and Macdonald believed it to be fate, and tried to woo her once more.

The British North America bill began its wretched halting progress through the Commons and the House of Lords, and the delegates spent their time visiting the sights. McIlvoy was grateful for the time, which he spent walking incessantly, breathing in the smoke and dust of civilization, hoping it would stay with him when he returned to North America.

On Oxford Street one day, he saw Macdonald walking with Agnes Bernard. He was talking, his hands waving, chopping the air for emphasis, and she beamed at him. That night, Macdonald called McIlvoy to his room. When he arrived, he could tell the sort of summons it was: Macdonald wanted someone to drink with. McIlvoy was no great drinker, but he was content to sip as Macdonald emptied his own glass repeatedly and spoke at length about the genius of the British North America Act. But his real subject was Agnes.

"As you have gathered, McIlvoy," he said, "we have been spending some time together. We passed a few hours in the British Museum, extraordinary, the world in one building. We shall have to do something like that. Capture history, put it on display." Macdonald stared across his room, which would have held McIlvoy's room and seven more like it. "I intend to marry her," he said. "A man needs a companion. To go through life alone, even steeped in purpose, is to die slowly each day."

It wouldn't occur to the politician that this was precisely McIlvoy's plight, although his purpose was muddier than Macdonald's. His purpose might be said to *be* Macdonald.

When McIlvoy left, it was early morning and Macdonald was almost insensible, though this time out of sheer happiness. An hour later, McIlvoy was wakened by Cartier's hammering at his door, summoning him at once to Macdonald's quarters. McIlvoy ran out in his nightshirt to find the space empty, though it was filled with smoke and the bed still smouldered. "Get some water, man," Cartier whispered to him. "Attend to that fire." McIlvoy filled a bedpan with water and threw it on the bed, which hissed and then fell silent. He opened the window, closed the door behind him, and then went to Cartier's room. Luce Cuvillier was sitting on the edge of the bed in a red silk housedress, smoking a cheroot, coolly staring. Macdonald sat looking like a bewildered animal. His hair was singed, which gave its normally wiry wildness even greater drama. His eyebrows were burnt as well, and when Macdonald gingerly put a hand to his face, McIlvoy noticed that his palms were blackened, as if he had used them to pat out the fire. His nightshirt was burned partly away, revealing a flannel shirt beneath it.

"It was like the devil come to claim me," he said. "I woke up and both my bed and nightshirt were aflame." Macdonald and a candle, that combustible pair.

"We should speak of this to no one," Luce Cuvillier said. Her meaning was not to tell Brown. Or the hotel, though in the morning some explanation would need to be concocted, a job, most likely, for McIlvoy.

The following week, Macdonald married Agnes Bernard at St. George's Anglican Church in Hanover Square, and on March 29, 1867, Queen Victoria finally signed the bill into law as the British North America Act. Macdonald returned to Ottawa with a new country and a new wife.

3

OTTAWA, 1868

It was April, the last of the stubborn winter still here. D'Arcy McGee stood in Parliament and spoke passionately about the Fenian threat and the need for a united Canada. Annexation to the United States, he also argued, would produce an ignominious future of northern peasants supplying lumber for America, a feudal prison. By the end of his lengthy speech it was after midnight, and he and Macdonald went down to the parliamentary bar and ordered brandies and cigars. They drank warily with one another (Macdonald had once half-jokingly told him that the party couldn't afford two drunkards and McGee would have to quit).

"Admirable words, McGee."

"I wonder if they penetrated the thick heads across the floor."

"I should hope not, or we'd be out of business. Without the obtuse Liberals, what would be the point of us?"

"There are those who wonder our point as it is." McGee paused to take some of his drink. "I have nightmares, John."

Macdonald sipped his brandy and looked at McGee, a man filled with Celtic dread and a poet's imagination.

"I have nightmares that I'll be killed, though it's not my death that wakes me with a fright. It's the thought of leaving my family with my debts."

"Are they considerable?"

"They are."

Macdonald, of course, had his own substantial debts. Why was it more profitable to create a company than a country? They were in the wrong business.

"Beware of Irish Catholics," Macdonald said. "There's blood in that religion."

"There's blood in every religion. What better way to attract new sheep? The Fenians are a threat, though."

"Better a threat to the country than to your person, McGee. This murder ..."

"I can't bear to think of it, John. It's as if I'm dying each night."

"I suspect the brandy will take you before the Fenians do. Or you may be bored to death in the House, a fate that awaits us all."

Macdonald finished his brandy and took his carriage home.

McGee stayed for another drink and then left to walk to Mrs. Trotter's boarding house. He was wearing a black cashmere overcoat against the late-winter chill, and a white top hat that added a dandyish touch. He carried a silver-headed bamboo cane that had been a genteel affectation but was now a practical crutch for his sore knee. There was new snow on the ground and the air was fresh. A full moon threw light onto Metcalfe Street. He smoked a cigar and thought of his wife and family who were at home in Montreal. McGee was forty-two, in poor health and heavily indebted. He was still intoxicated by the newness of the country, but his own situation weighed upon him. How to rectify this? How to repay the debts? He had been having nightmares for weeks. McGee turned on to Sparks Street and looked for the key in his pocket.

His key turned in the lock and the door opened to the smells of cabbage and smoke and the punitive soap Mrs. Trotter used on everything. He heard a step behind him, quiet in the snow, and felt the presence of the gun, felt the violent Irish inevitability that had followed him to the New World. Then the explosion.

The .32-calibre bullet went into the back of his neck and exited his mouth, sending his false teeth past Mrs. Trotter's distorted face and landing with a clatter in the hallway. McGee stumbled and turned and fell on his back in the fresh snow, his arms angled out, legs spread-eagled, his white hat, surprisingly, still wedged onto his head.

Macdonald woke up to frantic knocking at his front door and received the news through a haze. He threw on his overcoat, got in the carriage, and sped across Sapper's Bridge to Mrs. Trotter's. McGee was still lying in the snow, the blood on his dark face darkening it further.

Macdonald knelt down beside him, removed the white top hat, and pulled McGee's head onto his lap. He looked at the diminutive body, almost childlike in death. His cane was lying beside him, and Macdonald stared at it. He thought about his brother James Shaw, whom he hadn't thought of in years. Macdonald was seven, James Shaw five, and they were taken to a Kingston tavern by a family friend named Kennedy who had been hired to mind them. Kennedy forced gin on them and then drank heavily himself. John grabbed his brother's hand and fled the tavern, heading for home. Kennedy lurched after them like an ogre from a children's book, weaving down the street, his face black with drink and rage. John pulled his brother along, hoping to reach their house, but James Shaw tripped and Kennedy was on him, drunkenly hammering the boy with his cane. John's cries were for nothing. Kennedy stood there, a drunken beast, as James Shaw convulsed on the ground. Hours later, his brother was dead.

The anger in this world, Macdonald thought, though he supposed he would have to include his own. A world filled with murderous thoughts. He had called McGee a brute, though not to his face, and used him to court the Catholic vote. The only man his equal in eloquence, and perhaps in drink, and in truth, it was McGee who had dreamed the nation, a rambling poetic construct to be sure, but here was the author, dead from an assassin's bullet. Macdonald stared into the simian face that had been caricatured a hundred times as an Irish ape in the newspapers and cleaned the blood from it with the tail of his nightshirt.

With the help of another man, he carried McGee into Mrs. Trotter's parlour, cradling his bloody head. They laid him on the couch, and Macdonald took off McGee's boots and had Mrs. Trotter fetch his carpet slippers and put them on McGee's feet. Macdonald wept uncontrollably for fifteen minutes, then composed himself and summoned the lawyer within. He asked Mrs. Trotter what she had seen.

"I opened the door," she said, her face still ghostly. "It was late but I stay up late, not one for sleeping my life away. And Mr. McGee, he was often out late." She gave Macdonald a complicit look that he ignored. It had been necessary on occasion to help McGee up the stairs. Sometimes she had to take his boots and hat off after he collapsed onto the bed unconscious.

"I heard his key turn in the lock and there he was, it was awful, he was shot just as the door opened. I heard the noise and there was blood coming out of his mouth and he fell."

"Did you see who fired the gun?"

"No, I just saw something slip away into the night, like a shadow of the devil. And then poor Mr. McGee laid out just like you found him. He was full of stories, how he made me laugh."

Macdonald talked to three men who had been on Sparks Street but they had little to tell him. Surely the work of Fenians. The country's first political assassination. A baptism in blood. He telegraphed the police, who arrived at 4 A.M.

A man was hanged for McGee's murder, a suspected Fenian, perhaps the wrong man, but the new Dominion needed to act with authority. Five thousand people turned out to watch James Patrick Whelan swing. He proclaimed his innocence on the gallows and asked that God bless Ireland.

McGee's funeral was held in Montreal, and McIlvoy attended with Macdonald. There was a sea of keening black, the largest crowd the city had yet produced, and Macdonald's grief poured out and joined the deluge.

Macdonald's government was like Macdonald himself, ruthlessly managed, with extended moments of chaos that threatened to unseat it. One of the questions he had to deal with was the North West. One quarter of the continent was still owned by the Hudson's Bay Company. Five million square miles. The Russians had just sold Alaska to the Americans for $7.2 million. God knew what the Americans would pay for Rupert's Land. McIlvoy had heard the figure $40 million.

"Brown believes the North West is our birthright," Macdonald told McIlvoy. "That alone would be reason enough to abandon the territory to the Indians. McGee, bless his dead Irish heart, romanticized it, as he did everything. For myself, I see endless and endlessly difficult space. However, if we don't claim it, the Americans surely will. We are bound to take it. The British government will ease our way, I suspect, push us, even, toward the arrangement." The two men were eating lunch. Outside was the sunshine of May, one of the beautiful months.

"The North West presents as many problems as opportunities," Macdonald said. "And there are the Indians as well. A burden."

Macdonald looked up briefly, and McIlvoy stared with him. It was a familiar rhetorical tic, looking heavenward for a moment while he marshalled his arguments. But Macdonald's face looked suddenly stricken, frozen into a frightful mask. Then he collapsed like a pile of dry sticks falling off the back of a wagon, and lay there motionless.

McIlvoy dropped to his knee and listened for his heartbeat, which was still present. He stood and yelled to the parliamentary guard for help, and two uniformed men came and hovered beside McIlvoy. "Place the prime minister on the chesterfield," McIlvoy said, and they picked him up awkwardly, aided by a third guard who helped shore up Macdonald's slumping body. He was carried to the East Block and laid on a cot. McIlvoy called for Dr. Grant and waited nervously. Macdonald seemed to be conscious, but in a state where he recognized nothing. Only a soft gasp came from him, then his eyes shut and McIlvoy once more listened for a heartbeat, comforted by its muffled sound.

Grant examined the unconscious Macdonald and pronounced that the problem was gallstones. He recommended rest, an obvious prescription since Macdonald appeared capable of nothing else. Agnes was summoned and stayed beside him as the hours stretched into days. He came in and out of consciousness, but didn't speak. After four days he looked like death, having taken no food and only what little water could be placed on his lips. He hadn't left the East Block and it was assumed by almost all that he would die there. His presence had taken on the macabre cast of a head of state laid out for viewing. It needed only a grieving public to complete the picture. Agnes wept for hours on end. She finally poured some whisky on his chest and rubbed it, not knowing what else to do. She poured more onto her hands and caressed his face, lightly marking the rugged contours, and pushing back his damp, unbrushed hair at the temples. Macdonald's eyes opened.

"Do that again," he whispered softly. "It seems to do me good."

His full recovery took several months. Lying in the East Block, Macdonald requested oysters. They had curative properties, he had been told, and Dr. Grant allowed him half an oyster at each meal, saying it would be dangerous to indulge himself.

"Sir John, the hopes of Canada depend on you," Grant told him.

"It seems strange," Macdonald said, "that the hopes of Canada should depend on half an oyster."

When he was sufficiently recovered, Macdonald spread out a map of the North West on the large table in the room he was occupying. It was an uncredited version of David Thompson's map, his signature errors in evidence. McIlvoy stood nearby, nominally as a political aide, but more like a nurse.

"Maps create reality, McIlvoy," Macdonald said. "You see what is there, and it ceases to be imagined. I spent some time in the British Museum examining maps. They are extraordinary things. Have you ever seen Champlain's maps?" As usual, Macdonald wasn't expecting an answer, though McIlvoy had in fact seen them. The detail was indeed exquisite, made with primitive means, yet surprisingly accurate. "What maps do is dispel fear," Macdonald said. "They are replaced by new fears, of course. The unknown becomes known and soon becomes a commodity. Once it is a commodity, there is the question of who will buy it, and what will they do with it. Others will want it, as they always have. Champlain was the first cartographer of Canadian reality, his maps the beautiful templates." Macdonald took a large sip of his drink. "Have you heard of the Italian priest Francesco Bressani? A Jesuit. He drew a map in 1657, a map that shows Indians praying to God, of course, but also hunters, animals, houses, plants, and the peaceful, productive Hurons. All of that. Bressani lived with the Hurons but was captured by the Iroquois and creatively tortured for two months, burned, beaten, and mutilated daily with the persistent genius of men who understand pain, whose own lives are defined by it. His map was drawn with a hand that had only a single finger left, the others lost to the knives of his torturers." Macdonald stared out the windows, down to the city below, Ottawa long asleep. "Maps can tell you a great deal."

4

LOUIS RIEL, QUEBEC, 1877

The North West was his mother and God his father. At the
top of Mount Washington, God appeared to him in a cloud
of fire, as He had to Moses, and told him, "Rise, Louis David
Riel, you have a mission to accomplish for the benefit of
humanity."

The name David wasn't his own, but had been granted
by Him. The name of a king. The expectations were great.
But what would he accomplish in here? What could be
accomplished in such a place, a storage shed for the mad?
Within these stone walls were the weak minded, the
imbecilic and the alcoholic, as well as criminals, masturba-
tors, and drooling enthusiasts. The doctor was a Methodist
who felt dancing was the devil's pastime, yet he allowed it

at the Beauport Lunatic Asylum. He organized balls for the inmates. What grotesque sport. Twitching like dying animals, or gliding in and out of dreams, falling onto the hard floor and staring into the next world or foaming in this one. Did he think this would exorcise their demons, or did he think they were already lost to the devil? Riel wasn't lost. God still whispered to him.

Riel examined the walls of his cell. The stone was cold against his skin. His clothes were in the corner, ripped to pieces. His iron cot torn apart, the bars used to smash the walls, sashes, and ventilator. From the fevered blows against the stone a light dust covered the floor. He examined his naked body, its impressive bulk, as white as alabaster. Had the Philistines come to strip Saul? Perhaps not. He had done it himself. Yesterday, or was it this morning? The doctor had said he had delusions of grandeur. He was the Messiah of the New World, a secret Jew, and he had drowned his old soul in the Mississippi River and would lead his people out of the desert.

"Are you conscious of the times?" the doctor had asked him.

Conscious of the times? How could he not be? He *was* the times. To the south John Brown was trying to free the slaves. There was blood and revolution. Fenian raiders. Everywhere some form of madness. Here the Metis were Israelites persecuted by Egypt. After Riel set his people free he would appoint Archbishop Bourget to be Pope of the New World and move the seat of the Holy Roman Empire to Montreal.

Even a fool could see God's hand in this. The signs had come early. Riel returned to the West in 1867—the year the country was born—to find a plague of grasshoppers, surely a judgment on that misguided creation. They had come in a dark cloud that stretched across the horizon. It looked like a thunderstorm but didn't sound like one. As the dark mass drew nearer there was an ominous sound, like the mechanics of a music box, whirring, a sound that grew louder until they arrived like stinging hail. The grasshoppers ate everything. They were in chamber pots and pantries and shoes, and they hit the windows with a violence that sounded like gunfire. Riel walked by the banks of the Red River, where dead insects drifted like snow two feet deep against the willows, a fruity deathly smell rising from them.

God cannot create a tribe without locating it, Riel thought. We are not birds. The land was theirs, it belonged to the Metis who had tilled it. God had intended the land to be theirs and had given them warm summers and delivered good harvests. The year the Dominion of Canada was born, He sent a plague of locusts. What else would arrive? Surely He would deliver victory as well.

Riel saw himself as a bull, a red bull, and he roared like one. He was solitary, brutishly strong, a prophet. He saw the light of civilization grow from the Orient, the Euphrates, Palestine, and Rome. It was the New World's turn.

"Mr. David." It was the voice of Beaupré, the orderly. "Your dinner." Beaupré pushed the tin plate through the opening. "You've made another mess, Mr. David."

Riel took a spoonful of the mush in the bowl and tasted mould.

In the morning there was a meeting with Dr. François-Elzéar Roy. Riel sat on the wooden chair in Roy's office, a large space that seemed cramped by all the specimens he had collected. Brains in jars, pickled and shrunken. A skeleton of a man. Charts with measurements and diagrams.

Roy stared outside, beyond the stone walls. "I cannot satisfy myself, Mr. Riel, as to whether you are mad or acting the part of a man who is mad."

"We are all acting parts, Dr. Roy."

"Were you acting a part when you murdered Thomas Scott?"

"As you well know, I didn't murder Scott. He was tried for treason under the government I set up in a land that had none. A legitimate government. I was not on the jury, nor was I judge. I wasn't on the firing squad. I didn't give the order or pull the trigger."

"Still, Scott is dead."

"Deservedly so, doctor. He had no delusions of grandeur. He believed he was sane, a delusion of another sort. Delusions of normalcy. He was a rabid dog and died like one. Scott was politics, Doctor, not medicine."

Roy pondered this. "Your father's death had a great effect on you, didn't it."

"That is hardly an indication of insanity, Doctor. Mourning your father."

"No, but I wonder how it contributed to your condition."

"A father's death changes the life of the son." Riel shrugged. It was common sense.

The sun was coming in the window of Roy's office, a pleasant place. "If you are looking for madness within me, Doctor, you won't find it today. Perhaps you should travel to Upper Canada and look within the Orangemen. You'll have better luck there."

"The Orangemen don't have visions, they don't roar about God."

"They have a vision of taking the Metis' land." Riel stared at a brain shrivelled in its alcohol, the grey wormlike channels. "I have had visions, it is true. Hallucinations, even. I laugh at them myself. They come not from madness but from persecution. The Orangemen are Protestant fanatics. The Metis are a poor tragic people, the Indians even more so. My blood, my people, are starving. When I think of them, my own blood boils, my head is on fire. If I am mad, then I have reason."

"What is the cure for this, do you suppose, Mr. Riel?"

"There is no cure. But if I think of other things, the symptoms abate."

"Yes."

"You know that I was elected to office. A man who cannot go to Ottawa, who has a price on his head, who is considered mad and sits in a lunatic asylum eating mouldy bread. He is the choice of the people. That tells you something of our times, Doctor. If I am mad, then perhaps the country is mad as well."

There were other episodes at Beauport. Riel smashed the window of the chapel door, fought with three guards, insulted the sour Sister Superior. But his lucidity finally overshadowed his occasional mania, and he was released on January 21, 1878. As he stood waiting to be escorted through the gate, he noted how like a prison it looked, with its massive stone walls. Inside was a city, governed by the reason of science and administered by the healing intolerance of the cloth, the grey nuns checking the state of every damaged soul. They cherished the sinners, who needed punishing. Riel pondered his options, which were few. There was a still a price on his head; he couldn't stay in Canada. He decided on the American West and made his slow way to Montana.

In Montana, he became an American citizen, a member of the Republican party, and married Marguerite Monet, a Metis girl. He taught school and lobbied for Metis rights. The air in Montana was bright in the spring, and the old religion stirred. He could feel it moving through him, lurching through his veins, singing to him. He spoke in parables to the Metis, and announced that he was a prophet. He intended to reform the church, and made Saturday the Lord's Day.

Riel's short-lived Metis rebellion in Manitoba had failed, but he was planning his return to Canada to do God's will, to mount an epic battle, to stage Armageddon on the plains and ride through the Red River Valley with John A. Macdonald's head on a stick.

He would need the Indians to join him. The Metis would follow Riel, but he needed the Plains Cree and the mighty Blackfoot nation to join his battle. They had been fighting one another for millennia, but they were at peace now, and through fate (and divine intervention) both were in Montana. The Cree chief, Big Bear, and the Blackfoot chief, Crowfoot, had led their people south to find the last of the buffalo. Was this not God at work? The chiefs of the Metis, Cree, and Blackfoot, all together. It was providence. If Big Bear (who loved war, it was said, loved it like a son) and Crowfoot aligned with him, they would be powerful. The Queen's servants, those obedient men in red coats, those scarlet targets, how many were there? Twelve thousand. The combined Indians and Metis nation could field an army of fifty thousand warriors who had watched their children starve and whose anger would leave the prairie wet with blood.

Riel rode to a meeting with Big Bear. The Cree camp had maybe fifteen hundred people, spread along the valley in tents in the lee of the mountains. He was surprised to find a small, bowlegged man, his face pinched into a dark circle, a blanket wrapped around his shoulders. Big Bear was sitting near the fire, reading a newspaper, his chiefs and advisers on either side of him. Riel sat down and he and Big Bear smoked.

"The men from the Great Mother are on the prairie right now, measuring it, drawing lines across it, and giving it to strangers," Riel said. "You know this."

Big Bear sat without expression.

"The buffalo are gone. The Cree are starving. The Blackfoot are starving. The Metis farmers have had their land taken from them. They are selling us whisky to kill us off."

Big Bear waited for the proposal he knew would come.

"I am asking you to join me. The Metis will follow me. They did before and they will once more. If the Cree join us, we will have an army that can defeat the whites."

"My people are dying," Big Bear said. "Crowfoot's people are dying. Our army would be one of dying warriors."

"What better army? Dying warriors have no fear of death. Who can defeat death? Only one man has done it."

But Riel could see that Big Bear wasn't going to join with him. He wasn't young, had seen dozens of battles and had no taste for another. He no longer loved war. Riel subtly turned his speech toward the younger chiefs around Big Bear, where he could see there was some interest. They understood the romance of war, its possibilities, not its sorrows.

"The Great Mother has enough children to care for," he told them. "She will not weep if there are a few less to feed in the North West. The meat they sent you isn't enough. This is not an error, but a military plan. They appear to be helping, but they are killing you. They starve you because they fear you. But they don't fear the Cree—they fear the Other. The Metis, the Gros Ventres, the Blackfoot, the Peigan. They fear alliance and they fear a battle that will chase away those who come to raise cattle and grow wheat. We must deliver that fear. When the children of Israel asked the Lord who would fight the Canaanites, the Lord said, Judah shall go up, and behold, I have given the land into his hand. And Judah said to Simeon his brother, Come up with me that we may fight the Canaanites and they defeated ten thousand of them at Bezek. And they took Jerusalem and set the city on fire."

Riel paused to assess his audience. Big Bear would counsel peace, Riel could see it in his dark, unchanging face. But the young chiefs would go to war. He would meet with them again.

He rode back to camp, plotting his return to Canaan.

5

JOHN A. MACDONALD, 1885

Riel was a threat, Macdonald thought, but perhaps a useful one. He had wandered the desert for seven years and was returning as a prophet. If Riel managed to enlist the Indians to his cause, the North West could become a battlefield, blood spilled over a land Macdonald hadn't wanted in the first place. In truth, the Canadian government's claim to the North West was tenuous. Still. Macdonald had wandered his own desert after his government was forced to resign in disgrace. He had been caught taking money for his campaign to build the railway, a scandal, but even a fool had to know the money must come from somewhere. And that the railway was a necessity. It was the iron band that binds the barrel staves. Without it, the staves would fall uselessly in separate directions, without purpose or strength. Yet there was still opposition to the railway. (More than a million words had been spent on the issue in Parliament, more than the Old and New Testaments combined, as one blockhead calculated.)

His political undoing had been that one telegram to Hugh Allan, the shipping magnate who supported Macdonald's campaign in order to get a piece of the railroad. Macdonald had received $35,000 from him and then wired Allan that he needed another $10,000. The Liberals had gotten hold of the telegram by bribing a clerk (for $5,000, a princely sum) and they used it with the sense of triumph that the corrupt save for the corrupt. Macdonald's government was ousted, replaced by the Liberal Alexander Mackenzie, a man of such excruciating dullness that Macdonald took his election as a personal affront. As a former stonemason Mackenzie possessed the virtues of honesty, hard work, and a bottomless lack of imagination. One brick followed another. He would turn the entire country to stone with his plodding speeches, a modern Medusa. But the country woke up when Mackenzie began to talk annexation. The Americans, those wonderfully dangerous friends, could still stir the country's fears. And so Macdonald was prime minister once more, he and Riel both back from the desert.

Riel was dangerous, possibly delusional, and as such, useful. A wild man on the plains, rallying the Indians, plotting war. How to keep the settlers safe? How to get troops out there? They couldn't march; it would take too long, and the settlers would already lie bleeding on the prairie, tortured inventively. Parliament might not pay for a railway, but it would pay to put down an Indian and half-breed rebellion. Carefully managed, Riel would help build Macdonald's railway. That was his prophecy.

Through his study window, Macdonald saw the nurse approaching, pushing the wheelchair that contained his daughter, Mary. Agnes had piled Mary's hair on top of her head, making her hydrocephalic head appear even larger. Mary's withered body was confined by a black satin dress that fit snugly over her upper body, making it look fragile and almost birdlike, the skirts billowing down over her bottom half and covering her feet. The wheelchair seemed to be part of her body, some growth to compensate for her ailment. Macdonald believed she would recover from her hydrocephaly, that she would rise up and assume the graceful carriage of her mother. The nurse wheeled her through the house and up to Macdonald, and he observed her hopeful smile with his usual heartbreak.

Mary was one of the disappointments that Agnes had to bear. Another was the house, which had faulty drainage and smelled faintly of shit. How appropriate for a politician, Macdonald thought as he poured another glass of port. But the miserable state of the house plagued Agnes, who had imagined something much grander. He could ill afford better quarters, though. He had finally mustered the courage to inquire at the bank the full extent of his debt; a surprising $79,000. Repayment seemed impossible. He was drinking port with renewed appetite, beginning most mornings. Mary was wheeled into his study and he stared into her doomed child's face, though she was no longer a child.

"My love," he said. "You are the only flower in my garden today."

6

LOUIS RIEL, 1885

I have seen the giant, Louis Riel thought. He is Goliath.

But Riel was David. He was the future king. The visions came like flashes of lightning, each one briefly illuminating an Old Testament landscape littered with the corpses of his enemies. But in 1885, Armageddon came to this: 135 Metis facing 800 government troops at Batoche. Big Bear hadn't joined him. Nor had Crowfoot. His only ally was God. The settlers had finally fallen away. The newspapers, which had sided with him initially, were now crying for his blood, their editorialists quietly bribed by the government. And the clergy had abandoned him, having no taste for the mixture of politics and religion, a mixture embraced at their convenience. They already had a Messiah. In response Riel renamed the days of the week and denounced Rome. Everyone would be a priest in the New Order, and Batoche would be the City of God.

Riel walked among his soldiers, holding a silver crucifix. "Fire!" he yelled. "Fire in the name of the Father, the Son, and the Holy Ghost." His eyes were glazed. He hadn't slept. "The King of Syria," he told his men as they fired at the red targets, "demanded of Israel all its gold and silver, all of its women and children. And a prophet came to the King of Israel and said, 'I shall deliver the army of Syria to you and you will smite them in a great slaughter so that you know I am the Lord.'"

Riel's military commander was Gabriel Dumont, a marksman of legend. He had counselled guerrilla warfare, and had wanted to blow up the train tracks, both a symbolic and strategic strike. But Riel wanted Armageddon, a battle of biblical proportion. And here it was, his handful of men awaiting the inevitable.

The government men finally charged the Metis. And in that charge, Riel saw his empire vanish. His men disappeared into the woods, and he followed. The red-coated soldiers came looking, and first found Dumont sitting in a copse, his rifle resting on his knees. "I got ninety rounds here for any man wants to come and claim me," he called out. They left in search of easier game.

When they found Riel he was wild looking though oddly peaceful, the mania having passed, and they took him to a jail in Regina. It lacked the penal majesty of Beauport; the jail was overflowing, filled with Indians and Metis.

In prison, Riel heard that Dumont had escaped to Montana, the place everyone seemed to escape to at some point, the West's refuge. Dumont's marksmanship was prized and he was working in Buffalo Bill's Wild West Show as "The Hero of the Half-Breed Rebellion." History written as entertainment even as it was happening. Such was the modern age, Riel thought.

Riel's conscience was in good repair. He had done what he could. The half-breeds were deprived of responsible government, and he had made petition for one. When petitions failed, he had created his own. When that failed, he rebelled. I have been blessed by God, he thought. The half-breed hunters could foretell many things, an aching arm meant no meat that day, a twitching leg meant rain. Riel felt not despair, but something else.

John A. Macdonald weighed Riel's political value. Upper Canada was braying for his execution. It was unreliable political territory for Macdonald's Tories, and hanging Riel would likely bring it on board. In Quebec, however, Riel was seized as a hero, a champion of French Catholic rights. Quebec was Tory and would remain so, Macdonald reasoned. There would be cries in the streets when he was hanged, but they would forget Riel eventually, and they would remain loyal to the party. It was a calculated risk, but hanging Riel was his decision. He summoned McIlvoy.

"We have a problem," he told McIlvoy. "Politically, Riel must hang. For the good of the Dominion. However, we need a law." Riel was charged with treason, which wasn't punishable by death. "Our man must swing legally."

McIlvoy blinked once, taking this in. Macdonald could be ruthless, but this was new territory, a kind of viciousness. Was Macdonald asking him for a means to legally kill Riel? It seemed so. Cold-bloodedly so. This was ethically questionable at best, but it was also, uncharacteristically, politically risky. What would Quebec think of the government hanging a French Catholic? Riel was a hero. If his death was seen as political calculation, it might take a generation, perhaps longer, to restore their trust.

"Would this not be a grave political risk, Sir John?" McIlvoy asked. "Perhaps, if I may, an unnecessary, even a foolish one."

"Quebec will be angry, to be sure," Macdonald said. "But he shall hang though every dog in Quebec bark in his favour. The province will waver but won't fall. In the end, the sheep will return to the flock."

This seemed to McIlvoy a reckless assessment of his support. The country was, in his own view, a bloody-minded electorate, as happy to vote against something as to vote for it. To give them a cause was a dangerous notion.

McIlvoy spent two days reviewing British law until he found something Macdonald could use: a 1342 law that stipulated high treason as punishable by death. The trial was planned for Winnipeg, and McIlvoy pointed out, against the misgivings he had with the whole enterprise, that the Superior court judge in Winnipeg was independent and his independence was guaranteed by law. West of Manitoba, in the territories, the judge was simply a stipendiary employee of the government. Try him in Regina and they would own the judge. Then Regina it was.

There was one last hurdle.

"In order for him to hang," Macdonald noted, "he must be found sane."

"That may prove difficult," McIlvoy said. "He believes he is the Messiah."

"I have had the same thought of myself on occasion," Macdonald said. "Am I mad?"

McIlvoy looked at Sir John, his hair dry as straw and cut by his wife to resemble a recently harvested field, his face lined, his mouth, in unguarded moments, hanging in autumnal gape. He had created an ungovernable country, then tried to govern it. Who but a madman would do that?

"I have the honour to answer that I am not guilty," Louis Riel said to the Regina courtroom. It was July and the prairie heat descended on the proceedings like a shroud. Beneath their black suits, the men sweated heavily.

Riel's lawyers intended to plead that he was indeed insane. The evidence supported the claim, and recent events helped. Will Jackson, a Protestant who had sided with Riel and acted as his secretary, was declared mad after a thirty-minute trial. Like Riel, Jackson had made no plea for insanity, but the six Protestant jurors concluded that for a Protestant to follow a Catholic lunatic was itself a form of madness.

But Riel wanted no part of insanity. On this, he and Sir John were allied. His mind wasn't fevered now. And he realized that if he were declared a madman, his cause would be deemed a foolish one. In order to give the rebellion legitimacy, he must be found to be sane. And he was. In the peace of his cell, he didn't feel the demons, their agitating heat and spiked trail through his consciousness. He was the founder of Manitoba.

The next afternoon, Riel addressed the court. "There are those who brand me a madman. And to them I ask, 'Who is mad; the person who rises against an injustice or the person who perpetrates it?' If you believe the plea of the Crown, that I am sane and responsible for my acts, acquit me. I have acted reasonably and in self-defence, while the government, being irresponsible and consequently insane, cannot have acted wrongly, and if high treason there is, it must be on its side and not on mine."

Riel was found guilty, though the jury pleaded for mercy on his behalf. When asked if he had anything to say to the court, Riel stood. "When I came into the North West in July of 1884, I found the Indians suffering, I found the half-breeds eating the rotten pork of the Hudson's Bay Company. No one can say the North West has not suffered. I am no more than you are. I am simply one of the flock, equal to the rest. I say my heart will never abandon the idea of having a new island in the North West, inviting the Irish; a New Poland in the North West, a New Bavaria, a New Italy. The Belgians will be happy here and the Scandinavians and the Jews who have been looking for a country for eighteen hundred years will perhaps hear my voice one day on the other side of the mountains. It is my plan, it is one of the illusions of my insanity. My thoughts are for peace. This is what I have to say."

The judge stared at Riel and coldly announced, "You will be hanged by the neck till you are dead and may God have mercy on your soul."

Nine days before Riel's scheduled execution, Donald Smith, who looked like Methuselah and was as rich as the devil, hammered in the ceremonial final spike of Macdonald's railway at Eagle Pass in the Rocky Mountains. Smith distrusted Macdonald and was in turn hated by the man, and this animus filled his swing as he hammered the spike in. The transatlantic wonder. In little more than a week the country had an enduring symbol of unity in the railroad and an equally potent symbol of division in Riel's execution. A foundation for the uneasy tension that nations crave.

It was clear and cold on November 16 as Riel stood on the gallows. He said a short prayer for Macdonald. "I pray that God will bless Sir John and give him grace and wisdom to manage the affairs of Canada well." The hangman's hand rested heavily on the lever as Riel stared upward and began to recite the Lord's Prayer. "Pater noster, qui es in caelis: sanctificetur nomen tuum; adveniat regnum tuum; fiat voluntas tu

7

CATHERINE MOUNTAIN HORSE, MONTANA, 1881

Catherine Mountain Horse lay in the tall grass with her silent father, Jamieson. David Thompson begat the illegitimate Tristan who begat Jamieson who begat Catherine, an eleven-year-old girl as thin as a sapling, her black hair tied around an owl skull, wearing a long red skirt made from a blanket. The September sun was behind them, and she could feel it warm her back. The Sharps .45-calibre rifle was almost as long as she was. Her father was sighting along its octagonal barrel, resting on a tripod fashioned of sticks and pointed at two buffalo that walked warily in the valley below. The two buffalo in the Judith Basin were a remnant of the last great herd in North America. To the south, General

Sheridan had encouraged its slaughter as a military tactic, to starve the Indians into submission. Buffalo hunters killed thousands in a single day. The Sioux burned swaths of land along the border, destroying the grazing land in an attempt to keep the buffalo from moving north. British and German sportsmen shot thousands of buffalo from trains and left them lying on the prairie. Coyotes and carrion birds gorged on carcasses spread over miles. Bleached bones were shipped east in boxcars to be made into fertilizer.

The breeze moved her hair slightly as she lay on her stomach with her arms folded, her head resting on them, one elbow reassuringly touching her father. One of the conditions of this outing was silence. If she wanted to spend the day with her father, hunting the last buffalo on the continent, she had to remain silent. No girlish laughter, no foolish questions, no idle observations could escape her lips. No movement that could send this last, perilous food supply stampeding through the valley into the waiting guns of Big Bear or the Sioux. Catherine had taken this oath, the price of being near him. As they lay motionless, she conducted a conversation between them in her head.

"What is the colour you love above all others, my Flower?"

"Blue."

"Do you know where the snow goes?"

"No."

"It vanishes in the night, travelling to the north, running from the summer sun. It hides in the mountains and then comes back when the leaves turn, it creeps along the ground in the night and when you wake up, it is there."

"Why does the coyote sing to the moon?"

"Coyote first sang to the sun, because he loved its warmth

in the morning. But the sun heard Coyote's singing, and it turned its back to that terrible noise. Coyote was hurt. He thought his singing was the most beautiful on the plains. From that day on, he only sang for the moon."

"What else?"

"What is the colour you love above all others?"

"You asked me that."

For an hour they lay still, watching the bull, which was seven hundred yards away. Jamieson thought the bull would wander toward him, the wind at its back, and that the cow would follow. The west wind was coming off the mountains and scoured the valley in twisting gusts. When the bull was a hundred yards away, he aimed high and slightly into the wind and squeezed the trigger. The explosion made Catherine jump slightly, and Jamieson was jarred by the recoil. There was a brief delay, then the muffled thud of the bullet hitting the buffalo. It walked two more steps, then sat down, as if confused, the huge head the last thing to hit the ground. The cow started toward it, unsure of where the sound of the rifle had come from as it echoed off the hills. Jamieson fired into the cow and it fell.

Catherine watched her father skin the male buffalo, his knife moving in a deliberate sawing motion then twisting and cutting, an intricate dance. They walked back to the Blackfoot camp as the sun rose high in the sky. From the hill Catherine saw their tents spread along the lower slopes. Once they had been the most feared nation on the northern plains, her father had told her. Now they huddled in fear, of hunger, disease, and, when the whisky traders came, fear of themselves.

Men and women both went to where the buffalo had fallen and hauled them back. The animals were cooked, every scrap of meat roasted, the fat used for pemmican, the bones broken open for the marrow, the hides tanned into robes. Catherine sat by the fire with her father, the hunter, who was at a place of honour beside Crowfoot, their chief, a lean, tall man with a nose as thin as a knife. The fire was lulling and Catherine ate until she was full, something she hadn't done for a week. She fell asleep and her father carried her to the tent.

When winter arrived, Catherine saw fewer buffalo. She walked with her father in the deep snow and most of the time they came back to the camp without anything. She noticed the faces becoming thinner, the lines deeper. Perhaps her own face was doing the same. There were nights when she crawled under the buffalo robe and was cold and knew she would be colder. Her mother had died when she was an infant, and when she thought of her, she thought of warmth, a warm mother who would come into their tent and banish the cold.

There was an outbreak of measles during the winter and families died. They burned the grey cloth tents and blankets and possessions of the dead families. Sometimes they burned the families. In the spring the whisky traders found them again. Warriors traded buffalo robes and horses and women and reeled on the plain under the stars. The whisky took what starvation and disease hadn't. Most of the horses were gone. Many of the children dead. The old and the weak were culled. Brothers killed one another in drunken brawls, warriors humbled by whisky made with potatoes, tea, and molasses.

In the heat of summer, Crowfoot came to talk to Catherine's father.

"There are no more buffalo," he said. "The whisky traders have taken what little we had left. We cannot last the winter.

We must walk north and hope for the protection of the Great Mother."

Her father nodded.

The Blackfoot set out on a warm, dry morning in the middle of summer, fewer than half of the seventeen hundred who had come to Montana. Catherine walked behind her father. They made almost twelve miles that first day, walking until the sun set. There were some who were sick and many who were weak with hunger, or shaking from the absence of whisky, men who sweated and screamed for spirits that had vanished, who suddenly fell to the earth, flopping like fish taken from a stream.

At first it was the weak and sick that held them back, and the whisky-headed warriors who collapsed onto the grass in their own peculiar pain. Then it was the dead. They stopped to place withered bodies in trees, lashing them to branches.

On the fourth day, Crowfoot came and talked to Catherine's father and the two of them disappeared, walking back along the trail they had just walked. She found out later that her father had shot one of the horses that a whisky trader was riding. A warning.

Catherine could see her father getting thinner, slowly disappearing. Perhaps that was what happened to her mother; she was less and less and then she was nothing. They walked for more than one full moon and she woke one morning to find frost on the grass. When the first spot appeared on her father's face, she felt a cold wind inside her.

"It is nothing," he told her.

But then there were more. He was already as thin as he could be. There didn't seem to be many places to put spots, and maybe that would help. That night he talked as she lay beneath the robe. He told her how the stars got into the heavens, and pointed out which one was her mother. In the night Catherine woke and touched her father's face. It was cold and Catherine shook him and whispered into his ear but he didn't wake up. She told him a story about how the bear came into the world, a story he had told her when she was a child, then she laid against him and wept until morning. When the sun rose, three men took him away. They placed him in an aspen tree and Catherine sat beneath him until they carried her away. She walked north behind Crowfoot, and her father joined the line of blackened bodies rotting in trees that stretched into Montana.

Catherine walked as if in a dream, imagining her father's voice, his touch, those things she needed to preserve. She was empty with hunger, and her head ached and she felt, as she saw Grey Eyes hoisted reverently into a tree, as she watched Fierce Owl foaming on the ground, his skeletal body seized into a sinewy fist, as she saw her people shuffling northward, bent, that she was already in the spirit world, that she would find her father standing, smiling, at the end of this. His arms would be open and she would walk into them and stay there. For a week she uttered not a word, hoping that if she didn't engage the real world, she wouldn't be part of it. When her father was alive, she felt the protection he offered. Now, there was no protection. The nation couldn't protect itself. She hungered for the spirit world.

They trudged across the buffalo grass, through rivers, along alkaline coulees, past juniper and dusty bushes. A creek valley had turned to powder and it rose as they crossed it, a fine mist that caught the wind and coated them, making them appear as ghosts. Catherine saw a large shape on the ground ahead of them and smaller shapes around it. When she got closer she could see that the large shape was a buffalo. The other shapes were wolves that had been skinned, their still shiny carcasses wet under the sun. They were twisted into strange shapes, their teeth bared, turned in upon themselves. The wolfers had been here. They shot the buffalo and slit it open and laced the meat with poison and waited for the wolves. After eating the meat the wolves began to writhe, trying to rid themselves of the poison. Catherine had come upon them once with her father, howling madly, twisting like wild horses, leaping, briefly standing on their hind legs in a grotesque dance, as if they were in the throes of becoming human, then flopping onto the ground. The Blackfoot were starving but if they ate this meat they would dance like the wolves.

It took six weeks to walk to the Cypress Hills. A government man gave Catherine some bread and a bowl of soup and she sat and ate them both as quickly as she could.

There was another migration. Fifty miles west of the Blackfoot, heading north out of Montana, were thirty cowboys driving 6,800 head of polled Black Angus and Shorthorns to the Cochrane Ranche, the first large-scale cattle-ranching operation in the West. Senator Matthew Cochrane had 360,000 acres of grazing land. The cowboys drove the cattle hard, making eighteen miles a day. Calves were lost, cows with broken legs abandoned. By the time they arrived, they had lost a thousand head. They went back to Montana and got a second herd, driving them north through winter, getting caught in heavy snow and waiting for chinooks that didn't come. The cattle instinctively tried to move southeast, to find something to graze, but the cowboys had orders from Montreal to drive them north, damn the consequences. They lost half the herd, and in the spring the carcasses filled the coulees where the cattle had become bogged in deep snow. There were stretches where you could walk on the bodies for a mile without touching the ground. The meat was tainted but the hides could be salvaged. The foreman went to the Blackfoot camp and asked for skinners; they were paying twenty-five cents a hide.

It was another walk, this time without the red dress, dressed as a boy, twelve years old but grown. There were sixty of them, and Catherine could smell the job before she saw it, a thick taste of death. She had helped her father skin buffalo and she surveyed the expanse of spoiled meat beginning to bloat in the spring sun, and then set to work amid the men of her tribe, steering the large knife around the distending flesh, finding the lines that defined it and pulling the hide away and dragging it to dry in the sun. Ravens hopped nearby, picking at the faces. Magpies pulled at soft red threads and danced away. The smell infected the air, and the western breeze couldn't carry away the rot. The sound of flies changed in pitch, subtle notes that inflected upward as they moved, a screaming feast that covered the exposed meat like black blankets. A million beetles invaded from below. Sixty Blackfoot covered in blood, skinning the casualties of Senator Matthew Cochrane's eastern management. Catherine laboured until dark, her arm finally too tired to cut the stinking hide. She washed in the stream that ran through the hills, careful not to drink from it in case there were dead cattle upstream. She cleaned her knife, sharpened it on a stone, and then fell asleep by the fire.

8

DEXTER FLEMING, 1882

The crossing wasn't pleasant, a slurry of gin and vomit, the ship pitching in the waves, the aristocracy as miserable as the cattle. Four deaths followed by burials at sea, the last one—an infant with the misfortune of being born on the ship—poorly attended due to violent weather. Dexter Fleming was tall, with dark hair, a weak mouth, and a voice that sounded as if he was judging you, even if he was only asking for milk in his tea. He was coming from London, heading for the North West on the slurred advice of Bertie Beckton. Beckton's grandfather had made a fortune in textiles (and been Lord Mayor of Manchester, an ambitious man in all things) and left that fortune to his three grandsons: Bertie, William, and Ernest. Their plan, divined one evening after several bottles of port, was to go to the Canadian North West. They had read of an aristocratic farming community started by Captain Edward Pierce, who was recreating a utopian version of England on the endless prairie that he named Cannington Manor.

The Becktons had already gone there and built a twenty-six-room mansion out of limestone and blue rolling stone. They christened it Didsbury, a reminder of Manchester. Inside were hand-carved mantels, Turkish carpets, and oil paintings sent from their grandfather's country place. The bunkhouse had room for eighteen men and the kennels were filled with foxhounds imported from the Isle of Wight. They had poached a jockey and the head groom from the Lincolnshire stables of Lord Yarborough, and the stalls for the racehorses were lined with mahogany, the horses' names engraved on brass plaques. All of this situated on 2,600 acres.

Pierce was recruiting the English aristocracy and those who aspired to it with ads in British papers. "With a few hundreds a year, a gentleman can lead and enjoy an English squire's existence of a century ago!" At Cannington, Pierce had established a trading company, general store, dairy, cheese factory, flour mill, a land titles office, and an agricul-tural college to teach these young gentlemen how to farm.

Dexter Fleming couldn't imagine Bertie Beckton as a farmer. And when he finally arrived—after an interminable train ride and an uncomfortable slog on horseback—Bertie was standing outside the limestone mansion, cradling a drink, dressed to shoot.

"Dexter!" he said. "Welcome to the New World!"

"It looks somewhat like the old one," Dexter said. "Only without the scenery."

"And without the dreary convention, and without the

dreary relatives, dear boy. And those nagging laws. No nagging in-laws or nagging laws. You look like a pile of buffalo dung. Got you out here just in time."

Bertie, Dexter was suddenly reminded, was the kind of person you tired of rather quickly, his boundless energy for mischief eventually a burden.

If this was his prison, Dexter thought, it could be worse. He had quietly failed at several things—school, the military, a legal career—and his father had finally sat him down in his barely illuminated study and presented him with this opportunity: go to the colonies. They both knew it wasn't an invitation. Go to the New World or be cut off. He may shame them there, but it would be a distant and diluted shame. And perhaps, Dexter thought, in the way he thought of all new beginnings, and since his life was made up exclusively of beginnings—a life of fresh starts and routine failure—he might actually accomplish something here. Maybe what he needed was this blank canvas. Also, to succeed at something might send his father to an early grave, reward in itself.

"Let's get you a drink and a weapon," Bertie said.

His valet brought out a glass of gin and a shotgun, handing Dexter the glass and following the two to the stables with the gun.

Dexter picked out a horse and the stable boy led it outside. Dexter examined the shotgun, then slipped it into the sheath and finished his drink.

"Do you have any idea how free you are?" Bertie said.

Cannington wasn't the only social experiment in the North West. There was Benbecula, a Scottish crofter colony, the East London Artisan's Colony, New Sweden, Thingvalla, and the Harmony Industrial Association. Inspired by the writings of John Ruskin and William Morris, this utopian putsch into the New World replaced the state with a sense of brotherhood and co-operative labour. A dozen visions of man's higher instincts, most of them slowly failing. The Barr Colony, like Cannington, had a British theme, although it was more imperial in its aim: "Let us take possession of Canada," it counselled. At Cannington there were fox hunts, cricket matches, tennis, football, and gin.

Bertie and Dexter played billiards at Didsbury, sipping their drinks.

"This is a novelty, Bertie, but it's bound to become tiresome," Dexter said. "Then what?"

"I can't wait for Pierce to die," Bertie said. "Then Cannington will be paradise."

"I'm not sure of that," Dexter said. "He does rather a lot."

"The man's a dictator. He's in the wrong colony. He should have his own African state to bully."

Pierce was an autocratic leader, certainly, though he was also the driving force behind the various industries that had grown up at Cannington Manor, and effectively the force for moral order. There was still an element of education under his tutelage. Dexter had taken some instruction in farming and ranching, and had a loose sense of how to manage an enterprise out here, a tenuous grasp of crops, markets, and weather.

When Pierce did die, in 1888, the deterioration was almost immediate. The balance between industry and recreation veered suddenly toward the latter, culminating in a fox hunt that Bertie staged. Dexter sat his horse and examined his handmade gun, his head a pleasant buzz. Perhaps forty people milled, their horses skittering in the afternoon sun. It was autumn and the leaves were a sombre yellow, the whiff of decay in the western breeze. Eight servants loaded baskets with food and port that straddled their own horses. The horn sounded, the electric possibility of the hunt, the distant pull of blood, and Dexter rode west, the dogs yapping ahead.

He felt free of London's formal pall, the small pile of disappointments he delivered monthly to his father, and thought he could do something here, perhaps something grand. The plains spoke of possibility. If he started a ranch, made a success of it. There were ranches to the west that were half the size of Scotland.

On the other hand, pulling with equal force, was Bertie, with his gift for dissipation. He had been sleeping with women of the Whitebear nation, as well as the wife of the miller in town. He was drunk by noon most days. A witty companion, a decent sportsman, but dangerous company, and this dissolute life was veering into tedium.

The hunt moved noisily over the prairie. They would drive off everything, Dexter thought, would frighten buffalo if any were left. A few pleasant hours were spent riding, then they stopped to eat and drink and target shoot. Then they rode again into the lurid sunset beginning to glare in front of them. The dogs rousted a den of coyotes, and in the ensuing fight seven of the dogs were torn so badly they either died of their wounds or had to be shot by Bertie, who drunkenly wept when he blew Sadie's head off, a cherished dog. The coyotes, three adults and four pups, were also dying or dead and had to be finished off. The ride back was sullen.

Dexter finished the evening in Bertie's billiard room,

swanned on gin, a dozen men collapsing in the chairs that ringed the room, the floor wet with vomit, spilled drinks, and smatterings of blood. In the moment before he lost consciousness Dexter resolved to leave Cannington Manor, to go farther west, to a purer state, and there become a gentleman rancher. He would fill the space with purpose; he would put himself on the map.

9

JOHN A. MACDONALD, 1886

It hadn't occurred to Macdonald to actually ride on his grandest accomplishment. Agnes had already taken a railway trip through the Rocky Mountains and declared it a tonic. With an election looming, perhaps this would be a good way of drawing favourable publicity. The *Globe* wouldn't let Riel's corpse rest (nor would Quebec, as McIlvoy had predicted). The paper was as fervently against him as it had been when Brown was its publisher. Now Brown was dead, shot by an unhappy employee, and when Macdonald heard the news he had inquired only why it hadn't happened sooner.

On a bright day Macdonald climbed, with effort, aboard the *Jamaica*, the eighty-foot train carriage that had been named for Agnes's childhood home. Waiting inside amid the fresh-cut flowers, plush sofas, and wine were Agnes, McIlvoy, and a dozen others. Macdonald accepted a glass of wine and toasted their voyage.

The train lurched out of Ottawa and Macdonald pondered the landscape; the farmlands of Ontario, its occasional villages all giving way finally to cleaved rock where the dynamite had done its work. Macdonald did paperwork, read, and gazed outside at the hypnotizing forest. East of Winnipeg, the train emerged onto the prairie. In Winnipeg they stayed for a few days while Macdonald assessed the political terrain. Agnes shopped. She had once imagined a role in government for herself, an equal who discussed (perhaps even dictated) policy. But now she was content to shop.

The train crossed the eventless prairies to Regina, where there was a reassuring crowd. Not all of them were supporters, Macdonald suspected as he waved and shook a few hands. Some merely wanted to see the devil in the flesh, to see who it was they hated with such conviction. Macdonald went to Government House and met with local politicians and some Indian chiefs, and as he moved among them making amiable noises about their various complaints, he wondered if he had the stomach for another campaign, or another term for that matter.

The train stopped in Gleichen where a meeting was scheduled with Crowfoot. What would the Blackfoot chief want? Macdonald wondered. What they all wanted: a government that solved every problem. Macdonald had sent the largest share of rations to the Blackfoot—"Send the food to where the tomahawks are sharpest," he had ordered, and the Blackfoot were the mightiest of the Plains Indians. To the south the bloody purges had decimated the Indian and ensured a hostile relationship with the government. Macdonald had avoided the former but not the latter. With an Indian war no longer possible, the rations they sent had dwindled. There was a responsibility: The railway had driven the last of the buffalo off the plains, and the final hunting parties were a dreadful parody—drunken German sportsmen firing guns out of the windows of the moving train, shooting into the last herds.

As the train slowed to a stop, Macdonald looked out the window at hundreds of Blackfoot assembled in formation. At the head was Crowfoot. Macdonald stepped off the train and approached the Blackfoot chief with his hand out. Most of those present were men, and their faces were painted. For war? Macdonald wondered. No, the time for war was gone. In its place, theatre.

Where are the rations? Crowfoot asked.

"The Government Treaty signed by the illustrious chiefs"—in truth a series of Xs after a selective explanation of what the contract contained—"didn't promise food," Macdonald said. "It promised seeds. And on that count, we have delivered. It is time for your people to join the other settlers in this beautiful land, to grow crops, to enter into the new spirit of the West. You can grow crops to feed your people, and sell the surplus to provide for your other needs."

The railway burned the land near the tracks, Crowfoot said.

"White men work hard for their food and clothing," Macdonald said. "And we expect the Indians to do the same."

There were low murmurs among the several hundred Blackfoot. Crowfoot stood motionless. All of his twelve children were dead, of tuberculosis, smallpox, or starvation.

More Blackfoot would certainly die; they were a nation of warriors and hunters, not farmers.

There followed a perfunctory exchange of gifts, Macdonald motioning for the servants to come forward with rolls of canvas sheeting and tobacco. One of the Blackfoot men beat a drum, a beat that was insistent and rose in tempo. The Indians began a kind of keening.

Back on the train, Macdonald watched the Blackfoot get on their horses and ride alongside the train, firing their Winchesters into the air. This spectacle had an element of menace, Macdonald thought, but their moment had passed.

10

DEXTER FLEMING, 1905

Dexter Fleming woke in the crisp autumn air to see the shimmering perfection of his uselessness, his frivolity set in bold relief against this place, which rewarded practicality and perseverance. He saw this with the clarity that nearly two decades of heavy drinking brings. He occupied the landscape like spilled gin at a summer party. The sun shone through the window onto the four-poster bed and its messed bedclothes. He dressed with deliberation, finally pulling on the polished boots that had been made in London by his bootmaker. He debated taking the dogs, but when they charged out of the house, he had no choice. The air was fine and the sun warmed his back as he walked west, first along the path that led past the barn, and then through the grass that was still wet. The dogs yelped ahead of him.

He recalled that first winter when he had taken Catherine in as a domestic to clean the house and tend to his dogs and horses. She arrived wearing her red dress.

For a year she was quiet, existing between the spirit world and the real. She did his laundry and cleaned up after his parties. She worked the horses and walked the dogs, three black Labradors that leaped on her as they meandered through the foothills. She polished his silverware. For two hours every morning, she went to school, a three-mile walk, her favourite part of the day. The school had been Fleming's idea; literacy was a civilizing force. In the small house that was the school, she practised scratching shapes on paper, and the meanings slowly became clear, like an animal walking hesitantly out of the morning fog.

Catherine would never love him. Dexter knew this but had kept this secret from himself for as long as possible, knowing he couldn't bear its impact. His love had grown so quietly, stealthily, watching her do the books in the evening, the way the soft light played against her face. He had sold almost all of his land and still there were debts. There wasn't enough acreage left really to call it a ranch anymore. It supported a few head, a hobby. It had always been a hobby, he supposed. By the time he realized he had some attachment to the land, to this life, that he wanted to occupy his own life as something other than a squatter, it was too late. It wasn't mismanagement, but rather an absence of management that had done it. Without Catherine, he would have lost the place years ago. His mother was gone, thank God, and his father had cut him off, tired finally of sending money after reading his letters describing the empire he was building in the New World. His father had heard the truth from Gallagher, who had returned to London to settle his own parents' estate. Gallagher outlined the dwindling assets, the house in need of repair, his fine furniture and sterling silver service and endless gin. The parties and dead cattle. The gambling debts, and of course Gallagher told his father of Catherine. Your son has gone native, sir. Hate to be the one to say it, but it must be said. Two whelps into the bargain. He thinks it's hush-hush, whole world knows. Frankly, sir, the gin isn't helping. Made a bit of a mess of things out there, I'm afraid.

Yes, a bit of a mess. The letter came from his father's solicitor: we are informing you of the immediate cessation of funds, etc. The house certainly wasn't grand, but it was adequate. He supposed the silver was worth something. He had five good horses, a few cattle. The sheep experiment had been a failure, one that invited ridicule rather than admiration for attempting something bold.

There was much to ridicule. He had been to the grand house of the Vincenzy brothers, both of them counts (or so they claimed), their house with its silly turrets, its fine china and dark paintings, the trappings of the Austro-Hungarian Empire out here in the foothills. They had dreadful parties, though the wine was good. The German, what was his name? Baron Liepzeig, more nobility. Everyone who owned a pig in the old country was nobility here. Liepzeig had indeed roasted a pig and invited the local ranchers. They all drank the sweet, lethal home-made wine and played a drunken game of croquet that had been set up over several acres, croquet on a grand scale to suit the land. The balls were lost in the grass, or disappeared into groundhog holes. Dexter finally had someone throw one of the wooden balls up in the air and he shot at it. This prompted a shooting party, tossing up the croquet balls and firing at them until they began to lose their light. In an hour of shooting only three balls were hit, each prompting a great cheer.

The smattering of European royalty was overwhelmed by the earnest ranchers who had come up from Montana or Virginia and who understood horses and cattle. They were building another society that was practical, refined, God-fearing, and, most surprising, profitable. Among this company, Dexter felt like a fop. This wasn't England; the West didn't tolerate eccentricities and failure. It wasn't a question of society (from which he'd been subtly excluded) but of the elements. Nature wouldn't tolerate him. He had been rejected by the seasons, by the weather, the soil, by God.

Catherine was thirty years old, Dexter forty-nine, though he supposed he looked older. Stanford was four, Michael only two. He had no idea how to be a father to them. He couldn't really. There wasn't the advantage of distance that he had known as a child. As an infant he had lived on the third floor with the nanny—Kempy? Could that have been her name, as unlikely as it seemed? Odd that he couldn't recall it. He remembered her smell: lavender soap and starched clothes. She had shown him some kindnesses. Raised in captivity in South Kensington until school age, and then off to Scotland to be educated and tortured. And finally the colonies, the place where those of little promise come to sort themselves. Michael and Stanford were two silent, perfect reproaches that were never far. He was reminded daily of his irrespon-sibility, of his cowardice. He was their biological father but they were Catherine's sons. He had become the drunken uncle pulling pennies out of ears.

The pleasant cloud that the gin brought wasn't enough anymore. It had been, a decade ago, when the ranch was still the semblance of one. He had squandered most of it. The money, the friends even. He supposed he had squandered Catherine too, though she was never his. He hadn't seen his own love creeping up, had failed to recognize the signs. The education he had insisted on, perhaps it was as early as that. The spindly child, first an employee, a colonial responsibility, then becoming something like a daughter. The daughter grew up. And what did she become then? From the age of sixteen it was clear that she was a better judge of horses than he. At twenty she was effectively running the ranch. For two perilously besotted years, a period of drunken fox hunts (substituting the clever coyote), polo matches, summer parties where he sometimes awoke in the damp grass, miraculously uneaten: For those two years he congratulated himself on having hired her, on educating her. He was bursting with nobility. It was when she was in her early twenties that he noticed her light step, the slight, delicate curves beneath the dress. He noticed her skin, its unblemished, copper-hued perfection. The light softened it even more, until her skin seemed liquid, something he could fall into. Those dark eyes that gave up so little. She was keeping the books by then, tending to the horses, buying the cattle. The dogs ran to her. She was the ranch. In his pleasant alcohol dreams she had become a mirage, some shining idea of paradise that moved within the house just out of reach.

And then he touched her. His hand lingered, a kiss. Those few seconds. What was contained in them? On days when Fleming was bedridden, his head an anvil, his limbs aching and useless, swearing off gin, a promise that lasted until the evening, she was the employer and he was the invalid who had come with the property, an inherited burden. The taste of her, he should have known then certainly. A taste that was elemental, like a dream that one can't quite recall upon waking, a world suddenly vanished that contained every secret. At first it was simply business as usual, an Englishman in the colonies, sampling the local sweets. A national pastime, like cricket. She always withheld a part of herself. His face gluey with effort, out of tricks. He should have seen the signs. Perhaps that was what divided the successful ones from the failures. The successful ones saw the signs, and acted accordingly. He could live with his failure, with his regret, perhaps (though perhaps not), but the longing was too much.

The sun was higher, and would bring a late-summer heat by afternoon. He had walked three miles, he estimated. The mountains were bright and clean looking, polished blue and grey. The breeze was picking up, the gun heavy in his hand. It was a good thing he'd brought the dogs, or that they had brought themselves. They would find their way home and then bring someone out here. It wouldn't come as a surprise, certainly. Still, they would need proof.

MICHAEL MOUNTAIN HORSE

1908

So Macdonald creates a country in his own image. Messy, sprawling: the father of us all. English and French sharing a country. In Europe they wouldn't share a pot of tea. It took a lot to bring those two together, but the Americans were a lot. All that patriotism just across the border, those dark imperial dreams, and finally, those soldiers. At the beginning of the Civil War, in 1861, the Americans had an army of thirteen thousand: reluctant farmers, the indigent, the disturbed. An army like most others. Then suddenly there were two million soldiers hardened in battle. It was a violent time. And larcenous. The Americans stole Florida, California, and Texas and were prepared to take the rest of the continent. Maybe they didn't need to invade Canada. We'd get tired of the stuffy British and want to join the life of the party. We hoped the Americans would destroy themselves through war, but they didn't; it only made them stronger. The four colonies united for protection against this compelling beast, but there still wasn't any real shared nationalism. We knew what we were against but not what we were for.

The hope was that this would come with westward expansion (an old trick). Thompson mapped the West, Macdonald claimed it, but it still had to be filled with people. In that vast empty space was the grandeur of empire. Or so they hoped, anyway.

Michael looked at Billy, a few hairs sprouting from his unblemished face, the hint of manhood. His Indianness, a word Michael had heard in the teacher's lounge, seemed accentuated, the gift of silence now official.

How do you lure the millions to the wilderness? In 1900 Wilfrid Laurier's government sent out a million pamphlets, sunny fraudulent offers of free land, a balmy climate, freedom from persecution. They hoped for British and Americans, and there were some of those, but not enough. Germans and Scandinavians were next on the list. Then, finally, Ukrainians, Doukhobors, Jews, Galicians of every stripe. No one's first choice, but the landscape was so pure, it would change them. They would become clean and Aryan; the winds would scour them, the snows cleanse them, and a Protestant empire would rise up on the plains. What the pamphlets really offered was Christian redemption.

Michael pondered Billy's life. Bathed by the nurse every week, his black hair cut once a month, occasional visits from friends, friends that would stop coming soon, if they hadn't already. The visits from relatives would be less frequent too; his father off working the northern oil fields, his mother worn out. The baths would become cursory; occasionally they'd forget to bathe him. His green gown held the faint generic stains of suffering: leaking wounds or bad food that couldn't be removed even with the hospital's abrasive soap. Without the attention of others, what was he?

It was mostly British and Americans around here. The Ukrainians had gone farther north to farm. The Mormons stayed in the south. Among the local ranchers, my mother was a curiosity, the Indian widow of a British aristocrat whose nickname was Lord Gin. You don't always pick up on the nuances of adults when you're six years old, but you feel something. The men liked my mother. She was beautiful then. The women didn't invite her to join the baking circle or the Theatrical Group, or any of the other clubs they formed to keep rural loneliness at bay.

All the kids in the area went to a one-room schoolhouse just south of here. It's gone now. There were twelve of us, ranch kids who walked or rode to school every day, arriving at different times, an odd crew; the youngest five, the oldest seventeen. My brother, Stanford, and I walked to school each morning. The teacher might have been twenty and she knew that most of us would only need to read well enough to get through an operating manual or a cookbook, to be able to calculate the weight gain of a heifer. She did her best with us.

I was happy to lose myself in books, even then. One day she came over to help me with the letter G, which I had trouble writing. She knelt beside the desk and took my hand in hers and wrote a dozen Gs, breathing in my ear. When she softly let go of my hand and I mechanically produced more Gs, she whispered, "I knew you could do it." She smelled like soap, like flowers. I was so overwhelmed by her that I burst into tears. After school, Rory, the seventeen-year-old, teased me about it. He kept at it, wiping his eyes, pretending he was crying. Stanford was thirteen then and he told Rory to stop but he wouldn't. Stanford hit him in the face. It surprised everyone, Rory certainly, but I think even Stanford. That punch opened up something inside Stanford, and out spilled the violence that was coiled there. He went after Rory, knocked him down and kept hitting him. It took the teacher and half the class to pull him off. Everyone was screaming. Stanford's face looked like he was somewhere else, as if part of him wasn't there. When it was over, the whole class lay in the grass, *including the teacher, for five minutes, no one saying anything. Then we all went home. Stanford didn't say a word over those three miles.*

Once in a while, Stanford and I would sneak out at night hoping something mysterious would happen in the darkness. One night we walked to Rory's ranch, more than five miles away. The sky was clear and we had that energy that comes with doing something illicit. When we got there, we stared down from a small hill and saw two figures in the moonlight. The wind was blowing hard so we couldn't hear anything. We crept around and got as close as we could, maybe thirty yards away. It was Rory and his father. His father was screaming something and he had a gun. Rory was throwing tin plates up in the air—the kind they used to feed the ranch hands—and his father was shooting at them with a pistol. The wind would take the plates and move them on crazy, sudden tangents. They were impossible to hit. Maybe the father was drunk. He was screaming but you couldn't hear what. You could see Rory was scared. A plate came zipping back toward him and we thought Rory's father might shoot his own son by accident. They were out there for half an hour, then the father sat down on the grass and buried his face in his hands and Rory ran away. It was like witnessing a secret but not knowing what it was. I asked Stanford if everyone had secrets like this and he told me they probably did.

Of course, we had our own secret: our father's death. It wasn't a secret for long. It was the kind of story that sustains people in a small community, one that gives them a chance to point to their own work ethic and Christian values and to sit in judgment, saying it was a terrible thing but thinking secretly that it was inevitable. It confirmed that their way of life was God's chosen path. For years Dexter existed like a lesson from the Bible, his story repeated by the righteous.

When you enter history, you don't know it of course. You're born into famine or war or peace and think: This is the world. As you get older you start to piece it together; x led to y, which created z, and z took its toll on all of us.

1

ALBERTA, 1908

Just to be part of this crowd, with its wary hick yearning. Two boys hiding under the bleachers, shaded from the August sun by five hundred bodies, the town reassembled in orderly rows, waiting to be dazzled. A few shards of sunlight penetrated. Michael Mountain Horse and his brother Stanford stared out onto the bleached infield, its thin coat of dust sitting lightly after twenty-two days without rain. Michael lay on an angled support beam with Stanford standing behind him, sharing a sightline that looked past a woman's ankles (themselves an unspoken entertainment).

The cowboy moved his rope in a sinuous dance, interrupted by twists that sent the circle spinning over his theatrically smiling face. He brought the rope to a vertical position, creating a doorway that he stepped in and out of, a jig he kept up for a minute, the rope glancing onto the hardtack and sending up sprays of dust. He had leather chaps with silver studs down the sides, boots with red hearts sewn on the front, and a white hat. The wide circle of rope tightened into a smaller, faster, more sinister circle, moving above his head as he walked around the infield until it landed softly, like a living thing, around the budding corpulence of Percy Wedgewood, a Methodist preacher.

"Got myself a sinner," roared Guy Weadick, and the crowd roared back. "What is it the Bible says? 'All we like sheep have gone astray,' well ..." He laughed.

Wedgewood smiled weakly.

Crouched in the half-light, Michael was transfixed by the spectacle. "What's he going to do with that preacher?" he whispered to Stanford.

"Nothing good, I imagine."

Michael held his breath in anticipation and then let it out slowly and deliberately.

Weadick waved his white hat and kept hold of Percy, whose face was bubbling with perspiration, his hands pinned to his sides, a baby's hands.

"A man who walks with God fears nothing, isn't that right, Reverend? But there is one thing he *should* fear. One thing that every manjack with a lick of sense, whether he is a man of God or the devil's spawn, should tremble at." Weadick paused to assess his audience, men in straw hats and women fanning themselves in the heat. *"And that is a woman!"* The crowd roared and Percy blushed, and on that cue a woman rode into the infield on a golden palomino. She had a white hat too. Dark-haired, with a crooked smile, the prettiest woman Michael had ever seen.

"This is my wife, Mrs. Flores LaDue, currently ranked the world's most accomplished horsewoman," Weadick bellowed to great applause. "She will commence to astound you with her skills."

At the north end of the field targets had been set up, rusted heart-shaped metal plates mounted on stakes. Flores pranced her horse and took off her hat and waved it to the crowd. She disappeared from Michael and Stanford's view and they raced around the beams and ducked under the crossbars trying to relocate her.

"I suggest, gentlemen, that now is not the time to get up and stretch your legs," Weadick announced. "You want to be as still as a mouse around a woman with a loaded gun!" The crowd cheered as Flores produced two pistols, spinning them on her index fingers. Michael watched her, his sight-line between a large man and his slender wife who had left space between them, out of habit perhaps. The pistols spun and caught the sun, and Flores gave her horse a dig with her boots and it began to canter. She took one of the pistols and aimed and fired at a metal heart and it fell with a thud. Flores dashed by and Michael and Stanford scrambled until they could see her again, Michael almost panicked at the loss of this extraordinary vision.

The two brothers ran to where the bleachers ended and peeked out, risking discovery to see Flores. But everyone else was mesmerized too. She turned around backwards in the saddle and took off her hat, waving it. With her other hand she drew her pistol, fired, hitting another heart. Then she holstered the gun and spun around in the saddle, tapping her hat on tight and prancing by the grandstand with that crooked smile.

Flores trotted up to Weadick and Percy.

Weadick addressed Percy in his stage voice. "Now you are a man of God, sir, and you will be happy to know that it is God Himself who guides the hand of my lovely wife." Percy's white shirt was wet through under his black wool suit, as if he'd been baptized in a river.

Michael retreated under the bleachers and found a sight-line behind two fat men. Another man entered the ring, carrying a hat, holding it upright with both hands as if he was carrying a cake. Sitting in the hollowed crown of the tall white hat was an overripe melon stained with its own juices. The man placed the heavy hat on Percy's head, who finally found his voice. "This has gone far enough. I demand—"

"Where is your faith, man?" Weadick boomed to the crowd. He had the solid psychological insight of the showman, and could sense that Percy, this small-eyed, plump man, was not popular.

"Is he a true man of faith?" Weadick asked. The crowd roared its response; a dozen sentiments that blurred, some calling out Percy's name, and one yelling "Shoot the bastard!"

Michael recognized Percy from his one visit to church with his mother. It was a small Methodist congregation that met in a white church in the foothills. Most of it had been confusing, Percy describing the terrible things that awaited those who strayed, but Michael had enjoyed the sermon. There wasn't a shortage of action in the Old Testament. Afterwards, while they rode back, Michael asked questions about God and his mother answered as best she could and then they rode in silence. And now here was Percy, looking damp and sacrificial.

Flores dismounted and gave her horse a pat on the rump and it trotted obediently back to the north end of the infield and through the exit. She walked over and planted a kiss on Percy's soft mouth and again the crowd roared.

"Reverend," Weadick yelled, "if God has decided to call you home, at least you can't say you never been kissed." Percy was at the threshold that divides liquid from solid, melting in the August sun. He imagined himself a wet essence given up to the Lord. Water pooled in his shoes and flowed down his chest like spring runoff. I will be water, he silently chanted, and when Delilah in the red boots squeezes the trigger, the bullet will pass harmlessly through me; He will not forsake me.

Flores marched off an exaggerated ten steps and winked when she turned around. Michael felt that the wink was for him, that she could see him with her sharpshooter eyes, see between the fat men whose dark suit jackets had been removed and were now damp heaps on their laps. She could pull out that gun and fire a bullet through the straw hat of the man in the first row, between the two fat men and between the faces of Michael and Stanford, faces that were only a bullet width apart. They would feel its heat but be untouched, a kiss almost, delivered to the ten-year-old boy and his twelve-year-old brother, a complicit kiss that implied confederacy and love.

She drew her gun and spun it around her finger and then lifted it slowly, as if it was being pulled by an invisible mechanical device, or guided by the hand of God. It stopped, steady as an April rain, levelled at Percy. The power of speech deserted him and his God, and he was once again the plump boy who was bullied in the one-room schoolhouse that held every age, the big, mule-brained farm boys tormenting him, and now he worked hard each Sunday instilling fear into them, using the Old Testament as a club, threatening famine and locusts.

The sound of the bullet hitting the ripe melon, the explosion producing a shower of juice, brought a collective exhalation from the crowd, then a roar. "You missed!" one of the fat men yelled, laughing and stamping his heavy boots, his musty wool pants shaking in front of Michael.

When the dramatically moustached face of the Royal North-West Mounted Policeman appeared suddenly through two slats of the bleacher seats, he and Stanford bounced under and over the beams like ferrets, launching themselves out into the sun and racing for the woods. They sprinted down a path and slid into some brush in an aspen grove, breathing hard and smiling crazily.

Over the next four years, Flores LaDue appeared to Michael, beckoning in half-dreams, riding toward him with her crooked smile, a smoking gun in one hand. She touched his hair, kissed him, and whispered *My sweet angel*. And now here she was again, her image blurred on the handbill, standing beside Weadick, and the news they were going to present the Greatest Show on Earth. It would be in Calgary, and Michael wanted to be part of it. He was fourteen now, Flores still his only love.

Stanford brought the handbill up to their bedroom. It was folded into a tiny square and tucked into his sock, contraband, and he carefully unfolded it on the bed. Near the bottom, it read, "Calling All Indians!" Flores and Weadick wanted an Indian parade.

"You think that means us?" Michael asked.

"I figure it does. We tell them we're eighteen if they ask."

"Who's going to ask?"

"I don't know. Anyone. If anyone asks."

"I don't look eighteen."

"Go to sleep."

Michael had been having the same dream for a week, submerged in the creek, which was infinitely deep, looking up through the clear water at the world shimmering there without him.

"Do you have dreams, Stanford?"

"I suppose everyone does."

"You're in them?"

"Sometimes."

"What happens in them?"

Stanford was quiet for a minute. "There are dreams I can't remember," he said, "and when I wake up I feel like something important isn't being told to me."

"What do you think they're trying to tell us? The dreams." Was he was going to drown?

"The spirits guide us in our dreams. It's the only time they can talk to us. Go to sleep."

"Am I going to drown?"

"No one is going to drown."

"Do you remember him, Stanford?"

"Who?" Though he knew who Michael was talking about. "Dad."

"I remember him walking around outside with the dogs."

"Why do you suppose he did it?"

"I guess he got tired of something."

"You think it was us."

"He didn't spend enough time with us to get tired. I think he was just worn out."

Michael wondered how anyone could get that worn out. He was glad it hadn't been him who found their father.

Stanford and Michael sat in the brush thirty yards from the Cochrane train station, waiting for the men to load up milk, cream, and beef to haul into Calgary. Stanford pointed to a boxcar with an open door. "That one there," he whispered. "Follow me when I go."

When the train shunted forward, they broke from their cover and sprinted across the open ground. Stanford ran to the open door and got hold of the steel handle and swung himself up, a sudden fear, his head filling with stories of legs cut off as men swung under the wheels, stewbums that missed their jump and were cut in half, men with stumps named Shorty. He got his body horizontal and his legs fought for purchase and found the floor. He rolled inside and then scrambled back to the door.

Michael was running alongside. There was a gully coming up in less than a hundred yards. The train would be moving too fast by then anyway. Michael's face was a frozen mask of fear, adventure, and trust in his older brother, some powerful algorithm of adolescence. Stanford leaned out and pointed to the handle. "Grab here, then throw yourself up." Stanford had a new fear: his brother cut in half, his death Stanford's fault, their mother silent for two years. Michael missed the handle but Stanford grabbed him and pulled him roughly and as Michael's legs swung up Stanford half expected to see bloody, footless ankles. Michael sat up, whole and thrilled. They sprawled on the scarred wood and watched the Bow Valley go by through the open door, the erratic stands of pine, the deepening of the valley, parched hills the colour of wheat.

"Have you done this before?" Michael asked his brother.

"A few times."

"Where'd you go?"

"Along the tracks."

"How are we going to get off?"

"The train slows coming into Calgary."

"Will we go to jail if we're caught, Stanford?"

"We're not going to jail."

"What if Mother finds out?"

"She won't find out if you don't tell her."

"I won't tell her but she'll find out."

Michael believed his mother had a connection to the spiritual world that gave her constant updates on the benign treacheries of her children. He felt calm in her presence, the same calm he had felt as a child sitting in front of the wood stove in their kitchen, his mother in the rocking chair peeling an apple. He played with small lead soldiers, a present from their father. He had meticulously painted wounds on some of them with tiny drops of his own blood applied with a splinter. The wood stove had a distinctive smell, and Michael could sit there for hours. As a child he had been quiet to the point where it worried his mother, despite her own gift for it. She took him to a country doctor, a heavy-set man with a thick moustache and blue watery eyes. He sat across from Michael in his collarless shirt and black suspenders, staring at him, and then asked him questions: What day is it? What is your best friend's name? Have you ever been to the moon? And so on. His brother was his best friend, everyone knew that. Most of the questions were obvious or absurd. He stared back at the doctor in silence. A moon child, the doctor finally said authoritatively. They live in their heads. They make good caretakers. His mother led him out of the doctor's office, past a girl whose hand was wrapped in red-stained gauze, her face empty of blood. Her mother sat beside her, holding a doll.

The train slowed through the city, staring onto backyards, clothes hanging, a jumble of smokehouses and weeds and outhouses and vacant lots, the town's hind end. A few black cars moved hesitantly along Ninth Avenue. The city lurched, a tangle of machinery and traffic.

"I don't know that I could live here," Michael said.

"No one is asking you to."

"Could you live here?"

"I could live anywhere if I had to, I suppose."

"Why do people come to the city, Stanford?"

"So they can disappear."

"Do you ever want to disappear?"

"Sometimes."

"What do you do?"

"There's different ways of disappearing."

Stanford had a scar on his chin that he said he got breaking horses at Dunstan O'Connell's ranch though Michael knew this wasn't true. Stanford's hands were sometimes scabbed. He came in a few mornings looking haunted and rough, getting in just as Michael was waking up.

Stanford grabbed Michael's hand and they jumped together. They rolled, got up, and instinctively ran though no one was chasing them.

At the fairgrounds there were a few hundred Indians listening to John MacDougall, a Methodist missionary who had been paid $390 by the Calgary Stampede Board to deliver two thousand savages for the parade. "There are Indians, and there are *Indians*," he said, thinking, as he looked over his crowd, that he should have asked for $500, a round number. "Now I'll be honest," he said, taking off his straw hat and delicately sponging his forehead with a handkerchief. "People don't come to a show to look at prize-winning wheat, or polled Herefords or Shorthorns or Clydesdales. They come to a show to see a *show*. And that, gentlemen, is what you are. You may not know it, you look around, maybe two hundred men standing here in your everyday clothes. But imagine *two thousand* of you. Imagine two thousand Indians wearing the same skins and paint your ancestors wore. Imagine the sight of all that colourful history parading down Eighth Avenue on horse-back. Now that, gentlemen, is a *show.*" MacDougall took off his hat and dabbed his forehead again. There would be dozens of these speeches to give, he realized heavily, out at the Sarcee reservation, the Blood, the Blackfoot, Peigan, the Stoneys.

Stanford pulled Michael through the crowd and brought him up to MacDougall, who stepped off the box he was standing on.

"We want to be in the parade," Stanford said evenly.

MacDougall looked at them. His first question, unspoken because he didn't want to know the answer—in ignorance lies innocence—was: How old are you boys? Instead he asked, "Can you boys ride?"

"Yes sir," Stanford said. "And shoot as well."

"Well I hope there isn't going to be any shooting," MacDougall said, smiling. He told them to be at the fairgrounds on Labour Day at daybreak, in full regalia, war paint, and on their own horses.

It was just after three in the morning when Stanford gently shook Michael, chasing away the dream of Flores in her red shirt and blue scarf.

"Wake up," he whispered. "We have to get moving."

Michael put on a cotton shirt and a heavy wool shirt on top of it. Stanford carefully opened the window, and they stepped onto the porch roof, dropped softly to the hard ground, and then walked out to the barn. Stanford had hidden two sets of ceremonial Peigan buckskins even though neither of them was Peigan. He knew there was a set of beaded buckskins in a trunk in the attic that might fit Michael, but he felt uneasy about drawing their mother into this in any form, even something as remote as using those skins. He packed the buckskins into two saddlebags along with some beef and bread, and they led their horses out of the barn.

Grey clouds staggered against a pale sky. The moon was three-quarters full, a bleached disk hovering over the mountains. They led their horses along the path, out the gate, walking a quarter mile before getting on them, and picking their way east, following the valley by the Bow River. A coyote skittered ahead of them and was gone. They rode silently toward the arcing dawn, a paleness that spread under the clouds against the horizon.

"You think Tom's going to take it?" Michael asked. Tom Three Persons out of Cardston was widely considered the finest cowboy in the area. Michael had seen a photograph of him, lean with big hands and a face that revealed nothing.

"A lot depends on the draw."

"But even with a bad draw."

"I figure he'll cope."

"You think we can get to see that?"

"Maybe."

"Because that's something I'd like to see. I'd pay to see it."

"Pay with what?"

"I've got money."

"How much did Dunstan give you?" Stanford broke horses for a local rancher, Dunstan O'Connell, and Michael had tried his hand at it, without much luck.

"I've got money," Michael said.

Michael felt some warmth from the sun on his face as they approached the city, moving south to come up through town along the banks of the Elbow. Even at its edges the city was starting to stir, wagons rolling along the ruts, delivering ice or milk, picking up rags or workers. The brothers rode to the fairgrounds and saw that there were already eight or nine hundred Indians there. Tents were set up, and some of the men had slept in teepees and were now making coffee over small fires. Stanford and Michael sat down and ate the sandwiches and a man who said his name was Jimmy Blind Weasel gave them each a tin cup filled with bitter coffee.

MacDougall arrived at nine and by that time there were probably fifteen hundred of them, some already in costume. MacDougall gave directions that couldn't be heard and were passed backward through the men who were applying paint to their faces, holding up small mirrors. They would mass at the end of the fairground behind Jimmy Blind Weasel and wait for the signal, then ride two abreast down Eighth Avenue.

Michael and Stanford were well back in the line, their horses dancing nervously. It was a pleasant day, warm, with a little cloud cover. The flies were on them, and everyone twitched. At eleven o'clock they began to move.

It took a few blocks to find their rhythm and they trotted north in a ragged line. When they turned onto Eighth, Michael could see the beginnings of a crowd, kids wanting the first glimpse, running alongside, doing imitations of war dances and laughing. Pointing their fingers like guns and then blowing imaginary smoke and holstering them. Eighth Avenue was lined with people four deep—eighty thousand, more than the city's population. They came from Cardston, Cochrane, Airdrie, Olds, from Red Deer and Medicine Hat, from Montana, Wyoming, and Oklahoma, men in dark suits and straw hats, women in long skirts, children on shoulders or looking down from the rooftops. The Indians had headdresses made of eagle feathers and carried spears, faces streaked with vermillion, blue, yellow, ochre, a narrow line of colour that ran along the trolley tracks.

The city was looking for a spectacle that expressed its tingling momentum, the accumulated heroism of its existence, a boomtown. Not far behind Michael there were Booster Clubs in open cars singing the praise of western skies. Tommy Burns lived here, the last great white heavyweight champion. Broke three of Jack Johnson's ribs but the negro cut him so bad they couldn't stop the bleeding: Burns yelling from his corner, unable to see Johnson through the blood, yelling that it wasn't over when the referee stopped it, but it was over, it was over for the whole race. The parade went by Tommy Burns's clothing store and there was Burns himself standing outside, his arms folded, head thrust outward slightly, a pug still, soft though, and shorter than you'd expect.

Michael sat on his horse and for the first hundred yards he hardly looked at the crowd. He was afraid to meet its alien gaze, but he finally stole a few glances, and then stared into the faces. There were children with their mouths open, watching a fairy tale. Cowboys and Indians. In those faces Michael saw meanness, mercy, awe, and boredom. By the time they hit Seventh Avenue he was uneasy. The line of eagle headdresses bobbed ahead of him, and he felt as if he was floating, no longer anchored to the rows of Indians almost a mile long, a grand, dignified line that whispered defeat. He looked at Stanford, who was staring straight ahead. His face was set like that day they'd killed all those catfish.

The procession turned south on Ninth Street and the crowd thinned out, down to kids once more, running alongside, whooping.

It took another half-hour to get back to the fairgrounds, the lines starting to fray. Stanford took off his buckskins and threw them onto one of the cook fires. Michael stared at him.

"You wish you hadn't come, Stanford?"

Stanford was silent.

"I guess it wasn't what I thought it would be," Michael said.

"I expect that's true of most things."

"It was a mistake, though, wasn't it?" Michael wanted some kind of confirmation.

"I'll probably make another one before I'm through." Stanford watched the buckskins blacken in the fire. "I don't know it was worth the trouble," he said. "But maybe we can find something that is."

"We can go see Tom ride?"

"Maybe."

Around them the Indian nation was deconstructing; sacred eagle feathers, buckskins, headdresses packed up, paint removed, hair unknotted to take out bones and shells. They sat and ate beans and drank coffee.

Stanford paid for two tickets to the grandstand. All that was left was standing room at the end of the field, but Michael was thrilled to be in the crowd. Cowboys roped calves and wrestled them down, and a group of kids chased greased pigs as the crowd screamed. The Americans were winning the prizes and it came down to the bronc riding. Tom Three Persons was standing near the chute, lean, short haired, with a black wide-brimmed hat he was slapping against his buffalo chaps. He had a long yellow scarf around his neck and deerskin gloves so tight Michael thought they were just his hands. He drew Cyclone, a black horse rank as a drunken wolverine that hadn't been ridden in 128 tries. Michael watched Three Persons ease onto Cyclone, tying his hand then nodding almost imperceptibly to the man at the door to open her up. Cyclone launched out of the chute, rose up and twisted in the air, landed, bucked, did another twist. Three Persons anticipated each move and went with him, as if they had practised this together, moving as one thing, a dance. Small angry clouds rose where they landed. Cyclone twisted again and for a second Michael thought he might flip onto his back. After the eight-second bell, Three Persons stayed on for three more seconds, then swung one leg over as Cyclone rose again and eased off, moving gracefully upward with the buck before landing on his feet. He picked up his hat, waved it, and allowed the smallest smile, his lips barely moving, his eyes showing a brief light. The crowd was on its feet, cheering madly, chanting his name, and waving their own hats in response.

After Three Persons was presented with his $1,000 cheque, a fancy saddle, and the gold-championship belt, the crowd cheered again and began spilling out of the grandstand and off the fairgrounds.

"Maybe we should we go home now," Michael said.

"I know what's waiting for us at home. We may as well stay in town and see a few things."

"What things?"

"I don't know. We haven't seen them yet."

"There's bad people in the city, Stanford?"

"No worse than anywhere, there's just more of them."

They went with the crowd, walking north on Fourth Street up to Tenth Avenue. They stopped in front of a place where the door was open and inside there were men drinking and the sound of a woman singing. Some of the men were out on the sidewalk, raising their glasses to Tom Three Persons, the hometown boy, the noble red man, the blunt pleasure of victory elevating everyone.

Stanford was over six feet tall and had a man's body and hands, the gawky teenager in him already gone. He could have been twenty-five. Michael was still unformed, growing into himself, a more elegant version of his brother, more vulnerable.

A man beckoned them into the saloon. "You boys look like you could use…. Charlie," he called over his shoulder, "a couple shots of Four Feathers for these boys." He was holding a half-filled pint glass.

Stanford said thank you but they had to be somewhere.

"It ain't going to kill you, son."

Stanford thanked him again.

"I'll give you some advice, boys. Don't refuse a kindness. You don't know how many they going to be. I'm just trying to show my appreciation."

"I don't need your appreciation," Stanford said.

Charlie came out with two shots and held them out. They hovered in the space between the two men, something between an offering and a threat. Finally, Stanford took both of them and downed them, one after the other.

Michael stood mute beside him.

"Jesus, this boy can drink," the man said. "Charlie, two more shots."

"We have to be gone," Stanford said.

"Well your round is coming up, son. It ain't polite. We're drinking to your man Tom."

"I just drank to Tom. I reckon he'll settle for that."

"You ain't going to drink with us," the man said dully, registering this as an affront.

Michael saw in that rhetorical question the thrum of violence, a sudden tensing, a barometric seizure that changes the air.

Stanford backed away, pushing Michael behind him. Charlie came out with two more shots and held them out obediently.

"Come here," the man said.

Stanford moved slowly backward, one arm gently nudging Michael.

The man made a quick bull rush, a bluff maybe, but Stanford held his ground and stepped into him and the man fell awkwardly down on one knee, and got up quickly.

"You saw that," the man said, and Charlie nodded, still holding the shot glasses. There was a split second when Stanford could have grabbed Michael's arm and lit out, dodging the slow-moving Fords on the street. They could easily outrun these men. But that moment ticked by.

Stanford warded off the first blow, which was unfocused and tentative. The men hadn't manufactured any genuine anger and their violence lacked purpose. Stanford fended off two more weak shots. Michael was scared. He rushed up and hit one of the men on the jaw, blindsiding him, the unprotected bone giving way with a sideways crack. This gave the mob the purpose they lacked and they went in hard, none of them natural fighters, not knowing whether to kick, punch, gouge, or grab and working on all of them at once. The brothers backed down the street, but Stanford caught his foot and went down; they were on him with their heavy shoes. Michael jumped onto the back of one of them, a big man who came in late to this. He threw Michael off into a car at the curb and he slumped against the warm coal-black door. The man rushed over and jammed his arm against Michael's neck, and said, not unkindly, "Stay down." Michael had both hands on the man's large forearm but couldn't budge it. Each breath was laboured, a separate twisting journey along his bent windpipe. Stanford lay on the sidewalk, covering up, being worked on. Michael kept one hand uselessly on the man's forearm, and with the other he found the leather snap clasp of his knife sheath. He unsnapped it, grabbed the smooth bone handle and brought it out quickly and hacked once into the man's arm, who pulled it away immediately. The man was watching Stanford and hadn't seen the knife, but he saw it now and scraped backwards with one palm up in defence. Michael scrambled up against the car and moved toward Stanford, slashing like he was clearing brush. The men yelped and move away. Stanford lay with his back against the storefront covering his head and Michael helped him stand up uncertainly. His face was wet with blood and one eye was closed. They stood in the doorway of E. H. Wentworth's butcher shop and Wentworth himself was out there standing in a blood-streaked apron, checking to see what the commotion was. Stanford looked around. The men backed up two steps and gathered in a semicircle around the brothers. The agonizing lull was filled with hard breathing and suspended intent. Stanford grabbed Michael's knife and stood there, breathing heavily. When the man circled near them, the first man, the one who had offered them the drinks, Stanford lunged at him and the man fell trying to get out of the way. Stanford was on him and he made a quick sickening movement with the knife and came away with the man's ear. The man screamed and grabbed his head, and the men danced around Stanford and Michael, looking for an opening, not wanting to be the first.

Stanford's face was bloody and focused and he grabbed Michael by the arm and they spun through the open door of the butcher shop which Stanford slammed closed before driving the deadbolt across it. They ran past trays of short ribs and thick steaks, past a hog hanging above a pan filled with dark blood, and ricocheted down a narrow hallway, slamming through a wooden door and coming out into the alley. Then they ran west, stopping in front of a shed with windows darkened by smoke.

Stanford bent down and cupped his hands and Michael stepped into them and was hoisted up to the roof, scrambling to get hold of something at the edge. He rolled up and then offered his hand to his brother. They rolled to the middle of the flat roof and lay on their backs and listened. Michael counted seven seconds before he heard the sprinting anger of the mob, hard-soled shoes scraping on the scree of the dirt alley. Voices overlapped, interrogative and outraged, trying to make collective sense: the boys didn't come out the west end; we've got men at the east; they couldn't be that fast. Did the Great Goddamn Spirit come and take them? Well fuck a buffalo, boys.

The brothers lay still, staring up, concentrating on each breath. It was after ten and the sky still held a trace of light. Michael identified the faint twinkle of Cassiopeia, Auriga,

Hydra, Gemini. Blood pounded through him. He looked at his brother's face, one eye completely closed, a gash on his cheek, blood hardening on his shirt. Michael guessed there were ten or so men who came into the alley. He listened to the menace in their threats, what they'd carve out of him and Stanford if they caught them. Had they all gone? Maybe they left two men, waiting for the boys to show themselves. Michael felt the back of his own head, which was throbbing and had a patch of sticky blood.

After ten minutes they heard the striking of a match and smelled cigar smoke. They'd left one man at least. Their story was being told right now breathlessly in the saloon around the corner. Boys, the injun come up with a knife, fuck he got it from, looking to take some scalps. It was cooling off, and the man finally moved down the alley.

After two minutes, Michael whispered, "You think they're gone?"

"I expect so. But we can't go out that alley. They'll have someone watching." Some kid they gave four bits to to stand there and watch while they drank their whisky. And they were still scouring the neighbourhood, checking the yards and streets, checking under porches and shaking the bushes.

"What do you think made them so mad?" Michael asked.

"Anger just sits in some men looking for a way out."

"Does it sit in you, Stanford?"

"It's in everyone, you scratch deep enough."

Michael stared at his brother. "Are you going to lose that eye?"

"No."

"It doesn't look good."

"Then stop looking at it. Where you hurt?"

"I'm all right. My head's sore."

"Let me see." Stanford examined his brother's head, looking at the blood that was drying on his hair.

"Have you ever drank whisky before?"

"It ain't the be-all."

"Why'd you cut off his ear?"

Stanford was staring up. He hesitated. "I can't say myself."

"He'll come looking for us. He's never going to forget that."

"I imagine he won't."

"You think the police will be looking for us?"

"I figure there's going to be bigger criminals out there tonight. If there isn't, this isn't much of a city."

"I don't want to go to jail."

"No one is going to jail."

"You think he's dead?"

"He ain't dead."

"Should we get rid of the knife, just in case?"

"We hang on to the knife."

They waited another twenty minutes before standing up. From the shed roof they could climb higher and they clambered onto the next roof. From there Michael jumped soundlessly, but when Stanford landed, he let out a loud gasp and grabbed his ribs. They kept to the alleys all the way to the fairgrounds and got their horses out of the corral. They went west along the banks of the Elbow until they cleared town and then north through tall grass. From the hill they could see the lights of Calgary, spread out like something that had spilled.

They picked up the Bow and walked near its banks. The moon hung heavily to the west. The mountains were mutely luminous and looked like they were within walking distance, as if they had moved closer. Snow glowed dully on the peaks.

Michael shivered in his wool shirt. Stanford was slumped in his saddle, and when Michael asked him if he was okay, he just grunted and kept moving. A mile later, Stanford leaned out of his saddle and vomited something dark onto the wolf willow.

It was almost four when they get off their horses and walked them through the gate to the barn. Stanford looked worse, his eye a ripe plum, his breathing rough. They tried to clean up with water from the well, but it didn't have much effect. When they came in the door, their mother was standing on the stairs and Michael knew enough to not say anything.

She led Stanford into the kitchen and lit a lamp and held it up to his face. The warm yellow light scanned the new colours and lines of his face, the plummy eye, the long red gash, a welt that was darkening. She put a cool cloth on his eye and lifted his hand to hold it there.

"Will there be anyone at our door tomorrow?" she asked. She opened Stanford's shirt and tested his rib cage and he let out a sharp gasp.

"No," Stanford said softly.

She took a sheet from the hamper and examined it and then tore it into strips and began to bind Stanford's ribs. "Just the same, you two stay out of sight until you heal." She tightened the cloth and tied it and then put her ear to his chest, leaning in, her hand lightly on his back, surprised by his masculine bulk. "Breathe," she instructed. "Deep breaths." Stanford took a deep breath and coughed, then managed a few without coughing. Catherine couldn't hear anything worrisome. If the ribs were broken they hadn't pierced anything. Maybe they were just bruised.

She went to the pantry and took out a few jars of dried

herbs and spooned some into the stone mortar. With a pestle she ground them to dust.

"Was it everything you hoped?" she asked, not looking up, twisting the pestle.

Stanford was beyond speech. Michael weighed the question.

"Did you do your race proud?" It was an accusation. Catherine's voice was harsh, and when she looked up, her eyes were dark with anger. She looked at Michael's handsome face that still carried traces of the boy.

"No one is dead?" Catherine asked, an afterthought. Stanford shook his head. She mixed the herbs with some water and made a paste and then took the wet cloth away from Stanford's eye and patted the paste around it. She took Michael's head in her hands and turned it matter-of-factly, as if it was a globe and she was searching for a specific country. She probed the damp spot on the back, making him wince. She washed it and applied a damp mixture of herbs and brought the lamp in close.

"Does your head ache?" she asked. "You feel like you're going to be sick? Were you sick on the way home?"

"No," Michael answered.

She looked at the two boys. There would be more to say, Michael knew that. She blew out the lamp. Outside, the eastern sky was lightening. "Go to bed," she said. "It's late."

LOYALTIES

1914–1918

*There was an inspector for the Indian agencies out here named
Markle who didn't want any Indians in the Stampede parade.
Most of the churches jumped on board, saying we were being led
back into barbarity by whites. So the Indian Act made it illegal
for Indians to dress up as Indians and ride in parades. Another
visionary piece of legislation. For Stanford and me it was more
complicated given that our father was English. But Stanford made
an instinctive decision to embrace his Indian past. I was leaning the
other way, I suspect, but I followed Stanford. At the time Indians
existed somewhere between history and entertainment, and we were
somewhere between Indians and whites. And then the war came
along and solved all our problems.*

*Billy's injury was immaculate; there was no visible wound, just
his silence. Michael had known men who came back from the war
like that; quiet and fragile, one wrong step enough to shatter them.
They sat in the back rooms of houses or in hospitals staring out
windows and smoking as their brains worked madly to erase their*

thoughts before they could articulate them. A few were still teenagers when they came back.

World War I was a watershed moment, the point when the country stopped being a colony. In war, a national character was created, or at least revealed (and certain fault lines were reinforced—French vs. English, that reliable standard). At any rate, the country came out of the war changed.

In 1917, the law stated that idiots, madmen, criminals, judges, women, and Indians couldn't vote. Three from that group were eligible to go to war, though. Stanford enlisted because it was the most logical thing for him. I went because Stanford went. Not everyone wanted to go. Patriots and the unemployed signed up first. But they disappeared into the mud in France. The Canadian general Arthur Currie didn't want to send his troops into battle at Passchendaele. He said they'd lose sixteen thousand men and it would be a meaningless sacrifice. It turned out to be one of the few accurate predictions of the war: They lost 15,634 men and gained three miles of wasteland that the Germans won back six months later.

We had the Ross rifle, a temperamental weapon that jammed if it got a speck of dust in it. It was designed to shoot clay pigeons at a country fair on a cloudless day. But there were deals and kickbacks and we were stuck with these rifles, useless as tits on a bull.

We were running out of soldiers too, and we'd run out of patriots and the unemployed to replace them. Next came the middle-aged, the suspect, and the deficient, but they weren't enough either. So we had to force people into the army. War gave us shape and tore us apart, a unique gift. It gave us a glimpse of the modern in all its destructive promise. On the first day of the Battle of the Somme, the Allies suffered more than fifty-seven thousand casualties. In the end there were more than a million casualties on both sides, and we gained eight miles of bog, the pins moving an inch on the map in London.

When my great-great-grandfather David Thompson walked through the West, most Europeans still saw it as a wasteland, what Voltaire called those *"few acres of snow."* Thompson tried to give it a shape. In Europe the opposite was happening. It wasn't just borders that were shifting. The landscape itself changed, bombarded into fields of toxic mud. It was the unmapping of Europe: towns erased, lines redrawn every week. And I wandered through the waste like an explorer, like Thompson, claiming it for the king.

1

COCHRANE, ALBERTA, 1914

Who was the Kaiser, so wonderfully caricatured every day in the newspapers? A fat boy in a spiky hat marching off the edge of a cliff or stuck in a sandbox, or the earth impaled on that spike and weighing him down. Men in town talked constantly about the Kaiser. When our boys get there the Germans will be taken out to the woodshed.

Stanford's integumentary system was good. Nervous system, joint and osseous systems, special senses. Teeth, gums, tongue. Good good and good. The doctor handed him a sheet of paper with a series of checked boxes and shook his hand.

He enlisted with the 31st Alberta Battalion, and in the optimism of that first autumn they left Calgary on a train to Montreal. A thousand people were at the station, hanging on to one another in small, shifting dances. All those boys. Stanford had grown to his full height, his blue-black hair combed back, and wearing the uniform added five years and Michael stared at this transformation. Catherine held Stanford tight and kissed him on the lips and touched his hair. "I'll be careful," he said softly.

Michael shook hands with his brother and they embraced and Stanford said, "You take care of things."

"I'll be there in two years," Michael said.

"It'll be over in six months."

Stanford got on the train, a crush of uniformed bodies, all waving and blowing kisses. The train pulled away slowly and half the crowd instinctively moved with it, sending their love.

Michael and his mother rode back to Cochrane with Dunstan O'Connell, who had said goodbye to his own son, Colin. Michael sat in the back. His mother was in the front seat, listening to O'Connell, whose wife had died five years earlier and who was now working his way toward Catherine's heart as slowly as a winter cattle drive. A gentle rain began to fall. O'Connell's big raw hands gripped the wheel like he was trying to kill it. After eight painful silent miles, he managed, "You're a handsome woman, Catherine." When she didn't respond, he just kept his eyes on the road and gripped the wheel tighter. Michael stared out on the pastures, wishing lightning would strike the car.

Every day Michael rode to Cochrane and checked the news of the war, which was posted outside the newspaper offices. At night, he sometimes woke up to his mother's fractured cries. One night he saw her in front of the house in her nightgown, staring at the stars, singing, and shifting rhythmically from one foot to the other. In his room, Michael plotted troop movements on a map of Europe that he had sketched onto four deer hides stitched together and stretched over a wooden frame. The map was drawn meticulously to scale from the Brown & Attlee Atlas his mother had given them; to the south, it ended with Spain, to the north, Russia. Who knew how much territory, how many countries would be involved? He wrote the names of the battalions in blue ink with red arrows and dates to show their progress. The symbol for Stanford was a delicately sketched red eagle feather, currently outside St. Eloi. In a notebook he listed the populations of Germany, Britain, Canada, and France, and the reported casualties from each. It was a race to see which country ran out of people first.

The months leading up to Michael's eighteenth birthday went slowly and each week the unspoken issue of his enlistment became larger. He didn't see that he had a choice. And he ached to be there, to find Stanford. Michael wrote him letters, telling him about O'Connell, who had come calling and who sat in their parlour for an hour looking like a heifer on the killing floor. Their mother told O'Connell that ranchers were like bulls in the bedroom, and that she had no interest in it, none. O'Connell looked even more doleful and ate another piece of cake. Michael thought that if he offered the man a pistol, he might happily shoot himself.

On Saturday morning, Michael rode out to Jumping Pound Creek and set up targets. The trees had begun to bud but the early-May air was still cool. He made crude wooden targets using cross-sections of fir picked up from the Ghost River sawmill. He drew detailed German faces on them, with black moustaches and helmets and menacing features and scars. These heads were nailed onto poplar limbs, fashioned into enemy soldiers that he placed on the flood plain. Closer in he had empty forty-ounce lard tins, and closer still were jars that had once held tomatoes and pickles, near enough that he could experience their comforting explosions. He had a rifle of his own, and a Colt pistol that was given to him by O'Connell that his mother didn't know about. O'Connell also gave him three hundred rounds for the pistol, part of the war effort, he told Michael, a bribe that had yet to bear any fruit. After school on most days Michael rode over to O'Connell's and worked the horses that he was raising for the cavalry. O'Connell had thick grey hair and sad brown eyes and every day he looked like he was mourning something. Michael could see that he expected help or guidance or at least complicity regarding his mother, and he was careful not to offer any. So O'Connell moped by the fence as Michael rode the horses, bringing them into line. Like Stanford, he had become expert at breaking horses, whispering and soothing and riding them until they were quiet.

Michael took a few long shots, lying still, the rifle propped against a piece of deadfall. Then he backed up and charged with his pistol, firing at the lard tins and jars, feeling the satisfaction of each hit. When the targets were all down, he walked over to the large rock that slanted into Jumping Pound Creek and sat there to bait his line. Above him swallows weaved tight concentric circles around the nests built on the rock face. The sun was warm and he was comfortable in his wool shirt. After an hour, he had three good-sized trout, which he gutted and filleted with his bone-handled knife and then fried over a small fire.

He set up all the targets again, arranging the Germans in new poses, grouped tightly and advancing toward him. He tried angling their heads slightly, making a smaller target. Another hour went by in glorious battle.

His battlefield heroics were interspersed with manufacturing the perfect girl to leave. He began with her sympathetic eyes, which were brown, and filled with a sorrow and pain (and muted desire) at his leaving, at the possibility of his not returning. She was beautiful and dark haired, and talked to him of war and its injustice. Michael comforted her, and during their long walks she whispered that she couldn't live without him. When he tired of going over the same territory and couldn't think of anything to refine (her face already like a goddess, her breasts perfection), he threw in arbitrary traits; she could ride, she made him a blueberry pie, she taught him how to waltz. Occasionally they had a baby who looked just like her.

When he got home, his mother said, "Go and change. We have company for dinner."

"Who?"

"Change." She returned to the kitchen.

Michael went up to his room and checked his map. Stanford went from Armentières to Ypres and then toward St. Eloi with the Alberta 31st, which was being used as a feeder battalion to replace casualties. Gas had been unleashed at Ypres, the drifting greenish yellow cloud hugging the ground, invading the French trenches, leaving grotesque corpses behind. One hundred and sixty tons of chlorine gas a half mile deep. The English hospitals were filled with men who had blood blisters the size of walnuts, their skin darkened, breath poisoned. This new style of warfare had caught them by surprise, and outside the post office in Cochrane Michael got uninformed versions of this horror from whoever was loitering there.

Company could only mean O'Connell. Who else? Michael put on his dark wool pants and the white collarless shirt with pale charcoal stripes. How did this come about, he wondered. He sat on his bed staring at the map and gathering his dread, then went downstairs.

When the knock at the door came, Catherine opened it and there was O'Connell, his hair slicked with something, dressed for church, a melancholy salmon come to dash himself against the rocks. In one hand were a bunch of wildflowers.

Catherine invited him in and took the flowers and disappeared. O'Connell joined Michael on the couch and they talked about the war.

At dinner, O'Connell said, "I think poison gas is about the lowest thing a man can do in war." He realized that he had articulated the danger their respective sons were in and a silence slowly filled the room. As he struggled soundlessly with the roast chicken, Michael imagined this silence expanding out to the foothills, where it would eventually quieten the coyotes, the cattle, the birds, the West. He knew his mother's epic capacity for stillness.

After what seemed like an hour, O'Connell looked up from his plate and said evenly, "I have my own property and I have never mistreated another human being and have never voted Liberal and I don't think I deserve this."

Catherine looked at him and for the first time, it seemed, noticed he was there.

Michael stood up and took the plates to the safety of the

kitchen. He did the dishes and swept the floor and could hear talking. Whether this was a good or bad thing he couldn't decide.

The parade down Eighth Avenue was led by a piper, a man with wild hair and a kilt, his face liver coloured, eyes mad with effort as he piped them along. Michael was on a chestnut mare that he broke at O'Connell's, trotting slowly past the grateful city, the stenographers waving shyly, the men applauding.

At the train station, Catherine held him for three full minutes, clutching him tightly, then turned to go. On the way home in O'Connell's car, she took out the photograph he had given her, taken in a Calgary studio in full uniform. Michael had reached his full height, more than six feet, slimmer and taller than Stanford, and with his mother's dark eyes. The backdrop in the photograph was a painted clouded sky, a Roman scene with broken pillars and pedestals, the pageantry of war. Michael's face had an unpractised grimness that the photographer had coaxed out of him, the boy inhabiting a foreign landscape that he had no claim to. Catherine examined it all the way back to Cochrane.

Three days later, a letter arrived. It was from Stanford, addressed to Michael, and Catherine waited a week before opening it.

July, 1916

The Ross rifles don't work. I picked up a Lee Enfield from a dead Brit and at least I can shoot. I walk on the dead, a carpet of dead men. There are pieces everywhere. No one should see this. No one should be here.

2

FRANCE, 1916

In the chalk hills that run southeast from Thiepval, in a cave dug into the earth, two German officers played chess on a large board with heroically sized military pieces. An oiled machine gun sat by the window covered with a piece of canvas. The morning sun came in through the narrow slit and landed on one of the Germans, bisecting him with a brilliant vertical stripe that bleached his sculpted head and turned his blond hair white. They'd spent months digging in, and now the hills were a honeycomb of caves and tunnels that bristled with weapons.

In September the Australians took Pozières and the Canadians were sent in to help take Mouquet Farm, north of Pozières.

Michael sat in the trench with the rest of his battalion, lined up in crooked, nervous miles. He had been shocked when he first saw this landscape, its barrenness, an abstraction of land, the prize itself a ruin. The horizon on all sides revealed not a tree or house or sign of life. A colourless world.

The artillery barrage began before dawn. Michael sat for an hour listening to the heavy explosions. The soldier across from him was half asleep, a slumped pile. He opened his eyes and looked at Michael. He was maybe nineteen.

"Those our guns or theirs?" he asked.

"Ours."

"That's a comfort."

It wasn't. Regiments had been wiped out by their own guns. That was the rumour.

"This doesn't look like any country I've ever seen," the soldier said. "I guess I imagined something different. Looks like hell after a rainstorm." He lit a cigarette, cupping it carefully. "I heard they're about ready to call her quits. I hope they pick tonight."

They stared at the sky, heavy grey clouds that were low.

"We go over the top this morning," the soldier said.

"That's the order," Michael said.

"First one has surprise on his side. Second man has a chance. Everyone after that is a target, I figure. I'm going first."

Maybe the first man was the target, Michael thought. The Germans had their rifles trained on the trench and the first thing that presented itself drew twenty bullets.

The sergeant, a heavy-set man named Cross, crouched along the trench, mustering them, motioning the men up the ladders. The first wave was torn apart by sniper fire and machine guns. Michael crawled over the lip and flattened against the earth, which was without any natural smell, a sponge for blood, lead, and gas. His hearing was deadened by the big guns and he could see Cross's mouth twisting out orders but couldn't hear anything. Machine-gun fire stitched Cross in a diagonal that began at his jaw, the words disappearing into his crumpled face, and he fell dead, ten yards away.

Michael ran in erratic lines, low to the ground, stepping over the dead. He slid into a crater and leaned against its shallow side. A minute later, he saw a figure rushing toward him, and then heard the sound of machine-gun fire; the man pitched forward and landed beside Michael, splayed in an awkward pose. His guts were exposed, leaking over the wool of his tunic. It was the corporal from Millarville. Michael couldn't remember his name. He looked for his papers. Lance Evans, a boy who worked his parents' ranch. He might have been fifteen.

After an hour Michael realized that no one was coming forward. The offensive had failed. He might be the soldier closest to the German position. He eased his head upward and a bullet hit a foot away, spraying dirt into his eye, and he slid back down. He lay against the crater and stared upward. The early-autumn weather was pleasant, the clouds had broken, the sun revealed. He was grateful for its heat on his face. Michael looked at Evans's tunic, the bloodstains turning a dull brown.

The sun continued its slow arc toward a pocket of cumulus clouds that floated in the west. Michael ate the only rations he had, a can of bully beef and some dry biscuits, and took a sip from Evans's canteen, his own lost somewhere.

Would the Germans try to advance? If they moved at all, they would overrun this crater within minutes. He could feign death, lying next to Evans, borrow some of his blood before it hardened completely. He could take his knife and cut a section of Evans's intestines and thread them into his own tunic and lie in an angled, unnatural pose beside the irrefutable evidence of Evans. It was the strategy of certain snakes to pretend they were dead. Michael had seen one once, lying in the grass, belly up. A hawk came down and took it. A risk. What if a German shot him, just to be sure? Or came up close enough to check his pockets, looking for a gold watch, and sensed breathing or a pulse. Would he rather be a prisoner or a casualty? Indians died in prison, Stanford had told him, simply languished. They were found in the morning cold and stiff without a mark on them.

Darkness brought relief. Michael felt less exposed and he whispered the story of Orion to Evans. His mother had told it to him years earlier, lying in the grass together, staring up at the sky. Orion was the hunter. You can see his belt and sword and his two dogs, Canis Major and Canis Minor, fighting Taurus, the bull. Artemis was the goddess of the hunt as well as of the moon. When she fell in love with Orion, the moon no longer shone. She neglected her duties, thinking only of Orion. Artemis had a twin brother, Apollo, and he was jealous and had a mean streak, and when he saw Orion swimming far out to sea, he said to his sister, who was a great shot, that she couldn't hit that tiny spot out in the waves. She took up the challenge, pulled back her bow and let an arrow go and it hit Orion and killed him. When Artemis found she had killed her lover, she was overcome with grief. And that's why the moon has so much sadness in it.

Michael closed the boy's eyes with his fingers, leaving dark smudges on his eyelids. He slept fitfully for short periods, dream-filled naps that he awoke from suddenly, his boots slipping down into the three inches of water at the bottom of the crater that smelled like putrefying flesh. The sky lightened and Michael was cold. Evans's face was reddened by the sun and he looked, briefly, like an infant.

Another hour went by. Michael felt vibrations that ran along his back. Were they tunnelling beneath him? He had heard rumours that the Allies were going to tunnel under the German lines and blow them to hell. Maybe it was the Germans tunnelling, and he would be blown to hell. Military information arrived almost exclusively in the form of rumour and kept everyone in a state of hope and anguish.

The vibrations increased, accompanied by noise and then a torrent of enemy fire. Into his sightline came the surprising geometry of a Mark I tank, first the long barrel, a slender snout that preceded its impressive bulk, the tracks grinding up dirt, moving forward at the speed of a man walking, a claw dragging away the wire the Germans had laid. Its gun fired and the percussion felt like a slap. It was passing to the left and Michael grabbed his helmet and rifle and scrambled up behind it.

He had heard of this tank, a mythic weapon that would end the war. General Haig had ordered a thousand of them, or ten thousand, and they were being assembled in a secret plant below the St. Lawrence River, or in the British Midlands, or the sewers of Paris.

Michael stayed low, crouched behind one track, which stopped suddenly, the other still moving as it made a tight turn and immediately let out another big round. The enemy fire was less noticeable, the machine guns quiet. It began to rain, softly at first and then harder and the ground softened into bog. The tanks were mired in the mud or slid into craters but the troops continued their advance.

There were corpses rotting in the mud, men lying in bloated sprawl, the gas swelling within them and straining their wool tunics. A horse lay almost cut in half, its intestines spilling out. The smell was a physical presence, an element like fire or water, and Michael held a handkerchief to his face.

Allied artillery began their barrage and the shells exploded in the distance. Machine-gun bullets whined. Michael wondered if his fate had been decided already, if the fate of every man was fixed. He had found himself searching men's faces for clues to their fate. An aura surrounded them, a flickering light. Stanford was alive, he felt. He was one of those who could ride through a blizzard of bullets unscathed. What of Michael's own aura? It was impossible to know. You couldn't see your own.

The stench came in waves, the heavy, damp smell of decaying flesh. Michael could feel the distant vibration of guns to the east, as if the earth had a pulse. He moved across the mud with difficulty and took out two Mills grenades and calculated the distance to the German trench. A head appeared and if he didn't throw them now he would likely be shot. He heaved them both and a guttural scream floated out of the trench. Michael gathered his gun and jumped into the trench to see a middle-aged man with shorn blond hair and blood splashed across his grey tunic in the pattern of a comet. His eyes were starkly blue, mad with historic pride and military destiny. A warrior, his mouth a hard slash, his head a muscle, clenched and bare. He stared at Michael and raised his pistol. Michael fired his Ross rifle and the man's face bloomed darkly and his perfect head sprayed as he fell. The other German face was that of a frightened child, maybe fifteen. There was no purpose in this face, no appetite, only incomprehension, and Michael's bullet hit his chest like a benediction. He fell immediately and looked like a young girl lying there. The four others in the trench were injured or stunned and Michael looked around quickly and nervously for weapons, his rifle trained on them.

Two men from his unit, Bristoe and Wesley, came into the trench and examined the carnage. They motioned with their rifles toward the prisoners and barked out commands. The Germans look bewildered, and hoarsely responded in German. Michael ordered them to be silent and finally said. "We have to take them back."

"To where?" Wesley asked.

"To our line."

Wesley pondered the logistics of herding four Germans back through no man's land. One of the them was an officer, perhaps forty-five years old. It occurred to Michael that those left here to defend the line were deemed expendable; the youngest and the oldest. The officer had a pleasant face and smiled at Michael as his hand emerged from a pocket. For an instant Michael thought he was going to offer him a cigarette. Instead he held a pistol and fired it at Michael, his smile unchanged. Bristoe saw the revolver come up and plunged his bayonet through the man's neck, which erupted in blood.

Michael fell backwards and slumped against the hard wall of the trench, his helmet off. The last thing he saw was Wesley shooting the other three Germans, who turned away, as if against a headwind. Wesley emptied his gun into all of them and stood over them, breathing heavily.

Michael woke up and saw a vertical swath of sky that was defined by the walls of the trench. He was lying on duckboards, his head resting on a folded tunic. There were bandages below his shoulder, stained red. A medic hovered.

"It's not too serious," the medic said. "A few weeks in hospital. You lost some blood. The bullet had a clean exit."

Michael looked up at the man's exhausted face.

"They'll take you to England," the man said. "A hospital there." He left a package of cigarettes beside Michael and moved along the trench.

3

ENGLAND, 1917

The whiteness of the English hospital was a shock, its
brilliant antiseptic gleam. It had been a school dormitory, a
three-storey building with a slate roof and large washrooms
on each floor. There were ten beds in Michael's room. In the
bed beside him was a man who had been gassed, and dark
blisters hung like clusters of dead insects along his body.
The skin of his face was rough, as if it had been lightly
sandpapered. On the other side, a man with trench foot.
Michael watched as the nurse came in and dressed one of
the man's feet in whale oil and the other in something else.
One foot was almost black and all the toes were gone, as if
eaten by rats. It looked like the foot died years ago, a separate
death, but was still somehow clinging to its host. Michael

watched the man receive an injection of morphine, then lie dreamily, staring slackly at the ceiling. Gas and Trench, he began to call them in his head.

On the second morning, the nurse took Michael's bandages off and cleaned his wound with warm water and sharp-smelling soap. The wound was painful, but her touch was so comforting—her hand lightly dabbing, her face lost in concentration—that he wished it would go on longer. He stared at her, a wide mouth, imperfect and slightly skewed, a sensual mouth. She had brown eyes and dark hair held up in a bun.

He expected her to say something, but she didn't. "Have you been here long?" he asked, unable to think of anything else.

"Not so long," she said.

"What's your name?"

"Nicole."

"I'm Michael. Michael Mountain Horse."

"It sounds like a name you'd make up. Boys playing a game."

"I suppose someone did make it up."

Nicole looked at the gas victim, who was asleep.

"It's bad. The gas," Michael said.

"There are worse things," she said.

Her face was only a foot or so from his. She smelled like soap, not hospital soap, something gentler.

His experience with girls was limited. His first memory was of going with his mother to a house in the foothills, visiting on a Sunday, one of the few times they ever did. His mother a widow who was invited out of Christian charity and curiosity; the Indian who seduced Lord Gin. The house had a dark piano against one wall and someone was playing.

He might have been six. There was a girl there, a few years older than him, and she led Michael out to the backyard and asked him to drink a glass of water. She offered him another and then another. Five glasses in a row, until he couldn't drink any more. He had never gone visiting before, and he assumed that this was what happened when you did. He and the girl stood behind the house, looking at the hills that gathered height as they rolled west. There was a garden in the back, flowers and a few hardy vegetables. The girl stared at him, waiting. When he said he needed to go to the bathroom, she unbuttoned his fly, pulled out his penis, and waited. For a minute, Michael was too surprised to urinate, despite his urgent need. Then he let go, a broad happy stream that the girl waved across the flowers, holding his penis as if it were a hose. She gripped him and directed the stream over the peonies and violets, and when he was finished she tucked him back in and buttoned his pants. They went inside and listened to the woman who was playing the piano and Michael ate a piece of dry cake. This memory came to him as Nicole bandaged the hole below his shoulder.

In the morning he dressed carefully and walked the grounds, smoking a cigarette, a habit he was toying with, unsure of its pleasures. The grounds were large and had a wide path of pea-sized stones with plane trees on each side forming a canopy. The sun was interrupted by long patches of cloud. Along the path men sat on benches, smoking, talking in pairs, or sitting alone staring with milky eyes.

In the field to the west there were horses. They reminded Michael of Stanford playing polo in Cochrane. The pitch was as smooth as a table, beautifully groomed. They had been playing in a tournament against teams from Fish Creek, Millarville, and Cowley, and the Cochrane team was short a man, their regular player laid up with a broken leg. Stanford was asked to take his place. He was a good horseman and probably the area's best athlete, and he had played a loose, Indian version of the game on occasion. He was seventeen. Fifty carloads of people had come from Calgary to see the match. They ate picnic lunches and drank lemonade and cheered. Michael stood on the sidelines and watched his brother race up and down the pitch, finding his swing with the mallet. Patterns formed and dissolved as they raced to the ball. Stanford was a muscular rider who attacked at every opportunity. A player from the other team rubbed Stanford, looking to take him off his horse, and Stanford chased him down and swung his mallet and knocked him out of his saddle. He lay on the field bleeding and there was that brief instant where the crowd thought the man was dead. He was helped off the field finally but it was the end of Stanford's polo career.

Michael walked to a bench and sat down and was joined by an Australian with crutches, a big man with a creased face who introduced himself as Crewson.

"Mountain Horse."

"You're an Indian," Crewson said, offering Michael a cigarette. "What kind?"

"Blood," Michael said, taking the cigarette.

The man smiled. "How appropriate."

They smoked for a minute. "There's another Blood over here. He was at Vimy."

Michael felt suddenly dry. "Left his battalion apparently," Crewson said. "Killed one of his own officers, cut off his ears apparently. You're not going to cut off my ears, are you, mate?" Crewson smiled.

Michael asked him if he knew where this Blood was last seen.

Crewson shrugged. "He'll be shot if your lot ever find him. If Fritz doesn't get him first."

Michael asked Crewson where his own battalion was headed.

"Wherever it's worst, I imagine. They use us colonials as cannon fodder."

They sat smoking in the pleasant late-autumn weather. There was a slight chill, a welcome freshness.

Michael was unable to sleep that night, thinking about Stanford out in no man's land, its lone living citizen, a nation of one. How did he survive? Rations taken from the dead. Perhaps he made forays back behind Allied lines to kill rabbits or steal a goose from one of the farms that still stood. What had happened? Some madness that settles on so many over here. He had already seen some of its guises: men who retreated to a primitive state, who liked this work, who killed with appetite and a sense of purpose. And those who were terrorized by the violence, by the fifteen-inch shells that landed and blew limbs away without effort. Stanford had brought his own demons to set loose in this hell; perhaps they flourished.

The war was a subject that disappeared for days at the hospital, then it would rise to the surface like a drowned body, bloated, impossible to ignore. At mess, a man named Dobbins said the Kaiser was a madman and madmen had to be stopped.

"Is that what they told you?" Crewson asked. "A madman that has to be stopped? What do you think the Germans are telling their boys? That the Canadians shoot prisoners. That the French eat them. That the English have no God. Let me tell you something." Crewson leaned forward, his menacing bulk aimed at Dobbins's soft surprised face. "The Kaiser *is* mad. So is Haig. Mad as a rabid dog. The same for Foch and Nivelle. They're all mad. The boys who are out there in the mud listening to a million tons of gunpowder explode every night, they're mad as well. The sixteen-year-old who stuck his bayonet through a man's eye. Madder still. He'll go home to Sydney and work as a bank clerk until he's found hanging in his basement. There are a million madmen in those fucking trenches." Crewson's face was red and he strained toward Dobbins. "Look at you, you fucking pasty-faced ponce. *You're* mad. You think there's a design out there, a plan? There isn't. God is off the job." He took a breath and reached for his crutches. "The Somme is the nightmare of a blind man chained to the wall of a madhouse." Crewson rose heavily and moved quickly away, his arms propelling him.

In the afternoon, Michael sought out Nicole, simply to watch her, trying to imprint her on his mind, a photograph that he could take out and examine when he was back at the front. That night, as she checked the men, walking past Trench and his morphine noises, ephemeral stories that escaped as sighs, she stopped and saw Michael, awake and staring at her. She sat on the edge of his cot and held one of his hands and placed the other on his forehead briefly, as if she was checking to see if he had a fever. She was older than he first thought. Perhaps thirty. He watched her mouth move as she explained the nature of his injury, the way bullets move through flesh, the damage they did, low foreign sounds that soothed him.

"Where are you from, Michael Mountain Horse?" she asked.

"Alberta."

She stared politely.

"Canada. The West, out by the Rocky Mountains."

"I would think the mountains would be comforting. To look up and see them there."

"I suppose. You're English?"

"London."

"What's it like?"

"Lots of history, lots of rain."

She wore a ring and Michael wondered if this was simply protection against the patients or if she had a husband.

"Your husband is in France?"

Nicole hesitated. "No. Not now, no."

There was a short, familiar silence that implied he was a casualty. "He was killed."

"Yes."

"I'm sorry."

"We all are."

They were quiet for a while and Michael touched her hand. There was no reproach, and she responded by caressing his. She leaned down and kissed him on the mouth. Beside them Gas and Trench moaned lightly. The room and its sleeping, happily drugged men, four empty beds that would be filled tomorrow. He touched her hair and they kissed again and Michael was caught up in her. After a few minutes, she pulled back.

"I have to go," she whispered, and stood up, straightening

her uniform. She walked away, looking at the sleeping men as she left.

An hour later, he was still awake, in love. She seemed like a dream. Beside him Trench let out a muted whine, some new horror in his head.

The sun broke mournfully through low clouds the next morning and a man with a moustache came and stood at the foot of his bed. "You'll be leaving tomorrow, Mountain Horse. Back to your outfit."

Michael nodded and the man walked away. He heard that the Allies were planning some new offensive to break the stalemate, building to something grand and final. The next day he crossed the Channel in a crowded boat, listing in the waves, thinking of Nicole.

4

FRANCE, 1917

The winter passed in occasional snow, small raids, and rumours that rose out of the yellow mud like vapours. Michael heard that the French army had mutinied, hundreds of thousands of men. Two hundred and fifty mutineers were rounded up and tied to one another in a field and shelled with their own artillery, executed for treason. Men with carts hauled away the pieces and fed them to the hogs. This was the rumour.

Michael went to a makeshift pub set up behind the lines with Stubley and Griesbach, aptly nicknamed Grievance, who outlined how he would initiate a pincer movement that would bring the Germans to their knees.

"Look, it's simple," Grievance said. "You take fifty thousand men. You land them up the coast. They come down on Fritz. We go up. Then we move along the front like a broom and sweep them back to Fritzland." Grievance had thin blond hair, and his eyes were perpetually red. He was born with sensitive eyes, as he continually explained, and always looked tearful or tired.

There was a long mahogany bar and the windows were blacked out. Small tables were clustered in the room. A few women lounged, and Michael wasn't sure if they were prostitutes and thought they might not be sure either.

Michael had a glass of beer and listened reluctantly to Grievance.

"I intend to come out of this war an officer," he said.

Michael stared at him. He was precisely the kind of man you wouldn't follow, whose judgment you'd instinctively distrust, the kind of man who would become an officer.

"You're officer material, no question," Stubley said. He was a short, dark-haired man from the East, a city man. "Who wouldn't follow you and your teary eyes into the gates of hell?"

"I have a condition, Stubley."

"You've got a condition, all right."

"It isn't your flaws that define your character. It's character that overcomes flaws."

"Oh, you're a character."

"Stubley, have you given a thought to your future? You haven't, I'll wager."

"Future? Jesus, man, the world is ending."

"Fritz is tired. I have it on good authority."

"Kaiser send you a note, did he. 'Dear Weepy ...'"

"Stubley ..."

Michael's head felt like it was filled with damp wool. "I

need some air," he said and got up. He could hear Grievance talking as he left.

He walked down the street and saw a brown rabbit dart out of a tiny garden. The sky was overcast, and the moon appeared briefly as stony clouds blew east. He stood near a window and watched an old woman sitting at a wooden table, writing by dim candlelight. She had a quill pen that she dipped into a bottle of ink and rubbed her thigh with one hand as she wrote. In the distance Michael heard the whine of a shell. The long-range shells could travel a fair distance but Michael assumed they must be out of range this far behind the lines. He hadn't heard a plane. The sound was suddenly closer and he ran down the street, not knowing if he was running toward danger or away from it. The shell whistled and he pressed himself into a doorway. The explosion shook the ground. A fountain of dirt and stone and splinters rained down. Michael looked out from the doorway and saw that the shell had hit the chateau that housed the pub. Men lay on the streets, numb from the blast, just arriving at the horror of what remained of themselves. Grievance was sitting against the wall of a house like a doll on a shelf, his head down. One leg was gone at the hip and blood flowed out onto the street and he suddenly raised his head, letting out loud gulping screams. Michael looked for something to stop the bleeding. He rushed over and used his tunic, holding it to the exposed meat. There wasn't enough leg left to apply a tourniquet.

"It's going to be fine, Grievance. We'll get a medic. It's fine now, fine fine."

The street filled with people, some of them bringing sheets to tend the wounded.

Five yards from Grievance was the naked body of a young woman. She had been working upstairs as a private hovered over her, clenched and grateful. Her customer was nowhere to be seen. She appeared unharmed, save for a scrape along her side that ran to her small breasts. She had short blond hair and looked almost luminous under a moon that found a break in the clouds. Michael stared at her and took one of Grievance's hands and pressed it against the wool tunic on his leg and went to the girl and put his ear to her heart to see if there was any sign of life. Her skin was warm but there was no heartbeat. She was the first naked woman he had seen. A woman covered the girl with a blanket and looked up sharply at Michael. He noticed dimly that Grievance had stopped screaming.

To the north of Arras was Flanders, reclaimed from the sea through cleverly engineered dikes and drainage ditches and now on its way to being returned to the sea through constant shelling. It was a country of swampland that extended to the horizon, a stinking waste with a few charred timbers that stretched out like hands from a grave.

A move was on. Michael heard about it in snatches of conversation, pieces that came together and formed an unlikely quilt. General Haig's final madness, an offensive that would break the German will. They'll abandon their weapons and run all the way back to Berlin, to their mother's milk, he said. Michael's battalion took a train to the coast and then marched back, a diversionary tactic that had the officers cursing the stupidity of the commanders.

At 5:40 A.M. on October 31, they entered the fog, creeping behind the barrage of Allied fire. Michael went over the ramparts, and could see thousands of others emerging along the trench line. There was a percussive symphony from the

Howitzers, railway shells, machine guns, rifles, and the odd bomb that dropped from the cumbersome German Gothas that flew over like carrion birds. Hissing, whistling, a roar or a pop, the sound of a wet sandbag landing.

The mud seemed bottomless. He slid off the duckboards that were laid in preparation and his coat was caked in it, weighing him down. He swam through the slime, a primeval crawl, struggling to breathe.

The objective was a French village that had become General Haig's private lunacy. German machine-gun fire raked over Michael's head and the concussion of the heavy shells made him think he was being ripped apart, his ribs separated and his jellied organs spilling into the mud. Packhorses lay dead, half-submerged. Michael continued on for two hours, tortured heavy movements through the mud. When the shell landed, Michael rose up briefly, and then slapped down into the ooze, unconscious.

He woke up coughing mud out of his mouth. Was it still daylight? How long had he been out? There was smoke, fog, and low clouds that looked like coal smudges, a contiguous grey. Could it be dusk? He felt hollow and nauseous. His head rang and his mouth was still clotted with mud. There were no stars to orient him. He crawled instinctively, wondering if he would find Stanford in this overcast charnel house. The mud stuck to his coat, and to the mud that covered his coat. He was indistinguishable from the land.

When they were children he and Stanford used to wrestle in the mud near Jumping Pound Creek and then jump into the clear water, cold even in August, the water coming down from the mountains. Afterwards they lay on the rock that faced south and slanted into the water. The sun warmed them slowly. They shivered at first, then felt pleasantly warm, and finally hot, thankful for the western breeze. What he wouldn't give for that feeling now. To be clean and slowly warming, the air moving softly over his naked body.

Once they were warm they would walk downstream through the shallow water looking for buffalo bones and arrowheads. On the southern bank a hundred-foot cliff rose up, topped with pine. It was where the Blood had driven the buffalo, and Michael and Stanford found ancient vertebrae on the creek bed, white discs polished smooth by the current.

In late summer, a priest named Heeney came to their door, dressed in black, like a crow. He and their mother talked in the parlour for some time. She didn't offer him tea or lemonade. He sat there in his black robe, his large blue eyes, his hands moving when he spoke. A week later he returned and Stanford left with him, gone with the crow, stealing something shiny and precious. He was going to the residential school on the Blood Reserve to be taught by the Catholics. His mother was quieter than usual for two months. After Stanford went away, Michael went down to the creek on his own, but it wasn't the same. A year went by and he pined for Stanford every day.

A boy named Albert Lone Thorn jumped from the cliff in late autumn, as the poplar leaves dried to paper on the ground. He landed on the stones covered by moving water and lay there for three days. There wasn't enough water in the creek to carry him down to the Bow River. Two deer hunters found him, face down, crushed by the landing. He was naked and his clothes were at the top of the cliff, neatly folded. The hunters left him there and went to the Royal North-West Mounted Police office and two constables rode out and took Albert away.

It wasn't long after that that Stanford came back from the residential school, surrounded by silence. Michael was overjoyed at having him back, but when they went to the creek to fish there was no wrestling. They fished in silence and Stanford was quiet for months. That winter they walked the spine that jutted a hundred feet above the creek where it formed a horseshoe, a narrow spit of land. Stanford picked up a large rock and held it over his head and threw it down. They watched it fall and when it hit the ice a crack echoed in the cold air. The rock left a hole but still skittered across the ice. They scrambled down to see how thick the ice was and at the hole there was a trout, stunned. Michael pulled it out, laughing. What were the chances, he asked, a trout hit by a rock thrown from a hundred feet up, from the heavens. The rockfish, he called it. The unluckiest fish in the stream. Michael suggested building a fire and roasting it and eating it, but Stanford threw it away. "We don't want its luck inside us," he said.

And now Stanford was here, somewhere, crawling in the same mud. Michael realized suddenly how hungry he was and struggled to find some rations. Every movement was an effort now, the act of raising his heavy, mud-coated arms a struggle. He had some beef left and as he was eating it the sky turned a strange, almost beautiful green, lit by German flares. Its light was otherworldly, and as it dimmed, the land looked gangrenous. He saw rats scurrying over the remains of a packhorse.

He wasn't sure how many hours he had been crawling. Beyond the bloated horse he saw shapes moving, maybe two hundred fifty yards away. Three men it looked like, though he couldn't tell whose they were. A helmet presented a brief profile, the familiar German angles, and Michael waited behind the stinking horse. They were coming toward him, it seemed. He got his rifle ready and sighted it. He was wet through, and shivering through the wool. In the stillness he felt lice inch along his scalp and in his clothes, a constant twitching march. The men were two hundred yards away now, bent at the waist, swaying slightly under the weight of mud, passing a small hillock of corpses, each footstep a separate labour. Michael sighted the one on the left and squeezed the trigger and watched him fall soundlessly. He pulled the rifle over to the second and fired and he too went down. The third vanished, maybe lying in the shelter of a crater.

Michael crawled to his right in a wide arc, hoping to come up below him. It was getting cold and the mud was beginning to stiffen. His elbows were raw and bleeding from rubbing against the wool. The shelling was quiet, distant thuds that must be three miles away. There was only the rasping of his breath and the suck of mud.

He stopped every ten yards to listen. What was the German doing? Was he crawling toward Michael's original position? The two of them in a crawling dance, a slug's trail drawn in the mud that would form a perfect circle. Michael crawled for thirty minutes, his head up as far as he dared, his breath visible in the early November chill.

The phosphorescent beauty of another German flare lit the mud, a bloom of sunrise in the land of the dead. In the retreating pallor he saw the face of one of the Germans he had shot, lying less than three yards away. Michael crawled another yard and the man suddenly moved, turning his mud-caked face toward Michael, his mouth a black hole that was screaming something in German, a name and something else. Michael levelled his rifle and fired but no sound came out. ("The Ross rifles they gave us are no good.") The man began to roll onto his side, a whinnying sound coming with the effort, and Michael crawled after him and then half rose out of the mud and stabbed him through the shoulder. He screamed and Michael wrenched the bayonet out and stabbed him again, this time through the chest.

Michael lay behind the man, whose last breaths came out in a soft wheeze, and scanned the horizon, trying to control his own loud breathing. He looked frantically for the man's Mauser but couldn't find it. The other man he'd hit couldn't be more than twenty yards away, but what direction? He crawled in an expanding spiral that used the dead German as its centre. The shelling was getting closer. Maybe it was approaching dawn and the Germans were planning an offensive. He was exhausted, and to move he had to wrench each side forward and pull the other half of himself even. He found the second man twenty-five yards away, lying face up, a bullet hole in his neck. His rifle was near him and Michael reached for the Mauser, its comforting Aryan precision. A bullet hit two feet away and Michael pointed the Mauser and fired back instinctively, two shots. He looked up but couldn't see anything. The German must be in a crater. He scanned the horizon, looking for the distinctive helmet. His own helmet was gone, lost in the mud somewhere, and his head was slick with clay. A head appeared and fired two shots and Michael fired back but there was only one bullet left. He felt for his Mills grenades but there was nothing there. Eaten by the mud like everything else. A figure came over the hill, standing, bayonet out, stepping awkwardly, trying to run, moving slowly, as if he was running underwater. The man yelled, a guttural sound, his face obscured by mud, a member of some primitive tribe, his eyes and teeth showing white against the darkness. Michael readied his bayonet and took an unsure step forward to brace himself for the charge. Stumbling forward, the German made a cutting motion, as if scything wheat, and Michael pulled back to miss the sweeping point of the blade and they both fell back. The man was on top of Michael's legs, struggling to climb up, his rifle flailing. His weight, along with the mud that had formed around Michael like a cocoon, was crushing. Michael writhed and gasped for breath and hammered weakly with his rifle. They lurched awkwardly, and Michael's boots pedalled the air, trying to find something solid. They were on the slight incline of a crater and tumbled down slowly with Michael twisting around and grabbing at the man's head. They settled near the bottom in three inches of water, the German face down, Michael's weight pinning him. He pressed the German's face into the mud and held it with all his strength, his arms shaking with the effort and the man finally stopped moving. Michael held him for another minute and then collapsed against the German's back and lost consciousness. Two men welded by mud.

Michael awoke and rolled off. There was a small patch of clear sky and a few stars were visible. He looked at the German's face, an inch away. It was hard to tell how old he was beneath the mud. His hair was grey. He might be fifty.

—What were you? he asked the dead man.

—I cleaned the streets of Magdeburg.

—You liked the work?

—I liked the result.

—You had a wife?

—Marthe. Homely and loyal. I loved her.

—Children?

—Our great tragedy. She was barren.

He drifted back into sleep.

Something shook him and Michael woke with a shudder and looked at Corporal Taylor, his thin officious face.

"Mountain Horse. Back with the living."

Michael looked around. He was lying down. A medic was looking in his kit. The sun was high.

"You were out there three days, Mountain Horse."

"Three days," he repeated blankly. He was thirsty, his throat burning. "Water," he said. Taylor handed him a canteen and he gulped the water.

"Patrol found you. Lucky thing. Damn near missed you. Covered in mud with the dead." Taylor stood up. "They'll take you back behind lines, get cleaned up. Few days rest. You must be hungry. Mess is over there."

Michael stood up, unsteady on his feet. He went to the mess table and got a plate of stew and some crusty bread that was soft inside. He ate quickly and drank more water.

An hour later, with a dozen men led by Taylor, Michael marched heavily toward a small farm near a village five miles away. There was an outbuilding that may have held hogs or chickens and inside were four wooden feed troughs that had been converted to bathtubs. The men stripped and gave their clothes to a French woman, who gathered them onto a cart and disappeared, unfazed by the dozen naked bodies. Michael scrubbed uselessly at the lice. After they were clean, they sprinted across the cold earth to a blazing bonfire. In the November air they stood telling stories and jokes as their clothes dried on makeshift racks by the fire.

"Mountain Horse, what the hell was so interesting out there you wanted to spend three days?" asked Poynter, laughing. He was a big man, heavy and meaty, his white skin chafed red in places. He looked like a farm animal. He was holding his testicles and shifting his weight from one foot to the other, swaying in and out of the heat.

Michael smiled. He moved with the flame, tempting it, moving back, feeling the cold air on his back, and repeating the dance.

"Christ must love you. Looked like two hundred pounds of mud when they brought you in."

"Who brought me in?"

"Soldier from the 31st. Don't know how he dragged you that far on his own."

"What did he look like?"

"Like you," Poynter said, laughing again. "Covered in bloody mud."

The men joked while Michael pondered this. Could it have been Stanford? If it had been someone else, they would have stayed, wouldn't they? Rested, been escorted back to their unit. But Stanford couldn't stay. He was alive, then. If it was him.

When their clothes were dry the men dressed and went to an *estaminet* where they drank wine and sang lewd songs half-heartedly. They were billeted in a barn at the farm where they'd bathed, and as they walked back uncertainly in the dark, Poynter listed the words that rhymed with Fritz. "Shits, fits, wits, sits, pits, hits, flits." Poynter took a long drunken breath. "Fritz shits in his mitts."

5

FRANCE, 1918

The winter was quiet, cold days in the trench, grey time that moved slowly. The two sides were at a stalemate, lined up against one another, sending shells, small raids that yielded little. In the hopeful sun of April, Taylor took Michael aside. "Mountain Horse. You can ride, I gather. Horses. You're a rider."

"Yes."

"There's going to be a cavalry run. Rather big. Royal Canadian Dragoons are looking for men. I suggested you."

"Of course, sir."

"Grew up with them, I imagine."

"Yes."

"Fine. I'll tell them you're on board."

Michael reported to the Dragoons, who were outside Amiens. Corporal Hensley, efficient and annoying, took him to his horse, a chestnut about seventeen hands high that reminded him of the one he rode down Eighth Avenue. Michael spent some time with the horse, talking in a low musical voice, patting its neck. There were hundreds of horses, moving regally in the large corral, sleek anachronisms. The war was about machines that delivered shells from a mile away, spreading gore, seeding the soil with guts. The cavalry arrived to find they were in the wrong century. But the tanks broke down, defeated by the terrain and abandoned in the muddy sea. And the horses were there, the beautiful relics.

There would be drills in the morning, Hensley told him, and then pointed out the mess tent. Michael got a plate of thin stew and sat at a table with two men. One of them was named Walters, with bristled hair and startled eyes. The other was Dawkins, a rounded, dark-haired man. Both were in their thirties and they had the thousand-yard stare of those who had been here since the beginning.

"Amiens. That's what they're after," Walters said. "The last battle."

"The Somme was the last battle," Dawkins said. "Vimy was the last. Passchendaele, *that* was the last. All of them are the last, Walters."

"But Amiens *will* be the last. There's a breaking point in every war and Amiens will be that point. Wars aren't won by generals or strategy. They are lost by troops. There is a moment when the troops simply can't take any more. They have killed too many, seen too many killed, been exhausted beyond endurance, been fearful for weeks at a time, lice-ridden, their nerves are gone. A kind of unnameable despair sets in. That's where we are now."

Dawkins's mouth was full of stew. "I felt that way two years ago," he said through his food. "The problem with your theory, Walters, is that there isn't any bottom to despair. That's the beauty of it. You're sitting in no man's land, frozen, haven't eaten in two days, lice eating you, nice case of trench foot, scared as hell. Your horse bloating beside you. Can't get much worse, can it. But then it *does*. Shell lands. Blows three fingers off. Shit. Girls in Paris aren't going to like that development. Well, hit bottom now, haven't we. No, another shell, shrapnel takes your eyes. Fucking blind. Well that's it, then. No, wait, fucking wait for it. Get back to the trench, don't bloody know how, Corporal Turdbrain reads a letter from home: Your girl just married Dick from down the way. Couldn't wait. Knows you'll understand. It can always get worse, Walters. And it always *does*."

Walters stared toward the flap on the mess tent. Michael guessed that they had had this conversation a hundred times. It was a sort of sport, a way of passing the time, of keeping madness at bay.

"It's mathematical," Walters said, "war. You have despair on one side of the ledger, purpose on the other. Where you have little purpose, when you've, say, *misplaced* purpose ... let's give it a value of four. On the other side, people are dying, hourly, despair is creeping up. It's at sixteen ..."

"Where would Flowerdew fit in?" Dawkins turned to Michael. "I expect you've heard of Flowerdew."

Michael shook his head.

"Gordon Muriel Flowerdew. Let's take a look at an actual case history. Last month, his objective is Bois de Moreuil, six miles from here. Lord Strathcona Horse, whole squadron. Flowerdew leads the charge against the German line, cut down by machine-gun fire. They keep going, go *through* the line. Keep riding, galloping like Jesus on fire, two hundred yards to the second line, open field. More machine-gun fire. They go through *it*, turn around, firing their revolvers, sabres out, hacking away. The Germans flee. A victory? Well, Flowerdew is dead. Seventy percent of his men killed or wounded. Eleven horses survive out of almost nine hundred. Is this purpose or despair?"

Walters stared up to the ceiling of the tent, as if calculating. "Purpose."

"Seventy percent. Eleven horses."

"An objective was accomplished. That is purpose. Also, bravery is good for morale. Purpose."

"The Germans lost fewer men than we did. Despair."

Walters turned to Michael. "What is your view? What is your name?"

"Mountain Horse."

"Perfect," Walters said. "Which is it, Mountain Horse?"

Michael sat for a moment. "Both."

"Both. Well that's war, isn't it."

The three of them ate in silence.

Over the next few weeks Michael spent more time in their company, Dawkins and Walters talking endlessly, irreverently, a verbal sparring that began in the morning and continued into the night. Michael was young and quiet, the perfect audience. Dawkins and Walters had known one another slightly at McGill University in Montreal, and now each day brought fresh debate.

"Is it reasonable," Dawkins said one morning as they groomed the horses, "for French villagers to retrieve dead horses from the field of battle and then eat them?"

Walters, as he often did, looked up before answering. "Is the meat being sold to the cavalry?"

"It is," Dawkins said. "But it is sold as beef. Used in stew. The men don't know."

"But they *are* eating the very thing that they ride into battle on. They are eating a fellow soldier."

"Unwittingly."

"Meat is scarce."

"Unheard of."

"It is war. The trick is to survive with honour. Unwittingly eating horse doesn't betray that."

"Your own horse."

Walters paused. "Serve it to the infantry. They don't have the same attachment. There are no moral grounds to refuse."

"Thank you, King Solomon."

The way that men talked had changed, Michael noticed. When he first arrived, there was a shouldering of the wheel. The men in the trenches joked grimly, but they held to the same purpose. Now there was a sharpness. German deserters joined them every week. Canadians were taken behind the lines and shot for cowardice by their own men, or they deserted and were found in French towns and shot. The French had narrowly avoided mutiny. The Brits were fed up, both at home and on the front. Two weeks after he arrived— almost two years ago now—a man named Hapman lost his mind in the trench, thrashing and screaming and sobbing. He was taken away and the men held him in silent contempt. A month ago Liddle took an eerily similar turn. His thrashings were identical, the short run before being tackled. His face contorted by the same mixture of fear and anger, screaming for the same things, his home, his mother. But the response was different this time. Now they knew he was sane.

The morning broke clear and the early June heat was welcome. Michael enjoyed the drills, trotting in formation, lances out. There was a beauty to those focused lines, the horses' gentle nervous steps. Michael polished his saddle, groomed his horse, cleaned his gun, and then read the book that Dawkins gave him.

"Ludendorff lobbed one into Paris last night," Dawkins said at mess.

"What?"

"Just heard. Shell made it to northern part of the city. Some poor bastard is eating his baguette, bomb comes through the bloody roof."

Walters looked up. "Is this sound, aggressive military strategy, or the desperate act of a dying man?"

Michael told them about the Germans in the trench. One in his forties, the other maybe fifteen. And the man in the mud. Fifty.

"I've heard as young as thirteen," Walters said. "They're running out of people. I suppose everyone is."

"Who will be left to run the world?" Dawkins said. "The frail, the defective, the cowardly, the flawed, the rich. The invalids. The shell-shocked."

"The old," Walters said. "The female of the species. The lucky." He looked at Michael. "It'll be up to you, Mountain Horse."

"Did you finish that book I gave you?" Dawkins asked.

A novel written by a Russian. "I did."

"Good, good. If you're going to run the world, you should read a book first."

Riding toward Amiens, a gentle trot, a real army, the sun behind them, they came up Valley Road and the people of Domart and Hangard waved and cheered. The faces of the villagers were carved by grief and hunger. Old women held their hands up to them, empty, offering something unseen. This was something they could understand; three thousand men on horses with swords.

They crossed the Luce River flanked by Whippet tanks, the iron impostors waiting to inherit the language of death. The horses galloped past the Whippets, spreading out and picking up speed, forming their lines, pennons flying now, lances out. Ahead of them was Beaucourt-en-Santerre, heavily fortified, the Germans dug in, waiting for them. Dawkins was to the side, Walters farther down the line. They were flying. The German guns fired and formations began to fray. Michael concentrated on the familiar movements of his horse, the syncopation of the hooves landing on hard ground, and that split second when all four were aloft and they were briefly suspended, in flight. In Michael's mouth there was an unfamiliar taste, hard and metallic. He rode into the bullets without fear.

Two thousand horses were cut down in a few confusing minutes, sprawling, collapsing, skidding and trying to get up, failing. Men were thrown and pinned and lay broken among the animals. Michael raised his revolver and aimed where flashes of machine-gun fire appeared. Ahead, their commanding officer pulled up, his sabre raised. He turned in his saddle and yelled something, then dismounted and took cover. Michael galloped past him, and when his horse was shot he was thrown forward into the ground. He lay in the dust for a few seconds then scrambled to the cover of his dying horse. He assessed his injuries, his shoulder bruised, his knee swelling and cut, hands scraped, wrist jammed. His horse was still breathing. He could feel the damaged bellows of its lungs as he lay against it. Its forelegs were broken and a pink froth of blood and saliva pooled at its mouth. Michael lay against the horse and felt its laboured breathing beneath the warm coat. They breathed in tandem for short periods, a shared misery. He looked back across the battlefield. Could all the horses be down? Those magnificent targets. He couldn't see Dawkins or Walters. He found his pistol and shot his horse in the head to end its suffering.

After an hour, he heard changes in the gunfire. New guns had entered the battle. Men yelled and moved toward the village. He got up with effort and followed them. He stumbled over Chambers from Calgary, his thin moustache and easy charm, his pink brains drying on the earth.

The Fort Garry Horse had approached from the other side and routed the Germans. The Dragoons came up on foot and helped secure the village. At dusk, the 4th Division relieved them, and they walked, tired, horseless, back to their camp.

"Could that have been the actual last cavalry charge?" Dawkins inquired rhetorically at mess the next night. "After a thousand years, is this the last time men will attack one another with swords on horseback?" One of his arms was in a sling, and there were cuts along his forehead. "What commander could give that order now? How many horses survived? Fifty? Ten? Was that the final slaughter?"

"The tanks didn't do much better," Walters said. "We started with more than four hundred. Six are still working, I'm told. Horses don't work, tanks don't work. What does this mean?"

"It means we're living in the present," Dawkins said. "One of those rare moments in history where you know exactly where you are, right while it's happening. The horses are part of the past, officially relegated to history. But the tanks, they're still in the future. They don't work yet. But they will. It means that this"—he gestured around him—"this collection of death and sentiment and bad food and poor decisions, this is inescapably, undeniably, the present." Dawkins took a bite from a square of bitter chocolate, then offered some to Michael and Walters. They ate the chocolate and watched the sun glow red in the west.

During the autumn, the Allies advanced: Bourlon, Bourlon Wood, Pilgrim's Rest, Haynecourt, Canal du Nord, Cambrai. Sweating through bogs, laying corduroy roads under the afternoon sun, walking through abandoned villages of ghostly stone, seeing vague shapes in the fog that settled over skeletal trees the colour of bone. The smell of gas sitting lightly on the breeze, the hundred-year-old faces collapsing around bully beef as they ate in silence. They could sense the end. The Germans were in flight. Walters was vaporized by a shell outside Cambrai, a direct hit that left a pink spray that settled lightly on the earth. Tanks were angled on the horizon, rusting in farmers' fields. The Germans were inching eastward, going home.

Walking through the shattered streets of Cambrai, the dust rising in a grey mist out of the rubble, buildings cleaved

and looming jagged and black against the pleasant French
sun. A mad German sniper who was left behind to die fired
his Mauser from a window and was then blown to pieces. A
hundred men knelt in front of wooden chairs in the half-ruin
of a cathedral, the heavy candelabra intact and hanging in a
shaft of sunlight that came through the bombed dome.
Valenciennes, Marly, the buckled streets, huge splinters lying
across the stone, charred beams that the people carefully
stepped over as they came forward with flowers and tears,
embracing Michael, kissing him, holding his face like a
chalice.

6

STANFORD MOUNTAIN HORSE, FRANCE, 1918

In a cave in the chalk hills, beside the oversized chess set, Stanford pressed the cloth lightly against his wound and watched the red stain spread. Sunlight came in the vertical window, bisecting the space, illuminating the muddy rations scavenged from the battlefield that sat on the wooden table beside the tobacco. There was a revolver in a leather holster and a bone-handled knife. Two rifles, an Enfield and a Mauser, stood in the corner. On the floor, a collection of helmets. Stanford was slumped in the wooden chair and he reached for the dented canteen and took a long drink, and then breathed in sharply. Was his spirit getting ready to leave? A soft light that hovered, waiting to drift skyward like a feather on the wind. A warm breath dispersed in the cool of morning.

His mother had told him of Crowfoot, stories she whispered as he lay half asleep in his bed under the Hudson's Bay blanket. Crowfoot died in a tent east of Calgary. It was 1890, near the close of the century, certainly the end of their time. All twelve of Crowfoot's children had died of starvation or tuberculosis, and it was his mother, almost a hundred years old, who was at his deathbed. The generations working in reverse; first the children die, then the parent, finally the grandparent. She had seen the century come in and was there to see it end, one hundred years of gathering sorrow.

Stanford drank some whisky from the flask and discarded the bloody cloth. He took a grey rag torn from a German uniform, applied it to his wound, and watched it too slowly flower with blood. He observed the patterns on his body, the crude swirl of ink. He had been conscripted for a firing squad, the most loathsome thing he had done in the war. Eight of them, slipping out before dawn, lining up to shoot a seventeen-year-old boy whose nerves had broken like glass. He was sitting in the forest, unable even to stand, wet from the dew. He reminded Stanford of a crippled deer. The military police had captured him at a train station. One of the eight rifles had a blank round, cheap comfort that they may not have killed the boy. When they took aim at his heart (not his head), when they lined up the button on his chest pocket and squeezed the trigger, while the condemned boy rallied himself briefly, saying quietly, "It ain't right," they could convince themselves they weren't executioners. No one spoke on the walk back to their tents. The light had hardly broken, and no one spoke of it again.

How many had he killed since? There had been so many Germans. And so many of his own. Stanford took another sip of whisky from the small flask, lay back and closed his eyes. The hand that held the cloth to his side was sticky with blood. Who had shot him? A German, perhaps. Though almost as likely to be a Canadian or a Brit. Stanford inhabited the landscape like a wraith, behind one line then the other. He had begun to think he was invisible. Doing good, doing harm, doing God's work. This last thought triggered an ugly laugh that turned into a coughing seizure. He held the cloth to his mouth and noticed the fresh blood when he took it away.

His thoughts drifted back to the first battle, the beginning of his own war, years ago. (Was it the beginning? Not truly. A war begun before his birth, fought and lost and resurrected, handed down through blood.) He saw the door slightly ajar, the light leaking out, coming from the small window in the room and being swallowed by the dark polished wood of the school hallway. There was Heeney's naked form, his face both surprised and angry, the whisky priest. Albert Lone Thorn's eyes were desperate and uncomprehending. He was crying. Heeney closed the door. Stanford was paralyzed, and stood there hollowed, a void that grew inside him and was filled with shame and anger and a betrayal that finally rose like black bile and filled every sense. Albert was gone in a week, vanished from school, from the world, sitting unclaimed in the creek for three days. Stanford spent time on the aspen bough, finding the right size, the right length and heft. He carved a design in the bark, a wolf's head. When Heeney's face received the first blow, there was surprise and something else, some dark wish for penance, a Catholic gift for pain. The wood hit him above the eye and then again across his nose with the sound of a tree splitting. He fell awkwardly to the floor, losing consciousness, and Stanford focused on an offending hand that lay on the bare wood floor and hammered until it was red shapeless meat staining the freshly washed boards. When the other priests came into the room, Stanford was crying and on his knees, his mouth against Heeney's unhearing ear, filling his head with ancient fears.

HOMECOMING

1921–1929

*When I got home from the war. How many stories began with
those words. When I got home I married my sweetheart, made my
fortune, wept for a year, joined a dance band.*

*At first, I didn't get home from the war. I stayed in France. I met
a woman there, that was part of it. I was at an outdoor market in
Paris, a place I liked to visit, though the markets in those years
were lean. Wooden trays with stunted potatoes and peppers that
looked like old faces, apples pitted with black spots that gave a
wonderful aroma. But there was something hopeful about the
market. After two years of rations, everything out of a can, it was
a joy just to see something that had been grown. I would go early
in the morning and have a coffee and walk around. One morning
there was a woman holding an artichoke. I'd never seen one and I
stared at it, and at her too, I suppose, and she smiled and told me
what it was. She spoke a little English, enough that I understood
her. She handed it to me and I examined its armour. She invited
me to her apartment and boiled it and then showed me how to peel*

the leaves off and dip them in a spicy oil and she fed one into my mouth and slowly withdrew it as I bit down on it. Afterwards we made love. You can't imagine the effect this had on me. It was overwhelming. Her name was Marie. There wasn't a woman like her out here, not then.

I spent a lot of time in Paris just walking the streets. I had this fantasy of running into Stanford. Absurd, I know. But there had never been any official confirmation of his death. His body hadn't surfaced; most likely it was swallowed by the mud like so many others, a prehistoric beast whose bones will be discovered ten thousand years from now. But I would imagine him walking down rue Marcadet, dressed fashionably in a camel hair coat, a girl on his arm, and we would race through Montmartre, running as we hadn't on that day in Calgary when we fought those men.

We used to shoot gophers together when we were kids. We had one .22 rifle to share, our mother reasoning that there would be less chance of an accident with only one gun. I was maybe nine. There was a bounty on gophers: Each tail brought in a penny. We lay in the grass, Stanford with the gun, sighting down the barrel, waiting for a gopher to show itself. Hours went by like this. Pleasant unprofitable days.

For all we knew, the whole world was like this. There was no radio or TV and we didn't get a newspaper. Our only connection to the world was what we could see. We were explorers. Maybe if Stanford hadn't had any contact with the world he would have been fine. Or maybe it was in his blood and it would have come out anyway: four generations of war, starvation, gin, and darkness waiting to escape. And what better playground than France in 1916.

I stayed in France for more than a year, and then I started thinking of home, like Domagaya and Taignoagny, the first Indians in Paris, who had come unwillingly. I was no longer fashionable, or maybe it's fairer to say no longer exotic.

Domagaya and Taignoagny and their father, the Iroquoian chief Donnacona, were kidnapped by the French explorer Jacques Cartier, along with seven other Indians—four of them children offered to Cartier as gifts. Ten Indians in the Paris of 1536. The children were cooed over, like all children of other races, embraced as perfect, and Donnacona was presented to King François as a visiting monarch. The two kings stood opposite one another, François in his splendid gold tunic that bulged absurdly around the arms, as if his power was matched by his physical strength. Donnacona slept in a perfumed bed and was invited to royal balls, dressed in clothes that were the royal tailor's idea of what an Indian king should wear—a red cape that dragged on the floor, as heavy as drapery, a purple sleeveless tunic with embroidered trees and animals; here was the noble savage. Perhaps it was Donnacona who first put that idea into the French mind.

It was true that Donnacona looked kingly. He was taller than anyone in the court. But after eight months of posing as himself, Donnacona wanted to go home, wanted the snow and the sound of his people's voices. In May one of the Indian children died, eaten by European disease. She was covered in sores. In death she was almost weightless, her spirit gone. Donnacona viewed the small corpse with sorrow and realized they had to get back before they all died like the girl. The food didn't agree with him, though he liked the pastry, and he would miss the women, the ladies of the court who moved through the hallways like a school of fish, the careless removal of all those layers of clothing. But death was stalking them. There was death in Stadacona too, of course, but there it had a familiar face: winter, hunger, an enemy with an axe. Here it arrived unseen. You awoke with your killer already inside you, eating your heart in victory.

Also, the Parisian curiosity was almost sated. Donnacona spent more time alone. There were fewer invitations. His sons, who often woke in the morning smelling of women's perfume, were less in demand. Donnacona met with a man named André Thevet, who asked him questions about where he came from. Thevet was a mapmaker of sorts, trying to piece together the world. They sat together and ate pastries as Donnacona conjured a world—not the one he had lived in but one he hoped the French would want to return to, bringing him and his sons with them. So he told Thevet that the Saguenay had spices and gold, and the men who lived there were white and didn't piss.

Donnacona told the king the same story. François had been reluctant to spend money on another trip to the New World. The last two had been costly and hadn't yielded much. Cartier stood beside Donnacona as he described this imaginary world to his fellow king. Cartier had spent the winter in Stadacona, and he knew there were no spices or gold or white men. The Saguenay that Donnacona described was north of where his men had frozen to death, the ground too hard to bury them. They covered the corpses in snow and buried them in the spring. But Cartier wanted to go back too, and so he joined Donnacona in this lie, the kidnapper and his victim allied.

While they were preparing for the voyage, seven more Indians died, and Donnacona was sitting in a scented bed in a small room coughing blood into a dirty handkerchief. His hair had grown out and he resembled a startled bear. His eyes were red and his head was fevered and filled with dreams of death coming as a raven. He was unreconciled to the idea of being buried in the earth—why go down when your destination was up? Also Thevet had told him of hell, described its horrors, though he would be grateful for the heat. Cartier wasn't ready to return until May 1541, and by then Donnacona too was gone, and the only surviving Indian was a little girl. Her eyes were large and dark and she stared at people, making them uncomfortable. They called her Temoin—the

Witness—and she didn't go back. She disappeared into Paris as so many do.

Perhaps the little girl survived. She could have grown up, gotten married, had children, and her ancestors live there still, her blood diluted, unrecognizable, carrying the ancient crime inside, long forgiven. Or maybe the blood doesn't forgive. Maybe it produced someone like Stanford or Riel, someone who emerged three centuries later carrying revenge in his liver. A receptacle for every historic wrong.

Anyway, I was no longer exotic and Paris was grey. I longed for some of the things Donnacona had longed for: the first taste of snow, the sound of my own language. I think I'd been putting off coming back alone, without Stanford, as if it was a failing somehow. What would we be, my mother and I, without him?

After the war, the world was redrawn. Thirty countries met in Paris to sort out the new maps of Europe. Everyone lined up to claim their lost luggage. The Poles and Serbs arrived with maps that went back to the fourteenth century. Not to be outdone, the Bulgarians went back to the tenth century. The Italians wanted the Dalmatian coast. The rhetoric of maps has rarely been shriller. Everyone shouted that their bloodlines went back further and were purer, that their God was more righteous, that their map was proof. But maps are rarely proof; they're more like opinions. In 1919, land was given out like toys among children, and in that new map a new war was born, though it didn't start for twenty years.

Back here, things hadn't changed much. The big news was that the Prince of Wales had visited Alberta and fallen in love with the scenery. He bought the old Bedingfield place out by Pekisko, and suddenly the future King of England was our neighbour. When I got back I got a job working at his place. He called it the EP Ranch—for Edward Prince.

Edward looked like an illustration of a prince taken out of a children's book. A bit spoiled, aloof. His family were originally German. A vain man, always beautifully dressed. He usually had a cigarette going. I looked at him and thought about all those pink countries on the map—the colour of the British Empire—that would be under his patronage, more or less. And I looked at his face, a bit vacant, like a toy soldier, and I knew, even then, that the maps would be redrawn again.

In the meantime, we went to the movies. Everyone had had enough of reality: The war and the Spanish flu had seen to that. Cars and movies swept us off our feet. Movement and fantasy. It gave America the chance to sell its relentless promise to the world, and we weren't the only ones that bought into it. Germany, England, France, everyone sat in the dark and entered that celluloid world like children. Even in black and white, America was seductive.

1

ALBERTA, 1921

He was trim, a compact man with no fat. His posture gave him the illusion of height, his hair immaculately combed, standing in a checked shooting jacket, tan riding pants, and gleaming boots, nimbly taking a cigarette out of a silver case.

"This is the man I spoke of, Your Royal Highness. This is Mr. Mountain Horse."

Michael looked at Edward's face. The Prince of Wales had an expression that looked as if he had just received bad news but was taking it well. Edward extended a hand.

"Very good to meet you, Mr. Mountain Horse." The Prince stabbed out his cigarette after only a few puffs. "I understand you were overseas."

"Yes, the Royal Canadian Dragoons."

"Hellish, hm."

"Yes."

"Back in God's country, then. Very well."

The fog along the river valley was contained by the banks as if it was liquid; the air cool, too early to be warmed by the sun. Michael walked softly through the tall grass toward the poplar groves in search of deer. To his right Edward marched with his exquisite royal gun cradled downward. On his left was Ballantyne, Edward's royal handler. The dawn showed clear skies but Michael could see a slight massing of cloud near the mountains. This early walking was his favourite part of the hunt. He had no appetite for killing anything. In his rucksack, Michael had their lunch: two bottles of Pétrus, jellied pheasant, gherkins, grainy mustard like the kind he had in Paris, and bread. Michael observed Edward, who was walking slightly ahead of him. His nose was turned up at the tip, foxlike, giving his face a natural snobbery and a look of perpetual expectation. Let him bag his deer and he'll go away, Michael had been told by a local. There was something in Edward, the impending throne, the implied formality of a palace thousands of miles away, that made people tense. Michael saw it in the eyes of the cattlemen. Some part of them was watching themselves with the Prince, as if they were on stage and in the audience at the same time. Still, Edward had a democratic bent. He talked to the locals, rode the boundaries of his property, and even spent a slightly staged morning chopping wood. He was a curious man, balancing glamour with a common touch, unsure of his role. Perhaps a bit shy, Michael thought, aware that he embodied something distant and shimmering to those who rose before dawn and wiped the snot from their children's noses and saved suet in a can by the stove.

The west wind was picking up, coming over the mountains with its hint of snow. They were downwind; whatever was out there wouldn't catch their scent. The clouds rolled toward them, the light still radiant, glancing off the royal guns.

They walked uneventfully for four hours, then, at eleven, Edward stopped and said, "Lunch, gentlemen, don't you think." There was no hint of the interrogative. Perhaps it was a form that had passed out of use among the royal family, an evolutionary casualty, like the useless gills that some lizards retained as reminders of their days as fish.

Michael put his rucksack down and spread out the blanket. He handed Ballantyne a bottle of Pétrus and three tin cups.

"How do your rate our chances, Mountain Horse?" Ballantyne asked. "Haven't seen hide nor hair." Ballantyne had a heavy face, small veins joining in a dense network at the nose and spreading onto his cheeks in the pattern of a butterfly. He might have been forty-five, a military background, now a royal minder, managing Ed, as the ranchers called him. Enjoying the comfort and collateral luxury, eating and drinking what Ed ate and drank, faced daily with Ed's lofty emptiness.

Michael pointed to a stand of poplars that ran along a ridge to the northwest a mile away. "There might be something there. On the other side there's a clearing."

Ballantyne poured a glass of wine for Edward, who sipped it, and then stared blankly, assessing it.

"This is fine land, Mountain Horse, some of the finest I've seen," Edward said. "There are aspects of the Scottish

Highlands, a bit of Switzerland. Marvellous. Marvellous spot for one to be raised."

"Yes." Michael had abandoned the Highness appendix to every response, which felt alien and comic here in the foothills.

"Are there grizzly bears in this part of the country? I should like to get one on my next visit. Perhaps you can arrange a hunt."

Michael nodded.

"I'm told they can stand to a height of ten feet. Enormously powerful. You've seen one, Mountain Horse."

"Yes."

Grizzlies were a rarity this far south and east, preferring the mountains or the northern bush. Years ago, when Michael was twelve, a bear had moved into the foothills, its path unmistakable: a shed swatted into kindling, a calf taken, its remains found two hundred yards away, dogs broken like toys. Maybe it had exhausted its own territory and kept shuffling east, or had been forced out by a larger rival, though this seemed unlikely given its apparent size. Men gathered and spoke of this new threat and hunts were organized. A rancher named Granger claimed he put four bullets into it but they didn't have any effect. The bear became mythic and its singular menace grew. It was spotted in a dozen places, the sightings vivid and unreliable and occasionally coincident. Over the months its threat evolved, no longer mere nature but something primeval, conjured out of the dark imagination of settlers who recognized their essential puniness in God's country.

After the first snow, the ranchers assumed it would hibernate and in spring they'd have another chance. But the killings kept up through December. Two calves from the Bar

C, another from the Double D. A bluetick hound was found with its stomach missing. The tracks in the snow, widened slightly with the sun on them, showed the bear was as big as they thought. The fact that it wasn't hibernating fuelled its mythology. Like all evil, it was relentless.

It was Stanford's idea to track the bear. Winter was the best time; they could pick up a trail in the snow. He drew a map—local, unscaled, idiosyncratic—that showed sightings of the bear on it. It spanned an area of roughly twenty square miles. Stanford made a dot where he calculated the centre of the sightings to be, and he figured the den was somewhere nearby. The next day he and Michael took blankets, food, and a rifle and walked the ten miles to Stanford's dot. They set up camp, cutting spruce boughs for a mattress and gathering wood for a fire. At dusk, they moved through the forest, sliding through its darkness, silent and thrilled, the ancient ritual sitting in their heads like a promise. It was early January, a warming wind coming down from the mountains. They walked for eight hours until Stanford saw a track. There was no mistaking it. They picked it up and followed carefully, tingling with fear and purpose.

They came on it in the dead light of a quarter moon: the grizzly standing in a clearing, its humped mass swaying over the carcass of a black bear, its muzzle red and glistening. The sight transfixed them. A bear eating a bear. Michael had never heard of this. The cannibalism seemed human in its wickedness. It stood up slowly, a graceful unfolding, and looked around, like a giant suddenly aware of interlopers. Stanford slowly raised the rifle to his shoulder and sighted along the barrel. Michael held his breath, waiting for the shot. Maybe Granger had been telling the truth; he put four bullets into it and it didn't blink. Maybe it was unkillable, a monstrous totem that had endured through millennia and couldn't be stopped by man. Stanford held the rifle there for a full minute. He had the shot, his cold finger on the trigger, the finger growing numb and less trustworthy. In that moment of hesitation he felt unsure of this kill. They were hunters, they had killed deer, patiently taking a large buck in September and watching it fall soundlessly. They bled and field dressed it, carving off pieces like a bloody puzzle, and then drew two lines of blood on one another's cheeks as a private initiation. But killing the bear would be something else, somehow unearned; two adolescents following a map made of fear and rumour, and with blind luck they'd found the beast. Perhaps it was some nagging juju drifting back from the Bloods: They weren't worthy of the bear. And maybe something else, Michael thought: Stanford realizing even then that he had more in common with the bear than he did with the ranchers. By the time he left for the war, Stanford was an uneasy presence. His temper was unpredictable, and he made people nervous and they shied away from him. And maybe Stanford weighed all of this in that minute he had its heart in his sights.

When he lowered the gun, they both stood motionless. Fifteen minutes later the bear moved off, going north in its threatening waddle. They waited another five minutes, freezing, their faces mottled with cold, and then walked over to the dead black bear, a male, not fully grown, torn apart like a chicken. They walked back to camp and made a fire and warmed themselves. What was left of the night passed slowly and they set off for home in the morning. A snowstorm blew in from the northwest, unable to penetrate the coniferous forest with any power, but waiting for them on the plain.

"Grizzlies don't come this far south, usually," Michael said to Edward.

Ballantyne surveyed the poplar along the ridge. "We'll go to the east of that stand, Mountain Horse. You come in from the south and drive them out into the open. If there are any."

So Ballantyne was taking care of the hunt now. It was fine with Michael.

Edward lit a cigarette, drawing deeply, and stared at the scenery. The Prince ate little of his lunch and had drunk more than a bottle of the Pétrus.

"This country, what you can see of it from the train, will be the future of the nation," he said. "It is up to the Empire to see that its population is British and not alien." He stabbed out his cigarette and stood up. "It's a real life out here. I envy you that, Mountain Horse." Edward and Ballantyne began walking. Michael packed up the remains of their lunch and followed.

An hour later Ballantyne and Edward split off to come from the east. Michael kept his western tack and approached slowly, curling up from the south, climbing the incline with effort. The cloud had rolled over them and the afternoon light was flat. Michael stepped carefully on fallen leaves that weren't dry enough to rustle. There was deer scat on the ground, desiccated, a week old. Edward and Ballantyne would be set up by now. Michael edged to the east, staying downwind. He stood for a minute, looking through the trees, the dappled grey light sitting like a fog. Eighty yards away a schematic of horn bobbing lightly, the rest of the stag obscured by trees. Michael moved toward it in an arc, quietly stepping, keeping his eye on the deer. He came at it from the east, between the deer and the Prince, then broke into a run, spooking it westward, away from Edward. The haunches propelled it quickly through the trees, its magnificent silent speed briefly on display. Then it was gone.

Michael sat down and leaned against a poplar trunk. He wondered if Dunstan was bringing his mother any happiness, if happiness was possible. A part of her died with Stanford, and it would take an effort to animate what was left.

After twenty minutes he walked out of the trees and saw the Prince standing disappointed in the meadow among the last of the yellow flowers, a boy denied a sweet.

2

ALBERTA, 1923

"You whisky-kneed squaw-mongering deertick fuckbox," said Alhew, an American horse trader who had brought his substandard nags to sell to the absent Prince. "You snivelling King-sucking stoat-shit mongrel." Alhew was drinking shots of whisky in the bar at Longview, his curses delivered to his own reflection in the sepia mirror, though his target was Michael, standing farther down the bar. Michael had passed on every one of Alhew's nags. The prices were inflated and the horses flawed.

"You think King Shit of Limeyville is going to even see the damn horses? What's it to you? The price is fair, you can ask anyone. This could be a good arrangement for both of us."

"What did you do with the good horses?" Michael asked, staring at Alhew's reflection in the mirror, which revealed a slightly distorted version of his apoplectic eyes, his hat pushed back to reveal a high sweaty forehead.

"You know the pig-sticking son of a bitch is German. Whose side are you on? Them royals been inbreeding for two centuries it's a miracle they ain't born with two heads. Crap-eating Kraut defective and you're taking his side. Why do you think we fought the war?"

"What outfit were you with?"

"Christ."

Alhew downed another shot. He now had a string of useless horses that he couldn't sell. He had heard about absentee royal money and thought he could cut a deal with Michael. Charge an inflated price, kick something back to Michael, and everyone benefits. The Prince visits six years from now and they're dead of natural causes anyway.

"You wouldn't know a deal if it lit a fire under your ass and fanned it."

"But I know horses," Michael said. He put his glass down and walked out of the bar.

"Blightfuck titty-brained money-killing shit-twit!" Alhew called out after him.

On Sundays Michael went to his mother's house for dinner. In the three years he'd been home, it had remained a house of mourning over absent sons, Stanford, and Dunstan's son Colin, who had died at the Somme. It wasn't just the two men who weren't there but the wives and children that would have arrived, the babies filling the space with hope and noise and shit. Michael's failure to fill this void himself, his failure to arrive with a willowy girl who was shyly introduced, and then to arrive with news of a child on its way, threatened every Sunday. It was an unwelcome lacuna that waited for him on his mother's porch and followed him into her parlour.

They ate a pleasant dinner discussing the price of beef and feed and the new McLaughlin-Buick Touring car. Afterwards Michael played chess with O'Connell, who had a guileless defensive game.

"They are out there, Michael," O'Connell said, pondering his knight, one finger on the equine head, rotating it slowly in preparation of a reluctant move. "There are lovely girls. Practical. Loose if it comes to that. All kinds. But they aren't going to set on you like hounds. They aren't going to tree you."

Michael nodded. He was familiar with this narrative. Dunstan would mention how he saw Sarah Arthur at the post office looking lovely, or how he had seen Olive Banks— a woman who was taller than Michael and moved like a crane, in jerky movements that seemed to apologize for her height—and how Olive was coming into herself.

"What about that French girl?"

"Marie." He had written them about a girl he'd met in Paris, a mistake. Now she had taken on life in their heads, had become perfect.

"Nice name. I'll bet she's a swell girl."

"She is."

"You could bring her out here."

But he couldn't. Marie, what was the phrase he had heard so often in France? She wouldn't translate. At any rate, she was gone. Perhaps married now, pushing a large pram through Paris, a baby girl with her mother's smile. Michael won another game against Dunstan and drove back to the EP. The moon was distant and small, an afterthought.

It was late fall when he headed south. He didn't have much of a plan but he had a little money saved and thought he'd take a look at the continent, perhaps go to Mexico. He wanted distance as much as adventure. He had thought that taking care of Ed's horses would be the ideal job. Ed hadn't returned to the ranch, and Michael was left on his own. But he had come to find it isolating. He needed movement or people, a change. His mother said her goodbyes at the house, telling him it was a vacation. He could come home when he wanted.

Dunstan drove him to the train station in Calgary. An early heavy snow had fallen in the night, and in the pale morning Michael saw a house being towed on skids down Fourth Street. It was being pulled torturously by two teams of horses, each team with ten horses yoked in twos. It looked like a funeral procession, the three-storey house being hauled away for burial.

On the train Michael sat across from a man with a meaty Irish head and thin lips. He reached a hand across. "Makin," he said. "Bob Makin." He was an American who worked in Hollywood and he'd been scouting locations in Alberta. They were thinking of making a movie here. "Beautiful country," Makin said. "Look good on the screen."

He asked Michael what he did and Michael told him he had worked for the man who was going to be King of England, Edward, the Prince of Wales.

Makin told him there was another version of royalty being created in California, made up of the sons and daughters of farmers and factory workers made royal by luminous skin, expressive eyes, and a winning smile. They had millions of subjects. An artistocracy to be reckoned with.

"Ed's going to be out of a job soon," Makin said. "You aren't going to need English princes or dukes or lords or any of that. This is the new royalty: Pickford, Chaplin, Fairbanks. These are the kings and queens. And the other ones, they'll just disappear. You know why? I'll tell you. Two reasons. First, let's face it, they don't do anything. Right? Second, even if they did, who cares? No one sees it anyway. The new royalty, they're in every town in America, the world practically. Every theatre, every magazine. You can't pick up a newspaper."

Michael watched the country go by in ordered lines, cattle huddled near the fences.

"Mike," Makin said. "You won't believe the skirt down there. You look out that window. Every hick town has one pretty girl, one girl who everyone knows is going to leave soon as she's of age. She's too pretty to spend her life being gawked at by squarehead farmers. That girl goes to Holly-wood. Skirt, I'm telling you."

"Is there work there?"

"For the girls? Hell no, not what they came for anyway."

"For me, I mean. You think I'd be able to find something?"

"You Italian? I know they're using Italians in the movies to play Indians. Ride around without a shirt, look fierce."

"I'm not Italian."

"You could pass."

Michael slept for a few hours and then watched the ripe promise of the Midwest, its dormant fields, the shining towns sitting primly beneath the afternoon sun, a country in bloom.

3

LOS ANGELES, 1924

The California sky, the religious ascension of its blue volume and distant descent onto the Pacific Ocean. It formed a kind of receptacle, a brilliant illusion of space and possibility, and fifty thousand people arrived that year to empty themselves into it. It was the year Charlie Chaplin married a sixteen-year-old girl. There were more than a million people in Los Angeles. The motion picture business was luring rubes from every hamlet in America. A dream had been articulated and there was no reneging on its promise. The clouds above the city looked like frayed gauze, an aureole of sun illuminating the western contours. The clouds blew east and suddenly Griffith Park was filled with light.

Michael was prepared for war, sitting on the back of a Ford truck that had been outfitted with two lines of wooden benches bolted to the flatbed. Twelve men jostled pleasantly. Michael was happy for the bright emptiness of Los Angeles, the sparkling void of the ocean. The Ford laboured through the hills of Griffith Park. Above them the Hollywoodland sign undulated along the curves of Mount Lee, advertising a new housing development.

King Vidor was shooting his World War I epic, *The Big Parade*, in Griffith Park. Vidor was steeped in movies. He saw the world as film. During lunch one day, he mixed with the soldiers, an unassuming dark-haired man with a pipe, a contemplative Christian Scientist, a Texan who didn't match the bombast of his name. His picture wasn't about glory, he said, aware that some of the men were veterans. "I want the guts of war," he told them. "I want the audience to leave the theatre and think they were in a war." This movie wasn't going to be like the ephemera that filled the nation's theatres, short, disposable entertainment that was gone in a week and never remembered. *The Big Parade* would leave an impression; it would be, Vidor announced, American art, an art that would make millions.

Few of Michael's fellow soldiers had seen action. Sitting beside him was a boy from Minnesota, his cloudless expression broken by an incongruous black eye patch.

"Is that thing real?" one of the men asked the boy.

"Real enough, mister."

"You don't need it though I'm saying."

"Maybe I need it today." The kid bristled slightly. They had been told not to shave but the kid's blond whiskers were invisible.

"But I tear that thing off," the man continued, "I'm not

going to see some hole in your face where your eyeball used to be. I'm just going to see another blue eye, ain't I?" The man was about forty, and his stubble was grey. He took a drag of his cigarette and dropped it carefully on the dusty road. They had been warned about fires.

"Maybe it'll get me noticed," the kid said. "Maybe I'll stand out."

"I reckon Vidor found his next leading man. Then what, you get hitched to Mary Pickford?"

"Then I won't be forty years old bouncing on the back of a Ford for three bucks a day."

"You watch your goddamn mouth, kid," the man said, leaning forward aggressively, but then sagging back into his seat.

The sun and the slow lurching rhythm of the truck were soothing. A breeze came from the ocean. They were filming in the evening, arriving at four to get ready for six o'clock.

At the location, a small man in an argyle sweater vest walked in front of the hundred or so extras dressed as American soldiers. "The King wants humanity," he boomed through the megaphone. "This is what the King wants." He paced theatrically, an agitated walk twenty yards one way then turning to retrace his steps, an argyle panther. The sun caught his round spectacles and his eyes disappeared briefly, replaced by mirrors. "I have two pieces of advice," he said. "Those of you who were *in* the war, I want to remind you that this is not war. *This* is a moving picture. Three men went to the hospital yesterday. Three. And for those of you who were *not* in the war: *This is a war*. Don't stand around like you're on line for a soda." In the truck Michael had heard that Vidor was going to Texas to shoot epic battle scenes using the Second Division of the U.S. Army. But he needed more intimate war scenes, and for them it was cheaper to shoot in the thousands of acres of Griffith Park.

The soldiers were given their instructions. They would move out of the trenches that had been dug by Mexican labourers and walk tentatively toward the trees. Explosives were concealed among the trees, safely percussive props that went off, the cue for some to die. Others would be victims of sniper fire. They would die in one of three prescribed ways: falling sideways, backwards, or stopping dead and pitching forward. "You, Blondie," Argyle said to the Minnesotan, "you're dead."

"Me?" he said. "I can't die."

"We all die, kid, and take off that pirate patch."

The blond stared resentfully as Argyle went down the line, separating the dead from the living. "You're dead. You. You." They also needed men for corpses, men who would be lying in the woods before the cameras rolled, denied even the chance for a dramatic death. Argyle jabbed the air with an insistent finger, "Dead, dead, dead, dead, and dead." The men had to advance with purpose, carrying their guns with a sense of familiarity, and the dead had to die convincingly. "Get to know your guns," Argyle yelled. "I don't want to see you staring at them once we're rolling."

Michael took in the sprawling set, a hundred people dotted over the scrub, equipment and lights being set up. It looked like a military operation. He was given a corporal's uniform and at dusk he advanced carefully through the woods and motioned for the plumbers, bartenders, and veterans to follow him. They spent five hours creeping through the woods, being killed by German snipers.

Near Amiens they had marched through woods on a warm autumn day, the sun coming through the leaves. Each step was a separate act of will, moving forward, carefully waiting for the bullet that would land with precision in the centre of their faces. There would be a one-second delay between hearing the sound of the Mauser and the impact of the slug, the unfortunate head erupting in the dappled light. They were tortured by their own acquiescence, to march into a wood that had no strategic value and won at a terrible cost.

King Vidor sat on a chair surrounded by people, under a blanket, wearing a white shirt and tie and a dark tweed jacket. Behind him the huge lights glared, a camera on a small platform beside him, the look of a command post, the general in the field, directing his troops. Vidor was more than a general, though. He was a god who raised the dead after each take and returned them to their fate. Michael walked toward the woods, moving cautiously among the trees, then crawled noisily in his unfamiliar uniform among the others.

At three in the morning they broke for lunch and Michael ate his chili con carne among the other extras in the big craft tent. Most of them were complaining about the work, or saying they could easily do what the star, John Gilbert, was doing. Seen from this perspective, in its minute, belaboured steps, it was true that Gilbert's job was difficult to appreciate. His worth became clear only when you viewed him through the camera, when his face—likable, handsome in an unthreatening way, a regular guy—took on its trademark radiance, an inner meaning that conveyed something incalculable to the audience.

Michael noticed a woman carrying a clipboard, walking purposefully. She had short black hair that gleamed, helmet-like. She was tall and there was a dancer's sensuality to her movements, even in the way she held herself when she stopped at Vidor's table, one foot at a balletic angle, her body coiled, languid. She bent down and whispered to Vidor and showed him something on the clipboard. They talked for a few minutes and her face suddenly opened up with a crooked smile. It dented the armour that her walk presented, and it gave Michael the idea that it might be possible to approach her. The woman got a coffee and walked to a separate table and sat down.

After a few minutes, Michael walked over to her. "Can I get you anything while I'm up?" he asked.

She stared intently at the clipboard. "No," she said without looking up.

It occurred to Michael that she might have thought he was a waiter, even though there weren't any. "I died four times tonight," he offered, the only thing he could think of.

The woman didn't look up. "Let's not make it five, shall we," she said. Michael was rooted for two long seconds. Unable to think of a winning response, he slowly fled.

He got another coffee and took it outside the tent and breathed deeply, staring at the hills.

After lunch they regrouped and walked through the forest once more before dawn, then the Ford drove them back to the MGM lot. The morning sun was pale and cars briskly filled the Los Angeles streets. Michael got in his Buick 44, which he had bought second-hand, and drove home. He had rented a small, decaying bungalow with chipped red clay tiles on the roof and a curious gothic window in the tiny living room. It was ten years old but aging badly. A billboard that Michael had passed near a new housing development proclaimed "A Castle For Every King!" Perhaps that was what had inspired the builders of his bungalow. A striped awning designed to keep out the afternoon sun was supported by two grand spiked poles and lent a mocking majesty. The lawn was untended and shrubs grew randomly against the house. Michael made toast and coffee and sat at the small kitchen table. He wasn't tired enough to sleep. The dark-haired woman from the set was on his mind. What did she do? Some kind of underling. Every film had hundreds of them. Outside, the sun began to bake the city and a hot wind moved the palms.

A few days later during an afternoon shoot in Griffith Park there were camera problems and Michael heard prolonged yelling. He saw an intense-looking man no older than himself; Irving Thalberg, the Boy Wonder, a twenty-six-year-old producer, the new head of MGM. It wasn't Thalberg who was yelling though. It was the man with him, who was almost frothing, his hands jabbing the air like Dempsey. Thalberg looked contemplative as he walked around the set, taking it in, while his sergeant threatened everyone.

The extras were told they had two hours. Michael walked through the hills and hiked to the top of one of the wooded ridges. A woman was sitting beneath a pine tree thirty yards away. It was the woman from the craft tent. She was wearing black pants and a white shirt, looking at the same view, smoking a cigarette. Michael watched her for a moment, then approached.

"You won't remember me," he said.

She examined Michael. "The recurring casualty," she said, smiling slightly.

"Yes."

"It seems you may be spared today."

"Equipment problems?"

"By the time they get back with what they need they'll have lost the light. The errand boy, all that urgency down there, the death threats, all that. That was for Thalberg. To make it look like we're worried about the studio's money."

"Aren't you?"

She blew smoke and stubbed her cigarette into the dry earth. "As worried as they are about *my* money," she said.

Michael introduced himself and she stood up and held out her hand. "Marion," she said. They began walking along the ridge. Marion made a gesture that took in the park. "Colonel Griffith J. Griffith owned this land," she said. "Everyone has a movie name here. Three thousand acres. It was a ranch once, and the owner, Antonio Feliz, died here. Legend has it he haunts it still. His ghost spooked Griffith anyway. He gave the land to the city, all of it, then he shot his wife. Under everything in this town you find ghosts and blood. Or fake blood. The battle scenes for *Birth of a Nation* were filmed here."

Michael looked at her. She somehow retained her balletic glide even as they walked the uneven hills. Her skin had the whiteness of porcelain, a challenge to maintain in Southern California. Her hands moved gracefully through the air as she talked, elliptical paths that left a thin trail of smoke. Her face had a slightly feral quality.

"You were there," she said. "France."

"I was with the Canadian army."

"And did you fall in love with a French peasant girl the way John Gilbert does in the movie? Every soldier in the movies seems to."

"I think everyone fell in love with a French girl."

"What could be more lovable than a girl who doesn't speak English," Marion said.

They walked in the hills for an hour, her hand resting lightly on his forearm as she told him intimate Hollywood horror stories. She briefed him on Chaplin, the scandalous genius. "Do you know why he married a sixteen-year-old? Because he couldn't find a fourteen-year-old." She went down the list: Fatty Arbuckle, charged with raping a starlet with a champagne bottle and then crushing her to death under his lucrative weight (though there was talk he was actually innocent and was being set up by the Hearst newspaper chain—"Who wants to read about the innocent?" Marion said). She had stories of the studios giving its stars morphine to stave off pain and working them like pack mules until they collapsed. "It happened to Wallace Reid. He died of it. A martyr. The industry's first." Abortions, incest, and murder, Marion was steeped in it. A man was murdered and two of the suspects were Rudolph Valentino and Mack Sennett, she told him. At least one of them was innocent. The funny ones carry a lot of anger inside. She went on for an hour.

Marion was the continuity girl, ensuring that there weren't any glaring discrepancies between shots, that makeup, hair, and costumes were right, that cigarettes hadn't disappeared at an impossible rate, that drinks were consumed at a reasonable pace. She said she had come to Los Angeles to be an actress but you needed a leather hide and it was difficult to know what the camera would love. Mousy girls flowered in the alchemy of light. The pretty became merely ordinary. A velvet voice was useless, while a screechy voice, an unfortunate accent, a speech impediment even, were all forgiven in the silence of film. Intelligence wasn't prized. Like so many people, Marion was near the flame and she assumed something would come of it. She had the King's ear every day, however briefly.

They ate lunch together the next day. Michael attacked the indifferent food, hungry after his crawl through the woods, while Marion listlessly picked at her plate of vegetables.

"Does it remind you of the war?" she asked.

"The waiting, maybe."

"This picture will be the war for a lot people. You know that."

"I suppose. Better this version than the real thing."

"I wonder."

After lunch they walked toward the woods. There was a latrine thirty yards from the craft tent. She led him there by the hand and pulled him inside, locked the door, and then kissed him. She pulled away, appraised him briefly, then kissed him again. She reached down and undid his belt and moved his pants down over his hips and they fell to his knees. She coolly took off her own pants and hung them on a nail, then slipped out of her white, unadorned panties and hung them there as well. Michael was immobilized, had stopped breathing, the continuity girl stopping time. She climbed up as if scaling a mountain and then settled on him. Michael needed all his strength to keep their weight balanced and to stay upright, his legs bound by his pants at the knees. He leaned lightly against the wall as she held his head with both hands as if she were sculpting it, making a small determined noise in his ear. When she came, she clutched his hair as if she meant to tear it out. Then she climbed down, dabbed herself with the white panties, threw them away, and put her pants on. Michael was still standing, semi-erect, his pants at his knees. She opened the door and disappeared.

When the movie came out in November, Michael and Marion went to see it at Grauman's Egyptian Theatre, sitting in the back row. *The Big Parade* was already a hit, celebrated as the first realistic depiction of the war. *Time* magazine said it was "easily the greatest war picture, one of the greatest of all pictures." John Gilbert became a star, and King Vidor was sought after. Irving Thalberg was declared a genius for going against popular opinion. No one wants realism, he had been told; the American public wants escape. *The Big Parade* gave them both and now MGM was financially secure and Thalberg was a genius. From the back row, Michael watched the story unfold in earnest folksy scenes. Three men from diverse backgrounds go to war. They become close, compete for the favours of French girls. It was almost comic in tone for the first half.

Marion sat restlessly smoking, occasionally offering criticism. The second half had the battle scenes. Griffith Park had seemed like playacting: unconvincing and childish. But on screen, bolstered by the martial music that played as the soldiers walked toward the woods, by the solemnity of black and white, and by the distance of the camera, there was a grudging grace. Explosions went off, gas crept along the ground, extras died. Michael couldn't see himself anywhere on the screen and was relieved. He understood the appeal of the film-going experience, the collective huddling in the dark. The interior of Grauman's was exotic, a glorious tomb with Egyptian detail, filled with the congregational hopes of a thousand people. A perfect refuge. Even Marion's whispered cynicism failed to erase this. Michael had the yokel's joy of being deceived, and movies were a harmless deception. They sat and read the subtitles:

Jim: Do you think he'll make it all right?

Bull: Sure! Slim'll come back wearin' the Kaiser's mustache!

In the end John Gilbert lost his leg but got his French peasant girl. They embraced, the music swelled, and the crowd wept and applauded and then filed out into the cool evening air.

Marion walked with her arm linked through Michael's. They went back to her Wilshire apartment and she made a messy omelette.

"Sentimental nonsense," she said. "I can't imagine that's what it was actually like."

"Parts weren't far off. What they missed is the horror." But you couldn't get that with a movie camera. And who would want to?

"You look like a movie star, Michael. You've got something that John Gilbert doesn't have. My God, he's as sexy as a piece of cheese. But women in the theatres don't want sex. They want to be comforted."

They went out onto the fire escape and climbed onto the roof and made love. Michael lay on the flat roof, his skin dotted with black cinders that were pressed into his back by Marion's thrusting weight. He looked, she said, like a side of beef that had been peppered, ready for the coals. In the realm of sex, she was wholly alien, but he was thrilled by her appetite. When she came, her face sometimes went numb, she told him. Afterwards, she lay there detached from him, from herself even.

4

1925

On the weekend, he and Marion drove out of the city, north along the coast until they passed a faded wooden sign.

"Stop," Marion said. "Back up."

Michael put the car in reverse and backed up along the shoulder until they could read the sign: LAZY J RANCH HORSES BY THE HOUR THE HALF DAY OR ALL DAY.

"Let's go," Marion said. "Let's ride. It's a perfect day."

They drove to the Lazy J, a somewhat down-at-the-heels ranch, the fencing in need of repair. Marion told the man at the desk, "We'd like two horses for half a day. None of those half-dead tourist nags either."

The man took them out to the stables, and they walked down the lines of horses. Marion examined them silently.

"That one," she said, pointing to an elegant grey.

"Can't let you have that one," the man said.

Marion walked up to the grey and whispered into its ear, stroked its neck. It nuzzled her. Michael had assumed she was an urban girl. She'd been vague about her background, dismissing it as boring. Instead she pried details out of Michael about his Indian mother and the many ways soldiers died in France, which parts did the rats eat first. It was clear she was familiar with horses. The man let her have the grey and they rode toward the mountains.

"So now you know my secret," she said, looking over at Michael. "A farm girl. Iowa at that. An unbearable cliché."

"You rode horses on a farm in Iowa." Michael repeated the thought dumbly. He couldn't imagine her in a checked shirt milking cows, couldn't picture her without a cigarette.

"I rode horses, fed pigs, milked cows, hoed fields, and cut the nasty empty heads off chickens with a rusty hatchet. I'm full of surprises."

She told Michael that she used to have conversations with movie actors as she did the chores. When it started, they were in her head, but then she began to talk out loud. "Mr. Fairbanks, that's not how you milk a cow, you silly thing. Let me show you." Her mother heard her one day and prayed for her. When her father heard about her imaginary friends he feared the worst. He was a German immigrant, devout, heavy-set, humourless, a Lutheran whose life closely resembled that of a farm animal. He told her to stop her foolishness, but her conversations became symphonic, talking to Gish and Pickford as confidantes, to Fairbanks as a lover, Harold Lloyd to make her laugh. Her weekly visits to the Rialto theatre in Des Moines ("Temple of the Silent Art") were cut out, which only intensified her relationship with the movies. Her father thought the devil was in her and threatened to beat it out of her. He was genuinely afraid. "You can't beat all of us," Marion said to him smugly. Her father took off his belt and hit her with it and she yelled louder, summoning her allies. Fairbanks! Pickford! Barrymore! Mack Sennett would arrive on a fire truck moving loopily through the hayfield and reach down from a swaying ladder to pluck her up. Her father went to work with the belt, putting his bulk into it, approaching it as he did every chore, strength devoid of imagination. But she wouldn't stop, shouting her faith like a missionary at the stake. He finally threw her against the barn with such force that she lost consciousness. Her mother watched from the house, cringing in horror, and after her father walked deliberately back to his chores, she came out weeping, fearful that her daughter was dead, that her Karl had killed their baby. She wiped her tears with the apron that smelled of onions and knelt down and cleaned the blood from Marion's face and went back to the kitchen and returned with a pitcher of buttermilk and a cloth and bathed her body to keep the welts down. Marion regained consciousness and let her mother bathe her, not listening to the whispered explanation of her father's rage. Her mother tried to find some bridge between the three of them, a logic that would bind them, would preserve the family. Marion offered only a weak heroine's smile that her mother interpreted as forgiveness, but the smile wasn't for her, it was for Douglas Fairbanks, who was looking down at her, brushing a tear away with a monogrammed handkerchief. Three silent days later, Marion got on a bus out of Des Moines.

Marion told Michael about looking out into the pasture at night from her bedroom window as a little girl and seeing a cow walk in circles in the moonlight. "It had some kind of a disease that made it walk that way," she said. "In the morning my father took me by the hand and sat me down to watch as he slaughtered the cow with an axe. My first movie." Her first kiss was with a German Lutheran boy who stood immobile, tensed as if waiting to be hit. "It was like kissing a statue," she said. She had sex with a man who ran a photography studio in Des Moines. "Only it wasn't really sex. Just him groping me and himself at the same time and then his face looking like he ate something that didn't agree with him and then giving me chocolate. The perfect date."

5

1929

They got married in the lacuna that formed in the heat of August, an arid gap when everything was still. They went to a party in the hills one night, the home of a director. Michael didn't like parties, they were a burden. He felt like he was underwater, that everything was muffled somehow and he was slowly suffocating. Marion loved parties. She loved conflict, and parties were a good place to find it. Michael walked around the sculpted backyard, a drink in his hand, moving past the periphery of conversations about who was making money, who was addicted to morphine, who had a fifteen-year-old girlfriend. He could feel the suffocation starting in. Marion came up beside him and took his hand and led him to their car parked on the street. She got in the driver's seat and drove through the hills, not saying anything, then stopped at a graveyard that had a view of the valley. She pushed him gently down onto the fresh earth above Harold Ledbetter (1868–1926 Our Dear Harold). Michael was reluctant at this indignity but caught up in Marion. He stared at the stars while Marion hovered with that sense of predation. She was both aloof and carnal and the combination bewitched him. "I rescued you," she whispered as she moved faster. "You would have died." Marion was a wonderful affliction and few men want to be rid of all their demons. It was then that he asked her to marry him.

The next day they went to a justice of the peace. He had the sickly sweet smell of rum on his breath and rushed through the ceremony. He and Marion had been drifting slightly—through the film industry, through the California landscape—and marriage seemed like something that would define them. That was three years ago and now Michael felt himself drifting, wondering who had rescued who.

In the fall Marion got a job on a western that was shooting on location in New Mexico ("If there's enough landscape," she said, "you don't need a story") and asked Michael to go with her. She disliked being alone, especially in a place that would have few distractions. She could get him work as a stuntman.

Michael didn't want the job, didn't want to dress up as an Indian and ride in mock threat across the desert, shaking a spear.

"Michael," she said, drawing sharply on her Black Cat. "You could do it for me."

He wasn't sure that he could.

Marion blew smoke toward the ceiling. "It's a movie, Michael. That's all it is. It's a movie that no one is going to see."

"That isn't the point."

"It's a chance to work on the same film, to be together. I think we need that."

The re-creation of the war was one thing, but the thought of riding in war paint brought back the sour taste of the Stampede parade. She couldn't understand his reluctance, was unable to understand any world that wasn't celluloid, Michael thought. He had enjoyed this work at first, but now it seemed unhealthy, re-creating the world as something its inhabitants could stand.

"Can you do it for me?" she asked.

They left Los Angeles in September, and the New Mexico heat was still a shimmering threat. The star was Vince Fontaine, whose bland face was collapsing into alcoholic ruin. The pancake makeup hid some of it, but his eyes weren't those of a fearless sheriff. They had never been masculine; they had once been the eyes of an ingénue and were now nervous looking, an old man's eyes. Michael was dressed in Fontaine's white hat and white clothes to do his riding, or to manage the leap from horse to stagecoach. Some of the Indians were local Apache and Navajo, and a few were Italian New Yorkers who had moved to Los Angeles to work in the building trades, putting up flimsy houses in Hollywoodland. They oiled their hair and darkened their faces and whooped in pantomime. The Italians were ordered to shave during the course of the day to hide the bluish shadow of their beards.

He and Marion stayed in a hotel on the main street of the faded town, its red brick made pink by the sun. The heat invaded the room during the day and was hard to disperse at night. Marion's mood was sour most of the time.

They were shooting a scene where Fontaine had to ride across a stretch of desert and catch up with a man dressed in black. Michael rode while Fontaine was shot sitting on a saddle mounted behind the truck. He whipped the reins from side to side and tried to look determined. In the afternoon, Michael and the Italians attacked the mocked-up town in war paint.

After they wrapped, Michael went to the white canvas canopy that was attached to Walter Scarth's tent. The director liked Michael, who fit his notion of the masculine ideal. He appreciated Michael's stillness, a quality that was rare on busy sets. It had become a habit to have a drink with some of the men after the day's shoot, and when Michael arrived, a few of the Italian Indians were already sitting, sipping Scarth's excellent whisky. Scarth was in the middle of a story about a fight in a Spanish bar. Michael poured a drink and sat down. He saw Fontaine approach, still in costume—white pants and shirt, a red bandana, his makeup making him look old and eerie.

"Gentlemen," Fontaine said. "Another overpaid day behind us."

Fontaine was a type that Michael had seen before on film sets, men publicly courting failure. Fontaine poured four ounces into a glass and sat down, smiling.

Scarth laughed loudly at his own punchlines. He wasn't an artist, he insisted, merely a tailor. They supplied the cloth and he shaped it into something they could wear. Eight hundred movies were made in Hollywood that year, more than two a day. The Shit Factory, he called it, and he knew his place in the hierarchy: a dependable fifty-eight-year-old man who could tell a story and stay on budget. He worked with marginal actors making marginal movies, fodder that the studios needed to fill their theatres. The Million Dollar Theatre in downtown Los Angeles had 2,345 seats. Samuel "Roxy" Rothafel was building a 6,200-seat theatre in New York. The national hunger for brave cowboys, tragic waifs, corrupt tycoons, and innocent girls was bottomless. Scarth churned them out at a reliable pace and earned a good living.

Michael remembered that he was supposed to meet Marion at a roadhouse just outside of town for dinner. He was already late, and her anger would be starting to build. She hated the town and Scarth and the asinine star, Fontaine. She was seen by most of the crew as standoffish and had no allies on the set. Michael waited politely for Scarth to finish his story, then stood up.

"Marion's waiting for me at the roadhouse, Walter. I'm late."

"Never keep a woman waiting, son," he said, a segue to another story.

Michael walked past Fontaine's still-pancaked face, a drunken doll perched on a crate, feigning attention as Scarth started talking about a woman from Bakersfield.

Marion was sitting in a booth, sipping bourbon and smoking. She appeared not to have eaten. She ate very little anyway, though occasionally, late at night, she would display a ravenous appetite and would grill a steak, or fry eggs and potatoes before coming to bed. Michael was more than an hour late.

"How was the drink with your lovely wife?" she asked.

"I'm sorry I'm late," Michael said. "Scarth got going on his war stories and it was hard to leave."

"Of course it was." Marion wasn't slurring, she almost never did, even when she was very drunk. But her voice was husky and loose and Michael suspected she had had at least three increasingly resentful drinks while she was waiting.

"Fontaine joined us."

"All the fairies having a drinky after playing in the desert."

This was becoming a standard evening for the two of them. Marion growing bored and drunk, looking for a place to sink the knife in. His resentment at playing cowboys and Indians out here where Sheridan's men had cleared the land was growing every day. "Maybe New Mexico wasn't a good idea," Michael said.

"Maybe *we're* not a good idea. Maybe you and Walter should settle down. Get a nice place. A pool maybe. Of course there will be the problem of who the man is. Won't there, darling."

Michael looked around for a waitress and motioned her over. Marion was a train moving down the track, incapable of swerving off her subject. "You could adopt Fontaine. He's like a four-year-old in so many ways. Let's see—his dependencies, his intelligence, his charming child's ego that thinks the world gives a shit about his talentless, embalmed self."

Michael ordered a steak from the waitress, a girl of maybe nineteen who lingered to hear whatever blasphemies the movie people would utter. "How would you like that done?" she asked Michael, though she was staring at Marion.

"Just knock the horns off and wipe its ass, honey," Marion said sweetly.

"I'm going back to Los Angeles," Michael said.

"Scarth said he'd keep you on until the end of the shoot."

"He can use one of the Italians."

Marion stared past him. She would be here for more than a week, bored, angry, and alienated. "Maybe I should use one as well."

Back in Los Angeles, Marion saw her opportunities narrowing. The extraordinary success of *The Big Parade* hadn't translated into anything for her. She had imagined a rise through the ranks to a position of influence, if not power, but now she was stalled, working as a minion. She deserved more, and was surrounded by people who deserved less. She knew her frustration was poisonous, that it had infected her life with Michael, which had stalled as well. She felt as if she was encased in amber, like a prehistoric insect. At work one day she had had a sobbing fit that went on for half an hour, a gulping heaving jag that she couldn't control and which frightened her.

Marion used to trace her finger along the scar on Michael's face, mapping his history, she said. But she had no real interest in history, even in what had happened the day before. She was one of those people who moved to California to obliterate the past, a habit she kept up with great skill and determination. Each moment disappeared, along with its consequences and guilt, replaced by the false hope of the present.

When Harry Shearling, a producer with Rayart Pictures, started courting her, Marion didn't mention Michael. Shearling had thinning sandy hair and wore tightly tailored double-breasted suits that presented a masculine silhouette. Rayart Pictures was a Poverty Row studio, a far cry from mighty MGM. It had taken over the old Selig Studio offices in Echo Park, a glum operation, but Harry understood the business. He could list the grosses of every major film released that year, and he studied Thalberg as if he were the Talmud. Harry was close to forty, too old to be a boy wonder, but he was determined. He talked about the national appetite for entertainment and how there was something inside everyone, whether they were William Randolph Hearst or Nanook of the North, that wanted stories. Movies, he told Marion, reaching for her hand in a calculated way, were a map of the American soul. Marion listened, her natural cynicism held slightly at bay. She knew Harry would never run MGM, but there was money to be made even at the fringes if you played the angles, and Harry looked like he could manage that. So as their lunches went on, his hand clutching hers lightly, he became more attractive, the light shining off his beatific scalp. They had sex in his office, which occupied a dusty corner of the building and looked onto a parking lot. She felt his flesh beneath his shirt and undershirt, which he kept on, small handfuls of unkneaded dough wherever she clutched. He stared to the side and laboured briefly, then showered her with grateful kisses and offered her a job as associate producer.

Driving out to Rayart Studios to meet Marion, Michael wondered what to expect. She was working on a dismal western that was being cranked out in a few weeks. They had been circling some kind of reconciliation. It was after nine when Michael got there, and the soundstage was empty. Crudely painted scenes of dramatic rock formations and garish sunsets filled one wall. The whole thing was being shot in the studio. Marion appeared at the far end of the cavernous space and walked across the concrete floor, the sound of her shoes echoing off the walls.

"Marion."

She was ten feet away when she pulled out the gun and fired it six times into Michael's chest. Her face was expressionless. She dropped the prop pistol and left the studio. Michael felt the percussion of the blanks and stood rooted, too stunned to move. The adrenalin coursed through his body in lightning bursts. A mural of a dying desert town stood in front of him, oversized and unconvincing, and he stared at it for fifteen minutes before walking out to his car.

WILDERNESS

1935

Marion and I were never divorced, but I never saw her again after she shot me. I left Los Angeles a month later, suddenly a foreigner. The sun bleached the city and it looked like a photograph that hadn't been developed properly. When Marion and I started out, we were full of hope. What couple isn't? You set out on this journey together, unmapped, an adventure. It was perfect for a while. And then we lost our way. An old story.

Billy Whitecloud lay mute, unshaven, a dusting of dark hairs on his upper lip. What will come of these sessions? Michael wondered. Will Billy rise up one day and blink his eyes and thank him for not giving up, like in some weepy movie? Or was this a kind of therapy for Michael, an audience that wouldn't give up his secrets, though there hadn't been many.

The Jazz Age was ending; all that postwar optimism had to go somewhere. Josephine Baker grinning as her breasts wobbled in black and white. But few people actually lived in the Jazz Age. They went to work and saved and had kids and got their Buicks stuck in the mud. They argued about baseball and went to church and had picnics and drank lemonade. And then the Depression hit.

You could see it on people's faces. In their homes you knew there was saved string and candle wax and pennies and coupons and a suspicion of good fortune. My mother had already seen starvation and had adopted the usual defences: She raised a few cattle, grew a garden, canned the excess, wasted nothing.

The Depression tested the faith of a lot of people, though it probably strengthened the faith of just as many. For one thing, the world looked like the Old Testament, at least around here. Dunstan O'Connell's ranch was blown out and dead, a foot of sand piled against the barn. It was eight miles south of here. The provincial inspector came by one day and tested his cattle, what remained of them, and found two of them were diseased. I remember getting up early and riding out to the coulee and we herded them into that natural pen, driving them down the incline. A dozen men, neighbouring ranchers who had the sense not to say anything, stood at the top of the small ridge, loading their rifles. The cattle were skittish and a few fell. O'Connell gave the sign and fired the first shot, and a dozen shots immediately followed. Dust rose as they stampeded in useless circles and dropped in heaps. They bellowed and panicked and we kept firing until every steer was down, and then searched for movement among the brown and white carpet and aimed for heads. I remember O'Connell staring down at the carnage. He was sixty-six and it would take three years of hard work and perfect weather to reclaim the land. He was finished and he stared at that lifeless mess and knew it. We carefully spread lime over that mess and rode back.

Dunstan bought my mother a radio in the thirties and she used to listen to Amos 'n' Andy, a show that came up from the United States about two negroes who were always getting into some kind of jam. It was her favourite show. She never laughed; she said she just liked the sound of their voices.

There was a family that lived a few miles south of us—the Clancys—a hard-luck clan. They came to town in 1906 on their way to Banff. Cochrane was quarantined then because of smallpox, and when they got off the train to get some air and stretch their legs the conductor wouldn't let them back on. Maybe contaminated, he said, wasn't going to take the chance. Clancy threw a fit but it didn't do him any good. Their bags were taken off and the family was stuck in a town of three hundred people. They never left.

Mary Clancy had an army surplus phone set attached to the fence near her house. It was hooked up to the barbed wire that went all the way to our place. We had a phone set too and my mother and Mary talked to each other along the barbed wire. The government had quit paying for phone lines because they blew down and were too expensive to repair and there weren't enough people out here to make it worth their while. You had to yell sometimes to be heard. It was mostly Mary yelling into the phone and my mother on the other end listening to her tales of Irish grief. They were a curious pair.

Mary's husband died of pneumonia in the winter of '32. They loaded him onto the wagon to take him into town but he was dead before they got there. It was thirty-five below. There were seven kids in that house. It was built on a hill and it took the west wind full force and in the winter it just blew right through the place. They put newspapers up on the walls as insulation. They'd gather papers from town and make their own paste and glue them to the walls, one on top of the other. They had a neighbour, a widower named Levant, a man in his sixties, living alone. One day he was at the Clancys', staring at those newspapers. There's a photograph of a cow standing on a railway track and he wanted to know what happens to that cow. He can't read, he's illiterate, not that unusual for the time. So he asks the eldest daughter to read the story to him. She starts reading, "A heifer belonging to Lucas Porter of Cremona wandered down the spur line last Tuesday" etc. This girl was maybe eighteen, she wasn't pretty but she had a beautiful voice, the kind of voice where you don't want the story to end. She reads him the whole story. Not much of a story but he's hanging on every word. He asks for another one, then another. He starts coming by twice a week and sits in the rocking chair as she reads the newspapers on the wall. They keep getting new ones to paste over the old ones. They might be three inches thick. He pays her a dollar each time. Men working as navvies made that in a twelve-hour day. It wasn't the news that kept him coming back; some of the papers were six months old. It was her voice. She'd read him a story about a man who had his thumb cut off at the Quigley sawmill, or a lost pig, or a calf that fell through the spring ice, floating downriver, its brown eyes staring up as though through a window. She read comics and cattle prices and wheat futures, and he lived for the sound of that voice.

During the Depression everyone talked politics. They beat the subject until it was bloody and useless, then brought it up again the next day. I guess we were hoping someone would come along with an answer, but no one ever did.

Mackenzie King was prime minister for twenty-two years and yet Willie (as he was known) was almost invisible. His reign was like a magic act where no one ever figured out where the lady vanished to. There were moments when I thought King had vanished as well; the magician's final trick. He was as placid as a bowl of porridge. Had we known his actual thoughts, we would have run for the hills, but that's probably true of most people. So we had a leader who didn't lead and we convinced ourselves that this was progress.

1

MACKENZIE KING, 1935

Physically, William Lyon Mackenzie King was ordinary, scrupulously, almost aggressively so, inclined to stoutness (who would have guessed at the athleticism of his youth?), his hair sparse and flattened onto a spherical head. He was staring at Mrs. Etta Wriedt of Detroit, a serious and slightly pinched woman whose prosaic face stared upward, studiously vacant, though her words came out in quick conversational rhythms. She was speaking the words of Sir Wilfrid Laurier, the former prime minister, dead for sixteen years. She reminded King of Laurier when the light was fading in him, his feminine beauty betraying him near the end. Laurier had been a great leader, possessed of an enviable charisma, a quality no one accused King of having.

There had been trouble at the last seance, and the unresponsiveness of the spirits was put down to a lack of receptiveness among those present (a lack of faith, really, and certainly King wasn't guilty of this). Or perhaps there had been a mysterious absorption of ectoplasm in the twilight. It happened on occasion, he was told. The spirits unable to communicate, like a static-filled phone line. The session before that had been so electric! From the grave Laurier praised King's loyalty (though he had also stressed that he must redouble his efforts to learn French).

—What is the best course, Wilfrid?

—The best course is to follow history, Mackenzie. History is a like a swift river. You can fight the current, but you rarely win. The Conservatives inherited the Depression, and they have become the Depression. People are afraid. They are looking for certainty.

—How can I give them that?

—You can't. Any certainty you utter may come back to haunt you. We can never be certain. But you can bring them calm.

—Will I be re-elected prime minister?

—You were predestined, answered the voice from beyond, coming from its resting place near the corseted sternum of Etta.

—Wilfrid, will I be loved?

King waited for the reply, patient with the spirits. Five silent minutes, Etta's expressionless face staring upward. Then, a faint sound of something. Trumpets, perhaps, thought King, ever hopeful.

"I'm afraid he's gone, Mr. King," Etta finally said, her face drained and pale.

Laurier was right; it wasn't a good time to be in power. The last five years had seen locusts and dust storms. The Nile turned to blood, frogs raining down, a darkness over Egypt. A million men without work. In Quebec, priests were charging fifty cents to say Mass. Out west, men were setting forest fires in order to get work putting them out. They were burning the wooden sidewalks on the prairies in winter to stay warm. The barter system had returned; rural doctors delivered babies in exchange for live chickens. And through this torment, men made alcohol out of potatoes in their kitchens. It was the colour of milk and made them blind and they sat on their porches and felt the seasons change against their skin while children spooned oatmeal into their slack mouths. Out in the relief camps, men were busy doing useless work, simply a way of quarantining their misery from the rest of the nation, keeping them hidden. All those men without women, a constant war between flesh and spirit, skirmishes that went on for months. King understood that battle: the eternal struggle.

What politician could save these men?

He would bide his time, consult the dead. His campaign slogan came in a vision, "King or Chaos!" He would bring a judicious stillness to the country, a determined lull. His rhetoric was as flat as a Presbyterian hymn; he roused no one. This was his gift, to keep the country unroused, to keep it from rising up against the impossibility of itself.

2

MICHAEL MOUNTAIN HORSE, ALBERTA, 1935

Michael's first ride was with a truck driver carrying a load of sallow horses, their bony frames visible through the wooden slats. The spring was dwarfed, unwilling to bring much life, and Michael looked at the wreckage of the prairies go by. A grey farmhouse sat abandoned, sandy soil drifting to the windows. There had been reports of topsoil ten thousand feet above the Atlantic Ocean, a black blizzard that moved a million tons of earth across the continent, the last grains taken out to sea.

The driver talked about women the whole trip. "Thing about women is, they like a man with the gift of the gab," he said. "I got regular work, and I got the gift, and that makes me Rudolph Valentino."

Michael looked at him, maybe sixty, a short man with an honest homely face and small hands that gripped the large wheel like a child's. "What they got, most of them, is loneliness. Got it like the Spanish flu. Some of them have husbands. That makes them twice as lonely. You know why?"

Michael stared at the brown fields. Unhelpful clouds scudded east, dust swirling in the dry wind. "Why?"

"Their husbands are in the relief camps or on the railway. They're gone and there's a hole to fill. They need someone to come along, tell them they're swell, show them you know what they feel."

"And what do they feel?" Michael asked.

"Alone, mister. Every day is hard and there ain't any relief."

"You're relief."

"That's it. They're sorry to see me go. I get in my truck, they go back to their kitchens and cry in their aprons. Some of those gals, they learned some tricks somewhere. Take me all day and a chalkboard to explain."

Michael had heard versions of this story from dozens of men. The whole world was filled with lonely housewives, all of them panting and inventive, and judging by the storytellers, not too choosy. How was it that Michael never encountered them?

"Good-looking boy like you. You don't have work, don't have a girl. Some times we live in."

"If I had a girl, I wouldn't tell you," Michael said.

"You'd be smart," the man said, laughing. "They get tired of good looks. It's a scientific fact. Me, I make an impression."

Michael stared at the hair growing out of the truck driver's ears, his erratically shaven face, grey skin drooping at his jaw. He thought about Marion. Love is a flame, they say. Love is a woman with a gun. Love, you murdered my heart.

The truck stopped outside of Gleichen to let Michael out, the driver implying with a broad wink that he had a romantic liaison to attend to. Michael walked along the road in the spring heat. A family slowly passed him, their small house on wheels, being pulled by four draught horses, the caravan moving only slightly faster than Michael on foot. Michael guessed from their clothes that they were Ukrainian. A girl, maybe twelve, stared at him from the side window for fifteen minutes. Michael waved to her but she didn't wave back. Another team pulled a few pieces of farm equipment and Michael supposed they were heading north, to where the drought hadn't caught hold, though the land was unbroken and less arable there.

Michael walked until ten that night, the red glow faint behind him, and then lay down in a copse of elm trees that were half a mile off the road and slept. In the morning he ate the last of the bread he had taken with him and hesitantly drank from a slow, small stream, the water tasting faintly of wood. He walked until noon and then stopped at a gas station. A man pulled up in a Model T that was so covered in grasshoppers it looked like a living thing. The man offered Michael a dollar if he'd clean off the hoppers, and he spent an hour with a rag and a bucket of kerosene before he got them all.

Michael walked for three days, sleeping outside and occasionally taking a fish from a stream with the line he had. Outside Brooks he set his bedroll down beside a rusted truck that sat in a field and slept. When he woke up, the sun was a muted glow over the flat horizon. He walked east until late afternoon and then approached a farm that was a half mile off the road. The white paint had almost completely faded and there was a stain on the west wall the colour of tobacco where grasshoppers had congregated and left their sticky juice.

The soil outside the farmhouse was patchy and eroded but it wasn't buried in sand like some places Michael had seen. As he got closer he saw a field behind the house that was a lush green. It seemed like a mirage. He hadn't seen anything like it on the prairies. It was on a slight downward slope behind the house and barn, hidden from the road, hoarded.

Michael walked up to it and felt something like awe. When he stooped down to examine the miraculous crop, he saw that it was Russian thistle, a weed, an extraordinary field of useless green.

"Come to see the miracle, mister?"

Michael turned to see a woman who looked to be about forty but was probably closer to thirty. The Depression scoured faces. Her skin was raw, as if scrubbed with a stiff brush, and she had a man's hands. She was pretty though, or at least capable of prettiness. So many faces were occupied with more pressing wants. Her eyes were a pale blue.

"I was wondering what could grow like this."

"There's the devil's trick for you. Green as paradise and useless as sin."

"I'm also wondering if you have any work," Michael said.

She looked at him, assessing—he wasn't the first to stop by—then looked past him to the barn and the slouching fence. "I got lots of work, mister," she said. "What I don't have is money to pay you for it." She gave him another hard look. "I can feed you," she said simply.

Together they stared out to the property. "Tools are in the barn," she said. "That might be as good a place as any to start."

Michael retrieved the tools and laid them out on a piece of stiff canvas. There were some grey timbers outside the barn and a few pieces of odd-sized wood inside. He spent three hours patching the barn where the boards had rotted through, straightening bent rusty nails on a stone and reusing them. As the sky darkened into heavy blue, clouds collecting in the west, the woman came out with a bowl of thin stew and some bread and introduced herself as Hannah. Her husband had gone off looking for work and maybe he'd found it or maybe he'd found something else. He'd been gone six months, she said.

After he ate, Michael took his bedroll to the barn. In the morning Hannah gave him some tasteless porridge in a shallow bowl. The heavy clouds from last night had come to nothing. The house was plain inside, with a few photographs on a small varnished table that had a tissue of lace on it. There was a photograph of a balding, unsmiling man who Michael assumed was her husband. There was a piano, and when Michael asked if she played, she said no.

He worked for three weeks, repairing what he could, working the garden, spreading poison for the hoppers. In the evenings they sat on the sofa in the parlour and one evening she undid his shirt buttons and pulled her dress over her head. Her breasts were heavy and her skin was white and milky and shone almost. They made love on the sofa and afterwards she got up and walked naked over to the piano and sat down and played "Flying Down to Rio," singing the words in a sweet tenor. Michael asked for another song.

"You just get the one," she said, smiling.

There was a knock at the door and for a moment Michael thought it might be her mirthless husband, though he realized it would be odd for a man to knock on his own door. He scrambled into his clothes and Hannah slipped on her dress and answered the door. It was still light, and in the doorway were two boys, maybe ten and six, obviously brothers. They each had the same homemade haircut, and each one carried a pail filled with dead gophers.

"They're a nickel apiece," the older boy said, the smaller one just staring ahead. Both their faces had the dark cast that came with strong winds blowing dirt into their pores and a monthly bath.

"A nickel," Hannah said.

"Yes ma'am, killed fresh today."

Michael wondered how far the boys had walked. The nearest farm was two miles away, but they would have come farther than that. Michael felt a light breeze trying to move the dead air.

"Good for stewing," the boy said. "Or frying. You can fry them up."

Hannah looked at the two boys and said, "Give me one pailful."

"I can let you have a better price on the second pail," the boy said, not relishing carrying them all the way back home.

"Let me see how this first one works," Hannah said. She went into the kitchen and came back with a tiny purse, counting out forty-five cents for nine gophers.

The boy thanked her and he and his brother walked off down the road.

Hannah cut up the gophers and rolled them in flour with some salt and pepper and heated the skillet. She served them with some bread and they sat down. From the radio came the folksy tone of Bible Bill Aberhart, a preacher who was running for premier. "So now, radio friends," Aberhart said, "let us sit close to the radio and get a little more friendly with each other." He paused to let everyone pull their chairs closer. "You remain in the Depression because of a shortage of purchasing power imposed by the banking system. This is a wealthy province, no question, yet you don't have access to that wealth. I am challenging you today, then, to do two things. *First*, to commit yourself to the God of Heaven. *Second*, ask God to maintain the prices of grain and livestock this year. Let us ask *Him* to help make our religion practical."

Michael had seen Aberhart preach once. The founder of the Prophetic Bible Institute was a stout bald man with large liver-coloured lips, an unlikely-looking radical. His plan to pull everyone out of the Depression was to print money, a childish, magical solution. But who didn't love magic? Especially in these times.

"That holy roller is going to get himself elected," Hannah said. "People get desperate enough, they'll believe anything. I hope he prints some money for me." She stared at her plate. "My God this gopher is awful."

On the weekend they took a picnic down to the small creek that trickled through her land. It had dried up in '34, she said, disappeared without a trace. The heavy snows had put a little moisture in the ground and it was running now, though barely. They unpacked in the shade of some trees and laid the lunch on the blanket. They ate bread with two trout Michael had caught and drank homemade beer they'd gotten from a Scandinavian neighbour. Afterwards, they made love.

"Do you think God can see us?" she asked when they had finished.

"I hope not. You'd have some explaining to do."

"My mother used to say that's why there was so much wickedness in cities. It was because people were hidden away in alleys and basements and they could get away with anything. Out here God can see everything and people don't stray as much."

"I don't know what kind of God can't see into a basement," Michael said.

"The kind worshipped by farmers, I guess."

"Maybe farmers are just too tired to sin."

"Oh, they find the energy somewhere," Hannah said. "You scratch hard enough you'll find the seven deadlies all across these plains. And worse. Sloth is about the only sin they don't claim. You hear whisperings. Someone heard something about someone. A hundred rumours. Then we all get together at church and look around and wonder how true any of it is. That's human nature. It doesn't give you much hope to lift us out of this mess. And God isn't helping. But He'll get tired of punishing us at some point."

They lay on the blanket staring up at the unyielding blue sky.

"You know my husband Horace wasn't always the way he is," Hannah said, after a silence. "You don't start out farming already defeated. That comes later."

"You think he'll be back?" Michael asked.

"I suspect so. I doubt it's a woman if that's what you're thinking. He's a practical man, Horace, not much for romance. He's probably wearing the same suit of clothes he was wearing when he left, hasn't found but a little work and he's too ashamed to show himself. This farm was my father's, one of the first ones in the area. Horace wasn't feeling too successful before all this and he's feeling less so now. But I think he'll be back. There'll be better times."

They were still naked and Michael stood up, the breeze unfamiliar on his exposed skin. He pulled Hannah up and they slow danced naked, which felt more sinful than sex. "Do you know why Presbyterians disapprove of sex?" Michael asked, her head nuzzled in his shoulder.

"No."

"They're afraid it'll lead to dancing."

She laughed and they danced for a few minutes, made love again, and then fell asleep on the blanket.

Michael woke up to a strange light. The sun was red in the west but storm clouds rolled toward them, an unholy combination. Michael woke Hannah up and she stared at the black sky and the red behind it. "For our sins," she said. The storm looked like it was still a few miles away but the wind had picked up and it was closing fast. The rain would help the crops and the garden, and anything that kept the soil down, even if only for a few days, was welcome. As they neared the farmhouse, the sky was dark with glints of red. Michael hadn't seen anything like it. Then he felt the first sting on his face. They were still three hundred yards from the house and he yelled at Hannah to get inside but his voice disappeared in the wind. Hannah turned around and felt the same sting and instantly understood. It wasn't a thunderstorm; it was a thousand tons of topsoil being driven by a ferocious wind. Some of the soil was essentially sand and it picked up the red sunset and reflected it, like a blood mist descending on the land. They ran for the house, the dark grains swirling in small eddies and mixing with dust that was briefly suspended then swept east in a fury. It felt like sandpaper on the back of Michael's neck. By the time they got to the door, the storm was on them and it was hard to breathe. Michael pulled his shirt up to cover his mouth. They ran inside and quickly closed the door, and Michael raced through the house closing the windows; he could feel the grit under his feet on the wooden floors. He sat on the couch and watched the colours shift in the cloud, red and black and grey that billowed up a mile or more, symphonic in their movement, strangely beautiful.

It took a week to get the house clean and repair the damage. Michael thought he could feel Horace getting closer somehow, working up his nerve to come home. He thought Hannah felt it too. What would that house be like in January with eighteen hours of darkness and the thermometer reading forty below, the wind moving through the parlour. When he left, there weren't any tears. Hannah stood in the doorway and waved to him. She was holding one of the homemade dolls she had in her bedroom and she took its hand and waved it too.

Michael returned to Calgary, getting a ride from a sullen farmer who drove wordlessly for three hours before letting him out on Eleventh Avenue. The city's sandstone buildings were solid and ornate and it looked like a desert city conjured from a children's book. On the train tracks a freight sat with a few hundred men lounging on top of the cars. A banner nailed to a boxcar read ON TO OTTAWA. Michael asked a man in an ill-fitting pinstriped suit what was going on. He told him they had come from Vancouver, hundreds of them, on railcars, twenty-three hours over the mountains. They were going to ride two thousand miles on the rails to the nation's capital and then march straight up to those Parliament Buildings and say their piece to the prime minister.

"Mr. Richard B-for-Bastard Bennett will listen to us. You wanna believe that. He ain't going to have a choice."

Michael worked his way through the crowd, mostly refugees from Bennett's work camps, he guessed. They flowed through downtown toward the river, and in Bow River Park they laid out their bedrolls and some of the men walked tentatively into the river to bathe, bracing against its glacier-fed June cold.

Michael sat down beside a man who was eating beans out of a can. He might have been in his late twenties, Michael guessed, though he looked older, a big slope-shouldered man with reddish hair wearing a mismatched suit who introduced himself as Dusty.

"I don't figure the prime minister aims to let this train get all the way to his front porch," Dusty said.

"You think he'll call in the army?" Michael asked.

"He'll call in something. That's for sure."

A wooden stage was in the park and Michael could see three negroes setting something up on it. A banner was stretched across two posts at the back of the stage. KNIGHTS OF HARLEM, it read.

"What he does, see, if he's smart," Dusty started. "What he does is, he blows up the train."

"Blows it up."

"Damn right. He blows it up when it's on a bridge maybe. It's rigged to look like an accident. Then Bennett, see, he has a funeral for a thousand dead men and he says how these fine souls were taken by God and maybe he squeezes out a few tears. The papers get a picture of him and he gets two things—one, he's rid of us, and two, he looks good doin' it. Suddenly he's God's own angel weeping for a thousand men who smelled like dead cats headed for his parlour."

Dusty rolled a cigarette. He was filled with the wisdom of the road, the repeated lore of men who had nothing but stories to occupy themselves.

"You watch," Dusty said. "Bennett is sitting right now in that government house figuring ways to get rid of us."

The Knights of Harlem took the stage, a saxophone, banjo, guitar, trumpet, and four men who sang. The instruments lurched into step and the singers began marching in place.

"Black as coal," Dusty observed. "I hope they can sing some."

The Knights of Harlem high-stepped into their first song and the singers wagged their fingers in unison and sang through oversized smiles.

It was after midnight when the men began to get into their bedrolls. Michael stared up at Cassiopeia, the vain queen. He could feel himself drawn to this endeavour. It was partly the train, the promise of movement in these stagnant days. He slept with his hand in his pocket, clutching the nine dollars that was there.

In the morning the men straggled to the river and washed and drank, kneeling on the stones. Michael put his head underwater and let the river flow around him, then stood up and ran his hands through his hair. He started walking toward the rail yard and Dusty pulled up beside him.

"They ain't going to blow it between here and Regina," Dusty said. "My guess is somewhere east of Winnipeg, north shore of Superior. I bet Bennett's already got someone working on a statue for the fallen men. So I figure we're safe until Winnipeg."

"That's a comfort," Michael said.

"You goddamn right it is. Those men stay on past the Lakehead are done for." Dusty scrambled a bit to keep up with Michael. "You got a woman?"

Michael didn't say.

"Me, I got woman troubles," Dusty said, then paused, hoping Michael would want to know all about them. "Two women on the coast both trying to horsecollar me. They got me like TB but I ain't the settlin' kind." Michael was looking at the York Hotel. A few dandies lingered outside smoking their morning cigars and watching the hordes fill the streets like water, moving south toward the train.

When they got to the boxcar, Michael instinctively went on top. The sun was high, there would be a breeze, and it was harder to talk up there. Inside, they'd be crowded like cattle and a thousand stories would start. Stories of hard luck, remarkable skills, abandoned women who looked like movie stars. The train shunted east, pulling slowly through downtown and the small houses of the east side, then suddenly onto prairie. The farms looked as if a fire had gone through. In three hours they approached Medicine Hat and there was sand blowing in the wind, a taste of grit. He wondered how Hannah was doing and whether Horace had come back. Lying on his side, he watched the prairie go by, whorls of dead land collapsed under the June sun.

In Regina, they camped at the Exhibition Grounds and it was agreed that three hundred men would go to Market Square on Dominion Day and hold a fundraising rally. The rest would stay put. Too big a presence would intimidate the citizens. Their biggest sympathizers were women. An army would frighten them.

Michael walked to Market Square with Dusty and a man named Eberle, short and wiry with a few days of hard bristle on his face. It was dry and the heat had already settled in on everything.

"The worst job I had," Dusty said, "was hauling coal. In winter it'd freeze the balls off a brass monkey. So cold I had to walk with the horses. Sit on the wagon and you'd freeze up solid. Pick up the coal west of Taber, take half the day just to get it to town. Walking around black as negroes from the coal dust. I hauled ice in the summer and that was a damn sight better. You're loading ice into some woman's icebox. She gives you a glass of lemonade. Maybe she tickles your feather. So hot in August, you don't know if you done it or not."

"I worked as a navvy in northern Ontario," Eberle said. "Laying track fourteen hours a day for a dollar. You'd buy your boots from the company, your gloves, food, bed. End of the month be lucky to have ten bucks. Swinging those hammers. Jesus, the blackflies would drive you mad. Taking pieces of you all day you'd wonder what was going to be left but too damn tired to care. The straw boss we had was mean as a snake. He'd get after you, bend right down in your face, tell you to swing that hammer or go back to the goddamn farm. He was on this one fellow, big Scandahoovian, hardly spoke English. But the boss just had it in for this guy. Be on his case all the live long. One day, it's July, bugs are on us, heat something fierce and this big blond Scandahoovian has got the boss in his face too, leaning right in there yelling some fool thing. The Swede finally blows a gasket. He lets go with that hammer, and you swing that thing all day you can hit a dime nine times out of ten with your eyes closed. Drive a spike into granite with a single shot. He brings up that hammer and drives it right through the boss's forehead. Sinks in like it was a pile of manure. Then he just walks off into the bush. We're all standing there staring, boss is lying on the ties, deader than Christmas in July. What we do is, we all take a break. Get a little water, roll a smoke. Christ we earned it and you don't get many chances like that and not a one of us missed the sound of that man's jaws flapping. We sat in the shade and played cards until dinner while the boss lay there on the track with that hammer sticking in his head, the flies gathering. Never saw a cop. Never saw that Scandahoovian neither."

"That was the worst," Dusty agreed.

"It was the worst for that straw boss. But that wasn't the worst job, no sir. Bad as it was." Eberle took off his hat and wiped his brow and stared up at the sun. His face had a glaze of sweat on it, and looked polished, the colour of teak. "The worst was the killing floor at the Burns slaughterhouse. You're standing in blood all day. Lord help you if you fall. Jesus, it's ugly work. You kill something all day long. It don't matter they're dumb as hell and headed for your plate—it's one living thing after another and none a them are looking to go quietly. They ain't the smartest mammal on the ark but the whole place smells of death. It's in their nose. They don't need to form the thought. Every animal understands death."

"But it was a paycheque," Dusty said.

"It was a paycheque."

"It kept you and yours."

"It kept me," Eberle said. "The wife run off. It hardens you, that work, and I'd come home with blood on me, looking like John Dillinger and smelling like death and not a kind word for anyone on this earth. I guess she was within her rights."

"I'd kill for a paycheque now," Dusty said. "I'd kill a steer anyway."

"I'd kill just about anything," Eberle said, then turned to Michael. "How about you?"

"I worked for the King of England," Michael said.

Dusty laughed. "Well, King of bloody England. Now there's a job I'd like. Someone offers me the job of king it's where do I fucking sign."

"Pancakes every morning," Eberle said.

"And beer," Dusty said.

"Whisky."

"I'd shoot ducks from the car," Dusty said. "Pay my wife to drive it."

"You'd have to pay someone to be your wife first," Eberle said. "I'd sit in that castle in my long johns and play cards till I was too drunk, then get the butler to take my hand."

"You'd get all the skirt you want, that job."

Eberle turned to Michael. "So we're talking to royalty practically."

"Edward, the king in waiting," Michael said. "He had a place by Pekisko. I took care of his horses."

"What kind of king he going to make, you figure?"

"The kind who can't find his ass with both hands and a map," Michael said.

The men moved in orderly bunches, conversation leaking out, dust bouncing behind them.

"We get to Ottawa, Bennett's going to have to make a stand one way or the other," Eberle said.

"We ain't getting to Ottawa," Dusty said, spelling out his theory about blowing up the train.

"I don't think he'll blow it," Eberle said. "I figure Winnipeg is where he makes his move. No shortage of police there and an army barracks if it comes to it."

"Or Regina," Michael said. "He makes his stand here. It's farther away. Not so many newspapers. He uses the RCMP. He rounds us up and sends us all to relief camps on the coast, only they're closer to prison camps this time out."

"They were close to prison camps last time out," Eberle said.

They were sweating when they got to Market Square. Maybe a thousand people were there, some of them waiting to hear what they had to say, some of them, Michael sensed, just looking for distraction. There weren't any police, which seemed strange. There had been militant talk from the government, stressing the need for law and order, for soldiers if necessary. A few men stood up and made speeches about equality and fat cats and socialist hope. The air was dry and still. It felt like the city was in suspension. Michael was midway back in the crowd, and the stillness made him nervous. The evening felt poised, waiting to break.

At eight o'clock, a shrill whistle blew and forty or so Royal Canadian Mounted Police spilled out of three large vans. A garage door opened and two dozen Regina police rushed out. From around the corner, RCMP on horseback trotted through the crowd. Some plainclothes police arrested the men who were on the speaker's platform. Michael instinctively looked for cover, edging toward the surrounding streets. In the square, they'd be cut down. The RCMP on horseback had clubs and were swinging them. A few of the police had their revolvers out and some shots were fired above their heads.

People moved in waves of panic, seeking escape in undulating shapes that formed and then dispersed. Michael broke away from the pack down a side street, then darted into an industrial yard filled with rusting, unfamiliar machines. A man was stripping one of the machines, tearing it apart with a wrench. "Tar-maker," he said. "Grab some of them pieces." The man worked quickly and within ten minutes he had a pile of metal to be used as weapons, bushings and bolts to throw, longer pieces of steel to wield as swords. Two dozen men were in the yard, fashioning weapons from whatever they could. Others found rakes or hoes in garages near the square. Michael heard shots, the dull pop of the police revolvers. "God, they going to kill us all," the man said. He spun his wrench in a counter-clockwise motion and tugged at a steel spindle and gave it to Michael. Michael tested its weight against the air, then ran toward the lane. Crouched behind the fence, he could see into the square. A dozen bodies lay there, moving with a slight limbic twitch. Four policemen were carrying a man, one on each limb. A fifth came up, blood streaming down his face. In the lane a man swung a hoe that caught a cop across the forehead. Another policeman came around the corner and shot the man, who fell down and crawled ten feet.

Michael followed the laneway and came out on Thirteenth Avenue and went east toward Osler. Now hundreds of men were moving through the alleys and streets in packs. Michael saw Eberle standing on Twelfth, taking a stone out of his pocket. Two policemen rushed him and Eberle let go with the stone and hit one of them but the other one was on him, flailing with his billy stick. Michael rushed up and swung his steel spindle and the policeman fell, bleeding from his head. Michael knelt down and saw that Eberle's skull had been caved in near his eye. He was rocking back and forth, his mouth open. The policeman was holding his head, blood leaking. Michael couldn't do anything for either of them.

He spent an hour circling around to Rose Street, where a pitched battle was going on, policemen firing their revolvers at men who were throwing bricks and stones and any piece of metal they could lay hands on. Tear gas carried on the evening breeze. Broken glass littered the sidewalk and Michael saw a dozen typewriters lying broken in the street. He turned south on Halifax and saw two RCMP riding toward him. He ducked into an alley and sprinted, then went into a garage and sat on its dirt floor in the half-light, his breath coming out in sawing gasps. His eyes adjusted to the darkness and he saw a man sitting against the wall near the corner. One side of his face was dark gore. He held a rag over one eye and with the other he looked at Michael.

"They ain't going to stop, you know," the man said. "They got the blood lust in them now and they don't know how to quit."

"I imagine you're right," Michael said. Those RCMP must have been sitting in the vans for an hour or more, he thought. It would have been stifling in there. They came out hard and almost overwhelmed the crowd in that first rush.

"They ain't no issue now," the man said. "No law, no order. It's just kill the first thing you get your sights on."

"We can't stay here," Michael said.

"We go out there, we'll get cut down sure."

"If we stay we'll be cornered. Out there we have options."

"I don't think options is anything I got," the man said. "This one eye's gone or near enough. I figure I wait until they killed enough, maybe it gets quiet. I go out now, they'll just shoot me."

"If we can get back to the Exhibition Grounds, we'll be safe. They won't follow us there. They don't have the manpower. They don't want a war."

The man thought about this. "I don't know how good I can move."

Michael heard a door slam and a shot fired. He heard yelling no more than twenty yards away, and the sound of wood splintering. They were kicking in doors. Michael put his ear to the wall and heard the whinny of a horse and two shots. There was scuffling and yelling and then silence. Michael waited for another sound, like he and Stanford had on that roof, but there wasn't any and he fell asleep sitting up against a stud.

When he woke up, the other man was gone. He ventured outside. It was early morning and the sun was rising pale and tentative to the east. He walked down the laneways to Market Square, which was littered with debris. A newsie stood beside a stack of newspapers. "Biggest story ever to hit town, mister, yours for a nickel," the kid said. Michael looked at the front page, which said there were hundreds of injuries and one death. The police claimed thirty-nine injuries, many of them grievous, they said. A million dollars in damage, though Michael suspected that most of those numbers were either guesses or political calculations. The paper said a dead horse was found in the alley behind Dewdney Street with a slogan painted on its side but didn't say what it was.

AWAY

1936–1939

⤬

Before the Regina Riot we sent a man to Ottawa—Slim Evans—
to negotiate with the prime minister. Evans was a union man,
though he'd stolen union funds and been caught at it. Maybe not
the ideal negotiator. Prime Minister Bennett was a wealthy man
who spent his evenings answering all the letters people sent him. At
first they'd asked him to end the Depression, but faith in govern-
ment had disappeared and by the time Evans went to see him,
people were asking him for a new coat, or three dollars, or ten
pounds of flour. Bennett told them to buck up, the worst was over.
Bennett feared communism. Most people did, and they were
probably right to. Not many of the men in Regina were commu-
nists, but revolution comes from hunger and they were hungry.
Bennett told Evans they'd bring the law on him and Evans told
Bennett he wasn't fit to be head of a Hottentot village. So much for
negotiation.

When things go bad, men turn on each other; your own country
comes after you with a billy club. I wasn't a communist but I went

to Spain anyway. The whole world seemed adrift and maybe I was looking for purpose. The Spanish Civil War was billed as Good vs. Evil. But they all are, aren't they. It's where Stanford would have gone, though maybe for different reasons.

Part of the reason I went was Norman Bethune, a Canadian doctor who went over and wrote about his experience in the newspapers. Spain seemed like something concrete, and Bethune was a hero. But when you get close to anything, it looks much different. From five thousand miles away, communism looked like a brotherhood of man; up close it looked like three drunks fighting over a bottle.

1

NORMAN BETHUNE, MADRID, 1936

King or Chaos, that Hobson's choice. King had won, but chaos still ruled, Norman Bethune thought. Politics was a cesspool you threw money and principles into. As for his personal life, well it had always been chaos, hadn't it? The divorce from Frances (not once, but twice), his love for Marian. Married Marian. Perhaps he needed torment. There were men who did, God knows, and Bethune came from a long line of them.

Bethune was a doctor, a brilliant one—though what doctor, no matter how incompetent, was not brilliant in his own mind? A revolutionary in both medicine and politics. With his mobile blood transfusion unit, he would change the nature of triage. Outside, the Ford station wagon Bethune had bought in London held the gear, the Electrolux refrigerator that ran on kerosene, the autoclave, incubator, vacuum bottles, blood flasks, drip bottles, Froud syringe, microscope haemocytometers. On the side of the car was painted "Service canadien de transfusion sanguine à Madrid." And what better country for his experiments than Spain, with its ancient blood-mystique.

The fifteen-room flat in Madrid where he was billeted had eight thousand books, gold brocade curtains, and Aubusson carpets. It had formerly been occupied by a German diplomat who had fled to Germany to embrace fascism at its source.

When Bethune arrived in Spain he was detained and questioned by authorities because he had a moustache. War is filled with absurdities. In London he had ordered a half-dozen monogrammed silk shirts, deliciously inappropriate, but he was against all convention, even socialist fashion.

"Why are you dressed as a fascist?" the man said, as if he was a famous detective. "Why do you favour a moustache?"

"Why are you an idiot?" Bethune answered, his response thankfully untranslated. So he sat, looking less like a fascist than a Hollywood actor, trying to convince his accuser that he was on his side. But the bureaucrat was filled with the hot stupid blood of war, his childish self-importance suddenly dangerous. God save us from these fools.

He could feel Spain fading already. He had lost Canada, he thought. A man without a country and without love. How do you lose a country? The same way you lose a woman: inattention, misunderstanding, the passion becoming complacency. Maybe Russia would be his next love. Russia, that great imperfect woman giving birth to an ideology. She

sat splayed, one leg wet from the Barents Sea, the other
tickling Germany, and out of Moscow in a rush of pain and
blood came the Communists. Birth is always a beautiful and
ugly sight to behold, filled with agony. Grotesque, absurd,
magnificent, sublime. The attendants in Russia had been so
busy keeping the baby alive they hadn't cleaned up the mess
and this mess offended those timid souls who failed to see
beyond the violence of birth. Creation is not and never has
been a genteel gesture. It is rude and by its nature revolutionary, but this emergent spirit is the most heroic to appear
since the Reformation. To deny it is to deny our faith in man.
Though how much faith do I have? Bethune wondered. *Less now
than when I visited Russia two years ago.*

His attachment to Canada had been made more tenuous
by the election of Mackenzie King, an ass, a squat receptacle
of indecision and political expediency. The whole country
was hovering over an idea but wasn't ready to land, and the
complacency irked Bethune. The world was being redefined;
fascism was on the rise, capitalism was dying. It was time to
act.

At 6 P.M. the Junkers bombed the city. There was no
defence; the 250-kilo loads sank through the roofs of houses
and apartment buildings and exploded in basements,
bringing the structures down. It was a lottery, one place as
good as another. At midnight, Bethune left for the hospital
accompanied by an armed guard. It was dark and he heard
gunshots, though it was difficult to tell how far away they
were. They drove with the lights off through devastated
streets. Franco said he wouldn't leave a stone standing,
though they hadn't bombed the area where Bethune was

staying (the Westmount of Madrid, as he wrote Marian). They would want that for themselves.

The Palace Hotel had been turned into a hospital and the operating theatre was the cavernous dining room with its high ceiling, gold-framed mirrors, and huge crystal chandeliers. All that glass would be a problem in the event of a bomb, Bethune thought. To keep the interior dark, small spotlights illuminated operations. The small points of light reminded him of campfires in the woods around Gravenhurst where he'd grown up, cooking fish over the fire.

Bethune strode in, the Spanish assistants trailing with the equipment. There was a man lying on a stretcher and a doctor gestured to start with him. Bethune pricked the man's finger and applied one drop each of Serum II and Serum III to see how his red blood cells agglutinated. The man was French, in shock, and anemic. Bethune injected novocaine over the vein in the bend of his elbow, then cut and inserted a small glass cannula to run the blood in. He gave him 500 cc's of preserved blood that had been warmed in a bedpan of hot water and a saline solution of five percent glucose. Some colour returned to the man's face, and Bethune moved on to the next patient.

He did six more transfusions and at four o'clock got back into his car, sprawling exhausted in the back seat. Madrid is the centre of the world, he thought. What happens here will determine the future for the next century. It was the centre of the world in part because they had no news from outside. What was Marian doing at this moment? The car charged through the dark empty streets at alarming speed. He wondered if Marian was in bed with someone. With her husband, Frank? Or someone else? What would be worse?

In February, Bethune left Barcelona in the large Renault truck he had bought in Paris. Hazen Sise was driving. An architect from Montreal, he had worked with Le Corbusier in France and gotten caught up in the cause. The wind was up, driving wisps of dust along the road. Bethune saw the first of them west of Almería, a few hundred people walking wearily. German and Italian tanks and troops had taken Málaga, and its 150,000 residents were trying to make Almería. It would be a five-day walk for the healthy, but there was no food and they were being bombed by Junkers. The few hundred grew into thousands, the strongest at the front of the line, the weakest at the back. Many of the children were barefoot; some wore only a shirt. Men carried children on their backs. They dragged pots and pans in canvas sacks.

At first Bethune insisted that they push slowly through the refugees to deliver the blood to the front lines, but it soon became clear that both Málaga and probably Motril had fallen and no one was sure where the front was anymore. Bethune told Sise to turn the truck around. Immediately, mothers pushed children upon them, pressing sick, parched faces to the windows, their bodies wrapped in bloodstained rags. A woman of sixty had monstrously distorted legs, her varicose veins bleeding openly. These people had walked for two nights, hiding during the day from the bombers. Where did you hide 150,000 people on a plain? They were exhausted, old men lying by the side of the road, embracing death.

Bethune concentrated on families. Who to take? The child dying of dysentery, the ones without shoes, their feet swollen to twice their normal size? A hundred miles of misery. The largest exodus of modern times: families, goats, mules, people wailing for lost relatives. Bethune used his natural authority to advantage, assessing need, taking the children from the mothers and lifting them into the truck. He let Sise drive almost forty children and a few mothers back to Almería while he stayed on the road, walking with the people, doing whatever he could.

Medicine is the study of death, Bethune thought, though it disguises itself as a force for life. It is rooted in decay: gangrene's advance, a wasting cancer, the slow choking of tuberculosis. As a child, Bethune had killed a bird. What boy hadn't, especially where he lived, in a small town, close to nature? He watched it decompose, his first medical experiment. Every day brought subtle change. It shrank. One day he arrived to a mound of maggots. Then only feathers, and finally bone. In the spring, there was nothing. Claimed by the earth. Burial was superfluous. We are all claimed, we all come to dust.

In the 1920s Bethune lived in Detroit, working as a doctor, married to Frances. They had a bright, airy apartment, ate well, entertained as a doctor should. The city was wealthy and bustling with immigrants who had come to work in the car industry. When they got married, Bethune told Frances, "I can make your life a misery, but I'll never bore you—it's a promise." She wasn't bored, and her life was indeed a misery; they argued about money and sex, spending too much of one and not having enough of the other. She left him and filed for divorce. When he received the telegram he wrote back, congratulating her and proposing marriage. Had he stayed in Detroit, had Frances stayed with him, perhaps he'd be living in a mansion among the automobile executives, attending the symphony, eating roast beef. Instead he was in Spain, tending to the world's misery. The

Depression had ground people down, morally, spiritually, and war was its natural end. Spain knew this, and Canada would, in time.

The narrow coastal road was cut into the cliffs and these were vulnerable not just from the planes but from boats that lobbed shells along the route. When Sise came back with the empty truck, Bethune chose the largest families and packed them together, unwilling to separate them. For three days and nights Sise made trips to Almería, dropping refugees at the hospital of the Socorro Rojo Internacional. A scene of unbearable suffering and tension.

When he finally got to Almería, Bethune spent ten hours doing blood transfusions and triage, and when he went outside in the night for a break he heard the familiar whine. There were thousands sleeping in the street, huddled in packs, queuing for the milk and bread given out by the Provincial Committee for the Evacuation of Refugees. The bomb hit and a wall fell onto the street. Another hit a block away and Bethune saw the carpet of bodies heave. He ran toward them, the half-second of shocked silence now filled with shrieks and moaning. He picked up a dead child. She had no mark on her, as limp as a doll. His head was filled with hatred, the rest of him deadened by fatigue. He laid the girl down and attended to a man missing an arm.

In March, past Alcalá de Henares, the road was clogged with mule trains, donkey carts, bread wagons, lines of soldiers, and tanks. A cold wind came down from the snowy Guadarrama range. They were carrying the refrigerator and ten pint bottles of preserved blood in a wire basket.

Approaching the hospital, Bethune saw stretchers streaked with blood propped against the wall and a man cleaning them with a wet broom. Inside, Bethune saw Jolly, the inappropriately named New Zealand doctor.

"I've got a man here, can't make out his nationality," Jolly said. "He's not responding to any language. Hit by a bomb. One hand is gone, have to amputate the other. Blind as well. Can you give him a transfusion?"

Bethune hovered over the patient, a large man whose head was swaddled in bloody bandages. He heated the blood to body temperature and looked at the label—"blood number 695, Donor number 1106, Group IV, collected Madrid 6th March"—part of his elaborate collection scheme. "It's okay," Bethune said. "No hemolysis." In five minutes they moved to the next patient.

They spent the next eighteen hours on their feet, working with the wounded. That first man stayed in his head, a Swede it turned out. To be blind and handless. What could be worse?

I am a Modern who can see a man's soul through his open wound, Bethune thought. He was sitting in the semi-darkness of his Madrid apartment drinking a very fine brandy. Writing propaganda wasn't a noble job but it needed to be done to raise money, and Bethune sat at the Biedermeier desk and wrote about the heroism of the wounded, about valiant Spaniards, brave Swedes and Frenchmen, nurses who never slept and whose touch could repair a man's spirit.

He had never been at peace with Frances, he thought. Two divorces would attest to that. They argued in bed and were silent at breakfast. But he had loved her once (or maybe twice). He had loved the idea of her, at least.

He thought he'd found comfort with the woman from Alabama. She was married, but agreed to divorce her husband. Even when seeking comfort, he found turmoil. He must crave it. His own father certainly had. A small-town evangelist, unstable, violent, filled with conviction and wrong-headedness. There is something fatal and doomed and predestined in myself, Bethune thought. Marian might have been the only woman with whom he could live physically and spiritually in happiness. Perhaps he had chosen her because she was unavailable. Her impossibility made her perfect. *I am a solitary*, he thought, *I don't need a woman. Or a man. I am alone in the world. How perfect for a humanitarian!* Marian preyed on him, though. What do you do with your old loves?

Did they love? They weren't lovers. Her marriage was intact; this was Bethune's gift to her. But she may not have wanted that (the way his ex-ex-wife, Frances, didn't), that her love wasn't the consuming sickness that Bethune's was. Maybe she admired him as a man, as a doctor, and that was all, and she went along with the comforting fiction of their love. He was, certainly, the principal author of this narrative. If this love was inauthentic, then what? Bethune examined his opulent flat. A glorious exile. He poured himself another exquisite brandy.

He had been drinking more, and writing poetry, a bad combination, unless you were a poet. He was clashing with the Spanish doctors and authorities and even with his own colleagues. He had written few letters and so had received few. Why the impulse for solitude? Especially here, in this struggle, where everyone was his comrade, or at least had been. Now everyone was his enemy, it seemed—such was the nature of revolution. He was an internationalist: happier with nations than people.

Bethune's colleagues had written a letter asking for his recall from Spain. He was arrogant and irrational, they said. Perhaps he had been arrogant, but it was arrogance in the service of an ideal. It was the ideal itself that was breaking down, though at moments Bethune felt close to a breakdown himself: a race then.

The Republican government was an uneasy coalition of leftists and centrists, a smattering of anarchists, right-wing socialists, some secret misguided Trotskyites, and certainly more than a few Franco sympathizers. They suspected Bethune's secretary of being a spy. Kajsa! They suspected everyone. It was a poisonous atmosphere and the democratic ideal was unravelling into a handful of striving sects. *I am my own schism*, Bethune thought. Kajsa was asleep. Kajsa von Rothman, a good name for a spy. She was taller than Bethune, wore pants, rode a motorcycle, and had gold-red hair that suited the sun. She attracted more publicity than Bethune (and without the effort he put into it).

In Madrid he had both supply and demand for blood. The civilians rushed to donate, a symbolic blow against Franco. How these communists loved to mingle their blood, the brotherhood of *sangre*. There was already a transfusion man here, Dr. Frederic Duran-Jordá, though he hadn't worked on the front lines. That was Bethune's innovation—take the blood to where it was needed most. And organize the donors. But he had alienated his Spanish colleagues. They resented the press he received and disliked the movie *Heart of Spain*; or perhaps they only disliked the fact that he'd had a hand in making it. The bureaucrats were still bureaucrats; no amount of idealism would change them. They suspected him of spying because he had military maps. How did they suppose he would find his way around? He had photographed bridges and roads to facilitate their movements and now these photographs were being held as evidence of treason. Goodness is thwarted by idiocy as often as evil. The Socorro Rojo Internacional had welcomed him at first, but they were no longer his ally. Now the whole country was suspicion and treachery.

In his last radio broadcast, he had said that Spain was the opening battle of the world revolution. This was still true, but the revolution would have more than two sides. Why had he come to Spain? To enlist in a cause, to celebrate himself, because he was in love with death. And now he was leaving, another messy divorce.

Before anaesthesia, doctors only did triage. They tried to stem the flow of blood. But with anaesthesia came the leisure of time and doctors became artists. And with artistry came artistic temperaments. *I am an artist,* Bethune thought, *and the role of the artist is to disturb.*

2

MICHAEL MOUNTAIN HORSE, SPAIN

The volunteers crossed into the Pyrenees at Perpignan, walking at night in rope-soled canvas shoes on the steep paths. There was no moon, and they held hands like a group of schoolchildren. Michael hadn't been surprised to see Dusty among the volunteers; he recognized a number of men from the On to Ottawa trek, men like himself who were simply drifting, and ended up, finally, in Spain. Some shared Bethune's idealism; others followed the desperate herd. In Canada they would be living in shanties in northern Ontario laying track or following the harvest, or simply starving. It happened. Men without families who expired in alleyways or on roadsides.

"You think it's true what they say?" Dusty asked.

"What do they say?"

"Those fascists see us coming, they'll turn tail."

Michael looked at the weary, hatchet-faced men, arranged in a line, snaking through the Spanish mountains. All of them were over thirty, quite a few over forty.

"I wouldn't count on it."

"We put the scare into them Regina cops. We got Bennett voted out of office. I'll tell you one thing, those Spanish women, they got a treat coming."

Michael marvelled at Dusty's ability to see himself as victorious, a necessary gift, perhaps, the natural defence of the underclass. Without it he'd collapse under the weight of his bad luck. Maybe Michael wasn't so different, lured to Spain by the words of a doctor he'd never met and the chance to outrun the Depression.

"I figure I'll stay on after we win," Dusty said. "Be some Spanish woman's good news. I'll be honest, there ain't much back home. Not just the land that dried up."

"You going to learn Spanish, Dusty?"

"If it comes to that. Worse things in this life than having a wife who can't talk to you."

They walked for three nights, then a truck took them to Figueras. From there they went to Barcelona and finally Albacete, the marshalling point for the International Brigades volunteers. While Michael was being processed, veterans of the Abraham Lincoln Battalion returned to the camp: emaciated men with bloodshot eyes. They sat wordlessly among the recruits. Dinner was served and all of them ate chickpeas in olive oil with small sardines and drank a sour wine. When it was dark, a faded reel of Charlie Chaplin's *The Immigrant* was projected onto the white wall of a funeral parlour and the men watched in silence. The Little Tramp hopped comically in a listing boat and wrestled with a fish. The image was faint, and there were holes in the film that showed up as tiny explosions of light.

Belchite was a disaster. The Spanish 32nd Brigade had been the advance, but they were depleted after fighting the Moors at Codo. Michael was with the Abraham Lincoln Brigade and they hiked through the night, seventeen miles in thick heat. In the dust were thousands of leaflets. Michael picked one up and saw a picture of Franco posed beside Jesus Christ, his unwitting ally.

Belchite was well fortified and the Republicans had only one piece of heavy artillery, operated by a confused volunteer who killed seven of their own men when he incorrectly gauged the range. Their first objective was the church of San Agustín. They tried to cross the exposed plain but were cut down by machine-gun fire. Within an hour, every Lincoln officer had been shot. The survivors scrambled for cover. Michael lay beside a corpse, wedged tightly. His antique Steyr had jammed after the first shot. He recovered a rifle from a fallen Lincoln, a Ross, useless twenty years ago and no better now. They had Remingtons, Mexican Mausers, all manner of outdated rifles coming from a hundred different sources.

Michael crawled along a shallow ditch that smelled of industrial effluent to an abandoned factory. The heavy planks of the floor were stained and the factory smelled pleasantly of olive oil; the wood was imbued with it, the heat drawing it out. Michael was exhausted and slept for a few hours sitting up, his unreliable gun on his lap. He awoke to see an angled pattern of light on the wall, the afternoon sun coming through the high windows. The heavy scent of oil reminded him of how little he had eaten in two days; his last meal a cup of stew made from cat meat. He drank the last of his water, which was warm and brackish.

To the south two tanks lumbered across the plain, their dust funnelling upward in the wind. Out the east window he could see the church of San Agustín, the fascist centre of operations, its sturdy pink brick pitted with bullet holes. The streets were deserted. He sat down and leaned against the wall and drifted off again, overcome with weariness and hunger. A few minutes later he woke to the vibration of tanks. He looked out the window at the empty plaza. The long snout of the gun suddenly appeared, and the tank emerged onto the plaza, heading for the church. A few children came out and threw stones at it, a Soviet T-26, an alien brute bringing death to their doorstep. It turned abruptly and ploughed through the arched doorway that was too narrow for its bulk. It tore brick from the sides and moved heavily into the church. Michael heard machine-gun fire, and he sprinted across the plaza to the doorway, following the tank's deafening progress.

Inside, the light was dim. The arches held stone cherubs and intricately carved saints. Jesus was stranded on the cross, his beige plaster skin streaked with blood. There was a machine gun set up at the altar and the fascists fired at the tank, tearing up the wooden pews, small puffs of dust as the bullets hit stone. The tank let off a round that blew a hole in the wall, letting in a thick shaft of light. Michael scrambled up the stairs to the organ loft at the rear of the church and crawled along the aisle. The tank fired another round, this one hitting the altar and taking out their gun. The tank moved awkwardly, turning and hitting the stone pillars. Plaster dust was caught in the shafts of light and looked like fine snow descending. The pews splintered beneath the metal tracks and Bibles were ground to pulp. Michael moved to the front of the church where the remains of the machine-gun crew were splayed. The tank was still swivelling, a blind bull, unsure where to charge. There was a heavy smell of diesel and the sound of steel treads grinding on the stone floor.

In the rooms behind the altar, Michael saw evidence of the rebel effort: maps, a few weapons. He picked up a German pistol and some ammunition and put it in his belt. Against the wall, a painting of the Virgin Mary moved as if in a breeze, wafting sensuously. Michael walked over and pulled the painting aside to find a tunnel. He had heard that the town was filled with them, and the rebels would be escaping through this one now. He didn't follow the tunnel, fearing they might blow it up after they fled through it. The thought of being trapped underground was a horror he couldn't contemplate.

The tank lurched toward the opening it had made. More brick spilled, tumbling in small avalanches, pink dust hanging in the air. Michael followed the tank out into the plaza, then turned down a narrow street, walking past the shuttered windows. One of the houses had a hole in it and he could see the remnants of normal life inside, a wooden table, a chair. In the doorway was a starving burro tethered by a rope.

He was exhausted and went into the house and sat on the wooden chair. He felt hollow, and drifted in and out of consciousness. He woke to music followed by machine-gun fire. Then more music—was he dreaming this? He heard a few snatches of a speech in Spanish delivered over a loudspeaker, then furious grenade explosions. He leaned against the wall and closed his eyes and the explosions became louder. A last fascist offensive, perhaps. Michael crept out to the street. A fascist officer suddenly appeared at the corner and threw a grenade. It exploded near the burro and blew a hind leg off that was as brittle as a stick. A piece of shrapnel ripped into Michael's shoulder and he slumped onto the stone and lay there. When he finally got up he felt his head and looked at the blood on his hand. He found a sheet to use as a cursory bandage and a sling. The street was deserted. The remains of the burro were covered in flies. Michael inched along the wall with his gun out. The fascist grenade thrower was lying in the dust, headless, two birds pecking at the spray of blood.

A temporary hospital had been set up in Belchite in what had been someone's home. After the shrapnel had been taken out by a nurse and the wound cleaned and cauterized, Michael lay in a sweat and thought about lying in Jumping Pound Creek and letting the cold water run over his body. The floor above was a chemist's shop and he walked up the stairs to have his shoulder looked at by a doctor. In the main room a fluoroscope was set up to X-ray the wounded. A group of children sat on the floor staring at it. A man was led in by the doctor and told to take off his shirt. It was Dusty, looking older and thinner than he had in the Pyrenees. He saw Michael and said, "They say maybe I got the pleurisy." He walked behind the machine and his skeleton suddenly appeared, the bones bluish and grey, wavering slightly. His head and legs were normal but half of him looked dead, decayed. Suddenly there was less of him. The children sat open-mouthed at this alchemy and one of the girls laughed and quickly covered her mouth with her hand.

3

NORMAN BETHUNE, MONTREAL, 1936

"Political democracies are a shell and a sham," Bethune told his audience. He had surprised himself at how effective a public speaker he was, a bit clumsy at times, but passionate. Mackenzie King had passed a bill banning Canadians from enlisting in foreign wars, a denunciation not just of the Canadian men who were dying in Spain but of democracy itself. A Canadian battalion being formed in Spain bore the name of King's grandfather—the Mackenzie-Papineau Battalion—and yet this timid offspring shunned them. History was clogged with irony.

It had been Bethune himself who had helped inspire the Mac-Paps, and his tireless lobbying (some of it self-serving) for the Republican cause helped draw thirteen hundred Canadian volunteers to Spain. This civil war would divide the world, he argued, but it would help unite Canada by providing it with an international focus. Bethune was the face of all that. A surprise, if a slightly calculated one.

He continued the propaganda effort he had begun in Spain, writing articles and letters, cultivating reporters, showing his film, doing radio broadcasts. He was more huckster than doctor, and there was a danger of becoming the cause. The cause itself was splintering into warring sects, and perhaps Bethune was splintering as well.

Nine thousand people sat in the Mount Royal Arena listening to him, waiting for his words. "What's the matter with England, France, the United States, Canada?" Bethune thundered. "Are they afraid that by supplying arms to the Loyalist forces they'll start a world war? Why, the world war has already *started*. It's democracy against fascism."

The Allied powers had signed a neutrality agreement that kept them out of the conflict, while Germany and Italy were waging open war on the Spanish people, cementing their strategic interests. Mussolini wanted to make the Mediterranean an Italian lake. If Germany could install a fascist government in Spain, then they would look to France, and all of Europe would fall.

"Fascism has begun to rear its head in Canada," Bethune said. "No one can stand on the sidelines. No one can afford to be complacent."

He had toured the country, selling the Republican cause, raising $1,000 in the Orpheum Theatre in Vancouver, $1,800 in Winnipeg. The Depression could be felt at some of these events; in Sudbury, seven hundred people gave a total of $22.40. Sometimes he gave four speeches a day. As for his own plans, Spain worked better as an ideal: He wouldn't go back. His recall to Canada was tinged with disgrace in certain circles, though he was still a hero in the newspapers.

He had gone to San Francisco and Los Angeles with his film and his speech. There was a fundraising dinner in the home of Robert Oppenheimer, a nervous man with a birdlike skull who flittered around the room in a cloud of cigarette smoke. Joe Dallet's widow, Kitty Harrison, was there, as were other Communists. Oppenheimer pressed them for donations. He was giving generously himself, Bethune had been told, a man of inherited wealth, the perfect Communist.

Bethune's suit was cheap and his shirt unpressed. Where was the dandy that had gone to Spain? His bourgeois self finally gone. Perhaps this was penance. A vow of poverty, though there was no need to make promises; poverty would find *him*. His hair was thinning and grey, and he was almost gaunt. Yet there was something in him the crowd wanted; and who was not seduced by the attention of a crowd? As a boy he had gotten his father's attention at dinner with subtle blasphemies. His father was an Old Testament table thumper, and when Bethune questioned the Resurrection (Maybe Jesus wasn't really dead; did you ever think of that?) his father rose and undid his belt in a single, practised motion.

"The Empire is simply blocks of gold scattered throughout the world," Bethune told his audience. "And the coronation of George VI is just an advertising stunt for the next war. We'll be asked to go over there and fight for the Empire. And we'll fight. But we have to know what we're fighting for. Peace, that is the only thing to fight for."

4

MACKENZIE KING, LONDON, 1937

Prime Minister Mackenzie King went to London to attend the coronation of George VI, the shy, stuttering, dutiful man who found himself King of England after Edward VIII abdicated in order to marry an American divorcee. God knew what Edward's problems were, King thought, though certainly an alarming lack of duty was one of them. In these times of utter desolation, with fascism following like the plough behind the horse, a moment in history requiring moral leadership, Edward had run off with an American. By most accounts, a useless man.

After the magnificent ceremony, King went to the British College of Psychic Science and arranged for a medium. He

had woken up with a vision of his mother sitting at a piano—
the large one she had owned—and it seemed as if she was
communicating through music. Was the message about
Italy? Another country to keep an eye on.

The medium was a greyish, nondescript person (so many
of them seemed neutral in appearance, perhaps a necessary
trait for their work, their own personalities sublimated to
clear the passage for those calling from beyond). She saw
dark forces with King at the centre. How is it that I am in
this position? he wondered. There are abler men. But there
must be purpose to this. Mother and Father in their humble,
good lives were filled with the Holy Spirit and my life is the
result. When men are truly great they reflect the Holy
Family—the saintly Mary and humble Joseph, and their son,
the spirit of God upon him the source of all power. Each of
us, King thought, must be a little Christ.

The seance offered little illumination. She said his father's
voice was clearer than any she had ever received, that he knelt
and wept before God, overjoyed that his son was now leading
the nation. His mother sent her love. We bring back those who
have left us, King thought, so that we might move upward.

His conversation with Laurier was short.

—Wilfrid, what do you see?

—Clouds gathering.

—Will there be refuge?

—Birds scatter before a storm. You must stand.

Stand where? King thought reflexively. Could the dead
read his thoughts? He hadn't the courage to ask. The state
of man. Such a paltry vessel for God's work.

In the evening he wrote in his journal, the obsessive
history that he attended to each night, a version that
concealed and revealed in equal measure, like all histories.

London's greyness was soothing, a complex, comforting palette. It had been a surprise to get a call from the Germans, to be invited to lunch with Joachim von Ribbentrop, the German ambassador to the Court of St. James. When King arrived at the German embassy, he was shown in by a crisp young man. The embassy was marred by modernism, a stark, angled interior filled with functional geometric furniture. The modern instinct seemed to be to squeeze the life out of all it touched. There was just the three of them for lunch, Ribbentrop, his wife, and King. Ribbentrop had a thin-lipped smile and bright eyes, a man verging on handsome with an aura of weakness that his wife compensated for. She assessed King as she assessed all men, calculating the degree and nature of his vanity and how to exploit it.

Ribbentrop told King that he knew Canada. "I worked for your railway. This is a surprise to you, I am sure. I lived in Ottawa, a very stable city. I have great love for Canada's order and expanse." In this knowledge he saw a bond. Of course, the bond was greater than he thought. King told him he had been born in Berlin, Ontario (since renamed after Lord Kitchener, another casualty of the war), that he had been raised among those of German descent, could even speak a little of the language.

"Excellent, excellent," Ribbentrop said in that German way. "Germany has so few friends these days, Herr King. It would be to everyone's joy if you come to Berlin to visit with Hitler. If there is a world leader who can understand this misunderstood man, surely it is you." Ribbentrop licked his thin lips and glanced at his stern wife, as if for approval. "There are only two paths, friendship or war, and if there is war, it will be the end of civilization."

In his hotel King tried the "little table" as he was now calling it. He had become adept at table rapping, a way of summoning the departed without the services—or logistics—of a medium. It was a tedious exercise, as the answers had to be laboriously spelled out (one rap for A, two for B, and so on), but he had decided to avoid mediums. If news of his spiritualism were to get out, it would cause him political damage. What would the Conservatives say? That King has chosen Julius Caesar as foreign minister and Genghis Khan as minister of defence. And the papers. He could see the headlines: KING'S NEW CABINET: ONLY THE DEAD NEED APPLY, or some such. He was unable to raise his mother or his historic and beloved grandfather Mackenzie. He was finally able to summon Laurier, working his way slowly through his sometimes garbled replies. King would occasionally lose count (was it sixteen or seventeen raps, a P or a Q?).

—Wilfrid. War threatens once more. Are our memories so short? Who can forget the horror of the last one?

You have a sole (role) Mackenzie You qust (m?) walk cautiously weigh every vord (word) You will find yourself at the centre of mankinds darkness(est) hour Much rebinds (depends? reminds?) you.

—Wilfrid, whatever do you mean?

The lattice grows holy (??) Steak (speak) cautiously.

—I'm concerned about the German soul.

Flake well anod (?).

King asked once more but there was only silence from beyond, meaningless groupings of letters, Wilfrid off somewhere. King needed more information and surely Laurier would provide it in his own good time.

Berlin shone. King remembered mourning the death of Kaiser Wilhelm I when he was thirteen, the streets draped in black bunting, flags at half-mast, bells tolling at the Lutheran church. He had marched from Central School to St. Peter's and sat through the service honouring a German who lay dead thousands of miles away. His father, he recalled, wept manfully, a single tear rolling onto his starched shirt. Five hundred people crying in the spartan gloom of the church.

It was a pleasant evening and King walked through Berlin. He had grown stouter, he noticed, and was easily fatigued; walking was a necessary tonic. The city was vaguely familiar, and he sought out Kaiserin Augusta Strasse, where he had stayed as a graduate student. A line of women stretched before him, evenly spaced, soberly dressed, each adopting the same air of coincidence. As he approached the first, she attempted a tight-lipped smile that failed to disguise a dark tooth.

"Would you like to attend a party, Herr Doktor?" she asked in German. He remembered a little of the language, had laboured over German texts as a graduate student, even read the odd speech in German when he returned to Berlin, Ontario, expressing his love and understanding for the Germans in his riding.

"Party," King restated dully.

"I will be your party," she said with that smile.

King recalled the prostitute in Toronto. Velma, she had said her name was. Her thin cotton shift had faded blue flowers on it and her shoes were painted an unsuccessful red. Had he stopped then in a spirit of Victorian concern, to help Velma out of her wretched trade? He hadn't prevented her from disrobing in her tired room on

Madison. He sat on the edge of the small bed as she lifted the dress over her head. She sat on the bed beside him and he took her hand and stared into her pocked face. "What has led you here, my child?" he asked, his body at war, an animal straining within, straining against the sociologist, his first trade. What was it they called sociology—the whore of the humanities—it will be whatever you want it to be. It was what his enemies said about King himself. Two whores. But Velma wasn't interested in sociology, and she took his hand and pressed it between her legs and King recoiled from the soft dampness as if it was fire. He moved quickly and awkwardly out of her room and down the dark staircase, holding his hand as if it had been burned. He was on Bloor Street before he realized he was still holding it.

King looked at this parade of Germans, not the parade Ribbentrop wanted to show the visiting leader surely, not the handsome lines of blond youth gleaming like the future. He didn't need to respond to this German girl. She was already looking past him down the avenue, seeking less ambivalent custom.

He woke early, his dream lingering (they are not *dreams*, his dear dead mother had counselled, but *visions*). This time he was standing with his mother, arguing with her as they waited for a train. Mother was pleading for him to love her, and there was an unpleasant and unfamiliar tenor to her insistence. What could this mean? The train, clearly, was his journey through life. But his mother's behaviour? Her love was unselfish and spiritual. It must mean, he mused as he dressed (noting with some alarm his ample flesh, a melancholy thing, piled like sandbags against a flood), that she was making it clear to him—at the age of sixty-two— that carnal love was wrong, that it separated one from the divine and spiritual. His various alliances with women, whether the well-meaning matches presented by friends or his rare forays into the streets, were a mistake.

Over a pleasant, though overly large German breakfast, he read Joshua. At ten-thirty he met with Hermann Goering, who greeted him in a white general's uniform, the black belts crossing its spotless expanse. Goering's head was well formed, his mouth a bit wide, perhaps. He had recently banned all Roman Catholic newspapers in Germany—not an entirely bad idea, King thought.

"I must thank you for the bison," Goering said heartily, ushering King to his seat. "This was most generous." King's government had sent six bison for the Berlin zoo.

"Yes, they are wonderful beasts."

"I would like sometime to go to your Rocky Mountains to shoot one," Goering said. "You are a hunter?"

King smiled. "No. But please come at my invitation. It would be wonderful." It occurred to King that there was, in fact, no bison hunting. There weren't many left and most of those were in protected areas. He could offer elk or bear if it came to it.

"I noticed the theatres last night while out walking, General Goering. Dozens, it seems. You have an enviably vital culture."

"When I hear the word 'culture,' Herr King, I reach for my Browning." Goering smiled his improbable smile.

King was unaware that this line came, in fact, from a

German play. It was one Goering was fond of quoting, and it was usually greeted with laughter or agreement, either one an acceptable response.

Germany wanted raw materials, Goering told him. Canada was eager to trade, King thought, and its raw materials were abundant, but to what purpose would the Germans put that material in these days of rearmament? "In the last session of Parliament, Herr General," King said carefully, "I had to ask for an increase in the military budget. It wasn't what I wanted to do. But there is fear among the Canadian people. Fear of another Great War."

"Fear is expensive, Herr Prime Minister," Goering said. "But useful, no?" He attempted another smile. "England fears us. We fear England. Who has the greater cause? Let me ask you directly: If the peoples of Germany and Austria—being of the same race—should wish to unite, and if England would try and prevent them from doing this, would Canada support England?"

Canada, King replied, would examine the issue independently of Britain and decide for itself.

"I do not wish you to have the impression that we are planning to take possession of Austria," Goering said, though he was planning it, and Czechoslovakia as well, a nation of witless peasants who craved leadership and would welcome the tanks. Goering's stomach rolled, guttural noises issuing. What had he eaten the night before? A large piece of veal, an ambitious actress. Perhaps it was the cognac.

Germany was obsessed with the purity of blood, to protect it and revere it, a religion. Canada was the inter-mingling of blood, creating a new race, a global experiment. One was the past, the other the future. Which was which? King cautiously commented on these theories of bloodlines.

"I am a general," Goering answered, shrugging. "I think with my blood."

A general sees the world as a hierarchy of force, King thought, and Goering was no different. He and Goering had talked for an hour and a half. King would barely have time to drive to the old palace of Paul von Hindenburg on the Wilhelmstrasse to meet with Hitler. He thanked Goering for the coffee, repledged his friendship, and left.

At the palace, the Führer's elite guards saluted the arriving prime minister, and King congratulated himself on this diplomatic coup. What other leader had dared to view first-hand Hitler's worrisome nationalism, with its cunning marriage of order and barbarity? Hitler awaited him on the second floor. King walked across the marble floor that stretched out like a desert, his footsteps echoing slightly. Hitler's face was unlined and without expression, his hair still unclouded by grey. King had been warned of the man's charm; don't be seduced by the evil genius.

King felt uniquely qualified to talk to Hitler, to act as liaison between the dictator and an uneasy world. This was Canada's role, certainly. Did they not explain Britain to America and America to Britain? They would do the same for Germany and England. The Germans of Berlin, Ontario, were hard working and law abiding and peaceful (many of them pacifist Pennsylvania Mennonites, and perhaps too peaceful during the last war).

King gave Hitler a copy of Rogers's biography of him, and opened it to the page that showed the house he was born in.

"You know I was born in Berlin, Herr Hitler," King said.

Hitler sat immobile as Schmidt the interpreter translated.

"Berlin, Ontario." Schmidt passed on the punchline, and Hitler stared without expression.

King complimented Hitler on the tour that Ribbentrop had arranged and ventured some praise. "What you have done with the workers, it is remarkable."

"The workers are remarkable," Hitler said. "This is what is often overlooked by governments." The *Volk*.

They discussed their mothers; Hitler was as devoted to his dead mother as King was to his, a surprise. *He is certainly a spiritualist,* King thought, though he didn't bring this up. Hitler had the quality of a mystic, and a quality of greatness too, perhaps, though he was surprisingly modest. Still, there were concerns.

"As any man of responsibility, Herr Hitler," King began, "I cannot help but raise the issue of war. We have increased our own expenditures on defence. Reluctantly, I should add. But the reason for this is the increased outlay in German military spending and the growing unease in Europe. I had to give money to the military to unite my country."

"Then we have something in common, Herr King. I too was required to give money to the military to unite my country." Hitler offered a mirthless, understanding smile. "We are not arming for purposes of aggression, this I assure you. But you must appreciate what the Treaty of Versailles has done. Should we be held in indefinite subjection? Or do we assert ourselves and in so doing, preserve the self-respect of the nation? My interest is in improving the conditions of the German people. A war would certainly undo the work that we have already done. People respect strength. A simple truth. I saw what the last war did. With the weapons we have now, all of Europe would be devastated by war. There would be no winners, Herr King. There will be no war."

King had his assurance, something to take to London. But Hitler continued.

"I'm not like Stalin. I can't just shoot my generals and anyone in the government who disagrees with me." (Though hadn't he done just that during the Night of the Long Knives? Roehm controlled the *Sturmabteilung*, four million young men filled with revolution and blood. Roehm could have turned them on Hitler, and who is to say he wouldn't have—the wolf-hearted Roehm who would bury his mother alive for an ideology—so Hitler had him shot like a dog. At any rate, he was homosexual.) "I accept the Treaty of Versailles with all its indignities. What I don't understand, Herr King, is the Treaty of Alliance between France and Russia." Russia, the world's most dangerous enemy and worse as a friend. Perhaps this would prove ill fated for France. As for Russia, it was gloriously ill fated all on its own.

They spoke for over an hour. Hitler gave King a photograph of himself mounted in a silver frame that was warmly inscribed in remembrance of his German visit. They shook hands.

"I wish you well in your efforts to help mankind," King said.

Outside, in the courtyard of the Hindenburg palace, its oppressive grandeur, the dark lines of a Grimm's castle, King reflected that Hitler was, if nothing else, a patriot. King had his car take him back to the hotel, where he had lunch. The emotion in Germany was warlike; they were drunk with wild god. And Hitler was their god. *Perhaps*, King thought, *I am a medium for the forces beyond*. He had read Joshua at breakfast, the walls of Jericho coming down and all within slaughtered, men and women and children. (The only one spared was Rahab the harlot, another curious sign.) World history at its most perilous moment, and somehow King had a defining role to play. A confluence of events and coincidences had brought him to the centre of all this. He would need to keep in touch with the spirit world, would need advice.

There was a factory to tour in the afternoon, and when he arrived Ribbentrop was there to meet him. In his brown suit, he looked like a salesman, and he was a salesman of a sort, touring the world's capitals, asking them to limit their arms manufacture, asking them in a way that made them do just the opposite, allowing Germany to say that the world had turned down its pleas of disarmament, and that it had no choice but to keep pace.

There was a rumour that Ribbentrop was having an affair with Wallis Simpson. Perhaps it was strategic: In the event that Edward became king, he would have his ear. But now Edward was marginalized. He and Wallis were visiting Germany as well, testing world opinion on their tragic love.

The late June air was pleasant and the sun bounced off a thousand windows.

"I trust your visit with our Führer was altogether illuminating," Ribbentrop said.

"A surprising man," King said. "A patriot."

"His love for his people is without boundary. You can see now the import of our mission. If there is to be war, we will all be found guilty by history, yes."

If there is war, King thought, *England and Germany will clash, and France will be a casualty.* In Berlin he had toured the zoo, been to youth camps, and seen the grandeur of the Olympic Stadium. He stared at the sleek factory, its facade stretching for a hundred yards. "What do you make here?" King asked.

"Efficiency," Ribbentrop replied.

5

NORMAN BETHUNE, CHINA, 1939

Who would have guessed that China would become his mistress? Bethune had rejected Canada (too aloof), Russia (too dark, finally), and Spain (a tragedienne on the world stage). Near Chi-Shan he came across a mule that had its legs broken and ears and tail blown off by a bomb dropped from a Japanese plane. The beast was lying in agony on the side of the road because no soldier would shoot it, afraid the owner would claim damages. Bethune took out his jackknife and slit its carotid artery and it quietly expired. What kind of doctor murders a mule? a soldier asked Bethune's inter- preter. What kind? Bethune answered rhetorically. One who is arrogant in the service of humanity, that's what kind. He had cured his own tuberculosis. There is a little of God in every doctor.

In the spring he turned forty-nine. No longer young, and international brotherhood was no longer a youthful passion. He had come to China as he had left Spain: angry, troubled, abusing his colleagues and himself, drinking a bit too much. But he was happy in China, who wasn't his mistress finally, he supposed, but his last wife. Contentment rather than passion. That was the role of the last wife, was it not? You would read by the fire together, inquire how the garden was going.

He started a medical training school. There were 2,300 people in makeshift hospitals and a few doctors, but there was no money coming in from Canada or America. Perhaps he should have expected as much. For a year he had had no books, no radio, magazines, or letters; no English. The only thing he had read were weeks-old editions of San Francisco newspapers that had been used to wrap cakes and knives. He read about *The Wizard of Oz*, and its gamine star, Judy Garland, with whom everyone had fallen in love. The movie was in colour, like life itself. He knew the Yankees were on pace to win the pennant, but he didn't know if Roosevelt was still president. He didn't know who the prime minister of England was. No news from Canada at all. It would be too much to hope that King had been voted out of office.

He had been deaf in his right ear for three months. His teeth were neglected and he badly needed a Western dentist. His glasses were cracked and his vision compromised at any distance. On the border of northwestern Hopei, he was as isolated as if he were on the moon. Life was in the hospitals and in his head. Marian touching him at that party in Westmount as he left, her husband in the next room, leaving the party feeling loved, and happy in the mourning that had already begun for the loss of that love, walking downhill among the mansions, revelling in that delicious misery. Days went by when he didn't see a reflection of himself. He dreamed of coffee and rare roast beef, apple pie, music, and women.

In November he was planning to go across Shansi and down to Ya'an on foot, a distance of five hundred miles. He thought it would take six weeks. From there, Chungking, then to Yuman in the south, to Hong Kong, and finally San Francisco. In North America he could raise money and hopefully recruit some volunteers. Had he become an old man? he wondered He wouldn't know until he was back home. Everyone was old here, a consequence of war.

He had met Mao Tse Tung, a brilliant tactician. There was none of the divisiveness there had been in Spain. Mao would drive the Japanese out, marshalling those sheer numbers, waves of citizens joined by common cause.

A few days before he was planning to leave he cut his finger while operating on a soldier, and the cut became infected. A tiny wound, yet the most significant. We are undone by our greatest successes and smallest failures, he thought. He returned from the front, too weak to operate, and joined the 3rd Regiment east of Yin Fang. His fever was high and he was vomiting violently; it could be septicemia. The poison was spreading and it would attack the tissue and then the organs, which would hold out briefly before failing in their prescribed order: liver (a veteran of many assaults), kidney (an innocent), and finally the heart (scarred, remote, perhaps ready to die). He tried phenacetin, aspirin, woven's powder, antipyrine, and caffeine; all were equally useless.

He had already died once, in 1927, lying in the Trudeau Sanatorium with tuberculosis. He was thirty-seven, just divorced from Frances (one of the few things that got easier as his life went on), contemplating his own death. He took forty yards of brown wrapping paper and created a mural that he titled *The T.B.'s Progress*, modelled on Hogarth's *Rake's Progress*. Using oil pastels he painted nine panels. In the first, he was in the womb. The second showed him being embraced by a beautiful angel with iridescent wings. He drew his childhood as a dangerous journey through a wood, surrounded by animals that represented diseases (the measles were a tiger, he recalled, and a dragon for diphtheria). These were the real terrors of childhood, those unseen bacteria that ate lives.

He had written poetry for each painting. He was a dreadful poet, something he had known even as he wrote all those poems, yet he kept at it. He was young then, or at least not old, and poetry is a prerogative of the narcissist. At any rate, all he was able to do in the sanatorium was contemplate his unfinished life.

Perhaps his whole life had been a preparation for China. The Chinese embraced him in a way the Spanish were reluctant to. He hadn't been an easy man to love in Spain. Or anywhere. But he felt loved here.

He was the only trained doctor among thirteen million people. What a practice! Had he stayed in Detroit, he might have had a few hundred.

Outside Ho-Chin he came upon a boy with a bloodstain on his blue army jacket. He was perhaps seventeen and had been shot through the lung a week earlier. The right anterior chest wall suppurating, fluid in the pleural cavity as high as the third rib. Who would have believed this possible? An untreated gunshot victim walking around for a week. Each war was a medical laboratory, often grotesque, occasionally uplifting.

In Ho-Chin there were live carp in buckets, black pigs, barkless dogs, paper windows, and obsequious priests whose chants reminded him of High Church Anglicans.

Lying on the stained hospital bed, surrounded by wounded Chinese, he contemplated the body, how beautiful it is; how perfect its parts; with what precision it moves; how obedient. How terrible when torn. It goes out like a candle. Quietly and gently. It makes its protest at extinction, then submits.

He remembered walking among the pines near Gravenhurst early in the morning with his father when he was a boy. His father quoted Deuteronomy, a familiar ritual, the Bible delivered as they walked over fallen boughs under a brilliant autumn canopy. As Deuteronomy entered his ears, unwanted and abstract, Bethune scanned for deer tracks and dreamed of escaping his father's righteous temper that built as the day progressed, starting calmly then gathering force.

Bethune had found his highest fulfillment out here among the peasants, without love or comfort. Perhaps, he noted, he was a man of God after all, like his father. How lovely an irony. His head was a fiery pain now, his organs beginning to shut down, like a street of shopkeepers turning out their lights after the day's business was done. He wasn't a lover or an artist or a man of science as he had intended. As he firmly believed. Merely a missionary, and now, he thought, a martyr.

ALLIANCES

1939–1950

They were a curious pair, King and Bethune, the careful politician and the reckless doctor. When I went to Spain I was following Stanford's righteous anger as much as Bethune's, I think. I half expected to see his ghost there.

Thomas Carlyle had a theory that history was the accumulated biographies of great men. Was Bethune a great man? A messy, recognizable type: He was arrogant, drank too much, and embraced the world like a lover. Angry and restless, though I think he found peace in China. The Chinese considered him a national hero. He became one here, too, though that came later. He was too dangerous to embrace when he was alive.

And Mackenzie King? Who knows. He was insecure, a loopy spiritualist who feared women and envied great men. His charms were subtle, to say the least. Yet the country prospered under him. For a time we were defined by him (and perhaps we still are): the spirit of compromise. I wasn't a fan of Willie, but he endured, and you can't ignore that.

Endurance is part of the national theme: that humbling geography, its overwhelming scale, the sheer weight on the collective psyche. Though for most people (Thompson being the greatest exception), all that land is an abstraction. But it's the most obvious one and we cleave to it. We need to cleave to something; that's what sustains a nation.

When David Thompson first set out to explore, he went to Lake Athabasca with two Cree named Kozdaw and Paddy. Coming back on the Black River they hit a set of rapids and the canoe tipped. The two Indians got to shore but Thompson went under and scraped along the rocks. He lost his shoes and most of his clothes. They were able to recover his sextant, which was in a cork-lined box, and their cotton tent. The flesh was torn from the bottom of Thompson's foot, and he ripped the tent into strips to bind it and used the rest for clothing. It was September and already getting cold. They made a fire and Thompson thought about their situation: in a barren land, the canoe lost, without food, almost naked. They wrestled two small eagles from a nest and ate them, and Thompson and Paddy came down with dysentery. For four days they limped through the forest, eating a few berries, the dysentery sending their bodies into spasm. They were so weak that Thompson thought it was useless to go any farther. Better to die where they were. He was a young man and his life's exploration had come only to this: one lake, one river.

Kozdaw didn't get sick but he cried all day. Not for Thompson and Paddy but for himself: He knew he'd be blamed for their deaths when he got back. So using charcoal on a piece of birch bark, Thompson wrote an account of his own death, signed and dated it, and gave it to Kozdaw as protection. Sitting in the wilderness, writing his obituary with a piece of charred wood. I think of this image often. My great-great-grandfather, not much older than you. The mapmaker. It was the second time he had contemplated the end of his life, a short journey, its unfulfilled purpose, a hundred stories told by a dying Indian, and then a wisp, like an ash that wafts out of the fire, consumed. And yet, he endured.

Y ou could see World War II approach from a long way off, like a prairie thunderstorm. And then it hit and we were surprised by the awful power of war once more. Wars are bad for people but good for nations; we had another chance to shed our colonial status. In the end, we left the British for the Americans, a devil's bargain, perhaps, though it hasn't been a bad marriage. They're dangerous and entertaining, and God knows marriages have been based on less.

1

Mackenzie King, 1939

—Am I loved?

A silence from beyond, the discreet spirits.

—They *voted* for me, King said. The crowds when I spoke—I could feel something. I was their choice.

—A woman makes a choice but she doesn't always love her husband. Few politicians are loved.

—And I am not among the lucky, Wilfrid?

—They will love you after you're gone, Mackenzie. It is the way with most men. Resented, then mourned.

—Perhaps if I had a wife.

—The political wife is a rare thing. A woman who understands your world but lives in the other. A medium. Ha. But even they aren't enough for the politician. He needs the crowd, that roar of approval.

—Will I will feel it again? Will it be enough?

—You will feel it. It won't be enough.

King knew that the people didn't love him. That's why he didn't lead; he knew few would follow. In the West, Bible Bill Aberhart was a demagogue who understood his people at the level of their private fears, staring into the dark centres that contained failure and shame and a moral strength guided by lack of opportunity. And Aberhart worked these truths like the preacher he was.

King understood the people at a level they couldn't comprehend and therefore didn't fully appreciate: balancing the delicate factions of the country like a conductor bringing in the strings, signalling the oboes, keeping peace among the temperamental violins, ensuring the lonely triangle felt wanted, and making all of this move forward, if not in the pleasing strains of his favourite composers (the lulling Brahms—even his name was lulling), then the emphatic lurch of the Russian, Shostakovich. The people weren't consciously aware of this, but at another level, at the level of the spirit lusting for balance, they knew. And they knew King, the rationalist, the appeaser, the delicate crackwalker of Berlin, Ontario, was the one to keep this fragile alliance on course. If he could not overcome the forces of geography and history that tore at the nation (and he couldn't, but then, who could?), then he could at least stay them. His peculiar genius was like the spirit world, impossible to see but powerful nonetheless.

King decided that Hitler was too shrewd to go to war. He would get what he needed simply by preparing for war, assembling all those people (that enviable unity!) and massing that German steel along the borders. The threat would be enough.

The medium said Hitler would die this year—perhaps assassinated. Mussolini too was being called. King asked her to examine his hand, to see if she saw marriage there. She took his hand in both of hers, and King thrilled slightly at her touch, the finger tracing lines along his palm. "You are destined to live alone," she said. "There is purpose to your life. It is being ordered in this way." They spoke to Leonardo da Vinci, whose advice was unfortunately Mediterranean ("To truly live, Mackenzie, you must embrace all of life"). Was he counselling hedonism? A genius, an artist.

There was a surprisingly casual chat with Philip the Apostle. A disciple of Jesus, an extraordinary breakthrough. (Could he talk to Jesus himself? King wondered. What would he dare ask?) Philip, who had been crucified, hung upside down on a cross yet he continued to preach. He was offered release and refused, and died on the cross. What courage, what faith! And now, according to the slightly mousy medium, a woman with grey streaks in her dead brown hair who was channelling Philip's Hebrew musings into a breezy American dialect, the disciple and King had begun a friendship of sorts. His friendships with the great: da Vinci, Philip, Louis Pasteur. They were a comfort, though it occurred to him that he had more friends among the dead than among the living, an imbalance he would need to address.

What of his dead dog Pat? What was God's plan for

terriers? Do dogs have souls? King was unsure what to ask the medium.

"My dog. Pat, I was very close to him," he said. "I'm wondering ... Is it possible to communicate ... I don't know the ... I'd like to try."

The medium stared at King.

"Your dog Pat," she said.

"My dear departed terrier."

A slight shrug. She sat motionless for three minutes.

Would Pat bark at the medium? King wondered. Did he now have the gift of language? A low sound came out, not a growl, a guttural sigh almost. It pitched lower and finally died out.

"Pat is well," she said quietly. "He misses you."

In the morning King walked his estate at Kingsmere, gazing on the ruins he had assembled—some of them taken from the Parliament Buildings when they burned in 1916, other pieces scavenged from old houses. He was comforted by antiquity; he welcomed his ghosts. King had asked Laurier if he thought Kingsmere was too large an estate. He had bought the neighbouring properties, and his land was now too vast to comfortably walk. Partly the purchase had been defensive. The Jews had wanted to buy near Kingsmere and they would have ruined it certainly.

In the morning, King reread Matthew. Almost an hour went by before he received the news that Hitler had invaded Poland.

The following evening his departed father told him that Hitler was dead, "shot by a Pole." His mother confirmed it. "War will be averted," she told him. This view seemed to be confirmed again by both his grandfather and Laurier, so it was disturbing to find Hitler alive the next day. What could this mean? That the spirit world was unreliable, or non-existent, a fraud? It couldn't be. He had *felt* it, felt it with Laurier, with his mother and grandfather. He sought ways to explain this lapse, to keep all he had invested in the spirit realm intact; he couldn't merely be chatting with a blank-faced Detroit housewife who charged him for every session. There were malicious spirits at play, he thought, spirits that were not yet divine, or simply mischievous. Perhaps there were wars in the spirit realm as well, good and evil continuing their joust. He must be cautious with future advice.

Britain immediately declared war. King waited nine days to announce that Canada would join them, a way to telegraph its status as an independent country. The First War had ended Canada's life as a colony; perhaps this one would complete the transformation to nation. It is odd, he thought, that German aggression played such a large part in Canada's sense of itself. But such is history, the currents difficult to detect when you're in its swirling waters, but when you look back, what seemed like coincidence or of little consequence suddenly gathers import.

2

MACKENZIE KING, OGDENSBURG, NEW YORK, 1940

Roosevelt was eating the largest steak King had ever seen, rare and bloody, a prehistoric slab sitting in a lake of pale red juices. King doubted he could finish a steak an eighth its size. Where did that appetite come from? A right that God gave Americans. The president dabbed at the blood on his lip and examined the napkin. "I have been having a dreadful time with Congress," he said.

Ogdensburg had been decorated for FDR's arrival, the streets lined with soldiers and citizens and a thousand flags. King wondered if the president knew that Ogdensburg had been burned to the ground by the British during the

War of 1812. This couldn't be coincidence, King thought. It
was part of a divine plan, an illustration of the eternal laws
of justice. What was destroyed in anger shall host a meeting
of peace, a peace and alliance that will reverberate for all
mankind. Roosevelt wanted to assist in the war effort
without being seen to do so. His political enemies would
accuse him of dragging the country into the war, but the
United States needed to defend itself, and if FDR went
through Congress it would take months of blustering
debate. Better to do it on his own. Canada was the conduit
through which all of this could be conducted, once again the
go-between.

"Mackenzie, I can give you fifty destroyers. We'll deliver
them to Halifax, fully crewed, then it's up to you Canadians
to get them overseas. There's the possibility of 250,000
rifles, though little chance of ammunition, I'm afraid."

The destroyers were World War I vintage, ancient hulks
on the verge of being scuttled, though this was left unsaid.
In return for this dubious gift the Americans got land on
Canadian and British soil to build military bases. King
realized that this agreement essentially shifted Canada's
primary alliance from Britain to America. It was logical
certainly, inevitable even. If King had learned one thing, it
was to seize upon historical inevitabilities. If you didn't,
someone else would and take the credit. Though how close
should they get to the Americans, those bare-knuckle
optimists, those uniquely sunny brutes? The polio-stricken
Roosevelt was a curious choice to lead a people who saw
health as a form of divinity.

King knew that the president was facing an election and
that it was much on his mind. He asked him if he was confi-
dent of his chances.

"I could only be defeated by peace, Mackenzie," he said through the haze of his cigarette. "In times of peace, the people want a manager. In times of trouble, they want a leader."

"There is no danger of peace, Franklin, I can assure you."

King marvelled at how alike he and Roosevelt were; both disdained pretension, sought simplicity, and trusted in God.

While King chatted amiably with FDR's secretary of war, Henry Stimson, Roosevelt drafted a joint agreement for defence between the two nations. He wrote it out in pencil on a piece of paper under the title "Permanent Joint Board of Defense."

"I wonder about the use of the word 'permanent,'" King mused.

"Who knows what the future will bring, Mackenzie," FDR said. "What if Canada is invaded? We would like to be able to get three hundred thousand troops onto Canadian soil within three hours."

They had wanted to get troops on Canadian soil in the past, but had been unsuccessful, thank God.

Before going to bed that night King read from Ezekiel, which seemed to be calling to him of late.

In the morning it was warm and the air heavy. King sat in the president's car as they rolled slowly past people waving flags. FDR inspected the Pennsylvania Regiment, which was assembled in a field. Afterwards they all sang "Nearer My God to Thee" and King felt his body swelling, as if it were preparing to rise upward. You completed one stage on this earth and began another. He had had a vision that morning while lying half asleep—the most receptive state—of climbing a staircase to find a blank white wall. It was not yet his time to go, that's what the dream was telling him. Too much to do.

When they parted, Roosevelt leaned toward King. "If anything more is needed, Mackenzie," he said through that winning smile, "let it be done without my knowledge."

3

QUEBEC CITY, 1944

Winston Churchill took King into the map room they had laid out in the Citadel and showed him the battle areas. "The British troops are here," Churchill said, pointing to a spot near the Adriatic. "They will go over the mainland and up the route that Napoleon took, driving into the Balkan states during the winter. Unless, of course, the war is over by the end of the year. God willing, it will be. I suspect there will be skirmishing in the Alps for some time, however. Hitler and his gang have nothing to lose at this point—they know they're condemned."

Churchill looked healthy. He was drinking very little (in contrast to King's London visit when Churchill was tight all the time). But Roosevelt looked desperate. His forehead perspired and his face was flushed, and his leg seemed to have atrophied further. All three men were facing elections, King mused. He wondered if Roosevelt would last that long.

In the dregs of his morning tea Mackenzie King saw what appeared to be a guardian angel with a banner. A sign of something. Also the number thirty seemed to be taking on unusual import. In the House a few days earlier he had stared at the opposition benches to see three occupied seats and one empty (3 and 0). When he glanced at his watch, it was *exactly* three o'clock.

At lunch, King scanned the newspapers for unfavourable cartoons of himself. The newspapers had made sport of his not being included in meetings between Churchill and Roosevelt despite Canada's being the host country. They failed, as always, to see the subtler and more pertinent role, King thought. Churchill didn't entirely trust Roosevelt, and that feeling was mutual. Both distrusted de Gaulle, and had no faith in Stalin whatsoever. And there was something comforting in King, in his neutrality, a neutrality that transcended politics. *I am the facilitator*, King thought, *the translator.*

So the facile cartoons didn't irk. What did was his woeful knowledge of history and events. Foreign issues were bad enough, but his knowledge of Canadian history was impoverished. *I have been too much of a recluse*, he thought, *my mind concerned with lesser things.* Churchill had the world crammed into that head, a brain fuelled by champagne and cigars for weeks on end. But war was the breath of life to him. He knew the details of a hundred wars and was certainly enjoying this one.

King remembered wandering in the rubble of London, the rain-soaked, soot-stained brick lying in heaps. He had had someone from the Canadian embassy gather stones from the remains of Westminster Hall and had them shipped to Kingsmere, a glorious addition.

He had had a vision the night before of ruins, columns lying broken, but it wasn't London. Perhaps it was Greece. In this vision, his brother, Max, appeared. When he was alive, Max had been a doctor, and his presence usually meant healing. He was always comforted by the appearance of Max, whether in dreams or at his table-rapping sessions. The other figure was disturbing, however. A woman, naked save for a pair of shoes, sitting on a fallen column (Doric, he suspected). She was clearly aggrieved, though showed no sign of any wound. Could this be Velma (or Ann or Dorothy or any of the other prostitutes he had attempted to redeem)? The fallen woman. But what could be the possible significance now? King went back to his vision, trying to recall the detail, which had evaporated so quickly. The columns were Doric, he was sure of it now. His mistake was thinking it was Greece, that it was antiquity. No, this was the Brandenburg Gate. Of course! What had been the gateway to the sanctuary lay in ruins. Berlin was in ruins! But the woman. Was she Germany? One of the few countries that eschewed feminine metaphor. *Die Fatherland.* They would need healing when it was all done; Max was telling him this.

He summoned Laurier in the evening, using the plodding, sometimes infuriating table rapping. He didn't want to chance a medium here at the summit.

—Wilfrid, it seems that we are finally at the very centre of this dreadful business. I'm afraid that Roosevelt may not see the end of it.

I tally blade (?).

—History will miss him.

Histry berry occidents (accidents) vbising (?) to be shut in odder (order).

—The French question plagues me, Wilfrid.

No response was forthcoming, Laurier distracted with something in the spiritual dimension, perhaps. What distractions existed there? Three minutes lumbered by. How did time pass among the infinite? Perhaps King lacked the spiritual connection to summon these people. Sixteen discouraging minutes, then finally, King felt a response.

I pricked everton. (Picked? Plagued? Everyone?)

—Is there no answer?

All rations (nations) are unanswerable questions Mackenzie though bost (most) disguise it fore (more) cleverly that (than) we do.

—My place in history, Wilfrid …

That tactful pause.

Luddy min snoot.

Over and out.

There was a disagreeable discussion with Ralston on the issue of conscription. King was loath to send men into battle. Borden had been loath to in the last war, but now they knew the true horror of what had gone on in Europe, and King was even more reluctant. And the natural forces that pulled at the country were aligned on opposite sides of the issue, which made it even more problematic. In Quebec, which had elected him with such emphasis, 73 percent had voted against conscription; in the rest of Canada, 80 percent had voted in favour of it. King's compromise, "Not necessarily conscription, but conscription if necessary," was inspired, but it would only hold back the waters for so long. He was free to implement conscription, but there would be both a political and a human cost. With luck the war would end before a decision had to be made.

But Ralston was agitating to send some of those who had been conscripted for home service only, the so-called Zombies. Quebec's premier, the masterful and worrisome Duplessis (King had heard that the man had given appliances to rural Quebecers in return for votes), gave a gallant speech for the sake of Churchill and Roosevelt, extolling the patriotism that soared in the heart of every Quebecer. It was only a few hundred yards from here where Wolfe's men had climbed L'Anse au Foulon and Montcalm had doomed himself, the battle for a continent decided.

Roosevelt was coming out of the sunroom with a cocktail in his hand, pushed by his imposing wife, who King thought looked like a painting of a defective Dutch royal from two centuries ago. A forceful woman, though, and an engaging dinner companion. Roosevelt had his cigarette with that long holder, though King noticed he rarely puffed on it.

"Mackenzie, join us for a drink, won't you."

"Of course."

As he toasted FDR's health (barely able to look him in the eye), King thought that it was essentially a religious war between those who denied God's revelation of Himself in Christ and those who accepted it.

They all sat, of course, on the bomb, that secret knowledge. It could prove to be an agent for total destruction. The Bible says we shall have forty years of peace, and then Armageddon. The Russians were working on their own, using research stolen from the Americans. The Germans hadn't made much progress, it was being reported. *God help us if they do.*

He read Ezekiel 31 at breakfast, the cutting down of the lofty cedar that tried to rise so high above all the others. Perhaps this was mankind. The bomb would lay waste to all life, a modern version of the Flood ... "for they are all given over to death, to the nether world among mortal men, with those who go down to the Pit."

King wondered if War Secretary Stimson was being seduced by the imperial notion of a Pax Atomica. Of course the U.S. would need to control the world's supply of fissionable material. The Russians wanted Libya and Tripolitania because it would give them access to the uranium deposits in the Belgian Congo. Canada was supplying the U.S. with uranium from the Eldorado Mines at Great Bear Lake. The U.S. government had first ordered 8 tons of uranium for the Manhattan Project. The next order was for 60 tons. Then 350 tons, and now 500 tons.

The alliance between Canada and America still troubled King. The Americans had built the Alaska Highway, a project that Canada couldn't have managed on its own. Still, they had access through the Canadian north and some claim to it now. The relationship was always going to be a question of balancing friendship and imperialism. At any rate, the complicity between the two countries was cemented with this atomic project, whatever it led to.

The uranium was refined in Canada, then shipped to New Mexico, where the scientists were working around the clock to build the bomb. King had heard that Eldorado was falling behind in its orders. The project had already cost two billion dollars and caused some awkward political contortions. Just look at Oppenheimer. If he wasn't a Communist he was the next best thing. But he was a genius, and one always forgives genius in wartime.

Oppenheimer said that no demonstration would be sufficiently spectacular to guarantee the primitive awe the weapon deserved; for that they would need a city. Yet General Eisenhower was lobbying hard not to use it. An irony: the communist scientist in favour of the bomb, the Republican general against it. Eisenhower was against dropping the bomb for two reasons: It was unnecessary, the Japanese were going to surrender anyway; and it would make a terrible mark in history, a black smudge beside America's name. Perhaps he was right, or perhaps as a general he disliked the idea that all he had dedicated his life to was suddenly null. Five thousand years of discipline and sacrifice, armies clashing with their steel, that bloody tradition that became noble in the retelling. The military become superfluous in one nineteen-kiloton flash; war now the domain of science and politics.

Oppenheimer had been seduced by its awful promise, the pure and instant physics: a fiery centre that produced a ring of black smoke, the fireball extinguished in a flash and the smoke rising up—24,000 feet in four seconds—a miraculous growth that grew to 36,000 feet in another few seconds, a plume of white, black, yellow, and red that punched through the clouds with the greatest force the world had seen.

The bomb was to deter the Russians as much as finish the Japanese, King mused. Already they had to look to the next war.

4

NUREMBERG, 1946

Mackenzie King sat in the gallery that looked down on the dock. Ribbentrop and Goering were the last to come in and they sat beside one another. To think these men had brought such destruction upon themselves, their country, and the world. King felt something for them; they had come under the spell of the devil, who wasn't here to answer for his evil. The German lawyer was plodding to the point of stupidity. Perhaps this was part of the plan: to arrange for them to be defended by a simpleton reading endless affidavits.

Goering seemed half his former size, diminished in every way. Ribbentrop was taking notes, weary looking, an old man suddenly, a shadow. He was planning to write his memoirs, King had heard, and there would be several volumes, everything done on the monumental Nazi scale. Surely he knew he would be executed. Did these men know of the burning flesh in the ovens, children clawing at the doors? Who can see inside their souls? Apparently a psychiatrist was trying to do just that. King doubted he would have much luck. He had met these men in the guise of gentlemen (von Neurath was educated at Oxford) and they had presided over hell on earth. Such was the devil's power of disguise. Hitler was a false god, Germany itself a false idol, and now the Germans were like Job, destined to live "in desolate cities, in houses which no man should inhabit, which were destined to become heaps of ruins … he will not escape from darkness, his emptiness will be his recompense."

The tour of the prisons had been dismal. That nauseating odour. And there was Hess in his cell, eyes burning like coal, possibly mad. King had spoken with him several years ago, but it was impossible to tell if he remembered him. He stared like a zoo animal, like those bison that had been sent to Berlin. The exhibits were ghastly beyond belief; using human skin to make shoes. If there was anything to be gained from all this, King thought, it was that there would be a newfound embrace of divinity in the world. What was in doubt will become accepted belief. The scriptures will become literal truth, the world will evolve to a higher plane, and there will be a Second Coming. King had been told of a medium that did materialization, which seemed somehow dreadful: to behold your dead mother (in the dress she was buried in? In a gossamer gown?). But it was said to be beautiful; it must be where the conception of angels came from.

It was a moral universe; if you let Christ out of your life, Satan rushed in. This was clear.

In King's vision that morning, a Mother Superior stood beside him. He was holding a roll of paper under his arm. Perhaps new commandments—King picked to be Moses, a manifesto to keep mankind from destroying itself in the twentieth century.

Goering looked up from the dock and met his gaze briefly, and King was relieved when he turned away.

Goering sat in his cell toying with the copper cartridge, which gleamed dully in the prison light. He had enjoyed sparring with the prosecutors. Ribbentrop hadn't had the will to respond to them with any vigour. He hadn't the will for much. As foreign minister he had been weak and indecisive, and in the witness box he gave the impression that he would fall apart at any minute. Goering recalled his first meeting in Dortmund when he declared that in the future he would be the only man in Prussia to bear responsibility, that every bullet fired from a police pistol was his bullet, and if that was murder, then it was his murder. A convenient moral loophole, and so many ran to embrace it. This, he mused, was the beginning of empire.

Hitler was gone, dead in the bunker. The people loved him, no one would doubt that. They fought with loyalty, self-sacrifice, and courage even though they didn't want war. The *Volk* never want war, this is understood. They hunger for leadership and complain when they have it.

Blood will tell.

Had it been Himmler who dreamed up the medical experiments? Such a tedious mind. A buffoon whose suicide was welcomed by all. Yet another shirking of his responsibility. And Ley too, hanging himself in his cell. So he wouldn't be hanged by England! Ley had tied the curtain to the toilet handle and then around his neck and stuffed his own stockings in his mouth to die choking over the toilet. He couldn't have contrived a more ignominious end. Another weak-minded fool in the dock, facing the smugness of the English. Ley was no doubt dying for a drink. Perhaps he died for a drink. A squalid drunk (and possibly a Jew—his last name, Goering had heard, was actually Lev). And who are the English? They should be German, their kings are German. Isolated on that soggy island, they lost their German soul, a race of pale shopkeepers counting change for the world. Where is their empire? Its remnants in that damp food turned to shit and used to fertilize the precious gardens.

If the Nazis committed atrocities (and of this, he had no knowledge, and what did it matter if he did—Hitler was his conscience), the Communists were inhuman, following a barbaric ideology. The delusion that all men are equal. What Russian peasant living in his thirteenth-century filth was his equal? Barbaric Asiatics communing with goats. Their kings, too, were German, or at least educated here. *Communism is a disease, not an ideology,* he thought, *and I am proud, yes, this is true, proud that I created the first concentration camps—they were for the Communists. Let them be equal there!*

Of course you needed a sensible wife for this work. Hitler lacked one, perhaps a critical failing. There were two Hitlers. The Hitler of the French campaign was charming and genial. The Hitler of the Russian campaign was suspicious, tense, and violent. Perhaps he possessed the madness he was accused of. Who can be sure? When there is nothing left to connect us to this world, what are we?

There was a darkness at the edge of Goering's dreams, if they were dreams. He was afraid to sleep. Who can sleep when they will be hanged at dawn? Those last hours so precious. There had been no thoughts of justice. Justice is a luxury during revolution, everyone knows this. Whenever things go badly, we have democracy.

Something moved at the edge of his consciousness, some shape, large and undefined. It lumbered, then disappeared.

Hitler was sent by God to save Germany, of that there was no doubt. How shall I give expression, O my Führer, to what is in our hearts? How shall I find words to express your deeds? Has there ever been a mortal as beloved as you, my Führer? Was there ever belief as strong as the belief in your mission!

In the camps for Russian prisoners he had heard they had begun to eat each other.

How had the story gone? His father had told it to him as a child. The man with twelve children has another that he cannot care for. Unlucky thirteen. In desperation, he goes into the woods (the place of refuge and fear for the German consciousness, and for this they must thank the clever Grimms) and there he meets God, who says He will take care of the baby. But the man refuses. "You give to the rich and starve the poor," the man says. "I don't want you as a godfather." He continues walking and comes upon Death, who says, "Give him to me. I will raise him. I will teach him. I will protect him. Who is better able to protect him than me?"

What else was in the woods? An ogre, or perhaps that was another story. The boy is given to Death, and Death is true to his word—he protects him. And the boy grows up and becomes a doctor, and Death says to him, "If you see me standing at the head of the patient, then you may cure him. But if I am standing at his feet, then he is finished and I must claim him." The boy finds a beautiful woman who is gravely ill, and he sees Death standing at her feet. She is finished! And who can bear the death of the beautiful? Certainly not literature. But the doctor turns her around so her head is before Death. He is fooled and she is cured! This was always his favourite part of the story. To outwit Death! But Death learns of the deception and grows angry and leads his godson to a cavern, a dark cave filled with tiny points of light. And he leaves him there, and each light is a human life and each light quietly disappears. And of course this story is true.

Goering separated the copper cartridge carefully and held it up. The sun was breaking over the scaffold. Ribbentrop had gone bravely, a surprise. His last words had been, "I wish peace to the world." It was impossible to know if he was being ironic, this minor aristocrat. Ribbentrop had the moral consistency of spoiled fruit. Himmler had taken the coward's road, and Ley, even the Führer. But Ribbentrop marched to the gallows without pause or tears (they should have hanged his wife) and left those words, whatever they meant.

Goering swallowed the fine grains that were contained in the cartridge, welcoming the faint bitter taste of almonds, welcoming the consuming heat (was this purgatory already?), welcoming even the nausea and searing pain in his head as his nervous system fought for the oxygen that was no longer there. He convulsed horribly, like a marionette whose strings were being pulled by a madman. O Pinocchio.

5

MICHAEL MOUNTAIN HORSE, ALBERTA, 1948

The first maps of the country weren't of the land but of the sea: Portuguese maps of the Grand Banks that showed where the cod were. The land was barren, distant, useless; the water filled with riches. Now it was the land that was lucrative. Geologic maps extending from Alberta down to Texas showed synclines and anticlines, fluid permeability and seismic markings, the bleak wizardry of science in search of buried oil.

The smell of diesel hung in a breeze that carried black clouds east and dispersed them gently over the rape crop. Engines droned in the dark. A few shapes moved in the field, antelope perhaps. From the drilling floor, Michael could see another derrick to the west, its lights perpendicular to the flat dark plain. Oil was an inevitability. You threw the slips into the hole, rammed the tongs into place, and they snapped tight and twisted the drill pipe apart. A new pipe stabbed in and tightened. Pull the slips and drill another thirty feet through the stubborn D-3 formation. Oil was the western subtext, waiting to erupt.

The war had taken the young, and Michael worked with men who were older than he was. He worked here and there. With a threshing crew that had come up from Nebraska, following the harvest to Cartwright, north of the Canadian border. He had worked as a ranch hand down near Pincher Creek. Briefly, he had lived in Toronto, framing houses with tireless Italians who mourned their homeland and cursed the bland food. He walked the ravines in autumn under the cover of fiery maples. There were deer and he found evidence of coyotes though never saw one. He read constantly, finding solace and companionship in books. His mother used to tell them stories and read to them, and Michael wondered if the white books had been for him and the native tales for Stanford.

She was alone now. Dunstan was gone. Michael was playing chess with him one evening, waiting on another of his sclerotic defensive moves, when the old man tipped over onto the floor, felled by a stroke. He survived for another five months, but he had been eaten by the melancholia that first set in when his son died in the war. Then his ranch gave out. Michael suspected that it was grief that finally consumed him. He settled Dunstan's affairs, and for a few years ran some cattle on the land left to his mother, but it was too small to work in country where you needed ten acres a head, and they sold the property to a neighbouring rancher.

It was March and Michael couldn't taste spring. His hands were cold, the wet gloves of no use. They made a connection on the drilling floor, then Abe Babiak, the driller, went into the doghouse. Michael and the other roughneck, Ennis Cowley, joined him. It was the middle of the grave-yard shift, and Isaacs, the derrickman, hadn't come down from the stick, not even for lunch.

"What's with Isaacs?" Ennis asked. "He's like a treed raccoon up there. Why don't he come down? He's smoking over the wellhead too. Blow us to kingdom come."

Michael had noticed that Isaacs was out of sorts. He might have been drinking. A career oil worker in his sixties, worn out.

Babiak lit a cigarette and blew the smoke upward. It hit the low ceiling and curled back into the small space. He had a hunched muscular frame and the face of an ogre, his thick nose broken by the spinning chain years ago. There was one naked bulb in the doghouse that threw a deathly light. Outside it was black.

"He's still stunned as a heifer," Babiak said. "You didn't hear. Jesus. Long Change, Isaacs heads home like usual. He's got a farm up near Rimby, don't know what the fuck you can grow up there but. Works three weeks, then drives up spends the afternoon in the Rimby bar, most of the evening. Decides to go home, see if he can talk the old lady into sawing off a piece of tail. Opens his door at midnight, what does he find? Doris lit out. And not just lit out. Christ listen to this. She takes every stick of furniture. Takes the goddamn fixtures. Curtain rods, door knobs, carpets, fridge, stove. House as empty as a whore's heart. His clothes in a pile on the floor."

Ennis thought about this for a moment. "I guess she was trying to tell him something," he said.

"You got that part right," Babiak said. "Took the car and the trailer too. Not even a note."

"How long were those two married?" Ennis asked.

"Too long, apparently," Babiak said.

They stood in the doghouse warming themselves and then went down to check the blowout preventer under the drilling floor. There were problems with the hole but the toolpush said orders were to drill dry and that was that. Sitting on top of all that gas with no circulation mud. Babiak had been against it. "If you had half a fucking brain you wouldn't be drilling dry going into the D-3 formation."

They were crouched in the half-darkness when they heard it. A guttural groan, less a noise than a feeling that came up through their boots. A burp of mud spilled over the drilling nipple and they all froze. "Get out," Babiak said, urgently and quietly, almost to himself. They scrambled out from under the drilling platform. Michael's hard hat banged off a pipe and he started to sprint west in his heavy rig boots, running through a foot of snow. The noise was like being inside an airplane engine. The well was blowing in, all that oil and gas sitting at two thousand pounds per square inch of pressure spewing out. The earth giving up its dirty secret. Fifteen feet in front of him one of the rotary table master bushings landed in the snow, three hundred pounds of steel suddenly settled deep in the snow like a bomb. Pieces of shale rained down as shrapnel. Michael ran to the boilers and shut them off. The air was gaseous. The fear of fire was in all of them. The very air could burn. They scrambled back up to the floor, got the string off the bottom, lifted it as high as they could, chained down, and took cover. The air was a roar, oil blowing southeast, covering the snow. Michael ran to the toolpush's trailer at the north end of the lease and found Isaacs lying in the black snow, covered in oil. He looked like a newborn seal. His neck was broken. He hadn't tied himself off and was taken with the first gush. Standing on the boards a hundred feet up, smoking a Belvedere, looking at the empty darkness and thinking of Doris and then the well blew.

Michael opened the trailer door and there was a woman standing there in a man's cowboy shirt. She had pale skinny legs that were lightly veined with blue. There were circles under her eyes.

"Where's he at?" Michael said.

"I woke up when I heard the noise," the woman said. She was cradling herself in the cold. The trailer smelled like kerosene.

"Well blew in," Michael said.

"It might take more than that to wake him," the woman said. There was an empty bottle of rye on the kitchen counter.

Michael walked past the girl into the bedroom at the back and shook the push until he opened his eyes, which were confused and then hot with anger. "Well's blown in," Michael said.

They waited until first light before going back up the steel stairs to the doghouse. Sand was blowing out and the air was gritty and wet. There were trucks and lights all over the lease now. The company men had arrived.

Inside the doghouse, Babiak looked through the cloudy circle of window out to the drilling floor and said, "I imagine we'll see some Chinamen come out of that hole soon."

The pipe had broken off in the standpipe, the threads stuck in there, and Michael put on the extra derrickman harness and crawled across the drilling floor with a brass diamond-point chisel and a hammer. Cement trucks were coming up the lease road. They had to regain circulation but they needed that connection to the standpipe, and it wasn't possible with a piece of pipe broken. Babiak and Cowley were holding on to the rope that was tied to the harness, ready to pull Michael back. In case there was trouble, Cowley said without irony. How could there be more trouble? The biggest blow-in on the continent. Michael slid around on the slick floor and tore his knee on a snag in the steel. He managed to get the chisel in place, crouching awkwardly, and began to tap. He wondered when the whole thing would suddenly flare into blue flame. Crouched there he could see a newspaperman picking his way through the oily snow, holding a pail over his head. He got a piece out and worked at the remains, reaching in with his hand. It was still too stiff to move and he chiselled some more, loosening the last pieces and rotating them out with his bare hand that was beginning to freeze. He crawled back to the doghouse. Below them Isaacs was laid out on the bed of a company truck, still covered in oil.

Atlantic No. 3 blew wild for six months, a million barrels of oil covering wheat fields three miles away. Newspapermen came from Europe and Texas and Toronto to witness its unceasing anger. Newsreels played all over the world. Clips were shown before every movie at the Palace Theatre in Calgary and got a cheer each time, the celluloid confirming that they were part of history. Locals came out to watch the blow-in like it was television.

Men came out to the well site from Texas and Calgary and Oklahoma, murmuring like shamans. There were men who would run anything down the hole: oats, diesel, sawdust, Ping-Pong balls. They flared some of the gas, but it kept blowing. They tried getting the Hosmer button over the hole and latching it tight but the steel lid flew away like a postcard in a hurricane.

There were few thoughts of waste. It was a celebration. With the big strike at Leduc the year before, oil had filled the imagination of the province. After digging 133 dry holes, Imperial Oil finally hit big and Calgary was drunk with possibility. Atlantic No. 3 was a baptism.

Michael worked as derrickman for a Commonwealth rig through the summer, coaxing the drill pipe toward him with a rope, struggling with the stand, staring ninety feet down to the drilling floor, his harness tied to the rail. You could see from up there and he liked that expanse. To the west the mountains appeared as jagged teeth, and to the east the receding fields curved into the horizon.

The stick wasn't for everyone. Heights were a problem, even for some of those who said they weren't. Michael had seen men climb the ladder—like scaling a ten-storey building—and they started out fast and then slowed and sometimes came to a dead stop, and someone would have to go up there and talk them down. Others could manage the climb but once they were up there, it was a new kind of vertigo. You stared east into a thousand miles of flat land. You had to tie the harness to the railing and then, trusting that double clove hitch, lean out over the drilling floor. Babiak told him that on Big Indian No. 3 he was working motors and the derrickman fell to the steel floor like a splayed cat. Not as much blood as you'd think but everything inside him was jelly. Even at his age, Michael floated up the ladder, not using the safety harness unless the toolpush was around. He felt liberated by the climb. Ascension. Wasn't everything based on it? In life, in death? He left his burdens on the ground.

At dawn the sun broke through the blurred line of grey clouds that hovered at the horizon, and Michael could see two antelope springing through the fields. The ordered lines of the land. The surveyors had laid it out in grids, each section defined by gravel roads, the land claimed by immigrants and handed down, each farm filled with death and hardship and the renewed promise of spring.

Michael stayed up in the derrick and watched the sun rise until shift change. In the change room, Babiak and Ennis Cowley were already stripping off their coveralls, putting them in bags to take home and wash. There was a new roughneck, Curtis, a skittish, pale nineteen-year-old with a homemade tattoo on his forearm that read Trouble. He was six feet tall and maybe 165 pounds.

"What you got planned for tonight, Trouble?" Michael asked him.

"I'll have some fun," he said, as if Michael might doubt it. "You wanna believe I'll have fun."

They had been paid the day before. Michael looked at Curtis, with his tentative pugnacity and hand-tooled boots, the kind of boy who cashed his cheque and asked the teller for fifty-dollar bills, and carried it all in his pocket. He'd want to pull a fifty out in the King Eddie and buy a round, let the waitress know he was serious business.

The day driller, Washburn, opened the door to the change shack.

"Babyduck, where'd you hide that log?"

"Same place I always hide it," Babiak told him. "In the desk."

"Well I didn't see it there." Washburn stood silhouetted in the doorway, the day bright behind him.

"Maybe take your head out of your ass."

Washburn walked away, leaving the door open. "Christ," Babiak said. "You move his plate over six inches the son of a bitch would starve to death." He pulled on his cowboy shirt and snapped the pearl buttons shut.

Michael grabbed his work clothes and walked out to his car and drove back to the hotel. The end of the graveyard shift brought the greatest relief. The sun coming up, the day beginning. Michael felt optimistic. It was the last week of August and cool in the mornings, summer's power nearly gone.

He showered, put on a clean shirt and new suede cowboy boots, and ate a big breakfast at the Royal Café, then went back to his room and slept for nine hours. He woke up at seven, and went back to the Royal for a dinner of meatloaf and mashed potatoes, then walked downtown. The town was warming to Saturday night, people on the streets with expectant faces and starched clothes. He saw Babiak standing in front of the King Eddie, waving him over. Babiak's hair was slicked down and his pitted face was freshly shaved and Michael could smell aftershave from three yards away. Babiak was wearing a black and beige cowboy shirt with diamond-shaped buttons and there was a crease ironed into his jeans. He had a wife, apparently, though no one had ever seen her. His daughter had run away, Michael heard. Babiak never spoke a word about his family.

"I'll buy you a beer, Mountain Horse," he said. Inside it was smoky and smelled of stale beer. A country band was on stage struggling through Eddy Arnold's "Texarkana Baby," the lambent eastern notes of the pedal steel curving in the air.

They sat down at a small table. Babiak ordered four draught and sat silently until they arrived, then he knocked one back in a single slug and started talking. "Was working High Tower No. 5, digging holes in the foothills, never found anything. They had a driller named Donahue, drank some. Not so much on the day shift, when the push was around. But slow drilling graveyards he'd get a skinful. Sometimes he was out cold, sleeping on sacks of sawdust and the motorman had to make the connections. Well they set up on the eastern slope, early summer. Donahue's crew. Around the end of shift change, he gets that derrick hoisted. The cable's holding it snug, except Donahue, he's had a few snorts in his coffee and he's a bit relaxed. And he doesn't put the pins in to hold it. It's just that cable holding twenty tons of fucking steel. The wind is blowing pretty hard over those hills. Donahue gets in his truck, takes a few shots from his flask, and he starts driving down the lease road. Looks in his rear-view, and he sees that derrick starting to sway. It hits him that the pins aren't in. He stops the truck and sits there. That cable finally snaps and the derrick kind of waves up there in the wind for about five seconds then starts to go. It just heads down, a hundred forty feet of steel and when it hits, you know it, man. The dust comes up. Derrick's twisted and buckled. Ain't worth shit now. Useless as three Arabs. Old Donahue sees all this in the rear-view and he takes a jolt from the flask and he just keeps driving." Babiak let out a big laugh and took a long pull of beer. "No one has seen the son of a bitch since. I heard he was logging for Schlumberger out of Oklahoma."

Curtis came in, dressed up, his face open and nervous, and stood at the bar. Babiak stared at him. "Kid don't have a lick of sense," he said. He drank the last of his beer.

"Hey, Trouble," Michael yelled, and waved. Curtis spotted them, looking relieved, and then got his face looking nonchalant as he walked over.

By midnight, there were six of them at the table, all telling stories. Wells that had blown in, sending pipe out of the hole like spaghetti. Water tanks that had rolled off the truck and into pig barns, farmers that had shot the boilers up, fingers lost in the spinning chain, drunken roughnecks that fell into sump tanks, grass fires, rattlesnakes in the doghouse, three-day poker games, waitresses who broke your heart and took your money, Cadillacs that caught on fire. They worked on the rigs every day and every day they cursed them, and on their break they talked about them for six hours straight.

But they never spoke of oil, Michael noticed. It was an abstraction. Sometimes they talked about women, though they were abstractions as well. This was a womanless landscape. There were maybe two hundred men in the bar and fewer than fifty women, drinking with their men, not saying much, clinging to the wreckage. The songs were all about women, though. The band was playing "Humpty Dumpty Heart."

Curtis said he had to take a leak and got up, and Babiak started telling them about a guy he worked with who got in a fight over a pool game in a bar up near Grande Prairie. "Ahern, Bobby Ahern, about five foot fuck all, but wide as a house. So he flattens this guy, and the guy's girlfriend picks up the eight ball and lets fly. And this girl's got an arm. Ball's coming at him from six feet away. It hits Bobby's forehead at about fifty miles an hour and it sounds like someone smacked the boiler with a ball-peen hammer. He just stands there, though. Don't go down. His eyes are glassed over like he just found Jesus in the Cecil Tavern. We lead him to his chair and he sits. 'Damn near knocked me off my feet,' he says about ten minutes later."

After every story, Babiak's head went back and he'd roar. Michael listened to a few more stories, then said softly, "Curtis." He hadn't come back.

"Shit." Babiak got to his feet quickly. He and Michael raced to the men's room. Curtis wasn't there. They followed the hallway at the back of the bar to the back door. They opened the door and there was Curtis lying on the pavement by the kitchen bins, groaning, his face bloodied. They didn't need to search his pockets. His hand-tooled boots were gone too.

Michael had kept the news to himself, but on the last day of August he told Babiak: He was going to university in September.

Babiak looked at him. "I figured you for higher things. But I'll tell you the truth, you're too damn old to learn anything. I hope you're just there for the pussy. I quit school when I was eleven. No fucking regrets. Who am I going to send up the stick?"

"Maybe give Curtis a try."

"Christ," Babiak said. "He'll blow away. Have to pick him off a weather vane in Drayton Valley." He lit a cigarette. "What they going to teach you up there, Studhorse?"

"History."

"Like we don't have enough of that."

6

MACKENZIE KING, KINGSMERE, 1950

His breathing was laboured and wet, as if each breath had to swim to the surface. If his brother, Max, were here, he would cure him. Or Louis Pasteur. King noticed that his skin had a bluish tinge. He coughed some blood into a handkerchief. The grey man of politics suddenly colourful.

What was it that Frank Scott, that miserable poet and dedicated critic, said about him? That King would be remembered wherever men honour ingenuity, ambiguity, inactivity, and political longevity. King was the longest-serving prime minister in Canada's history—twenty-two years, the longest-serving leader in the English-speaking world. His mother's faith had been well placed, his own doubts without cause. He had risen to the challenge. What Scott and so many of his critics failed to understand was that greatness lies in what you prevent rather than what you create. He had brought the country together, or at the very least, he was the prime minister who divided Canada the least.

Looking back on the state of the nation, he was rather pleased. Communism had been stifled, the war won, the Depression ended, French and English were living comfortably (if not happily) beside one another. Canada had inched further from Britain (though dangerously close to America). Villains had been punished. The events had been biblical, threatening the very globe. And in this maelstrom, Canada had flourished, and he had played an important role. Surely history would grant him this.

The war was the sorest test. It would be a pleasant reunion with Franklin, who he had already spoken to. He wondered about all those souls from Hiroshima and Nagasaki. That fearful demonstration would haunt the world, no doubt. The blast had imprinted people like shadows onto the sidewalk. Thank God it was the Japanese who received the atomic bomb and not white people. The Americans had dropped leaflets on Nagasaki, warning of the bomb's awful power, though they had been dropped after the bombing. To lessen the awful consequences, Truman told the American people that Hiroshima was a military target. He was already rationalizing. But Nagasaki had no strategic purpose, no military goal. What would history make of that? What was that Japanese slogan— "Extinguish Britain and America and make a bright new map!" It had been chanted by schoolchildren apparently. And in those flashes in August a bright new map had been created, one that would chart the future of mankind. King had found Truman a curious man, the Missouri haberdasher trying to grow in the giant shadow of FDR.

How would King be mourned? He knew there wasn't going to be the love that had spilled out of the nation's heart when Laurier died, or when the flawed Macdonald, or even the deeply flawed D'Arcy McGee, passed on. His accomplishments would be appreciated over time though, of this he was certain. No less an authority than Lorenzo de' Medici had assured him of it, a man who understood history. His legacy would form, gathering power like a summer storm, first a hint of breeze, a change in the air, then the deluge. And he would watch it, like a sporting event perhaps, seated with his mother, his dogs Pat I, Pat II, and Pat III (hopefully there won't be any trouble there), with Laurier, and his beloved grandfather. They would watch his stature grow over time. Like Laurier, he would offer his own counsel to those who were progressive enough to seek it.

His chest ached, a saw going through it with every breath. He was shaking with fever, chilled even under the blankets. Whither shall I go from thy Spirit? Even the darkness is not dark to thee, the night is bright as the day; for darkness is as light with thee.

His mother stood over him with her hand on his shoulder. "It's time to go," she whispered.

LULL

1961–1963

In the 1950s I studied history at McGill in Montreal, a city in its prime, the largest in the country then, still the richest, certainly the most complicated. The life of a campus is youth, young men and women filled with doubt and debate and sexual longing. I was fifty, older than many of the professors. I had a brief affair with a twenty-year-old woman in my class, and it made me feel even older.

Montreal looked like a religious city, governed by murmuring Jesuits, a city of spires, and like every religious city, reliably sinful. The presence of all those churches was oddly comforting, but I never went inside. Occasionally I went to a nightclub on Mackay to see country-and-western bands. I found that plaintive music soothing.

When I came back to Calgary in 1953 it wasn't quite a city. It was a conservative place, a wall of order, the hand of God visible, perfectly balanced between optimism and dreariness. It was in the 1950s that I found love. The fifties were the necessary lull after the bomb. It seems unlikely now that anyone could find love in that tentative time, especially at my age, but I did.

435

Michael looked at Billy's quiet face. Seventeen was all about yearning. Yearning for the girl who sat beside you in home-room and smelled like honey, whose pens were arranged in a neat row on her desk in the gradated hues of the rainbow, her eyes filled with kindness, her unattainable hair. Or yearning for your friend's mother, whose hand on your forearm was electric.

Michael had been pulled toward a hundred women. He remembered a woman he'd seen on a Paris street forty-seven years ago. A woman he'd never even spoken to who still clung to his imagination. Something in her face, the set of her eyes, her lips parted as if she was going to tell him something, the way she stood; he could see a lifetime in her. She smelled like straw when he stood near her, waiting to cross the busy street. Like an animal he read her through gesture and scent, attaching moral equivalents to these cues (she would be a wonderful lover, he thought as she delicately straightened her dress, and this when he was virginal himself). What if he had stopped to talk to her? They talk, have a glass of wine, fall in love, get married. His life goes in some other direction. But he was a bumpkin then, walking Paris with a soldier's numb relief, and he didn't have any idea how to approach a woman.

As for Billy, who knew? Maybe he loved Nancy Baxter, the blond distraction that sat in class curling her hair with her pencil, revelling in the desire that flowed from every boy in the room. Michael doubted this, though: Billy loved the idea of love. He was unfulfilled. But so were millions. People huddled together in the Depression out of necessity, embraced during war out of fear, allied on the prairies out of loneliness. Not every union was perfect. But the heart keeps seeking, looking for love in books, or old lovers, or strangers. We are all explorers.

I met Elizabeth at a party. A party I didn't want to go to, like all parties. It was in a small bungalow, filled with men in sports coats and women in dresses, most of them teachers. I was standing

by the hi-fi when a woman walked up and started flipping through
the records. She picked out a Fats Waller record and delicately laid
the needle down, then stood for a minute, listening to Waller tear
through "Honeysuckle Rose."

Elizabeth had thick blond hair that was fading into grey, and
a habit of drawing one hand through it, as if she was renewing her
own sense of its lustre. Then she would repeat the gesture, as if she
needed to be reminded again of its magnificence, its thickness like
a sheaf of wheat. It seemed flirtatious, as if we had mussed her
hair together.

Elizabeth talked quickly and her hands moved through the air
like a conductor's. She'd grown up in Montreal and for a while
lamented the loss of its mystery and romance. But she found solace
in the mountains. We spent almost every weekend there, hiking up
to the tea hut above Lake Louise, canoeing down the Bow River,
driving up to the Columbia Icefield. We swam naked in Emerald
Lake, its otherworldly colour giving the water the impression of
viscosity, as if it were a green soup, the very water where life had
first formed. We made love in our small tent, happy to wake up in
the fresh air, cool in the mornings, even in August.

Elizabeth was a nurse and there were more opportunities in
Calgary. But there was something else too, I think: She wasn't
particularly happy in the place she came from. She didn't really fit
in. Or she didn't fit into the romantic version of Montreal she
carried with her. Tall and wide-shouldered, on the cusp of big-
boned, she was more suited to the West, where her natural grace
wasn't eclipsed by the small, slim, dark-haired women that appear
in waves on St. Catherine Street, almost military in their numbers,
strutting with alluring indifference. Among that army Elizabeth
looked ungainly and plain. So she came west.

We were together for a decade. I don't know how it died. We
went to Montreal together and she gave me a tour of her childhood,

showed me the place where she first smoked a cigarette, where she went to school, lost her virginity, the café where she talked about Marx with an African exchange student until two in the morning. We drove through Notre-Dame-de-Grâce and I tried to imagine her as a schoolgirl, walking in her uniform smoking experimentally with her fellow Catholics, furtively checking to see if God was going to strike her down. But I couldn't. I couldn't summon her life there, or perhaps I just wasn't interested enough, and she sensed that. We drove past Ogilvy's, Schwartz's Deli, a café where she fell in love, all her landmarks.

Perhaps Elizabeth was an antidote to Marion. They were certainly opposites, both in appearance and temperament. Marion was feral, and that had an appeal, but it was exhausting. Elizabeth was a pragmatist. I never needed to worry about her shooting me in the chest six times with a pistol filled with blanks. If she were ever to shoot me, it would be with real bullets. But in the end, she stayed in Montreal and I came back home alone.

Sometimes people move to reinvent themselves. They move to Paris or Toronto or New York or Los Angeles and become something else. Marion was one of those. She scraped the cow shit off her shoes and disappeared into the movies and never looked back. I went to her funeral. It wasn't that long ago. I hadn't seen her in thirty years. Why go? It ended badly, of course, but I was in love with her once. And that's something. It took me a long time to get over her, two years, probably more. Eventually she faded from my thoughts. But she was a moment in my life. When you're in your twenties you think there will be a lot of these moments, but you look back and there aren't that many.

So I went to her funeral.

The service was held in a small Spanish chapel in east Los Angeles. There was a Mexican priest with a dark, heavy head and six mourners. Rough wooden beams spanned the ceiling and there was an emaciated Jesus on the cross beside the priest, an especially anguished version, his eyes leaking blood, his body a red wound. Marion's coffin was by the altar. It was closed and I wished that it wasn't, that I could see her face. I hadn't kept any photographs of her; I burned them in the desert thirty years ago, and all memory is flawed. What did she look like now? She would have been in her sixties, still slim. I didn't recognize anyone in the chapel, though I hadn't expected to. We didn't have that many friends; we were a nation, enclosed and fractious.

I tried to recall the taste of her, the feel of her skin, something tangible to bury. She had a specific stare, one hand up by her face, squinting through the smoke of a Black Cat, lost in thought. What had she been doing for the last thirty years? I constructed a loose narrative: three more marriages; living in a bungalow on the flats below Beverly Hills in the shadow of celebrity; wearing oversized sunglasses into the evening. She had too much white wine with lunch, did the crossword, owned a small dog that died of neglect, talked about moving to France.

Who was her last lover? I wondered. How long ago?

After the priest's unfelt eulogy, there was a short prayer and we stood up and bowed our heads and filed out into the light.

The priest came over and asked me if I would help with the casket. They were one short. Two of the pallbearers had been supplied by the funeral home, impassive men dressed in black suits. Three others looked like they had some affiliation with the church and had been pressed into emergency service, Mexican men in white shirts that were damp with perspiration. We picked up the casket and walked in a hesitant procession to a hearse, then drove to the graveyard and unloaded her. I was at the front, and my face touched the cool wood of the coffin. Marion's face, unglimpsed in decades, was only inches away. Would they have applied makeup? Probably not. Her face would be pale, hues of greys and blues, her lips thin and drawn, the lines gathered in small piles. I thought of the night when we made love in the graveyard and now here we were again.

*T*he 1950s were good for a lot of people. In 1958, John Diefenbaker became prime minister, landing in office with the largest majority in history. What luck for a politician to arrive on stage at the exact moment that history craves him. Dief the Chief was of the West, with a preacher's rectitude and a lawyer's tongue, an outsider when the country had tired of insiders. His name was given to your school. An easy man to mock; he looked and sounded like the Old Testament, and preached anti-Americanism. He berated them as the devil, wattles shaking, eyes burning, livid and righteous. If we didn't cast the Yankees out of the temple, we were lost, he said. They wanted to put nuclear warheads on Canadian soil. They were buying Canadian companies. Their movie stars were in our dreams and we lusted for them, but when we awoke Marilyn and her comforting breasts were gone.

Well, we hate what is most like ourselves: That's what makes civil wars so potent. The narcissism of small differences. Maybe that was part of my attachment to Stanford; he was my opposite in most ways. He was another world. Diefenbaker was worried the differences between the two countries would be erased completely. He found comfort in the British Empire and the Queen, in tins of Walker's shortbread bought at Eaton's, in lace tablecloths and Anglican ceremony, and millions shared this view. Though not many who were under sixty. It isn't just music that each generation throws away.

Diefenbaker understood the 1950s, a decade of order and prosperity and everyone singing from the same hymn book. But beneath that calm, forces were gathering, the kilotons assembling on our borders. *The world was a quiet hostage, the end of history at hand, a flash of light and physics that would take everything, though people didn't give it that much thought. It was incomprehensible. Who can comprehend that final nullity? It would take all human meaning with it. We would be a blip, that short, violent period between the dinosaurs and nuclear winter.*

Diefenbaker didn't understand those forces. He didn't understand the 1960s and still doesn't (he's still in the legislature, sitting in the back benches like a mad uncle they can't find an attic for). How can one decade be so different from another? But of course they aren't neatly divided in ten-year increments; we do that after they're gone.

Diefenbaker is lost now. He can see history moving away from him and doesn't know where it's going. But for a brief moment, he coincided with history, a lucky thing for anyone, especially a politician. He was the people; we were him.

1

JOHN DIEFENBAKER, WASHINGTON, 1961

Standing in the doorframe, John F. Kennedy had a look he'd been practising forever. He bristled with purpose and adventure, the tanned heir, the whole country suddenly young. Jesus, he was handsome. Not like Ike's comfy face, the face of a fishing guide. Diefenbaker had liked Ike, could relax with him, even if they hadn't always agreed. They were of the same generation. But Kennedy was forty-four, Dief sixty-six, and this gap loomed as they shook hands.

Diefenbaker had already built up a reasonable dislike for the man. The Prairie populist with crinkly hair flattened under punishing protestant brush strokes, those hawkish eyes with their hint of evangelical madness, had won in a landslide. Kennedy, on the other hand, had scraped through with the smallest margin in U.S. history—118,000 votes! On this count, Diefenbaker was ahead. He had campaigned on a vigorous platform of anti-Americanism, tapping into the public mood.

"Would I be right in thinking that the United States is not unhelpful to you for political purposes in Canada?" Kennedy asked, smiling, teasing. He pronounced it "Canader" in his Boston accent. (On announcing Diefenbaker's visit, he had mispronounced his name—Diefen*bawker*—a mistake, though curiously the original pronunciation before it was anglicized after his grandfather's death.)

"That would be a not inaccurate conclusion."

They chatted in the Oval Office, which had been redecorated since Ike left, and reflected Kennedy's naval background. There were paintings of the War of 1812, which Kennedy saw as a marvellous victory for the States.

"You know," Diefenbaker said, "the British frigate *Shannon* captured the U.S. frigate *Chesapeake* and took it to Halifax in 1813."

"If I had that picture," Kennedy said, smiling, "I'd put it up."

"I'll give it to you."

Kennedy had already shown him the sailfish he had caught during his honeymoon in Acapulco. What kind of president had a fishing trophy in the White House?

"Have you ever caught anything better?" Kennedy asked, teasing yet not teasing in that Brahmin way.

"I was in Jamaica," Diefenbaker answered. "I caught a marlin. Eight and a half feet, one hundred forty pounds. A fighter."

"You didn't really catch it." Smiling.

"I did. Three hours and ten minutes."

"Three hours." *Owahs.*

"And ten minutes."

The real point of the meeting, through the terse niceties, the subtle complaints of economic imperialism, the idle chat of dumping surplus goods, and the natural friction due to the gap in age, political belief, and privilege, was nuclear. If the Russians came over the pole, Canada would be the battleground. Kennedy wanted to put nuclear missiles on Canadian soil. Diefenbaker wanted to publicly stand up to Kennedy, but also wanted to have an adequate defence against the Soviet threat. He saw the grey light of compromise in every issue. (He was more decisive when he woke up; as the day wore on he dithered—it was a race to get to him early in the day.)

"We need you to accept those nuclear warheads for continental defence," Kennedy said.

"There is strong opposition to nuclear bombs," Diefenbaker said, wandering instinctively to a middle ground. "We will be a strong ally ... but we'd like to see the acquisition of warheads tied to disarmament talks." His nuclear position was a mélange of qualifiers, hypothetical futures, and contrary politics; his private language.

They talked of Latin America, and the Congo, where the Russians and Americans were circling one another like wrestlers. It had been less than a year since the Congo leader Patrice Lumumba had come to Ottawa looking for support and money. Lumumba asked External Affairs Minister Howard Green to send a girl to his suite in the Château Laurier. Green assumed he needed a secretary and sent one. When the naked, professorial Lumumba opened the door, the girl ran down the hallway clutching her steno pad. External Affairs hired a prostitute the following night and sent her over, then billed the cost to the taxpayer under the entry of "flowers." And now Lumumba was dead, murdered last month in the African bush, the Belgians standing by apparently, maybe even supervising the execution. A Belgian officer dug up Lumumba's remains and cut them up with a hacksaw, then dissolved them in acid, keeping his teeth as a souvenir. Geopolitics as a horror film. The Americans had wanted to kill him as well, and perhaps the CIA tried.

Diefenbaker wondered if they would have to get a girl for Kennedy when he came to Ottawa; he had heard rumours.

There were a few inconclusive areas of agreement between the two, and after the meeting Diefenbaker simmered with squalid thoughts. Kennedy's steamrolling confidence, imperious in every gesture. "He's a pup," Diefenbaker told his special assistant John Fisher. "He thinks he can dictate to us. He cannot. *I will not be dictated to by that man.*" Dief told Fisher to find a print of a British ship winning a naval battle during the War of 1812.

"Why?"

"I'm going to send it to Kennedy."

"Oh, I don't think that's a good idea. What are you trying to prove?"

"We must teach him some history," Diefenbaker said. "History must be taught."

Kennedy strode back to the Oval Office, hand in his suit jacket pocket. "I don't want to see that boring son of a bitch again," he told his brother Bobby.

Diefenbaker had the marlin mounted in preparation for Kennedy's first official visit to Canada, as well as a painting that showed the British winning a naval battle in the War of 1812. It was a brilliant day in May and tens of thousands clogged the streets of Ottawa to see JFK and Jackie. They attracted a bigger crowd than the Queen and traffic was snarled for miles. When they walked through the Parliament Buildings a phalanx of secretaries came out to watch, each of them silently dying for JFK, their angora hearts screaming. He stopped and flirted with a few who appealed, his handshake lingering, making eye contact, reflexively measuring their sexual worth.

"Where's your marlin?" Kennedy asked Diefenbaker, smiling.

Dief escorted him to his office and pointed to it triumphantly.

"That *is* big," Kennedy said. "And you caught it." A hint of the interrogative. He radiated privilege and success, this despite the fiasco of the Bay of Pigs only weeks ago. The American-trained Cuban exiles were defeated in a few days, a failure of both planning and nerve.

They went out and greeted the crowd. Diefenbaker stood on the podium and spoke of warm historic relations between the two countries, beginning in the French that hadn't improved in all his years in politics, the words coming out, as always, in single unrelated sounds, a stilted phonetic bleat. "I welcome you as a great American," Diefenbaker finally said in English, to everyone's relief.

"I am somewhat encouraged to say a few words in French," Kennedy said on taking the podium, "after having the chance to listen to the Prime Minister." His line got a laugh. Everyone loved him. Dief was relieved at least that Kennedy's French was little better than his own.

They shovelled some dirt at a ceremonial planting of oak trees at Government House, a symbol of the two nations' shared destiny and respective strength. Dief handed Kennedy a silver-handled shovel (how appropriate, he thought), and Kennedy stared at it, smiling. His bad back, a war injury, meant he had to be careful. He lifted four shovel-fuls, pausing to look up for the cameras. On the fifth came that electric pain, a spark that jangled like a hot wire through his back. He almost screamed. It had taken two years of physiotherapy to tame his back, to get him to a point where he didn't have to take painkillers every day. And now after shovelling dirt with this doddering menace it would take two more years of cortisone and corsets and massage to deal with it again.

Diefenbaker told the press the tree planting had been exhilarating.

"If that was exhilarating," Kennedy whispered to an aide, "I never want to get laid again."

He needed his daiquiris just so. The White House had sent instructions: two parts Bacardi Silver Label rum, one part lemon, one tablespoon sugar. And they'd had the gall to request Cuban cigars. After the Bay of Pigs, no less. He had banned them in the U.S., was pushing hard for Dief to do the same, but he needed his pleasures. He was, Dief decided, a man without principles.

"We'd like Canada to help out in Latin America," Kennedy said when they finally sat down to talk. Kennedy also wanted Canada to increase its foreign aid budget, wanted support on

Vietnam and Berlin. It wasn't that he wanted Canada to help; he *expected* the country to do as he asked. If Kennedy had his way the country would be reduced to birdwatchers, a neutralized puppet dangling between giants. The most critical issue was nuclear. Kennedy was meeting Khrushchev in Vienna next month and he wanted Canada to accept nuclear warheads on its soil. "It's really important," he said.

"There's a lot of opposition," Diefenbaker said. "But I'll see if I can turn public opinion around in the next few weeks. At the moment, it is a political impossibility."

Kennedy wanted the Bomarcs to be armed with nuclear warheads, and he wanted to store nuclear weapons at U.S. air bases on Canadian soil, and to equip Canada's NATO forces with a nuclear capacity. Khrushchev only understood muscle, and Kennedy couldn't have this vast hole—a peaceful, unarmed gap between him and the Soviets—when he was staring into Khrushchev's worker soul in Vienna.

Canada was of two minds. On the one hand, what if the Russians came over the pole? That dark-minded, perverse race, swimming in vodka and history. But there was a growing camp that sought disarmament. Diefenbaker was indecisive, and this issue had no clear answer, politically or morally. Anyway, the moral high ground was long gone. Canada had been supplying uranium for the American nuclear program for over twenty years; it brought money and jobs and it happened offstage, in the north, in towns that were grateful for the work. Diefenbaker stalled on the nuclear issue, crawling around the edges, seeking something soft to cling to.

Dinner was unpleasant. Kennedy had his daiquiri and chatted with Lester B. Pearson—"Mike" Pearson—Diefenbaker's political nemesis, the Nobel Prize winner, the lisping Liberal jellyfish. Of course Kennedy would chat with Pearson. They knew the same people, played the same sports. Kennedy had glowingly reviewed Pearson's book, for God's sake. *He's trying to humiliate me*, Dief thought. It was an insult, a deliberate one.

The next morning they stared solemnly into the cameras and laid a wreath at the war memorial. Afterwards there was lunch with just JFK and Jackie, Dief and Olive.

"Your husband's quite a fisherman," Kennedy said.

Olive smiled. Olive, the pastor's daughter who had taught high school on the prairies. Across from her that Bouvier with her squared sphinx head. At dinner the night before, Jackie had chatted with the Governor General, Georges Vanier, in her fluent French. She had gone to the Sorbonne, had come from money. Perhaps her money had the taint Joe Kennedy's had. These were careless people, Dief thought, and they had large, careless families.

Diefenbaker and his first wife, Edna, hadn't had any children, God's wish perhaps (or was it his own?). Otherwise, he had fulfilled every covenant, as his mother predicted.

"I'd like to come up here and fish," Kennedy said.

"Yes," Diefenbaker said. "Although it's, as you know, so much more than that, than fishing."

"Of course," Kennedy said. That smile again. When he smiled Jackie smiled. Sitting primly in her Oleg Cassini gown, looking at the furniture and china, judging, redecorating in her head.

Kennedy was the great hope for mankind, the dream made flesh. Diefenbaker pondered this injustice as Jackie put her fork and knife down with finality, most of her lunch untouched, the ghost of an apologetic smile. Dief had been among the first to move to isolate South Africa, to kick them out of the Commonwealth because of apartheid, and one of the few who hadn't gone along with the internment of Japanese Canadians during the war. He had implemented the Bill of Rights and given the vote to status Indians. He had done more than Kennedy for human rights. Look at the American negro. How was it that Kennedy was seen a saviour?

Jackie was a handsome woman, glamorous without being pretty. Impressive though, but it wasn't enough for Kennedy. Whatever he had would never be enough: Kennedy was an appetite. Diefenbaker had never strayed from Olive, had only rarely strayed with her. As a child his family moved from small-town Ontario to homestead in Saskatchewan. It was 1903, he was an eight-year-old whose world was both vast (that endless horizon, that limitless sky) and constrained by the confines of the small house that smelled of kerosene and smoke and earth, dark as a closet, and in the winter swallowed by a larger darkness, a world that killed and encouraged imagination in equal measure. It was in that shrouded cell that he first imagined himself, a slayer of mythic dragons that lay hunched on the plains.

His father had failed as a homesteader, a melancholy German lost on the prairie. Diefenbaker remembered sitting in the fields with his brother, Elmer, amid stunted tufts of wheat standing erratically on the infertile ground. Each harvest a funeral. Dief enlisted in 1916—what better way to erase the German name that had been the object of childhood ridicule?—but he was discharged honourably. There was an accident with a trenching tool while training in

England. (Though of course there had been no accident, no trenching tool; his injury was an illness, psychosomatic, like a crushing weight that made it impossible to breathe. His mother had told him of the night mare, the horse that rode through the dark and invaded our dreams, pressing on our chests as we slept. It was something like this that had overtaken him in England.) Kennedy was a war hero, but perhaps his heroism was as manufactured as Dief's discharge. Diefenbaker was the people, Kennedy what the people aspired to.

"This weather is such …" the First Lady said breathily, her hands fluttering upward. Her whispery voice seemed like an affectation.

"Yes," Olive said. "May is a lovely month."

"Washington can get so close."

"The winters …" Kennedy said.

"They stimulate the blood," Diefenbaker said.

"As long as they stimulate something," Kennedy said. That smile.

There were polite sounds, cutlery laid carefully on china, glasses placed on the table with care, the half-sigh of a conversation unbegun.

After lunch Kennedy gave a speech in the House of Commons. He took the stage and smiled that smile that radiated health and destiny while Diefenbaker sat and pondered the alarming shift that had occurred in three years. In 1958 it was Dief who had been the face of renewal. He was the logical sum of hard work and Christian values and sacrifice, a natural culmination of historical forces. But 1961 was the beginning of something, and Diefenbaker wasn't sure what that thing was. In 1958 experience was an asset; now age was a liability. He had been born in the nineteenth century and was, his critics pointed out, better suited to it. "Geography has made us neighbours," Kennedy said, "history has made us friends. Economics has made us partners, and necessity has made us allies. Those whom nature hath so joined together, let no man cut asunder." The House stood up as one and gave him a lasting ovation. When Diefenbaker had gone to the U.S. to speak to a group of governors on the same subject—the kinship between these two great nations—there had been only tepid applause. Politics wasn't about substance anymore. Kennedy had won the election on television; Nixon was the better man.

Diefenbaker sat amid the idiot sound of clapping and wondered if he had ever hated anyone the way he hated Kennedy.

"I don't trust that prick," Kennedy said to McGeorge Bundy, his national security adviser. "He's going to screw us on the nuclear." They were sitting in the Oval Office. Kennedy had a daiquiri and a cigar and his sleeves were rolled up.

"The book is he can't make up his damn mind," said Bundy. "He's going to be a running sore. He's getting it from both sides and he doesn't know which way to jump."

"I hope to hell Pearson wins the next election. I can deal with Mike."

"I wouldn't bet on it. I think we're stuck with Diefenbaker. I don't know what the hell they see in that man."

"My back is agony. That bastard handed me a shovel and told me to start digging ..."

"Rusk says he's all politics. You have to give him a political path on this."

"He's erratic, maybe unbalanced. I'm not going to have any more dealings with that son of a bitch."

"What, I wonder, will that do for relations between the two countries?" Bundy said pleasantly, familiar with this mood.

"Improve them."

"He's leaning both ways on the nuclear, a talent. You should call him."

"It's a waste of time. I'll send him a letter." Kennedy hated few people, but one of them was that cryptic fool in Ottawa.

2

NIKITA KHRUSHCHEV, VIENNA, 1961

Khrushchev, the unlikely victor. The turnip-headed peasant, his pants too short, that endearing simpleton smile and his quick grasp of kilotons, kill zones, and half-lives. But his country couldn't feed itself. We could feed the people, Polyansky had told him, if we didn't need to feed Moscow and Leningrad. Polyansky the genius. They were selling Russian gold on the London market to buy European butter. There was a joke going around the interminable lineups, "What nationality were Adam and Eve?"

"Russian."

"Why Russian?"

"Because they were both naked, had only an apple to eat, and thought they were in paradise."

They were slaughtering milk cows to solve the meat shortage. This was the kind of thinking out there. A party secretary came in to see Khrushchev and pulled down his pants, screaming his own failures, demanding to be whipped.

There was a housing shortage as well. Khrushchev wanted to build high-rises but was told there wasn't enough steel for the elevators. He knew whatever official was given the housing problem would produce not houses but numbers, numbers that were borrowed or conjured, snatched out of the ether and pasted reassuringly onto the Seven-Year Plan.

And he had promised the people that Russia would surpass America by 1970. So he was thankful for Gagarin. On April 12, cosmonaut Yuri Gagarin became the first man in space. They had beaten the Americans! The celebration was on the grandest scale, Gagarin escorted to Red Square by the ubiquitous tanks. Khrushchev observed the people crowded onto balconies above the parade of Soviet might. He had read the reports of substandard construction and was thankful the balconies didn't collapse.

Five days later, the Bay of Pigs. A Soviet success and, even better, an American failure. Kennedy was his antithesis (he had heard the jokes about Kennedy being prettier than Khrushchev's wife), yet he wanted to believe that it was the malevolent Allen Dulles, the head of the CIA, who was behind the Bay of Pigs, hoping to poison the scheduled summit between Kennedy and Khrushchev just as he had poisoned the last summit by sending Gary Powers's U-2 into Soviet airspace. Powers, of course, was a gift: His spy plane had failed to self-destruct as programmed and Powers had failed to take his prescribed poison. Life was filled with failure, that's what made it interesting. Discovered inside Soviet airspace and shot down with an S-75 Dvina missile. They interrogated Powers for months, and examined the plane at their leisure, the so-called weather plane. A rare insight into the vacant, appliance-mad American soul.

Dulles was like his Russian counterpart, Lavrentiy Beria, former head of the KGB, a man so treacherous Khrushchev had to kill him. Perhaps Kennedy could do the same to Dulles.

Khrushchev stood on the steps of the American embassy in Vienna amid the photographers, the diplomats, advisers, fixers, the worst-case-scenarists. Kennedy approached with his hand out and they smiled for the cameras. When Khrushchev smiled it was like opening a fissure in the earth, and the glimpse into that black maw showed the happy farm boy walking in pig shit.

The first day was, to be honest, a bore. Kennedy wanted to chat; Khrushchev wanted to negotiate. There was a weakness in Kennedy, he felt, a softness in the West. Between them, dangerously, the issue of Berlin.

"How is it that you can find the time to give long interviews to Walter Lippmann?" Kennedy asked. It was intended as a compliment.

"The system permits it."

"I spend all my time persuading and consulting," Kennedy said.

"Why don't you switch to our system."

Kennedy wanted to talk about test bans. Why discuss test bans, Khrushchev asked, why not disarmament? There was a missile gap and Russia couldn't catch up. The Soviet economy was a failure, the missiles a burden. To get rid of them would be a relief. "You should have the courage to embrace disarmament," he told Kennedy. Without warning, Khrushchev's face would detonate into that smile while Kennedy waited for the translator to catch up. There was a disconnect; the smile arriving with a new demand, or a veiled threat.

For a day and a half, it was cordial. Kennedy was the suitor, but Berlin was the sticking point. Kennedy seemed anxious, upset even, over Khrushchev's bluntness. He was carrying the disaster of the Bay of Pigs with him, lucky for Khrushchev. "We cannot abandon our occupation rights in Berlin," Kennedy finally said. "If the U.S. does not draw this line, it will lose its allies, its promises will be mere scraps of paper. I didn't become president to preside over the isolation of my country."

"If the U.S. tries to exercise its right of access to West Berlin after a treaty is signed," Khrushchev coolly said after weighing the translator's words, "there will be a military response. It is up to the United States to decide whether there will be war or peace."

"Then it will be a cold winter," Kennedy said.

3

JOHN DIEFENBAKER, OTTAWA, 1962

The nuclear age was a plague. It was unnatural for all of God's creation to be held hostage, all of human history leading to one stark mistake. Diefenbaker was handed a petition weighing twenty-one pounds, 147,000 signatures demanding disarmament. Meanwhile, Royal Canadian Air Force Wing Commander Bill Lee was running around the U.S. trying to discredit Diefenbaker, planting stories with journalists and politicians and the American military that Dief was soft, a waffling dotard on the central issue of the age, leaning with each new breeze. "He's a fucking weather vane," Lee told an American colonel. "He's a liability."

But Diefenbaker finally found the compromise he sought

in everything. "We will keep the Bomarcs here," he told Kennedy, "but the nuclear warheads must remain in the U.S. Right near the border. In the event of emergency, they could be transported into Canada." A political solution. "They could be here in half an hour."

Kennedy was exasperated. "It isn't possible. It would take fifteen hours minimum to transport and launch them." A millennium in nuclear time. Twenty million dead. "Our cities would be in ashes."

And now the nuclear question had passed out of the theoretical, where Diefenbaker was happiest. Soviet ships were heading to Cuba, hours away from the American naval blockade. The CIA had verified that the Russians were putting nuclear warheads on the island—ninety miles from U.S. territory. Forty-two Soviet missiles, each designed to carry a nuclear warhead with more than twenty times the capacity of Hiroshima. Kennedy had telephoned Britain's Harold Macmillan to seek his advice. He hadn't sought Diefenbaker's advice, hadn't even called him personally, simply couldn't bear to talk to him even at the brink of apocalypse. Instead, he called Pierre Sevigny, the associate defence minister.

Dief looked at the blow-ups of the photographs of the missile sites. At first he wasn't sure what he was looking at, the grainy shots. "I'd like to see more photographs," he told the Americans who had been dispatched to Ottawa to present the crisis. The photographs didn't seem as conclusive as he'd been led to believe. What if Kennedy was grandstanding, still smarting from the Bay of Pigs? What if this was simply wounded manhood? Khrushchev had treated him like a child in Vienna, had referred to him as "the boy." (And for that, Diefenbaker felt a kinship with the Russian.) Kennedy was capable of taking the world to the brink of thermonuclear war. He wanted to prove himself the man for our times, a courageous champion of Western democracy. Diefenbaker believed that Kennedy was irresponsible, that the natural parameters that harnessed our lives were absent in him.

"What?" The Americans couldn't believe what they was hearing. Every other Western leader was behind Kennedy. Even the irascible French were behind them; de Gaulle said he didn't need to see the photographs, Kennedy's word was enough. But Diefenbaker wanted to see more evidence. This, he sensed, was a moment of national import.

"I need to be sure."

"Everyone is sure. There is no margin for error."

"I'm not sure."

But Canada wasn't being consulted, merely notified. In two hours Kennedy was going public. Diefenbaker read through Kennedy's speech and suggested taking out a paragraph about the Soviet Foreign Minister Andrei Gromyko that was needlessly inflammatory. It was taken out, a surprise.

Canada could be at war within hours. There was another problem. The old Canadian War Book, which set out the procedures for war, had been cancelled, and the new one had yet to be approved by cabinet. They were, temporarily, without rules of procedure. Diefenbaker recalled that the old Defence Scheme No. 1—which outlined how Canada would defend itself in the event of an attack from the U.S.—was only cancelled in the late thirties, little more than twenty years ago. Our strongest ally and greatest threat.

America went to Defcon 3, and the rest of the Western nations followed suit. Except Canada. Diefenbaker called an emergency meeting of his cabinet. The minister of defence,

Douglas Harkness, said he had to follow the Americans immediately. "It is irresponsible not to," he said.

"*Irresponsible! I'm* not the one who is irresponsible," Dief shouted. "I am the voice of reason. Kennedy has taken us to the edge. Maybe Khrushchev is happy to push us off. We need to think this through." Diefenbaker thought about John A. Macdonald, his political hero, a man who thrived on persecution. Macdonald had created the country and now Diefenbaker embodied it. Dief kept a portrait and statue of Macdonald in his office, and sat in the man's old chair. He could feel Macdonald, his shimmering historical light, a companion.

"What would Sir John A. do?" Diefenbaker asked rhetorically. You have to take risks to create a country. Macdonald took them, and paid dearly, but look at the result. He willed this endless geography into existence, he collected these colonies into a single force, a nation. He would defy these aggressive neighbours. He had done it before; he would do it again.

Harkness stared at Diefenbaker. It occurred to him that Dief was a nineteenth-century man himself. Invoking Macdonald over the nuclear issue. Was he mad?

"If we go along now," Diefenbaker warned, "we'll be their vassals forever. We have to go slow." And remember Nagasaki. The recklessness that sits in the Americans.

"We can't go slow. *There is no slow.* We could be at war."

"There is nothing this man can teach me. *Nothing at all.*"

It was Kennedy, Harkness thought. Diefenbaker was obsessed with him. This was about him.

Harkness secretly issued the order to go to Defcon 3 himself, without Diefenbaker's or cabinet's authorization, and told the military to do it quietly.

The world held its breath. In schools there were bomb drills. Each day an insistent alarm, louder and shriller than the recess bell, the sound of adult urgency, and the children all solemnly filed into the hallway. They lined the walls and shut the doors so that the glass from the windows wouldn't fly inward and scour their flesh in that camera-flash instant. In the hallways they sat cross-legged and were told to bend their heads down into laps as far as they would go (kiss your ass goodbye, school wits announced). They waited like that for two minutes, the time not spent thinking that this time it was real, the Russians had finally lobbed one over the pole and they would all vanish: their pets, their baseball mitts and babysitters, the pink plastic hairclips in the shape of Scottie dogs, the lunches of tuna salad and two percent milk, all vaporized. Instead, those minutes in that awkward but oddly lulling position were spent dreaming of a perfect future: heroic victories, impossible romance.

In the end, the Russians blinked. Their boats stopped at the naval blockade; the missiles were disassembled and shipped back to Russia.

Diefenbaker issued a statement to the press. "We supported the stand of the United States clearly and unequivocally." The country wasn't so sure. The press castigated him, the opposition party vilified him as a quisling.

Perhaps it *was* only Kennedy, Dief thought. Certainly it had become personal. They had been opposed on almost every issue. Kennedy wanted Britain to join the European Common Market, while Diefenbaker wanted them to stay out, as it would mean less British influence on Canada and in the growing void, more American influence. When Dief went to London to state his position, he was ridiculed in the papers (the world's cruellest, surely), denounced as Colonel

Blimp, a man poorly briefed and out of touch. British Prime Minister Harold Macmillan disliked him, and could no longer disguise it. Canada had once been the go-between for Britain and America, the interpreter, a logical mediator holding a piece of each culture. Now Kennedy and Macmillan were friends, united in their disregard for Diefenbaker. He was isolated abroad and increasingly at home. He couldn't vent his feelings about Kennedy because Canadians liked him too much.

It was on January 25, 1963, that Diefenbaker finally unveiled his nuclear position, unspooled in the House of Commons, two hours of baffling rhetoric, words that circled and curved in on themselves, each new thought eating the one that came before it. "We know that the way to prevent nuclear war is to prevent it," he said righteously, comforted by this tautology. His tone was emphatic, his words minced into opposing positions and mingled with theocracy. "My prayer is that we will be directed in this matter. Some may ridicule that belief on my part but I believe that the Western world has been directed by God in the last few years, or there would have been no survival. I believe that will continue." God would be the arbiter; He would make the decision. Dief told the House that both Kennedy and Macmillan had agreed at the Nassau meeting to move away from nuclear warheads, to return to conventional weapons (though they hadn't said that, and Dief hadn't been at the meeting). "If nuclear arms are necessary for defence, we will take them," he thundered. If not, we would not abide them, for they were unabidable.

At the end of the speech, his own party was divided as to whether he had come out in favour of nuclear weapons or against them. The press was equally unsure and printed both versions, pro and con. But the U.S. State Department was furious; they issued an official press release accusing Diefenbaker of being a liar.

When Dief read the press release, he frothed, spit forming on his lips, aerated by his curses and flying in small flecks onto the leather-topped desk. A goddamned liar! It was an outrage. The government of one country officially and publicly declaring an allied leader to be a liar. This was Kennedy's work, that boastful son of a bitch. There was a federal election coming and Kennedy wanted Pearson to win and he was going to use his money and influence to get his man in office. He would treat Canada the way the U.S. treated the Congo or Iran or any banana republic and simply install someone they could do business with. He had heard that Joe Kennedy had bought the election for his son—118,000 votes, easily affordable—and now the son was trying to do the same here. When Diefenbaker's bile subsided, he realized he could use this. Here was clear evidence of American interference.

But his own party was leaving him. Diefenbaker was increasingly incoherent and isolated, consumed by the paranoia that nurtured him.

"Everyone's against me except the people," he told Olive.

"They're what's important."

"The country has no idea what is at stake here, Olive. The very borders are being redrawn." A border wasn't a wall, he thought, it was an imaginary line. You didn't need to send an army over it now, you could send radio and television signals and movies and money. Kennedy was a handsome salesman selling a bill of goods.

"You'll tell them, John. It's what you're best at. They'll listen."

He campaigned on his strengths. He wasn't a policy maker, he was a populist. And like many fine populists, he had a talent for hatred. He was a brilliant hater; he could develop and nurture hate and keep it at a high pitch. He could celebrate it and knead it into something ennobling, something that felt like love. Everyone was his enemy: Kennedy, America, the elite, the corporations, the Liberals, the press. *Newsweek* (whose Washington editor was Kennedy's friend Ben Bradlee) ran an issue with an unflattering photograph of Diefenbaker on the cover. (Macdonald had said *he* was the ugliest man in politics but he would surely have to take second place now.) Dief looked, as one pundit reported, like a cross between Queen Victoria on her death bed and a rabid owl. The caption read "Canada's Diefenbaker, Decline and Fall," and the article described him as a vacillating rube. "Britain's Prime Minister Harold Macmillan can hardly bear the sight of him and President Kennedy dislikes him cordially." They said he ran the country like a tantrum-prone country judge.

Diefenbaker had the magazine sent out to all his supporters as a rallying cry, evidence that the Americans were trying to unseat him, and by extension, trying to unseat Canadian democracy. He received a letter of sympathy from Richard Nixon, a Quaker with a gift for vendetta that rivalled Dief's own.

What Diefenbaker needed was the country to hate along with him. After Robert McNamara, Kennedy's defence secretary, said the Bomarc bases in Canada would be targets for Russian warheads that would otherwise be headed for American cities, Diefenbaker toured small towns and villages armed with McNamara's words, crying, "Decoys, decoys, *decoys!* A decoy duck in a nuclear war! That's what the Americans would reduce us to. Are we to be a burnt sacrifice?"

The cities had little time for him, but the rural people, the small towns and hamlets, still loved him. He took a train across the country and stopped everywhere and rejoiced in this rural reflection of his government, a reflection of himself. It was a government made not of policy or legislation but of the divine plebeian will of its leader. Diefenbaker understood the little man, and in his own night fears, staring bug-eyed as dawn spread dully in his room, he worried that he was the little man.

The papers had turned on him, the cartoons increasingly cruel, but Dief gathered strength from the attacks, and he was invigorated by the campaign. They had attacked Macdonald like this, he thought. After a few weeks, he could feel a change in mood; the country moving back to him, even if the party wasn't. He had remade the Conservative Party into an image of himself: against big business and corporate interests, anti-urban, a populist party that celebrated Diefenbaker himself. Pearson had started the campaign with a striking lead, but it was diminishing with each day. Pearson hated campaigning. He was an uninspired speaker whose natural private charm turned to something else on the podium, a stiffness, an off-putting principal chastising a child. Diefenbaker loved to campaign, and as the election neared, he saw a moment when the country was magically returning to what it had been in 1958, when the honest aspirations of its millions were parsed into clear and comforting lines.

But Pearson won, the lisping Nobel bow-tie nancy.

"Kennedy spent one million dollars and used four hundred

operators to defeat me," Diefenbaker told his wife. "This was not an election, it was a coup d'état."

On November 22, Diefenbaker was in the parliamentary cafeteria eating with five friends—telling them how Kennedy had phoned, and mimicking Kennedy's Boston accent ("When I tell Canader to do something I expect Canader to do it!"), how he had told Kennedy where to get off—when his secretary, Bunny Pound, came running up with the news. "Kennedy's been shot," she said. "He's dead."

"Ohhh," Diefenbaker said, slumping. "That could have been me." It wasn't clear if this was a private fear or a public boast.

Diefenbaker excused himself, and went and found his speechwriter and told him to put together a eulogy. He delivered it in the House hours later. "John Fitzgerald Kennedy stood as the embodiment of freedom not only in his own country but throughout the world," Diefenbaker said, with that preacher's delivery. "Canadians, yes, free men everywhere will bow their heads in sorrow. Free men everywhere mourn. Mankind can ill afford to lose this man at this hour."

An arrogant man, an imperious leader who won the Canadian election for the Liberals, the martyr that America craved, and history would hoist him to its golden heights and he would be forever Jesus. Their feud had lasted 823 days—his own tally—and Diefenbaker wouldn't betray his hatred just because the man was dead. He had a gift.

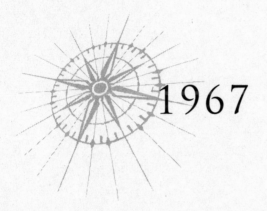

1967

The first maps were to dispel fear. We claim those spaces, piss on the trees to mark our territory. It's partly a bluff, of course; really, we're just hoping for the best. Each new map is eventually made a lie. Towns wither and die and that small dot lingers, inert, for years until Rand McNally finally erases it. Cities grow, empires die, continents shift, people change. Is the mapmaker reflecting the world's existence or his own?

I am a living map, Thompson's blood. I sought him out, I wanted that link. My father was never really there. Stanford was my guide, but he was gone so soon, and my mother retreated into the past, comforted by ghosts. We need to attach to something. In the end I looked to Thompson; I explored.

All history is suspect, including this one. What we include, what we suppress, what we remember, what we think we remember. How reliable are witnesses? The suspect was tall/short/medium build, and he was wearing a suit/jeans and drove away in a red Chevy/blue Ford. Not everyone sees the country the same way. But the centennial brought it into focus for a brief moment—that moment when people pose for a photograph: a beaming schoolchild, face washed, hair slicked, full of hope. Our national agonies— French, English, native—suddenly shone. The centennial is waning now, the country poised at the brink of something profound it can't quite define.

Billy Whitecloud's expression seemed altered slightly. Could he be experiencing some life inside his head? A flicker of joy? A memory?

My brother, Stanford, was about your age when he went to France. After he left I thought of him every day. I thought that was how I could keep him alive. As long as he lived in my head, he was safe from harm. I imagined his life over there as something noble and heroic. It's an easy fiction to maintain. That's the version that comes to us in paintings and books and movies (and sometimes history). It was different after I got there, of course. But even after the war, some small part of me wanted to believe Stanford was alive. He was out there; in Paris or Egypt or Brazil, somewhere.

Michael took the piece of paper out of his wallet, a compact square that he unfolded. This letter arrived a month ago. It was addressed to The Mountain Horse Family of Cochrane, Alberta. Michael read:

I don't know who I'm writing to. I served with Stanford Mountain Horse in the first war and it's taken me fifty years to write this letter. I wasn't sure it was the right thing to do and I'm still not sure but maybe the truth is best finally. I don't know what they told you. An awful lot of boys got changed by that war and I guess Stanford was one of them. I don't know what got in him or why. But he killed our

commanding officer, Sergeant Ryan Dair. They
had an argument about something, no one knows.
I didn't know Stanford, he was one of those who
kept to himself. Stanford stabbed him in the heart
and then cut off his ear. I don't know if anyone
'told you this. It was 1916. He lit out. They sent
a patrol but they didn't find him. Every night for
a month but there was no sign. A lot of boys
snapped over there in different ways. Some had
fits, others just got quiet, like they were frozen.
They couldn't move couldn't hear. They were in
some other world which was a mercy because that
world wasn't any place to be.

      But two years later I saw Stanford again.
We were on patrol. It was November 10th, the
day before the war ended. As far as most of us
was concerned it was over. We'd all been hearing
things. We were sweeping up near Bourlon. It
was night and it was raining. Just two of us me
and Danny Iron out of Swift Current. Raining
pretty good and you couldn't see much. We came
up on this house it was empty but we took a look.
The windows were all gone. I was just standing
by one of those empty windows looking inside. I
didn't expect to see anything. I guess I was just
standing there wondering who had lived there and
if they'd be back now that the war was ending.
You wonder about people's lives. Then I saw
him sitting on the floor. At first I didn't know
what it was. There was a blanket around him
and his hair hadn't been cut in two years and it

was piled on his head and wrapped around bones.
But when he turned around I knew right off it
was Stanford. He was thin, hardly anything on
him. His face was hollowed. I think he was
already somewhere else. His eyes were blank as
anything I've ever seen. He had a bayonet in his
hand and he started to get up. Danny he was
behind me and his rifle was out and Danny fired
and killed him. We went over to look. Under that
blanket he didn't have a shirt on. There was a
wound from a bullet probably only a few days
old. There were other wounds too. The strangest
thing was on his body there were drawings.
Tattoos he must of made himself. The whole
front of him. Everywhere he could reach I guess.
There were pictures of battles, and a picture of a
horse and maybe your house. It was a house
anyway and there were mountains beside it.
Other things but I don't remember them. He had
scars on his face but it looked like he'd put them
there himself. Lines made with a knife. Me and
Danny stayed there for a bit. The morning was
starting to break. It was a cold rain. We went
back to camp and by the afternoon the news of the
armistice had come and you can't imagine that
feeling unless you were there but it was like
waking up from the longest nightmare. Danny
said we don't tell anyone about this. There's no
point they'll just make us stay and fill in papers
and talk to officers and all we had on our minds
was going home and we said well they would of

shot him anyway. So I am ashamed to say we
left him there but I don't think he'd want to be
buried by the army whatever they decided. I'm
not making excuses I know it wasn't right. It
didn't sit too good with either of us but Danny he
just wanted to get home so I said I wouldn't tell
anyone what happened. Danny's heart gave out a
few months back and he was taken and maybe
that's why I'm writing. Or maybe to ease my
own mind. It's not a happy story and I hope
this hasn't brought a grief into your house but
there's lots who don't know what happened to
theirs and I've seen what it done to them so I'm
writing this late as it is. I hope you can forgive
us and find some peace.

Corporal Walter Dobbs

1

COCHRANE, ALBERTA

The montane forest swayed lightly, the air cool before the first snow. Autumn was aloof here; summer could turn to winter in an afternoon. The light was brittle and flattering. Starlings hounded a crow in swirling aerobatics, chasing it away from their nest. As a boy Michael remembered running past a nest and then turning to see a starling only a foot behind his head, motionless, gliding, escorting him out of her territory with extraordinary ferocity. The image was otherworldly and gave him nightmares. A week later he returned with a gun and fired into the nest, his sense of vindication immediately replaced by nausea as he observed the broken nest and tiny bird on the ground.

His mother's house was slouching toward ruin. The rotting roof had been repaired, but the porch was collapsing, and the wallpaper in the dining room was water-stained, the rust-coloured marks blooming within the baroque pattern. Michael had finally torn the barn down. It had become dangerous, listing to the east after a century of powerful west winds, its boards grey and desiccated. Tree roots bubbled up, heaving the stone walkway and attacking the foundation, probing for weakness. A root had come through the basement wall, the bricks helpless against its progress.

There was a marker over the graves of the two dogs, who had died within weeks of one another, like an old married couple. The dog that his father had morbidly named Erebus walked off in January and dug a hollow in the snow at the base of a pine. Michael had tracked him and found him curled up, gone there to die. He was worried that the dog would be helpless, near death, when the magpies descended on him, going for his eyes, or the coyotes would quietly tear him up. He picked him up and carried him back to the house, where he moped forlornly. Two days later, Erebus went back out to the pine, intent on dying. Stanford got the .22 and Michael burst into tears when he heard the shot. They put Erebus in a wooden crate that had once shipped English linens, nailed it shut, and left him on the porch until spring when the ground loosened up enough to bury him.

Inside the house, childhood smells drifted with mnemonic authority; the homemade glue they used to build crude wooden models, the smell of smoke on their clothing that hung over the chair, every compound used to make the house, the newspaper and sawdust that had been used for insulation. Missing was the faint medicinal tang of gin soaking through his father. It left a vapour trail like a jet, concentrated where he stood and dissipating behind him as he moved uncertainly through the rooms.

Upstairs, what had been his and Stanford's room was largely unchanged from sixty years ago, a clandestine world of damaged lead soldiers, painted and named and sent out to die in new ways each day. Two boys shooting at magpies with bows made from saplings and scavenged Blood arrow-heads, inventing Saracen armies they gallantly slew, pissing off a cliff beneath the moon, passing on the received wisdom of what lurked between Betsy Harrison's legs. Homemade weapons to be used against enemies manufactured in the dark as they lay in their beds: spears hardened by flame, buck knives, spurs. There was the deer-hide map that Michael had made, showing troop movements in the first war. On the dresser was a photograph of Stanford in his uniform, his face expressionless. In that neutral stare the collected rage of five generations or the warrior spirit incarnate or the weakness in their father's blood, their mother's sorrow: a weapon passed down through the ages.

His mother described the ghosts during his last visit. Crowfoot came sometimes, she said, though he never spoke. His lean face, that aquiline nose—like a scythe; he stood near the wolf willow that grew by the creek. Her ghosts were a wide-ranging group, and weren't limited to people she had known. When Michael asked when she had seen the first ghost, he was surprised to learn that it had been more than a decade ago. There had been dozens of sightings over the years, but now they were a fixture, a daily occurrence.

They weren't limited to humans either. She saw buffalo, deer sometimes, and wolves. Horses that had been dead for decades that she remembered by name. She saw the dogs. She wasn't afraid of the ghosts and most days was happy for their company, though she found it difficult to sleep. She had once seen Michael's sorrowful father, marching the land in his handmade boots.

"I think he was trying to be useful," she said.

His mother seemed to spend as much time in the spirit realm as the real world. From the upstairs window of his old room, he could see her in the backyard, her small form further diminished by this perspective. She turned and saw him there and he went downstairs to embrace her. She was as dry as a sarcophagus, like desert air. They sat in the parlour, an anachronism with its upright piano, a gift from Dunstan. It had bare spots where the finish had worn away, and the ancient ivory keys were concave. The floral-patterned sofa sagged dangerously, flanked by three hard wooden chairs. The heavy mahogany case with its glassed-in shelves that once held delicate porcelain now hosted a collection of feathers and medicine bundles and beadwork. Michael sank into the ancient cushions of the couch and his mother served brackish tea made with the leaf of *Prunella vulgaris* that she bought from a Stoney Indian and believed to be curative. They sipped the awful tea from the exquisite china that Dexter had brought from London seventy years ago, as thin as paper now, with spidery lines, the blue flowers faded.

His mother was ninety-seven, maybe older. There wasn't a reliable record of her birth, born with the nation still humming in the blood of its creators, giving sanctuary to the rude crowd, a sense of possibility conferred by nothing more than space. There were still a few dark streaks in her white hair, and her face, which had grown rounder in age, had now collapsed into a compact ball with lines radiating outward like a medieval street map. For decades she had seemed ageless, and now she looked like Crowfoot's mother must have looked, a diminutive leathery witness to a rapacious century. She had been getting quieter in the last year or so, her gift for stillness coming to its logical end.

"Do you see any ghosts right now?" Michael asked.

His mother looked out the window, scanning the long grass that stretched toward the mountains. "No," she said.

"Do you ever see Stanford?"

"I haven't seen him," she said slowly. She saw her father, Jamieson, on occasion.

Michael had made a doctor's appointment for her but she refused to go. Was this some form of dementia? She was lucid most of the time. It was a miracle that she could still take care of herself, isolated as she was in this house. She had never learned to drive and had refused Michael's offer to move in with him.

"Do *you* ever see Stanford?" she asked.

"He appears in dreams sometimes. We're out riding together, or fishing the Bow."

In fact, Stanford only appeared in grotesque dreamscapes that occupied ruined forests, corpse-strewn fields, charred, unfamiliar buildings, all of it joined in a grey dream light. He hadn't told her about the letter.

This business with the ghosts didn't concern him that much. Perhaps it was natural: She had lived as a ghost for much of her life; almost weightless as they starved on the march up from Montana, invisible to all who encountered them. With Dexter, she occupied a limbo: one life when they were alone, another in the face of the public. The mother of their two children, she retreated to the role of employee when he had parties, parties that started with aristocratic solemnity and some form of entertainment—polo or croquet—and degenerated into raucous toasts. There had been duels with rake handles, croquet mallets, and butter knives, ending in farce and nominal blood. At these parties, Catherine served drinks, and when the guests were settled she took him and Stanford for walks in the foothills, identifying wild mint, purple aster, fleabane, and fireweed, investigating fox earths and spotting deer or coyotes. When it got dark, they lay on the cool ground and stared up at the stars as she outlined the constellations and told them stories.

"Do you need anything?" he asked.

"No."

Michael finished his tea, which tasted bitterly of earth, and briefly thought of repeating his offer of staying with him, but he knew the answer and so didn't bother. He got up and kissed his mother's head. "I'll come by on Thursday," he said.

2

Michael observed his students, their tired Monday faces. The afternoon sun filled the classroom with a stifling heat. Nancy Baxter ran a pink comb through her lustrous hair, more performance than maintenance, the public rite of the beautiful. Hector Grayson was slumped in his seat, already asleep, his mouth open, saliva pooling on his pearl-button shirt. August Purvue stared out the window. Billy Whitecloud's empty seat.

"What is a map?" Michael asked rhetorically. Almost every question in his class was rhetorical. "A painting. You have the image in your head and you put that image on paper and a world comes to life. Some maps are truths in the service of a lie. Some are simply utilitarian. And some are art."

They stared at him dutifully, a primitive tribe striving to find meaning in the noises of a missionary, their heads filled with longing, the lyrics of John and Paul, envy for someone's jeans. Observing one another with scientific rigor and ignoring the larger world. "A map is a lament," he told them. "You lose something—that sense of possibility, and you gain something: knowledge, which isn't always a joy to possess. Maps were the first blow against Indian reality."

They now had a tangible history that occupied their interest: what happened to Billy. What had happened in that car? It consumed their imaginations and created a hierarchy of those who knew something, an event in a place where there were so few.

"I want all of you to draw a map of this particular moment in your lives," he said. "You can map your family, your bad mood, the person to your right, anything."

They rose out of their wooden seats, the student prisons that had grown too small for many of them, and there was bumping and tipping and scraping as they freed themselves. He could be talking about the Magna Carta or bran muffins or how to die of natural causes. It was all the same to them.

Michael drove to the hospital, the sun dropping bright and reddish behind him. Billy was thinner, and looked older; there was less of the boy. A week earlier Michael had come in when Billy's father was visiting, a surprise. Davis White-cloud's dark mass filled the room like a weather system. His large nose was bent to the side, his hair longish. But it was his hands that were his most distinguishing feature, like dangling machinery, scarred from years of careless use. Cuts ran across scars that intersected with small holes that hadn't closed. Davis was six-foot-six, maybe 270 pounds, and his nickname was FBI, for Fucking Big Indian. Michael had known people like Davis when he worked in the oil fields, men who sat hunched over their draught beer on Saturday night, a simmering rage inside. And every week they found someone who cradled their own anger like an infant, and in the sickly light of the Cecil Tavern, or the St. Louis, or the King Eddie, they recognized one another, and by the end of the evening there was blood.

When Michael came in, Davis was leaning over his son with a damp cloth, dabbing carefully at his face. Six small lines had been drawn at a slight diagonal, three on each side of his nose, two royal blue stripes separated by a yellow stripe, drawn with a felt pen. War paint. Davis pressed lightly, in soft repetitive movements as the blue began to run, combining with the yellow to produce greenish streaks. The paint moved in tiny rivulets down Billy's unlined cheeks, spilling onto the pillow and settling in small puddles in the hollow of his collarbone. Another trip to the sink to rinse the towel and Davis returned and carefully removed the lines that were left on his son's cheek, the small multihued streams. Michael could see the rage building in him, a rage that would likely find a target on Saturday night. Some man sitting in a Grande Prairie restaurant right now, eating a thirty-two-ounce porterhouse, unaware of what was to come. With a dry corner of the towel Davis dabbed at the water staining Billy's pillow and hospital gown, working carefully, as if restoring a painting.

3

Nancy Baxter sat with her parents in the RCMP office and explored the fine line she had drawn. She looked down at the dull linoleum floor.

"Was there anything special about your relationship with Billy Whitecloud?" Constable Edson asked her. He was a twenty-six-year-old recruit with a shaving rash that shimmered slightly under its veneer of oil.

In class Nancy had developed a fixed mournful look, like a beautiful widow, she thought. As the only real witness to the event, she realized that she was the owner of a commodity. She wasn't the first to fall in love with tragedy. Its comforting darkness, its scale and celebrity, the way it rose above homework assignments, silent breakfasts, annoying brothers, tentative hair styles, and the mundane crawl of the seasons; its rich public transcendence. Tragedy seduced.

It wasn't a conscious leap from loving drama to loving Billy Whitecloud. She didn't love him when he was conscious, of course, when he was slouching and lurking silently at school, never once volunteering an answer in class. She hadn't even noticed him then, would have been unable to remember his name. But now he was a tangible event, and her proximity made her suddenly tangible. Billy was an opportunity.

She pondered her course of action. What was it she loved now? Maybe his tragic maturity, laid out on the metal hospital bed like a war victim. His silence, which was moving, was a kind of wisdom, and each day it grew deeper compared to the words spoken around her. His wisdom ennobled her somehow; there was this bond, this pact that only they understood. And maybe that is what love is, carrying around this knowledge that you have a fortress to retreat to and in that fortress is a love so perfect that neither of you has to say a word.

She had implied that Billy Whitecloud's coma was a source of personal anguish. It hadn't taken much. The girls hovered around her, waiting for new information, which in turn empowered them. Nancy controlled the story; she *was* the story, and she shaped it in a way to emphasize that, ensuring it was passed on, tendrils that reached through the school and down Main Street to Cremona and High River and Springbank and maybe even Calgary. And each telling added flesh and detail: Nancy Baxter had secretly been dating Billy Whitecloud, which explains so much now that you think about it. The way he always lingered at the edge of things, stayed aloof, the way he looked at her, the way she looked at him. This story snaked through the foothills, a living thing that heralded Nancy's tragic loss. It didn't matter that she hadn't dated him, that she wouldn't have dated him if you'd put a gun to her head. Now he was the perfect date. No fumbling with her brassiere as August Purvue had, twiddling her nipples like he was trying to find a radio station. No holding clammy hands all the way through the movie so you ended up not enjoying the movie, no wet tongue in her ear searching for an opening. He was in a coma; her immaculate lover.

Her parents stared, waiting for her response.

"Billy was a friend," she said carefully, looking up at Edson.

"Nothing more."

"We ... were friends."

"Did you actually see him go out the window?"

"It was more I heard it. I was sitting against the door in the back. The music was loud. I just wanted to go home. That's all I was thinking. Going home."

"And you heard Billy go out the window?"

"He was already half out. He was singing, sort of yelling."

Nancy remembered being both afraid of this dangerous game and annoyed that the open window was whipping her hair in a kaleidoscopic swirl. Her constant attempts to order her hair, her hands moving rapidly, like a raccoon washing itself at a stream, were useless, lustre and body both being killed.

What she had been, more than anything else, was bored. She basked in the attention of these boys, but none of them actually talked to her. Billy didn't say anything, and Augie and Hector just talked loudly with each other, trying to impress her. She had measured this particular boredom against the boredom that waited at home: checking the jeans in her closet for fadedness, holding up her mother's earrings to her ears in the mirror to see what pierced ears would bring. Her father in the living room drinking a Molson Canadian and watching *Hockey Night in Canada*, Johnny Bower's quilted face stopping another puck for the Maple Leafs.

The convex shape of the gravel section road, graded to drain rainwater into the ditch, coupled with August Purvue's driving and the heavy Mercury Marquis—like being in a boat—combined to create a drunken rhythm, and she remembered thinking she might throw up. The radio was turned up loud, and a Van Morrison song that Purvue liked was playing. He tapped one hand on the steering wheel.

It scared her, having Billy hanging out of the car like that and Augie driving so fast. She huddled against the far door. "Pull him *in*!" she yelled. Had she actually said the words? "What is the *matter* ..."

Then Billy's legs scissored against the roof and she screamed. Purvue locked up the brakes and the car skidded to a stop and she threw up.

The sunlight came in the west window and captured the suspended dust in Edson's office, tiny grey particulate that swirled in abrupt clouds. The impression she wanted to give Constable Edson was that she had always loved Billy White-cloud and he had always loved her. She liked this version; it showed her in a flattering tragic light, as someone who had been living a larger, more interesting life than anyone imagined. A woman with secrets. Each day would bring its weight of sorrow, and each day she would rise to greet it in another well-chosen outfit. She would tell her girlfriends that his strength was within her, that he was her warrior.

This was the random thought that came to her when she reluctantly went to the hospital and stared down at his placid, unfamiliar face. She took the royal blue felt pen out of her purse and drew the war paint on, carefully drawing the lines at a diagonal, not pressing too hard on that innocent skin. She found a yellow marker, Sunrise Yellow, and drew a line between the two blue ones, and then stared at her work happily. The primary colours had a force, an energy. They conjured something private and tribal. She put the pens back in her purse and stared at Billy. My warrior, she whispered experimentally.

Billy's unheard version was a roar of wind, his body half out the window, his hip uncomfortably on the door where the window had been lowered. He had never been included in their listless small-town Saturday nights. He lingered at the edge of groups at school and didn't know what form his social being should take. He was sitting on the curb of the parking lot of the Esso station, without any plan, just there to avoid his own house. His father was back from the northern oil rigs for five days and everyone in their house was nervous. It was Saturday night, and his father had had a few drinks. Those huge hands, scarred, scabbed at the knuckles, swinging carelessly, like the knot at the end of a heavy rope. A lazy movement but the hand moved with surprising speed, fast enough that Billy's expression hadn't changed, a combination of fear and inquisitiveness (Why did you have to hit her?), and it was still there on his face when the hand arrived.

So he was sitting in the convenience store parking lot staring at the hubcaps of slow-passing trucks when he heard

Hector Grayson's voice. "Whitecloud, what're you doin', man!" Hector was yelling out of the Mercury Marquis driven by August Purvue. They were getting more Coke. Billy was invited along, swept up in the brotherhood that came from rye and Coke and the calming voice of Donovan on the car radio.

The Coke teased his throat with its caustic bubbles and the rye tasted of medicine. They drove out to the Ghost Lake reservoir and sat for an hour, then roared back in the Marquis. Purvue and Hector tried to impress Nancy by arguing about Muhammad Ali. Billy's own fear of her was so great that he hadn't said a word, not even hello.

They drove fast along the section roads against a half moon that sat near the mountains and Billy put his head out the window and let the wind hit him, suddenly removed from Nancy's petulance, and from the drunken brotherhood of August and Hector. He didn't have anything to add to their stories. The night air was liberating. He inched out farther, one hand hooked onto the plastic grip affixed to the ceiling, the other resting on the door. He could smell the sage growing in the ditches. In his head the rye and Coke formed effervescent half-dreams. He floated with the maritime movements of the big car, the air filled with a dozen scents, the coming of autumn, the taste of frost. The freedom that came with movement, a primitive, satisfying surge. The red-tailed hawk travels at a hundred miles an hour, almost motionless in its descent. A missile. *Buteo jamaicensis* coming to earth to claim its prize.

4

The November light hung over the hills, pale and empty. The wind was from the west, and you could taste the bitterness that preceded the first snow. Michael drove with the window open, letting in the cold air. He had visited his mother a few days ago and was alarmed at how pale she had become. He made her some tea and listened to the ghost report. She had seen a herd of riderless horses. His mother was ghostly herself now, almost transparent. One day he would arrive to find the trace of her shadow on the land, all that was left, like those victims at Hiroshima.

Michael had heard that Davis Whitecloud was on the lam. He had beaten a man to death in the parking lot of a Grande Prairie bar. The police were looking for him but he had disappeared into the working maw of the north, maybe doodlebugging on a seismic line near the Arctic, or roughnecking on a gas rig out of Medicine Hat, or he'd fled to Montana. One way or the other, he wouldn't be seeing Billy again.

Michael drove past the plant that made railway ties, the smell of creosote an assault that lingered until he reached the empty rodeo grounds. The main street was quiet. It was Saturday. Michael pulled into the school parking lot. The front door was open and Ed Usak, the janitor, was moving behind an electric floor buffer that hauled him in its wake. The mural was finished and mounted on the gymnasium wall. He had seen the panels that they had worked on individually, the wars, esoteric maps, the clumsy portrait of John Diefenbaker done in thick oils. What would it look like in its entirety, this folk art?

The light in the gym was flat, the fluorescent lights off, a pale illumination coming from three windows high on the wall covered with wire mesh. And there it was, the result of more than a year's work, the project begun with last year's students, who laboured until June, their work taken up by this new class. Its ten separate five-foot panels stretched across the pale yellow cinder-block wall. There was Cartier arriving, his ships small dots in waves drawn like slanted letter *M*s in slanting upper case. Samuel de Champlain killing two Iroquois chiefs with his oversized harquebus. A scene from the Plains of Abraham, particularly bloody in its sweep. John A. Macdonald was at the centre, his face traced from a photograph that had been projected onto paper. His nose was a foot high, an alcoholic beacon painted a sickly mauve.

He had expected maps of the town and the country, clumsy and idiosyncratic, and there were a few of those. There was a map of the world, missing continents and oceans, dragons drawn at the edges without irony, and one of that evening showing the car and the road, and local points: Ghost dam, the rodeo grounds, lines that showed the trajectory of Billy Whitecloud flying out of the car toward a heaven rendered in fluffy clouds.

Nancy Baxter had a map of her heart drawn in a simple valentine shape. It was, unwittingly, drawn as a Stabius-Werner projection, a style of map that came from the fifteenth century, the invention of a parish priest in Nuremberg. Inside her heart was a neat cursive script that followed the cordiform contours. In different colours, indicating a hierarchy, there were names: the contents of her small-town heart. At the centre, in red ink, was BILLY.

There was a drawing of David Thompson standing on the west coast, staring out to the sea. If the individual elements were irregular in scale, and the artistic sensibility discrepant and crude, there was a naive grandeur, Michael thought. It was huge, for one thing, and who doesn't admire the epic?

Michael drove along 1A, the wind listing him toward the median. The sun was obscured by cold clouds blowing swiftly from the west, bunches of slate grey among the off-white. A flat light, the fields dry and drained of colour. He drove past the motel on the highway with its small bungalows, an illicit meeting place for lovers. Why else would you stay in a motel on the edge of town? He had used it himself years ago, consumed with desire in that shabby room. A woman from town who flirted but when they got to the motel she sat on the bed and talked for an hour and finally asked, "I was wondering, your father, as I understand it, was white. I'm just, what would be the, if you had to put a percentage ..."

He looked at her. "How much of an Indian am I?"

She gave a relieved smile. "Yes, I suppose. How much of an Indian are you?"

For an hour she talked about her obligations, and he suspected that in the course of that hour he became another one.

Past the motel were rolling hills that rose up from the Bow River valley. The western edge of the city was a hive of bulldozers and earthmovers, pirouetting on the scraped land, creating contours for new suburbs. The city grew west toward the mountains as if there was some force in that rock, a magnetism that drew people. There was still pasture land within the city limits, holding a handful of horses that looked stranded. On the fringes, you could see how cities weren't imagined, but evolved like a child's fort, adding pieces as necessity or whim dictated, an ongoing accident.

They had moved Billy to a new room, and Michael assumed there was a reason. Maybe they felt he was going to improve. He was now installed in an east-facing room, the morning sun welcome. Did he sleep, and then wake within the coma, each morning a fresh disappointment? Or was it all some version of sleep? His whiskers were still spare and soft and clustered around his mouth. The two roommates that had been there on the last visit hadn't been replaced, and Michael wondered if Billy missed those wheezing, damaged bodies.

He paced around Billy's bed, and looked out the window to the city laid out in a sprawling grid of lights. What was left to say? History is a series of accidents balanced against inevitable forces. If Montcalm had just waited three hours, instead of sending his troops out to engage the British in 1759, Louis Antoine de Bougainville would have arrived with three thousand troops and the French might have won. If Billy hadn't gotten into that car.

What are we? Thompson's Great Map, Wolfe's reckless climb, Macdonald's drunken genius, the flaws of our fathers, the corpses of Passchendaele bloating in the mud waiting for the kiss of history. Laurier's genius, Mackenzie King's shrewd indecision, the threat of snow. The path of the wolf fleeing the modern, New France, the smell of mustard gas and wild rose, the dead at Batoche, the dust settling on a million bison. A railway, revolution, a gathering of the dead on a prairie night. Loves that form mysteriously and then vanish, leaving wounds we tend like gardens. A hymn heard in another language, brothers left to their madness, a car travelling a dark country road. The hope that this frozen space could be filled; four hundred years of blood and accidents forming a shape to comfort the world.

A map was the view from above: How high do we have to go before we can place ourselves? The scouring wind roared past the window. Michael adjusted the pyjamas that were misbuttoned and kissed Billy's forehead and turned out the light.

AUTHOR'S NOTE

Chief among the many challenges of historical fiction is finding a way to condense a huge volume of material into a coherent narrative. I relied on David Thompson's journals but collapsed the events for the purposes of my story. So his several tries at crossing the mountains become a single conflated effort, for example. Where possible I used primary sources (such as the thousands of pages of Mackenzie King's diaries, which make for interesting, occasionally disturbing reading). I used actual quotes but in some cases modified them slightly for the sake of rhythm or brevity. Dozens of books went into the research of *Kanata*, among them Knowlton Nash's *Kennedy and Diefenbaker: Fear and Loathing Across the Undefended Border* (McClelland & Stewart), Jack Nisbet's *Sources of the River* (Sasquatch Books), R. Douglas Francis's *Images of the West* (Prairie Books), and *The Politics of Passion: Norman Bethune's Writing and Art* (edited by Larry Hannant, University of Toronto Press). I am indebted to

Alan Morantz's fascinating *Where Is Here?: Canada's Maps and the Stories They Tell* (Penguin).

Thanks go to a number of people: Nicole Winstanley for her editorial skills as well as her extraordinary patience and generosity. My agent, Jackie Kaiser, who was so instrumental in the conception of this book. Gail Gallant for her perceptive reading of the manuscript. The Canada Council for their generous support. Special thanks go to Ken Alexander for his heroic efforts with the manuscript—reading, advising, and arguing Canadian history with the energy of a patriot.

And of course, my family, my wife Grazyna, my daughter Justine and son Cormac for their support and indulgence while I worked on the book.

Kanata

A Penguin Readers Guide

ABOUT THE BOOK

Spanning two centuries and countless kilometres, *Kanata* is a story both epic and personal in scope. Don Gillmor, co-author of the award-winning *Canada: A People's History*, brings the vast story of our nation into fine focus through the eyes of Michael Mountain Horse, a high school history teacher with a remarkable heritage and an adventurous past. Shifting seamlessly between Michael's story and insightful historical portraits, Gillmor delves deep into the hearts and minds of fascinating characters both real and fictional, inviting the reader to examine not only the nature of history but that of storytelling as well.

As the country celebrates the 1967 Centennial, Michael is ready to retire, but he hasn't given up trying to reach the easily distracted young minds in his classroom. Hoping to involve them in Canada's historical narrative, he assigns his class a new project: a commemorative wall mural that illustrates what the nation's past means to them. Absent from this project, however, is a fellow student named Billy Whitecloud, who is trapped deep in a coma following a tragic car accident.

Michael begins making regular visits to his comatose student, and it is here in Billy's quiet hospital room where the real story of *Kanata* is told. Starting with the life of his great-great-grandfather David Thompson, Michael delivers the lessons Billy has missed, revealing his own past in the process. Gillmor's skills as a historian shine as he furnishes the high school teacher's stories with narrative passages that invigorate hundreds of years of Canadian and world history and bring a vital human touch to men and women lost to the past.

Thompson's story sets the tone for the book and establishes many of its themes. Despite cruel hardships and seemingly insurmountable challenges, Thompson explored the vast uncharted country for the Hudson's Bay Company and made it his life's work to draft the first accurate map of its distant borders. Although his work wasn't recognized in his lifetime and he died penniless, Thompson's perseverance and pioneering spirit were essential stones in the foundation of the country.

Kanata's history lessons continue through the years leading up to Confederation, as John A. Macdonald, D'Arcy McGee, George-Étienne Cartier, and George Brown form a decidedly uneasy alliance and an unusual country. Gillmor presents a fascinating look at Macdonald and how this very fallible man took his place in history as our first prime minister. He also explores the inner conflicts of other crucial and controversial Canadian figures, including Métis revolutionary Louis Riel, battlefield surgeon Norman Bethune, and prime ministers Mackenzie King and John Diefenbaker.

But it is Michael's remarkable story that truly brings *Kanata* to life. As his private lessons with Billy continue, Michael slowly reveals his nomadic past and the events that made him a man. From his childhood adventures with his older brother Stanford to the bloody killing fields of the Great War and the Spanish Civil War, Michael's spirit remains restless. He tramps the railways across the prairies, learns about love and heartbreak in Hollywood, finds work on ranches and oil derricks, and finally applies his incredible life experience to a career as a history teacher.

Based on painstaking research, Don Gillmor's *Kanata* is an epic exploration of Canada and its greatest natural resource— our history. ■

AN INTERVIEW WITH DON GILLMOR

Q: How did the idea for *Kanata* originate? Did it emerge as part of the process of researching *Canada: A People's History* or did it develop afterward?

It started with *Canada: A People's History*. It was the story of David Thompson that seduced me. I had known a bit about his life, but after delving into the details I found his story both extraordinary and heartbreaking. At the time I thought it would be perfect for fiction. ■

Q: Why did you choose to use the fictional character of Michael Mountain Horse to provide the framework of the book, especially since many of its historical figures, such as David Thompson and John A. Macdonald, could have easily supported a novel on their own?

Certainly Thompson could have supported his own novel (as could Macdonald and Bethune and others), but once I decided to open up the subject, to continue past Thompson and up to the modern era, I needed a fictional character who would act as a narrative thread. Mountain Horse gave me that latitude. He had the Native background that allowed me to explore a critical part of the country's history, and he was born at a time when he could conceivably be part of many key historical moments. ■

Q: As a young man, Michael experiences war in Europe and love in America before eventually returning to Alberta. Do you think it's important to see the world in order to fully understand and appreciate what we have in Canada?

When I travelled to Europe as a student, years ago, I remember thinking it seemed so much more sophisticated. Nevertheless, after months of travel, it was a joy to return home. Canada has gotten much more sophisticated since then, without losing the essential force of its personality. Now it's a model for the coming century, a harbinger of the successful multicultural state. ■

Q. Many of the political figures depicted in the book, such as John A. Macdonald, Louis Riel, and Mackenzie King, have strong and complex personalities defined by what some may call serious character flaws. Why do you think such traits are so common in the political world? Do you think these leaders have earned their places in Canadian history because of or despite those flaws?

I suspect that Louis Riel's bouts of mania helped propel him through the hostile political landscape. They were what launched him and what defeated him at Batoche ultimately. He needed those flaws, but they were his undoing. Macdonald once remarked that the people would rather have John A. drunk than George Brown sober. His flaws and his gifts were wrapped up so tightly that they became indistinguishable. His energy was heroic for all things: politics, alcohol, and life. King succeeded in spite of his flaws. He was insecure, overly attached to the mystical, and curiously isolated. But his natural instinct for compromise helped govern an ungovernable country. Arguably, it was also what kept him from being great, however. ■

Q. *Kanata* covers almost two hundred years in our history and touches upon many important people and events. Were there other events or figures you wanted to include but simply could not find the space for? If so, do you have any plans to explore them in the future?

There were a lot of stories that I couldn't find space for. Some of them I wrote and then reluctantly cut. The stories themselves were fascinating, but they seemed to stray too far away from the central theme. I originally wrote a section dealing with the Dene Natives who worked in the uranium mine at Great Bear Lake. They were shipping the uranium to the U.S. to be used in the first atomic bomb. A third of the Dene miners died of cancer, and Deline became known as the "Village of Widows." It's a tragic story and historically rich, but I cut it, finally, because I felt there just wasn't room. It opened up too many doors; it needed a longer treatment. ■

Q: What were some of the practical challenges in creating a fictional interpretation of events that took place hundreds of years ago? Were you mindful of presenting a "truthful" fiction?

The practical challenges aren't as great as one would think. There was a wealth of existing description, especially in Thompson's exhaustive records. The literary challenges are more of a problem. The question of what is "truthful fiction" lurks. There is no hard and fast rule. *Kanata* was presented as "historical fiction," a term that means different things to different people. I wanted to have the book governed by central truths, but I took liberties with certain events, or collapsed events into a single scene. I used dialogue and descriptions from the historical record, but also manufactured my own. I tried to stay truthful to the spirit of the characters and to history—an impossible task, ultimately. All historical fiction necessarily takes liberties. It does so in the service of the story. ■

Q: Which of the historical figures did you find most interesting to explore? Did any of them present a difficulty or a challenge in capturing their voices?

I deliberately used characters who had left a written record of their own. Thompson's journals helped give him a voice. Bethune also wrote a great deal, and his voice and personality shine through in his work. Mackenzie King left an astounding archive—more than thirty thousand pages. My greatest affection was for Thompson, but I gained a surprising empathy for King. I don't think he was a great leader, but he was, in his way, very human. He was like a character in a Samuel Beckett play. Diefenbaker was another character I hadn't much liked as a politician, but I had sympathy for the man. He became, very quickly, a man out of time. It is difficult to be so beloved and then so ignored. And Diefenbaker had no other life. He was purely political. ■

Q: How do you respond to those who say that Canadian history is boring, especially when compared with that of the United States? Why do you think Canadians are reluctant to embrace or explore our country's history?

I think my generation was shortchanged as far as Canadian history went. I remember the Plains of Abraham being a compelling story. But I don't recall many other stories being told to us. Our history was presented as a series of inevitable battles, generically heroic figures, and dates. A lot of dates. I didn't sense a narrative, I didn't get a sense of the personalities. The drama had been removed, and the history felt neutered. So we looked to the south, where American history was being distorted in a thousand entertainments. ■

Q: If some of the historical figures in *Kanata* were able to borrow Mackenzie King's crystal ball and peer into the future, what do you think they would say about the nation that Canada has become and the state of their own personal legacies?

Well, Clifford Sifton—the minister of the interior under Wilfrid Laurier and the man charged with the task of filling the empty prairies with immigrants—would be cheered. Diefenbaker would be disappointed that the British legacy has faded so much. Thompson would be proved right (he predicted that the Natives would be pushed off the land in favour of settlers). Mackenzie King would look at our current political situation with its minority stalemates and think that what the country needs is a man like him. ■

Q: You have an impressive career spanning fiction, non-fiction, and journalism. Do you find that your approach to writing changes depending on whether a project is fiction or non-fiction? Is one more rewarding than the other?

At one level, non-fiction and fiction are a cure for each other. There are moments in non-fiction when you wish the character could be more interesting, or more flawed, or more something. But you're stuck with him. And there are days when the blank pages of fiction can be daunting rather than energizing, when one wishes for the prescriptive structure of non-fiction. But when it's going well, fiction probably offers the greater rewards. It is a purer act of creation, I suppose. ■

Q: Canadians share a certain national pride, but we often find it difficult to put it into words. Do you have any thoughts on why we have such a hard time defining ourselves?

The country is young, geographically diverse, linguistically complex, and increasingly multicultural. So it's hard to define. But like all countries, we have our foundation myths, from David Thompson's maps to Paul Henderson's goal. It's better to search for national meaning than to subscribe to uniform, sometimes jingoistic, notions of nation. As far as nationalism goes, I think we have one of the healthier versions. ■

Q. In an era of Google Maps and GPS, what place do you think mapmaking, as an art and as a medium, has in today's world?

It is less of an art, certainly. Though the bias and subjectivity that informed maps in the sixteenth century are still with us today. Back then, mapmakers would put drawings of spice trees or gold mines as a lure for explorers. Now we have MapQuest, which shows where the nearest restaurants are. In that sense, maps have always been less objective than we would like to think. Usually some point is being made. ■

Q. How has the novel been received? Does the literary reaction differ from that of the historical community?

The relationship between historians and historical fiction is generally troubled and needlessly territorial. I sympathize with the historians' position, that sense of violation they feel when a character they're familiar with is brought to life using fictional tricks. But the aims of novelists and historians don't coincide. One of the reasons I used historical characters who had left extensive records themselves was to bypass historians' interpretations, which can be sterile and subject to the same biases novelists are prone to. Australian writer Peter Carey, whose novel *Parrot and Olivier in America* was panned by historian Hugh Brogan, said that the historian "had no idea how to read a novel." I empathize with Mr. Carey. There is a great deal of territoriality in play, and novelists are seen as interlopers. But we aren't working the same side of the street. ■

DISCUSSION QUESTIONS

1. "History is a series of accidents balanced against inevitable forces." How is this statement illustrated in the novel?

2. Why do you think it's important for Michael to visit Billy Whitecloud in the hospital and tell him stories from Canadian history?

3. Throughout the novel, war and conflict are depicted in various art forms, such as murals, paintings, and movies. Discuss how any given representation of war reflects the time period in which it was created.

4. *Kanata* presents a fictional narrative based on actual people and events. Do you feel that this approach to storytelling is respectful to the historical figures in the novel and to their legacies? What does it say about the malleable nature of history itself?

5. Many of the historical figures in the novel suffer from such character flaws as alcoholism, violent tendencies, and mystical delusions. Discuss how these traits help or hinder the leadership of these men.

6. "Endurance is part of the national theme: that humbling geography, its overwhelming scale, the sheer weight on the collective psyche." How is endurance, in physical, religious, or emotional terms, explored in the novel?

7. "We knew what we were against but not what we were for." How does this statement reflect Canada as a nation, both in the past and today? How is this uncertain sense of national identity illustrated in the book?

8. "In the evening, [King] wrote in his journal, the obsessive history that he attended to each night, a version that concealed and revealed in equal